Ciara Geraghty lives in Dublin with her husband, three children and a dog.

You can find out more at:
www.ciarageraghty.com
visit her Facebook page at:
www.facebook.com/CiaraGeraghtyBooks
and follow her on Twitter@ciarageraghty

# LIFESAVING FOR BEGINNERS

She has lots of friends, an ordinary job, and she never ever thinks about her past. This is Kat's story. None of it is true. Milo McIntyre loves his mam, the peanut-butter-and-banana muffins at the Funky Banana café, and the lifesaving class he does after school. He never thinks about his future, until the day it changes forever. This is Milo's story. All of it is true. And then there is the other story. The one with a twist of fate which somehow brings together a boy from Brighton and a woman in Dublin, and uncovers the truth once and for all. This is the story that's just about to begin . . .

Books by Ciara Geraghty
Published by The House of Ulverscroft:

BECOMING SCARLETT

CIARA GERAGHTY

# LIFESAVING
# FOR
# BEGINNERS

*Complete and Unabridged*

# CHARNWOOD
Leicester

First published in Great Britain in 2012 by
Hodder & Stoughton
An Hachette UK company
London

First Charnwood Edition
published 2014
by arrangement with
Hodder & Stoughton Ltd.
London

A catalogue record for this book is available
from the British Library.


ISBN 978-1-4448-1949-6

Published by
F. A. Thorpe (Publishing)
Anstey, Leicestershire

Set by Words & Graphics Ltd.
Anstey, Leicestershire
Printed and bound in Great Britain by
T. J. International Ltd., Padstow, Cornwall

This book is printed on acid-free paper

For my parents, Breda and Don Geraghty,
with all my love

# Prologue

## 1 June 2011; Dublin

He knows he is driving too fast. Not over the speed limit. Never over the speed limit. But too fast for the way he feels. The tiredness. It's in his bones. It has seeped into his blood. It's in his fingers that are wrapped round the steering wheel of the truck. It's in the weight of his head on his neck. He feels himself sagging. He straightens and slaps his face. He blinks, over and over, training his eyes on the road ahead.

He'll be home soon.

He turns on the radio and takes a long drink from the can of Red Bull on the dashboard. The sun has warmed it but he finishes it anyway. 'A Pair of Brown Eyes'. He turns up the volume and thinks about Brigitta.

The truck roars down the motorway.

Later, he will deny that he fell asleep at the wheel. But afterwards, in the stillness of night, when he sits up in bed and wonders why he is shaking, he will concede that it's possible — just possible — that he closed his eyes. Briefly. Just for a moment. A second. Perhaps two. Sometimes that's all it takes.

He can't remember how long he'd been driving when it happened. Too long. He should have pulled over. Climbed into the back of the cab for a rest. Splashed cold water on his face in

1

a worn-out toilet cubicle at the back of a petrol station. He should have done a lot of things, he admits to himself when he sits up in bed in the middle of the night and wonders why he is shaking.

Instead, he drives on. The conditions are near perfect. The road is dry, the sun, a perfect circle of light against the innocent blue of the sky. It looks like a picture Ania draws for him with her crayons. She folds the pictures inside his lunchbox. 'So you won't miss us when you're far away, Papa.' A yellow sun. A blue sky. Four matchstick people. His face relaxes into a smile. He thinks perhaps this is when it happened. This is when he might have closed his eyes. Briefly. Just for a moment. A second. Perhaps two.

When he sees it, the deer is already in the middle of the road.

Some things are cemented in his memory. He remembers the beauty of the thing, the sun glancing against its dappled side as it runs its last run. The fear in the liquid brown eyes. Human almost, the fear. He's never seen a deer on the road before. He's seen the signs. The warning signs. But this is the first time he's seen one on the road. He knows he shouldn't try to avoid it. Shouldn't swerve. He wouldn't have, if he hadn't been so tired. He wouldn't have, if he hadn't taken on the extra shift. The Christmas-fund shift. He started it last January. Julija needs a new bike. And then Ania will want one. She always wants what her big sister has.

He grabs the steering wheel and swerves,

glancing in the mirror only afterwards to check the lane is clear.

The lane is not clear.

The thud as the front of the truck hits the animal. Hits it anyway. The sound of his brakes, screeching, the crash of the gears as he wrestles them down. He remembers the car. A bright yellow car. There's a suitcase on the back seat. Held together with a leather belt.

The truck gaining on the car.

The sound when he hits it.

The sound.

His body shoots forward but is wrenched back by the seatbelt. Later, there will be a line of bruises from his shoulder to his hip. The airbag explodes in his face and he will have to admit to the judge that he doesn't know what happened next.

The witness will know. He will describe how the car, the bright yellow car, is tossed in the air like a bag of feathers, rolling and turning until it lands in the shallow ditch the workmen have been excavating.

The technical expert will know. He will talk about the truck. How it jackknives as it swerves, hitting two cars, causing one to roll and turn and end up in a ditch and embedding the other against the crash barrier, like a nut caught in the steely grip of pliers. The technical expert will present these facts with the calm monotone of a man who never wakes in the darkest part of the night and wonders why he is shaking.

The judge will say it's a miracle. That more people weren't killed. That woman in the Mazda, for example. The thirty-nine-year-old woman. A hairline fracture on one rib after being cut out of the car embedded against the crash barrier. That she will live to tell another tale is nothing short of a miracle. That's what the judge will say.

And Brigitta. His beautiful Brigitta. She will be in the courtroom. Somewhere behind him. She will have asked Petra to mind the children for the day. When they lead him away, he won't look for her. His eyes, open now, will be trained on the floor.

He will be a long time getting home.

# 1 June 2011; Brighton

Mam says, 'Milo, you gave me a fright. What are you doing up at this hour?'

I say, 'I set my alarm.'

'Ah love, you shouldn't have. It's five o'clock in the morning. You'll be falling asleep in Miss Williams's class.'

'No way. We're making papier-mâché masks. If everyone knows their spellings.'

'And do you know your spellings?'

'Course.'

'Sorry for asking, Einstein.'

The kitchen is colder than usual. Probably because the sun's not properly up yet. Mam stands at the counter, with her hands wrapped round the mug I got her last Christmas. It says 'World's Best Mum'. I tried to find one that said 'Mam' but I couldn't. They probably sell them in Ireland, where Mam is from. Still, she drinks out of it all the time. She says she doesn't mind about the Mum bit.

'What time is the ferry?'

Mam looks at her watch. 'I'd better go if I'm going to catch it.' Her suitcase is on the floor beside the table. It's still got Dad's old leather belt tied round it. She was supposed to get a new case ages ago. She must have forgotton. The sticker on it says 'Elizabeth McIntyre' but everyone calls her Beth.

'I'll put your suitcase in the boot.'

She smiles. 'Don't worry, love, I'll do it. Besides, the boot is full. I forgot to take out the boxes of flyers I got for the café the other day. I'll put the case on the back seat. It'll be grand.'

I hand her the car keys and look out the window. There have been a few car robberies lately but Mam's car is still there. I don't think anyone would steal it. We call it the bananamobile. It's bright yellow. The writing is pink. Shocking pink, Mam calls it. It says 'The Funky Banana', which happens to be the name of Mam's café.

'So when are you coming home?'

'I've told you a million times already. I'll be home on Sunday.'

'I wish I could come to Auntie May's with you.'

'There's the small matter of school, remember. Anyway, you'll have a great time with your sister.'

That's true. Faith doesn't know how to cook so we won't have to eat vegetables and things like that. And Rob always gives me money to get DVDs and sweets when they have to go to Faith's room to talk. They're always going to Faith's room to talk.

Mam puts on her coat and hat. It's a beret, which is a French word and that's why you can't pronounce the t at the end. Her lips are red on account of the lipstick. She doesn't wear half as much make-up as Faith but she still looks nice. For an adult, I mean. She puts her hand on my head. 'Don't forget to brush that mop before you go to school, mister.'

I say, 'I won't,' even though I probably will forget.

'And you've got lifesaving class after school today, remember?'

'My bag's in the hall.' As if anyone would ever forget about that. I'm still in the beginners' class but

6

Coach says if I keep on doing well, she'll move me up to intermediate next year.

'OK, so, see ya Sunday.'

'Yeah, see ya Sunday.'

'Are you gettin' too big to give yer auld mam a kiss?'

Mam's mad about kissing. So is Damo. He says he's done it loads of times with girls but I don't believe him. I mean, he's my best friend and everything, but sometimes he makes stuff up. His mam says she wouldn't believe him if he told her the time. And last summer, he said he climbed Mount Everest but when I asked him where it was, he said it was in Spain. Near Santa Ponza.

Mam holds out her arms. Before I can duck, she squeezes me so tightly I can barely move. Her hair tickles my face. She smells like soap and toothpaste. She'll probably tell me not to forget to brush my teeth. She kisses me on the cheek and I rub it away with the back of my hand.

'Be good.'

'I'll try.'

'I mean it, Milo. No messin' with Damien Sullivan, OK?'

She's only saying that because of what happened the last time she went to Ireland. And that was only an accident. Damo's eyebrows have nearly grown back now.

'And make sure you brush your teeth.'

'I will.'

'I'll ring you tonight, OK?'

'Promise?'

She presses the palm of her hand against her heart. 'Cross my heart and hope to die.' She picks up her suitcase with the leather belt wrapped round it and

7

that's when I have the idea. About buying her a new case for Christmas. I still have most of my First Holy Communion money in the post office. I'll buy her a green one. Green is her favourite colour.

I stay at the window until she drives up the road and I can't see her anymore.

# 2 June 2011; Dublin

'She's coming round.'

'Thank Christ.'

'Kat?'

'Katherine?'

'Can you hear me?'

'Come on now. Wake up.'

'Don't crowd her.'

'Kat?'

'Easy now. Take it easy.'

'Thomas?' My voice sounds strange. Rusted. Like I haven't used it in a long time.

'Give her some space.'

'Am I in a hospital?'

'Get her some water.'

'What happened?'

'It's all right. You were in an accident but you're all right. You're all right now.'

'Tell me what happened.'

'Calm down, Kat. Take it easy.'

My breath is quick and shallow. Panic isn't far away. I move my legs to see if I can move my legs. They move. I can move my legs. I try to calm down, to beat panic back with both hands.

Someone puts a hand under my head. Puts a glass against my mouth. I think it's Thomas. 'Here, take a drink of water.' That's definitely him. The soft, low voice. It would make you

9

think of Wispa bars, whether you wanted to or not.

The water goes down, cold and pure. Panic falters. Takes a step back. Thomas's hand is solid against the back of my head. I keep my eyes closed, in case he's looking at me. In case he sees the panic. And the gratitude. I am weak with gratitude all of a sudden.

When I open my eyes, I say, 'I'm not forty yet, am I?' so that we can have a laugh and everything can go back to normal. It works because everyone has a bit of a laugh and the atmosphere in the room slackens and there's a chance that things can get back to normal.

Thomas says, 'You've still a bit to go.'

The light grates against my eyes as I look around the room. The hospital room. I'm in a hospital. I hate hospitals. I haven't been in a hospital bed since I was fifteen.

I do a headcount. Four people. They look tired, like they haven't slept, or, if they have, they've slept badly. My parents. My oldest friend, Minnie. And Thomas. Almost everyone.

I say, 'Where's Ed?'

My mother says, 'I had to send him home. He was too emotional. You know how he gets.'

'He's not on his own, is he?'

Dad steps forward. 'Your brother's fine, Kat. Don't worry. I brought him to Sophie's house and Sophie's parents are there. They'll look after him. You need to worry about yourself for now.'

'What's wrong with me?' I feel far away, like I have to shout to make them hear me.

Dad says, 'You got a bump on your head. The

doctor says it'll hurt for a while.'

Mum says, 'And you've got a fractured rib. You either got it in the accident or afterwards, when they cut you out of the car.'

'Jesus.' I curl my hands into fists so no one can see the shake in them.

Minnie says, 'It's not even a proper fracture. It's just a hairline one.'

Thomas says, 'You were lucky, Kat.'

I don't feel lucky. I feel far away.

Minnie looks at her watch. 'Well, now that I know you're not going to cark it, I suppose I should go back to work.' She sounds annoyed but when I look at her, she's got that pained expression on her face that she gets when she's trying not to smile.

It's only when Mum puts her hand on my forehead that I realise how hot I am. Her hand is cool and soft. I'd forgotten how soft her hands are. Her eyes are puffy, like she's been crying. But she never cries. The last time I saw her crying was in 1989, when Samuel Beckett died.

She says, 'We'll go too. We'd better pick Edward up.' She pulls at some strands of my hair that are caught in the corner of my mouth. I try to sit up but I'm like a dead weight so I stop trying and lie there and try to make sense of things.

The room smells of heat and bleach. The sheets are stiff and make a scratching sound when I move. There's a deep crack zigzagging along the ceiling. Like the whole place is going to come tumbling down. Right down on top of me.

Dad says, 'Get some rest, Kat. I'll call you later, OK?'

'Will you tell Ed I'm fine? Tell him I'll see him soon. Tomorrow.'

'Of course.' Dad bends, kisses the corner of my eye. I'd say he was going for my forehead but he's a little short-sighted.

Minnie says, 'The next time you're going to have a near-death experience, could you do it on a Friday? Get me out of the weekly meeting with the Pillock.' Pillock is what Minnie calls her boss, and the funny thing is that they get on quite well. She picks up her handbag and coat and is gone in a cloud of Chanel Coco Mademoiselle.

Now it's just Thomas and me and, all of a sudden, I feel sort of shy, like I've been doing the tango in my bedroom with an imaginary partner before noticing that the blinds are up and the neighbours are gawking. I grab the sharp edge of the sheet and pull it to my neck.

I say, 'Shouldn't you be spreading dung on some poor unfortunate turnips?' If you ask Thomas what he does, he'll say he's a farmer, even though he's a freelance journalist who happens to have inherited a smallholding in Monaghan where he grows impractical things like grapes that are never anything but sour, and sunflowers that, as soon as their heads poke above the earth, get eaten by his one goat, two pigs, three hens, a garrulous goose and a lamb-bearing ewe.

He doesn't answer immediately. Instead, he sits on the edge of the bed. Carefully, like he's afraid he might break something. I want to punch his arm and tell him he's a big eejit but I can't because of the wires attached to my wrist. I don't think I can laugh out loud either. My head feels funny: heavy and dense. When I touch it, there's a bandage, wrapped round and round.

I say, 'This is a bit *Grey's Anatomy*, isn't it?' My voice sounds nearer now but there's a shake in it. I clear my throat.

He smiles but only briefly. Then he puts his hand on mine. His hands are huge. Like shovels, they are. I pull my hand away. 'What?'

He says, 'What do you mean?'

'You look kind of . . . appalled. Is it my hair?'

He smiles a bit longer this time.

He says, 'I'm just . . . I'm glad you're OK. When they said the car was a write-off, I thought . . . '

'The car's a write-off?'

'Yeah. Sorry.'

'I love that Mazda.'

'I know, but it's replaceable.' He looks at me when he says that. A really intense look like he's cramming me for an exam. For a terrible moment, I think he's going to say something horrendous. About me. Not being replaceable. Something heinous like that.

But he doesn't say that. Instead, he says this: 'I thought you were dead.'

'Jesus, this is actually cheesier than *Grey's Anatomy*.'

'Can't you be serious for a moment?'

'I'm as serious as a car crash.'

'That's not funny.'

'It's a little bit funny.'

Thomas nods, thank Christ. He's not usually like this. He's usually got quite a good SOH, as Minnie calls it. Even though she's got Maurice and they've been smugly coupled up for years, she still reads the ads. For me, she says. I don't know if she does it anymore. The Thomas situation has been going on a fair while now. Maybe a year and a half.

Although I think Thomas said, 'Twenty-two months, actually,' when I mentioned it the other day.

Thomas says, 'Do you remember the accident?'

I nod. 'Sort of.'

'What do you remember?' He can be such a journalist sometimes.

'There was a deer on the road.' What the hell was a deer doing on the road? 'There was a truck. It swerved. Really suddenly. And there was a car. In front of me, I think. A yellow one. Really bright yellow. Something about a banana written on it. Then the airbag exploded in my face and then . . . I don't know . . . I don't think I remember anything else.'

'You could have died.'

'Are you going to keep on saying that?'

'That woman . . . the one in the yellow car. She . . . she died.'

'You're not going to cry, are you?'

'No.'

'Thank Christ.'

Thomas stands up. Walks to the door. Pauses. Looks back at me.

I say, 'Can you get the doctor?'

'Are you feeling OK?' He looks worried, like maybe I've got a brain tumour or something.

'I want to know when I can get out of here.'

'I'm sure they'll want to monitor you for another while. You've been out cold.'

'I just want everything to get back to normal.'

He looks at me then. Says, 'No.' Like we're in the middle of an argument.

'What do you mean, no?'

'I mean no. Things are different now. You could have died.'

'Can you stop saying that?'

'We've wasted enough time.'

I manage to prop myself up on my elbows. I ignore the pain in my head. My body. I need to nip this in the bud. I say, 'Look, there's no need for all this. I didn't die. I'm fine.'

'I don't care.' Thomas closes the door. Puts his back against it so no one can come in. There's a feeling in my chest and I think it might be disquiet. 'I'm just going to say it.'

'I wish you wouldn't.'

'I know. But I'm going to say it anyway. I love you.'

'Where are my clothes? I need to get out of here.'

'I want to get married.'

'Congratulations. Who's the lucky lady?'

'And I'd love to have a baby.'

'Good for you. They're making huge leaps in human biology these days so I'm thinking, any day now.'

15

'Can you stop joking around, just for a minute?'

'How about a peace settlement in the Middle East while we're at it?'

He sighs then. 'I'm going to get the doctor.'

'Good idea. See how she's getting on with that cure for pancreatic cancer.'

It's only when Thomas leaves the room that I notice how quiet everything is. Quiet as a grave, Thomas would probably say in his current maudlin form. There's pain down my right side. But other than that and the dull throb in my head, everything feels the same as usual. I'd love a cigarette. I don't know where my bag is. I need my phone. I need to phone Ed — he'll be worried — and tell him not to worry. Tell him that everything is the same as usual.

Nothing has changed.

Even Thomas, when he returns, seems to have gone back to his usual self. He couldn't find the doctor but he has somehow discovered that one of the nurses keeps hens in her back garden and they've been discussing feeds and eggs and coops and what have you.

It's only when Thomas is leaving — I have to stay another night for 'observation' — that he goes all funny again. He says, 'I want you to think about what I've said.'

I say, 'Can you put the telly on before you leave?'

Thomas hands me the remote. 'Here.' His tone is brusque but then he bends down from his great height and kisses me. Right on the mouth. As if I'm not lying defenceless in a hospital bed,

16

with no access to a toothbrush or toothpaste or mouthwash or anything. He just kisses me like he always does. No lead-up. No warning. Just his mouth on top of mine. It always gets me. How soft his mouth is. He's so big and farmer-ish, you'd be expecting dry, chapped lips from being out in all sorts of weather. He kisses me for longer than would be considered appropriate in a hospital visit sort of scenario. I don't tell him to stop.

'I'll pick you up tomorrow. Take you home.'

I think the accident has had some effect on me after all because, all of a sudden, there's a chance I might cry. I'd say it's the medication they have me on. Because of the shattered ribs. Well, OK then, a hairline fracture on one rib.

I nod and close my eyes as if I'm going to have a nap.

When he leaves, I open my eyes and — this is the strange part — I do cry. Not loud enough for anyone to hear. But still. There are tears. I'm crying all right. They gave me something for the pain and they said it was strong. I'd say it's that. I blow my nose and lie down and close my eyes. I want to go to sleep as quickly as I can so it'll be tomorrow as soon as possible then I can go home and everything can get back to normal.

# 2 June 2011; Brighton

I'm sitting on my bed.

The house is dead quiet even though Adrian is here. I know he's here because, a while ago, he knocked on the door and poked his head in and said, 'All right, Milo? You hungry, mate?'

He never knocks on the door.

Faith and Dad and Ant are gone to Ireland. I think they're staying in Auntie May's house. That's where Mam is supposed to be. I don't know where she is now. I hope it's not a morgue. I saw a morgue on the telly once. They put people in drawers and it's really cold. Mam hates the cold. Her hands turn blue when she's cold.

Dad said I couldn't go to Ireland with them. His jumper was inside out and his breath smelled like cigarettes, which is weird because he doesn't even smoke anymore. Not since he went to Scotland to live with Celia.

Faith said, 'Don't worry,' when she left. 'We'll be back tomorrow.' Her eyes were all red and puffy and her skin was even whiter than usual so I didn't want to ask, 'What time tomorrow?' I look at my watch again but it's still only twenty past nine in the morning. I think Adrian is in the kitchen but I don't want to go to the kitchen because that's where Mam is supposed to be. When she's not at the café, she's in the kitchen, baking something. Or just sitting down,

18

listening to the radio. Adrian is not supposed to be in the kitchen. He's supposed to be at the university in London with Ant. And I'm supposed to be in Miss Williams's class, probably writing some story, like My Plans for the Summer Holidays. Something boring like that.

Everything is sort of back to front. Like breakfast. Me and Adrian ate slices of pizza, left over from last night. We drank Coke as well. Even if it was my birthday, Mam wouldn't let me drink Coke for breakfast and my birthday is the same day as Christmas Day, which is sort of like two celebrations in one, I suppose.

People keep knocking on the front door. Neighbours, mostly. Mrs Barber from across the road left a gigantic bowl with a lid on the top. She said it was beef casserole. There's celery in it. I hate celery. I put it in the fridge. Mam would call it a terrible waste if I threw it in the bin.

The clothes I wore yesterday are on the floor. I'm supposed to put my socks and boxers into the linen basket every night. 'There're no skivvies in this house.' That's what Mam says.

I'm going to have to remember to brush my teeth from now on. Every day. Otherwise they'll rot in my head. Mrs Barber's teeth look lovely and white and straight but that's only because they're not real. Her real teeth rotted in her head because she never took care of them. She told me that one day, when she was in the house and Mam was giving out because I hadn't brushed my teeth.

Damo didn't call for me this morning. He always calls for me. Or else I call for him. Whoever's ready first. Usually me, because of Damo and the way he stays in bed way after his mam tells him to get up. She says one of these days she won't bother calling him. She'll call Mr Pilkington, the head master, instead. But she hasn't done that so far.

Here comes Adrian again. He knocks and pops his head round the door. He says, 'You wanna go out, mate? We could go to the park? Or the cinema? I think the new *Batman* one is out.'

I look at my watch. It's still twenty past nine. I say, 'The cinema's not open yet.'

'We could go to the park first.'

'*Batman*'s not out till next week. Mam said she'd take me. She said she'd be back on Sunday.'

Adrian walks towards me. He stands on my clothes but I don't think he notices. He sits on my bed. He looks like he's going to say something but then he doesn't.

I say, 'Half four.'

Adrian looks at me. 'What?'

'She said she'd be back at half four if the ferry was on time, which it usually is at this time of the year on account of the weather being nice.'

Adrian looks at me like I'm talking some foreign language. Italian, maybe. He can't speak Italian. He's not too bad at French, though.

We don't say anything for ages and then I say, 'Is today Thursday?' If today is Thursday, that means that Mam left yesterday but it doesn't feel like yesterday. It feels like ages ago.

Adrian doesn't say anything. He covers his face with his hands and, even though he doesn't make a sound, I think he's crying. His shoulders are sort of moving up and down.

Adrian never cries. Even when he was a kid and was

always getting into tricky situations. Like nettles, for example. He was always falling into bunches of nettles. Getting stung by wasps. And bees. And horseflies. Except I don't think horseflies sting. I think they bite. He even fractured his skull once. The time he cycled his bike along the back wall, pretending it was a tightrope. Mam said that was the last time she'd take him to the circus. He still has the scar on his forehead from the stitches. Mam said he could have supplied a blood bank for a week with the amount that poured out of his head. The doctor said he was very lucky.

But he never cried. Not when he got the stings from the nettles or the wasps, or the bites from the horseflies or even the fracture in his skull. Everyone says that Adrian never cried.

He's crying now.

I wish he'd stop.

I wish it were yesterday.

Wednesday.

I wish it was Wednesday and the ferry got cancelled because the weather was really stormy. But it's not Wednesday. It's Thursday. And the ferry didn't get cancelled because it's June and the weather is lovely in June. Glorious. That's what Mam says when the weather's good. She says, 'Isn't it a glorious day?' to the regulars at the Funky Banana.

The phone rings and I run down the stairs and answer it. I don't know why but I keep thinking it'll be Mam, laughing her head off and saying she's grand and there's been a mix-up and she's coming home and could I put the kettle on because she's gasping for a mug of tea. She's always gasping for mugs of tea.

I answer it and I say, 'Hello? The McIntyre

Residence,' in a posh voice cos I know that'll make Mam laugh, except it's not Mam. It's a woman and she wants to know what the arrangements are. I don't know what the arrangements are. She says, 'I'm sorry for your loss.' I think she means Mam.

I go into the kitchen and put the kettle on anyway. If it were Wednesday and the ferry got cancelled, Mam would be here and we wouldn't be eating leftover pizza and drinking Coke for our breakfast and Adrian would be at the university in London learning about science and Damo would have called at the door and I'd be in school writing a boring story about what I'm going to do for the summer holidays or something like that.

# 11 June 2011; Dublin

I say, 'Ouch.'

Thomas says, 'You OK?'

'You're rushing me.'

'I'm going at a snail's pace. In fact, no. Look, there's a snail, overtaking us.'

'That's a slug.'

'He's still pretty slow. Sluggish, you might say.'

'I'm glad you think this is funny.'

'You're not, though, are you? You're not glad.'

'It's an expression.'

'Here's another expression. Cheer up!'

'I hate people who say, 'Cheer up' . . . '

'What am I supposed to say to you in your current form?'

' . . . And 'Relax'. That's a horrible thing to say to anyone. Telling someone to relax never makes them relax. It makes them more tense. It's a stupid thing to say.'

'Here we are.'

We're at the restaurant. Thomas invited me when we were at the garage, ordering the Mazda this morning. He still calls them dates. He says, 'Do you want to go on a date tonight? Celebrate you ordering the new car?' I wonder how many dates we've been on. A fair few by now.

Before Thomas, I was — strictly — a three-date woman. First date I called the 'give it a go' date. I only ever went after unmerciful pressure from Minnie. She said, 'There's a Maurice out there for everybody.' Let's hope that's not true.

The second date I liked to call the 'benefit of the doubt' date. Again, usually Minnie-induced.

The third and often final one was when I usually said, 'It's not you. It's me.' Even though it's never me. Hardly ever.

On our third date, I said to Thomas, 'It's not you. It's me.'

He said, 'What do you mean?'

I said, 'My life is a bit . . . complicated.'

Thomas said, 'Isn't it well for you?' He used one of his gigantic hands to push his hair — long and grey and curly — out of his I'm-not-as-old-as-I-look face.

'No, I mean it's too complicated for a . . . a relationship.'

'A relationship?' He looked amused at the word and — in fairness — in his Monaghan accent it did sound a little absurd. 'I just asked you to come to the Galway Races with me. Do you want to?'

'Well . . . '

'Do you?'

'I suppose I might be able to . . . '

'Grand, so. I'll pick you up tomorrow at ten.'

And I nodded and said OK and I went with him. To the Galway Races. It was hard to say why, exactly. He kissed me there. At the races. Our first kiss. Up till then he'd just dropped me home and said, 'Goodnight now.' Like I was a farmer from whom he'd bought a calf of good stock.

He took me by surprise in Galway. After yet another horse he'd backed came last, he tore up his betting slip and said, 'Well, that's that!' and then, for no particular reason, he kissed me.

There was no ceremony. No sweet talk, thank Christ. Nothing like that. He just put his face in front of mine and kissed me. There was no form. No style. It was . . . well, it was all right, to be honest. Nice, even. He had to bend, although I have never been described as small.

That was our fourth date. The races. Then there were more.

*The Field* at the Abbey Theatre.

Climbing to the top of Bray Head. Thomas laughed when I called it a mountain.

Farmers' markets where the smell of the cheese would knock you off your feet.

A boat trip to Ireland's Eye. He rowed. I managed not to get seasick.

Minnie whistled and said, 'Oh my,' when Thomas went ahead and booked a mini-break at a cottage in the middle of nowhere. It actually wasn't that bad.

I followed it up with a disastrous night at the opera in Wexford. Thomas fell asleep and snored, loud enough for the usher to issue a stern 'Shhhh' towards our row of seats. He laughed that off like it was nothing and then proposed a day at the ploughing champions in Carlow, where he came second in a sheep-shearing competition.

'Kat?'

I look up. I look at Thomas. He looks the same as he always does. Everything is fine. I have the car sorted. We're out. Having our dinner. My rib is getting better. The doctor said I might have nightmares. About the accident. He said post-traumatic stress disorder was a possibility. I suppose I should be glad. That I haven't had nightmares. And no sign of any disorders either.

I think it's Thomas the doctor should be worried about. He hasn't been himself lately. It's little things, I suppose. Like the apartment, for example. Since the accident, he's stopped leaving his clothes on the floor and across the backs of various chairs and sofas. I look in his wardrobe and they're all there, the clothes. Some of them are rolled in a ball on the floor of the wardrobe but they're all in there. In the wardrobe.

Minnie said, 'So?' when I told her. 'Isn't that good news?'

'Yes, but he's never done it before. Why now? Why is he doing it now?'

Minnie shook her head and said, 'You're some contrary hen.'

And last week, he went and put his name beside mine on the letterbox. Up until then it was just my name, scribbled on a scrap of paper in blue pen. He went and replaced it with a card that has both our names on it. Typed in some fancy font, in capital letters. He asked me first and I said, 'Fine.' But it's a different story altogether when you come in from the shops one day and there it is. In plain black and white. No more scribbled blue biro on a scrap of paper. It's as stark as an announcement in the paper.

He looks at me over the top of his menu. 'You all right?'

'Why wouldn't I be?'

'I don't know. You're quiet. And you haven't given out yet.'

'About what?'

'About where we're sitting.'

'What's wrong with where we're sitting?'

'There's a draught.'

'Is there?'

'You hate draughts.'

'Why do you always think you know every single thing about me?' My tone is sharper than it should be but I don't think Thomas notices because he smiles.

He says, 'I know a fair bit.'

I study the menu.

'I know that you'll order the seabass.'

'Is that so?'

'But what you really want is the steak and mushrooms and the onions with chips and a dirty big dollop of tomato ketchup on the side.'

The waitress arrives and I snap the menu shut and say, 'The beef stir-fry, please.'

Thomas orders the bacon and cabbage and potatoes, just as I knew he would. I take a long drink from my glass of wine and try to loosen myself out a bit. I'm as taut as a violin string. I've been like this since the accident. The bloody miracle. Stiff.

After we order, Thomas sits back in his chair. He looks happy for some reason, like something good has happened. He says, 'Why wouldn't I be happy?' when I mention it.

'So,' he adds. 'Today was a productive day. You got the car ordered.'

I say, 'Yes.'

'The same make. Same model. Same colour. You'd think it was the same car.'

'Just because I was in an accident doesn't mean I should go and get myself a completely different car. There was nothing wrong with my old one. I liked it. I didn't want to change it.'

Thomas shakes his head and smiles. He leans forward and his grey eyes lighten to green in the candlelight. He says, 'I have a good idea.'

'Another one?'

Last week he suggested that we buy a new bed. Said our one — which is really my one when you get around to thinking about it — creaks. I said, 'It does not.' He said, 'It does. It creaks like the clappers.'

I said, 'It only creaks when we're . . . you know . . . '

'Having sex?'

'Yes.'

He said, 'Which is as often as not.' That happens to be true. You'd think by now we'd be bored with that caper.

Our dinners arrive. The stir-fry is more noodles than beef and there's way too much of it. I pick up my wine glass and empty it, then fill it to the top again. Thomas eats like he always does. As if he hasn't had a square meal for several days. Then he says, 'So. Do you want to hear my good idea or not?'

I shrug my shoulders.

Thomas says, 'Actually, it's a great idea.'

28

I'm pretty convinced that there won't be anything great about the idea. Although this is the man who introduced me to chocolate in chilli. Still, I say nothing.

'You OK, Kat?'

'I'm fine.'

The thing is, I'm not fine. But it's difficult to say why not, exactly. It's nothing really. It's just . . . well, nothing's been quite the same since he came to pick me up from the hospital in his beaten-up old Saab with the Get Well Soon balloons tied onto the roof rack. I wouldn't get in until he'd taken them down. He put them on the back seat of the car but they floated up and covered the back window. They weren't easy to burst. He had to stamp on them in the end.

I went to open the passenger door but he got there first. Opened the door. I was about to get in when he stopped me. Put his hands on my shoulders. He said, 'The apartment's been fierce quiet without you.' I came up to the pocket of his shirt. It was pale grey and happened to go very well with his black jeans, which were definitely new as well. No jacket, but, then, he hardly ever wore jackets. He was rarely cold enough.

I said, 'Did you go shopping?'

He is the only man I know who blushes. He said, 'Yeah. Surprise!'

'You never go shopping.'

'I knew you'd be pleased.' He put my overnight bag on the ground and gathered the lapels of my jacket in his hands and inched me towards him until I was close enough to see that curious ring of dark green round the grey of his eyes.

And then he kissed me. Right there on my mouth. As if we were in my bedroom with the curtains pulled and the lights off, and not in the middle of a public car park in broad daylight with everyone gawking.

I sift through the mound of noodles on my plate, trying to find a piece of beef. I wish I'd ordered the steak and mushrooms and the onions with chips and a dirty big dollop of tomato ketchup on the side.

Thomas says, 'So do you really not want to hear my idea?'

I think the wine has settled me a bit because I say, 'Oh, go on.'

He says, 'I think we should buy a place together.'

I put my glass on the table. 'I have a place.'

'I know. And I have my place. I just think it's time we thought about getting a place together.'

'I like my apartment.'

'See? It's your apartment. You just said it. But wouldn't it be nice to have a place that's both of ours? We don't have to start looking straight away. We could leave it till the new year. Prices are still going down. It makes sense to wait.'

I think about my bedroom. My kitchen. My bathroom. Even the cupboard in the utility room where I keep the brush and pan seems dear to me now, in the light of Thomas's latest idea.

'No.'

'No?'

'I'm not moving. I like living in my apartment.'

'And I like living there too. It's not about that.'

'What's it about, then?'

'It's about you and me. Setting up shop together, you know. Being a proper couple.'

I push the noodles to one side and put my knife and fork on the plate. Cover the plate with my napkin. 'Is it OK if we don't order dessert?'

'Are you OK?'

'I'm a bit . . . uncomfortable . . . the rib . . . ' This isn't true. But it will get me home and away from this conversation.

Thomas says, 'Of course,' and asks for the bill without even finishing his dinner, which makes me feel bad because he always clears his plate. Even Minnie says he's a pleasure to cook for.

He guides me out of the restaurant like I'm a bomb that's about to explode. He doesn't mention the apartment again.

The weird thing is that, until the accident, everything had been going well. I mean, I wouldn't go so far as to say fantastic or anything like that. Just, you know, quite well.

Like the writing. It was going really well. For ages, in fact. I suppose since Thomas moved in. I thought his moving in might have an adverse effect on the writing. I hate distractions and Thomas is a pretty big one. He moved in about a year ago, I'd say. Maybe even longer than that. I had just started writing the next book in the series. I can get a bit jittery when I'm at the start. Before I commit to it. Then Thomas sort of insisted on moving in and, six months later, the book was finished, and when I rang Brona, my editor, and told her, she thought I was joking, even though I don't joke as a rule and I never joke about my job. There'd be no point, for starters, because nobody knows about my job. Well, nobody except Minnie. And Brona, obviously. And now Thomas. I told him one day. Ages ago. Even before he insisted on moving in. I didn't intend to. It just happened.

That book — the one I wrote after Thomas moved in — ended up being the most successful one in the entire Declan Darker series. Brona said it was because Thomas was 'The One'. She was always saying crazy things, where Thomas was concerned. The day he moved into the apartment, for instance, she said, 'This is a great day for spinsters everywhere.'

I suppose, officially, you could say that Thomas moved in sometime in the summer of 2010. There he was, in my apartment, surrounded by boxes and black bin-liners and two cabbages that still had the muck of one of his five fields clinging to their stalks. In fact, some of the muck fell onto the carpet. The cream carpet. The cream, wool carpet. I had to walk past him to get to the Hoover. He grabbed my arm and pressed me against the wall and he looked at me without saying anything but all the while his hand moved up my leg until it disappeared inside my skirt and kept on going until his fingers reached the edge of my knickers and then he stopped. He smiled and said, 'You're wearing your fancy pants.'

'No, I'm not.'

'You are. They're those black ones with the lacy panel at the front. They're your good knickers.'

'I don't have good knickers.'

'You do. You wore them the first time I stayed over. I remember.'

'I did not.' Although I did.

He grinned. 'You're wearing your fancy pants because I'm moving in. Aren't you?'

'No.'

'Admit it.'

'I won't.'

'I won't play *Grey's Anatomy* if you don't.'

His fingers slid down the lacy panel and disappeared between my legs. He was close enough to kiss. His grey eyes were green that day. Bright green.

I said, 'OK, then.'

'Say it.'

'For fuck's sake, Thomas.'

'Say it.'

I sighed. Then I said, 'Fine, then. I'm wearing my good knickers.'

'Ha!'

'Are you going to have sex with me or what?' I made my voice sound bored out of my skull.

Afterwards, he said, 'You're going to love living with me.'

And back then, lying on the living-room floor with my good knickers down round my ankles and my skirt hitched over my hips and my breath coming in fits and starts, I thought . . . just for a moment . . . I thought . . . yes, I am.

And I did. I liked it. Not every day, obviously.

33

But most days. It wasn't as bad as it could have been. I liked it enough for people to notice. Like when Ed and I met Mrs Higginbotham in town about a month before the accident. We usually met once a month after Mrs Higginbotham retired from her job, which was minding me and Ed pretty much from the time we were babies. Ed used to get confused sometimes and call her 'Mum'.

Anyway, we met in town and Mrs Higginbotham commented on it. On how happy I seemed. She said, 'Watch out, Katherine. If the wind changes, your face might just stay like that.' I was smiling when she said it.

Even Mum noticed. She said, 'I don't know what's got you so cheerful.' That was shortly after she'd been nominated for the Kerry Group Irish Fiction Award. She's not a big fan of literary prizes. She says, 'It's not a bloody beauty pageant,' when the journalists ring and ask why she has demanded to be removed from various long lists and short lists. She's cantankerous during the literary-prize season.

So yeah, things were OK before the accident. Better than OK, really. Good, even. A lot of the time. Most of the time, in fact.

Later, in bed, Thomas says, 'Will you at least think about it?'

I say, 'I don't want to move. I like living in this apartment. I've lived here for years.'

'You never say 'home'.'

'What do you mean?'

'You never call this place home. You never say, 'I'll see you at home'.'

'I do.'

'No, you don't. You say, 'I'll see you at the apartment'.'

'No, I don't.' Except I do. I do say that.

I switch off the light and bash my pillow a couple of times with my fist. I keep expecting Thomas to say something. Something terrible. About marriage, maybe. Or wanting to have a baby. We used to talk about all sorts. Politics and books and plays and music and, of course, other people. I adore talking about other people. Then along comes the bloody miracle and all of a sudden I'm holding my breath, waiting for him to say the terrible thing, and my eyes are open but they haven't adjusted to the dark and it's like I'm in a cave. Or a tomb, and the dark is pinning me down, like hands.

But he doesn't say anything. I hear him turn onto his side.

I turn onto my side.

I close my eyes.

Eventually, I fall asleep.

# 13 July 2011; Brighton

We have to go to mass. Again. This one is called a Month's Mind or a Month's Mine. Something like that and you have to have it one month after somebody dies. I don't know why. This one is actually six weeks after because Faith didn't book it in time. The church is freezing and has a gigantic statue of Jesus on the cross with blood coming out of his hands and his feet, because of the nails.

I tell Damo about the statue and he wants to come to the church to see it but Faith says, 'No way.' She says, 'I've enough to be doing without making sure that fella doesn't drink the altar wine.'

Dad and Celia come all the way down from Scotland. That's what Celia says when Faith shouts at her later. 'We came all the way down from Scotland. And this is the thanks we get.'

This time, there's no coffin at the top of the church with a photograph of Mam on it, which I think is a bit better. I had to walk past it when I went up to get the Holy Communion and I was in a big long queue so it took ages. Some people touched it with their hands and some people blessed themselves when they walked past it but I didn't do anything. I just walked past and I didn't even look at it. I don't know why.

Ant and Adrian are wearing the same suits they wore the last time. Dad keeps calling Ant, Adrian and Adrian, Ant. Adrian says, 'Wrong again,' and Dad says, 'Story of my life.'

In the graveyard, you can hear the horns beeping and cars and buses whizzing past. That seems weird. Everything is just going on as usual. The priest is saying the rosary, which is like the Hail Mary about a hundred times, over and over and over. It's really boring. Faith's hands have gone blue because it's so cold, even though it's summertime. It's wet too. And windy. Mam would call that a fret of a day.

Back at the house, Celia asks where the bathroom is and I show her, and then she says, 'Is there any toilet paper?' and I go and get some from the cupboard under the stairs and then she says, 'I wonder would there be a clean towel anywhere?' and I go to the linen cupboard and get a beach towel because it's the only towel I can reach. Instead of saying, 'Thank you,' she says, 'Are you all right, Milo?' like there's something wrong with me, only there's nothing wrong with me except that I'm a bit wet and a bit cold from standing in the graveyard. I'm hungry too. Faith says I'm always hungry, which is not one hundred per cent true. It might be about ninety-two per cent true.

If Mam were here, she'd say, 'Get out of that gear before you catch your death.' In the kitchen, everybody is sitting round the table drinking mugs of tea and eating the sandwiches and buns that Jack dropped off before we went to the church. Jack is running the Funky Banana now and he's nearly as good as Mam at baking and cooking and coming up with new recipes with bananas in them. I take the banana and strawberry smoothie that Jack made me out of the fridge. My hands are too cold to hold the cup so I just put it on the counter and drink it through a straw.

37

Celia comes into the kitchen and Dad says, 'Ah, there she is,' like everyone was going mad wondering where she'd got to. Dad stands up and puts his arm round Celia. When they stand beside each other like that, they look like a father and daughter instead of a . . . I don't know . . . boyfriend and girlfriend, I suppose.

Dad always coughs like he's got something caught in his throat before he starts talking. 'I — that is we,' he smiles at Celia, ' — we have a little announcement to make.'

Ant says, 'Be careful, Dad. Last time you made an announcement in this kitchen, Mam clattered you over the head with a frying pan.' I don't think that's true because Faith, Ant and Adrian laugh as if Ant had made a joke.

Celia says, 'You should do this another time, Hamish.' She whispers it but I hear her.

Dad says, 'Och no, m'love. We need to tell them now. Besides, we could all do with a bit of good news.' He smiles at us. 'Couldn't we, gang?'

Nobody says anything. All you can hear is the tick and the tock of the clock on the wall; it's in the shape of Ireland. Dad bought it for Mam years ago. I've never noticed how loud it is before.

Then Dad says, 'Celia and I are going to have a baby.'

Nobody has anything to say to that so Dad keeps right on talking. 'The baby is due on the twenty-second of December and we're really — '

I say, 'That's three days before my birthday.'

Dad looks at me. 'Oh, yes . . . yes, son, it is indeed.'

Adrian stands up. He stands up so fast, his chair topples over. When he stands up, he's taller than Dad.

38

'Are you for real?' He sounds just like Mam when he says that. She never said, 'Are you serious?'

Faith says, 'Calm down, Adrian.'

Ant sits at the table, eating the icing off the top of a bun, as if Dad hasn't said anything about a baby coming three days before my birthday. As if Adrian isn't standing in the middle of the kitchen, looking mad as hell.

Dad takes a step back so Celia has to take a step back too. 'Your mother would have been happy for us, Adrian.'

Adrian walks right up to Dad, and when he speaks, his voice is really quiet. 'Don't even mention her name. I don't even know what the hell you're doing here. You and that girl.' He doesn't look at Celia when he says that but I'm pretty sure everyone knows who he means.

Dad says, 'Your mother would be glad I'm here.'

'What the hell would you know about it?' Adrian's voice isn't really quiet anymore. It's more like a shout now.

Dad says, 'I'm still your father. You should — '

'I should what? Respect you? A man who abandons his family and shacks up with a girl half his age and gets her pregnant and expects us all to be delighted with the news?'

Adrian is shouting so loud you can hardly hear what he's saying and that's when Dad says, 'You had better keep a civil tongue in your head, boy.' And that's when Adrian sort of lunges at him and grabs him by the collar of his shirt and he's still shouting but I can't make out what he's saying. I can just see specks of spit landing on Dad's face, and Dad is saying, 'Get off me!' and Faith is trying to step in between them and Celia picks up her handbag and hits Adrian with it a couple of times and shouts, 'Let go of him!' And that's when Faith shouts at her. Something like, 'Leave Adrian alone. He's upset.' And that's when Celia says, 'We came all the way down from Scotland. And this is the thanks we get.'

In the end it's Ant who sorts it out. He gets up from the table and walks over to Adrian and grabs him by the jacket, then pulls and pulls until Adrian has to let go of Dad's shirt, but he doesn't stop shouting so Ant keeps pulling him until he manages to get him out of the kitchen and down the hall and out of the house. Everything is quiet enough now to hear Celia crying but not so quiet that you can hear the tick and the tock of the clock anymore.

Dad is standing by the sink, leaning on the worktop, puffing and panting like he's just run a mile or something. Celia takes a tissue out of her bag and blows her nose really loudly. Faith sits down and puts her face in her hands.

After a while she says, 'I think you should go.'

Dad sighs and shakes his head. He picks up his jacket that's hanging on the back of the chair. He says, 'I just thought . . . you'd all like the idea. A new life. After everything that's happened, you know?'

I nod and say, 'A new baby will be nice, Dad.' Even though I'm really hoping it doesn't come late. Some babies come late. And if it came three days late, that would be my birthday and I'd prefer if it didn't come on my birthday because then it wouldn't really be my birthday anymore, would it?

Dad drags his hand down his face. He looks pretty tired. His tie is crooked and a button of his jacket is hanging on by a thread. He nods and tucks his shirt

40

back inside his trousers. He looks at Faith. 'Maybe you're right.' Faith nods. Dad says, 'I'll ring you when I get home.' It still feels weird. When Dad says 'home' and he doesn't mean here.

Faith picks up the chair that Adrian knocked over. Starts clearing the table.

Dad says, 'Your mother would be proud of you. Everything you're doing.' He nods towards me. 'Come here, wee man. You're not too old to give your dad a cuddle, are you?' I am too old but I go over to him anyway. I feel a bit sorry for him. The way Adrian sort of hates him since he went to Scotland to live with Celia and the way Ant just kind of acts like he's not here even when he is.

I don't think Adrian is right. I don't think Mam hated him. She didn't hate anyone as far as I know. She said hate was a tiring emotion and if you wanted to hate someone, you'd better get good and ready to put a lot of time and energy into it.

Me and Faith walk Dad and Celia to their car. There's no sign of Ant or Adrian, which is probably just as well. We wave and wave until they're gone. That used to be Mam and Dad's job. Waving and waving at visitors until they were gone. Once Ant and Adrian go back to the university in London, it'll just be me and Faith. I hope nothing happens to Faith, I really do. Otherwise, it'll just be me here, waving and waving until everybody is gone.

# 13 July 2011; Dublin

I am being driven insane. Insanity fuelled by Thomas's care. His consideration. His gentleness. It's on a loop: the care, the consideration, the gentleness. Like supermarket music. It's driving me crazy. The nicer he is, the crazier I feel.

And since he's living in my apartment, we're way past the third-date stage. The date when I get to say, 'It's not you. It's me.' Even though it's never me. Hardly ever.

If I said that now, he'd ask, 'What do you mean?' and I'd have to have something to say, because if I didn't, he'd say, 'I'm entitled to an explanation at the very least.' And he's right. He's right about everything. Except me. He said everybody is ready to settle down at some stage or another. But I'm not. I'm pretty sure I never will be. It's not something I want.

Everything was fine before. Before the accident. The bloody miracle. Now he keeps saying how lucky we are and how nothing should be taken for granted and how we need to appreciate everything we have and . . . Christ, it's enough to drive me to drink only I'm practically most of the way there already.

This evening takes the biscuit. Takes the biscuits, in fact. The lemon and ginger biscuits that Thomas has baked. From scratch. He has to buy most of the ingredients because there's never any call for flour or baking powder or what have you in my apartment. He buys some weighing scales too. And a spatula and a mixing bowl. He doesn't have to get a rolling pin. I have an empty wine bottle he can use.

I say, 'I thought we were going out?' when I come down from my office. I'd said I was writing but what I was really doing was playing Angry Birds on the iPad.

Thomas says, 'We're staying in!'

'Why?'

'Because we're celebrating.'

'What are we celebrating?'

'The day we met.'

'It's not the anniversary. Is it?'

'No.'

'Then why are we celebrating it?'

Thomas hands me a glass of champagne. 'It's the only excuse I could come up with for drinking bubbly on a week night.'

I nod because that's fair enough. We clink. Thomas says, 'To Aer Lingus. Where romance takes off.' And then he laughs because he happens to think that's pretty funny.

I only noticed Thomas after the pilot made the announcement. Something about the discovery of a 'suspicious package' in a cubicle of the mens' toilets in Terminal Two. I was in the aisle seat. I always pick an aisle seat so I can get in and out without having to talk to anybody.

We were sitting on the runway at Dublin airport. I lifted my head and looked out of the

43

window for the first time since I'd boarded at Heathrow, and that's when I saw him. In the window seat. I don't know how I'd missed him before. The height of him. The top of his head nearly brushing against the call button. He was wearing a well-cut suit that suggested a banker or a broker but there were spatters of muck at the ends of the trousers. His tie had been yanked away from his neck, like it had been choking him. It was a sombre navy with tiny pink sheep dotted up and down it. His smile was superfluous, I felt, given our situation. His hair was long, curly ropes of grey, all different lengths, as if it had been cut with shears by someone who may not have been a qualified hairdresser. He had a thick fringe that fell to curious grey eyes. His face wasn't just weather-beaten. It was much worse than that. It looked like it had been attacked by a gale-force wind. He had one of those 'Irish' noses: long and narrow. He had one of those 'full' mouths: wide and fleshy. The *Farmers Journal* was stuffed into his laptop bag and he was holding a copy of *Dirty Little Secret*, which happens to be the first of the Declan Darker books. A dart of something like electricity shot through me. I didn't know why. I had seen lots of people reading my books over the years.

That's when he looked up and caught me staring. He smiled. He said, 'Are you going to finish that?' His voice was unexpected. The tone of it. It made me think about Wispa bars, for some reason.

He nodded at the remains of the sandwich I

had ordered from the steward earlier.

I shook my head.

'Would you mind if I have it? It's just . . . they've stopped serving here and it's past teatime and I'm maddened with the hunger. I had dinner at one o'clock.'

I looked at my watch. It was thirteen minutes past five in the evening.

He said, 'I'm sorry. I wouldn't normally ask but there's no telling when we'll get off this bird, with the situation inside.' He nodded towards the terminal building.

I handed him the box. I said, 'It's not very fresh but . . . '

The remains of the sandwich were gone in two bites. He took a bottle of wine out of his bag, unscrewed the cap and took a long swig from it. Then he offered it to me.

I said, 'No thank you,' in a voice that suggested I wouldn't dream of drinking at such an ungodly hour.

He said, 'Oh, hang on a second,' and he rummaged around in his bag again. This time, he brought out a crumpled paper cup into which he poured a good measure of wine. He set it on my table top, thrust one of his enormous hands towards me and said, 'Cunningham. Thomas Cunningham.' His accent was midlands. Cavan, maybe. Or, worse, Monaghan.

I said, 'Kavanagh. Kat Kavanagh.' Not even Katherine.

He said, 'What decade are you on?'

'I beg your pardon?' Was this some new way of asking people their age? The cheek.

45

He said, 'Of the rosary. There're four of them. Or five. I was just wondering which one you were on.' I had forgotten about the rosary beads threaded round my fingers. I do that sometimes. On planes. And trains. In queues. They're a great deterrent.

'Oh.' I stuffed the beads into my handbag.

He said nothing then and I'd say that would have been that, which would have suited me fine. But then I said, 'Is that one of those Declan Darker books?' And, just like that, I turned into one of those people I have spent my life avoiding. People who strike up conversations with strangers on planes and trains and in queues.

He nodded and picked up the book. He said, 'Have you read them?'

I nodded. He opened the book. Inside the jacket was a photograph of Killian Kobain. Well, a photograph of an actor posing as the reclusive Killian Kobain.

Thomas looked at the photograph. 'It's funny, you know . . . '

'What?'

He shook his head and smiled. 'I read this one years ago. A friend gave it to me. It didn't have the author's photograph on the jacket and I just read the book without really paying any attention to who wrote it and I just assumed that the book was written by a woman.'

'Why?' Nobody had ever questioned Killian Kobain's gender. His sexuality, yes. Of course. You don't get to have bone structure like Kobain's without the occasional allusion to sides and which one you might be batting for.

Without skipping a beat, Cunningham-Thomas-Cunningham said, 'Because of the hands.'

'The hands?'

'The way he describes people's hands. He's always at it. Men don't describe hands. And certainly not fingers. Here, try me.'

He clamped the book over his eyes and said, 'Go ahead.'

'What?'

'Go ahead and ask me.'

'Ask you what?'

'Ask me to describe your hands.'

It was obvious he wasn't going to let up so I said, 'Er, what do my hands look like?'

And he said, 'No idea,' and he lowered the book from his face. 'See? Now it's your turn.'

And there I was, sitting on a plane that was squatting on a runway at Dublin airport on a wet, dreary Friday evening in August, with my hand over my eyes and, beside me, a man I'd just met saying, 'Go on, go on, give it a go, sure.'

I said, 'Big. Hairy. Gold band on the little finger of the left hand. Long scar running down the palm of the right hand.' I lowered my hand.

He examined his hands. Then looked at me, shaking his head. 'That's un-bel-eeev-able,' he said and I almost felt a sense of achievement, the way he said it.

'It's not. It's easy. Especially with your paws. No offence.'

He smiled. 'None taken. Hands like shovels. That's what the mammy says.'

He took out the wine bottle, refilled my cup. He said, 'I mean, Kobain once described a man as having smokers' nails.'

I remembered the character. Luka Brown. Second victim of Malcolm Beeston, a serial killer with a fondness for strangulation by washing line. If Malcolm hadn't killed Luka, the fags would have got him. Sooner rather than later, I'd say. He was a two-pack-a-day man.

'So . . . do you . . . ah . . . like the Declan Darker books?' I couldn't believe I was doing this. I never did this.

He nodded and said, 'Keep you guessing till the end. That's what I like about them.'

When we were eventually allowed to disembark, there was a mad scramble for the exits. Cunningham-Thomas-Cunningham stayed in his seat. I stood up. I said, 'We can get out now.'

He said, 'I always wait till the crowd disperses.'

When Thomas smiled, his eyes lightened and I noticed the ring of green round the grey, except the grey wasn't all that grey anymore. It was more like a pale blue. Like the sea when the cloud breaks and the sun filters through.

He said, 'It was nice meeting you, Kat.'

'You too.' The weird thing was, I meant it. That was strange.

I moved into the queue of people standing in the aisle of the plane. Thomas said, 'Goodbye now,' before he settled himself in his seat, opened his book — my book — and began to read. As the queue of people inched forward, I wondered, for the first time, why I do this. Why do I stand up as soon as the plane doors open and join the queue instead of waiting till everyone gets off before collecting my belongings and ambling off the plane? I've never ambled. Not once.

I looked back. Thomas was still there, still sitting down, still reading his book — my book.

I inched my way to the front of the plane. Eventually, I disembarked.

Thomas rang the next day.

He said, 'It's me.'

I said, 'Who?' even though I knew immediately. Definitely Monaghan, I decided.

He said, 'Cunningham. Thomas Cunningham. We met on the plane yesterday, remember? I was reading *Dirty Little Secret*. You were pretending to say the rosary.'

'I was not pretending.' The cheek.

'Anyway, I just wondered if you'll be hungry on Friday, around eight?'

'How did you get this number?'

'I'm a journalist.'

'So?'

'I can't reveal my source.'

'I demand to know how you got my number.'

'The telephone directory.'

'But . . . I didn't know I was in the telephone directory.'

'You have to ask to be left out of it. Otherwise, Eircom just put you in automatically.'

'Oh.'

'So? What do you think? Might you be hungry then?'

'I don't know.'

A pause. Thomas didn't fill it.

I said, 'Why?'

'Because if you were hungry, I could take you out for the bit of dinner.'

'Dinner?' I say, like I've never heard of it before.

'Or if you weren't hungry, we could skip dinner and go straight to the show.'

'What show?'

'The magic show. In the Button Factory. It's very good, so it is. I saw it last year. There're no white rabbits and no black hats. It's good.'

I'd never been to a magic show. 'Why?' I asked.

He said, 'Nothing like a bit of magic on a Friday night.' I was supposed to meet Minnie that Friday night. To celebrate the completion of the latest Declan Darker novel. A cocktail at the Shelbourne and dinner at One Pico.

I opened my mouth to say what needed to be said. Instead, I said, 'OK.'

'OK to dinner or OK to the magic show or OK to both?'

'Eh, both.' I couldn't get over myself.

'Grand, so. I'll pick you up at half seven, OK?'

'OK.'

'Great. See you then.'

'OK.'

Minnie said, 'I'm getting dumped for a muck savage from Monaghan?' when I told her.

I said, 'Yes.' I was as shocked as she was.

★   ★   ★

Now, I look around the kitchen and say, 'What are you doing?'

50

Thomas says, 'I'm making lemon and ginger biscuits.'

That could be true because there are bits of what could be biscuit dough on the counter, the table, the floor, the door of the fridge and all down the front of Thomas's shirt. There's also a pretty big lump of it in his hair.

'What about dinner? I'm hungry.' Minnie would say, 'Quit your whining,' if she were here.

Thomas doesn't say that. Instead, he says, 'I've made your favourite.'

I look around with suspicion. 'What?'

'Guess.'

'Takeaway.'

He smiles. 'No, I mean your favourite home-cooked meal.'

Before Thomas came to stay, I didn't have a favourite home-cooked meal unless you count cheese and ham toasties.

'I'm not guessing. I have no idea.'

He says, 'Goulash,' and lifts the lid off a gigantic saucepan to reveal a thick, bloody, boiling mass. He lowers the lid — so carefully, as if he's anxious not to disturb it — then looks at his watch and says, 'Dinner in eighteen minutes.'

I say, 'Why do you think goulash is my favourite home-cooked dinner?'

He says, 'Because you loved it when I cooked it for you the last time. Remember? You had a cold and I cooked you goulash and it was really, really hot because I put a bit too much paprika into it, and you said it was better than a bottle of Night Nurse because the minute you ate it, you were cured, remember?'

51

'No.'

He refills my glass.

He says, 'Don't worry about the kitchen; I'll clean it up.'

He says, 'Don't worry about the goulash; it's not as hot as the last time.'

He says, 'Don't worry about the lemon and ginger biscuits; they're supposed to look like that.'

I'm going out of my mind.

It's later when I come up with the plan. It's not a lie as such. It's more like self-defence. I throw myself a lifebelt. I have to. It's either that, or say, 'Look, it's not you. It's me.' Anyway, it's not like I want to break up or anything as drastic as that. I just need . . . a break. A mini-break. That's all.

I say, 'Brona is anxious to see some of the new manuscript and I haven't got much so far so I was thinking about barricading myself into the apartment, switching off the phones and just getting down to it.' I don't mention that I haven't written any of the new manuscript. None of it. Not one word since the accident. The bloody miracle.

Thomas smiles and says, 'Good idea. I'm glad you're getting back to work. It's a good sign.' He puts his hand on mine. His smile is one of those encouraging ones. His tone is a master class in tenderness. I feel like I'm being crushed to death in the back of a bin lorry.

I say, 'So I was wondering if you could . . . '

'You want me to make myself scarce?'

'Yes.'

'No problem. I need to spend some time on the farm anyway. It's coming up to harvest time. Need to make hay while the sun shines, eh?'

He leaves early the next morning, when I'm still in bed. I'm half asleep when he comes to kiss me goodbye. His hair is damp from the shower. He smells of my Clinique shower gel, which I'm always telling him not to use. He kisses me for ages and I worry about my breath because I haven't brushed my teeth yet, but he just keeps on kissing me, as if there's nothing to worry about at all. Then he takes off all his clothes again and gets back into bed and we have sex and Thomas calls it 'one for the road'.

He says, 'Give me a call. I know you're writing. But the odd time. OK? Just to let me know you're all right.'

'Why wouldn't I be all right?'

'Well, maybe you might be wondering if I'm OK.'

'You'll be fine.'

'A farm is a dangerous place, you know.'

'It's not a farm. It's five stony fields.'

'Five grand big fields.'

I say, 'See you next week.'

He says, 'Kiss me again, for luck.'

Then he says, 'Hang on, I've left my wallet in the bathroom.'

Then he says, 'Wait, I'd better take some of those lemon and ginger biscuits for the journey.'

'It's an hour's drive, for God's sake.'

After a very, very long time, he leaves. I stand in the hall and breathe it in. The silence. It's like something physical, the silence. Something you can get a hold of.

I am alone in the apartment. I can do anything I like. Nobody will say, 'Are you all right?' or 'How are you feeling?' or 'Isn't it such a bloody miracle that you're alive?'

Mostly, I do nothing. I watch a lot of telly and I eat Cheerios out of the box. I order a lot of takeaway and I make a fairly good dent in a box of wine. I don't think about the accident — the bloody miracle — and I don't think about my rib, mostly because it doesn't really hurt anymore. When I'm in danger of thinking about anything serious — like my deadline or how quiet the place is since Thomas left — I turn on the telly. Daytime television is enough to banish even the merest whisper of a serious thought right out of your head.

I do this for a few days and then I have to venture out for essentials. Cigarettes. Wine. Dinner. Dessert.

It's when I'm on my way back that I meet Nicolas. Nicolas from number thirteen, who always makes suggestive remarks when I meet him in the lobby downstairs. Today is no different. Nicolas is in the lobby, checking his post. He takes a few flyers out of his letterbox and straightens, which is when he sees me and smiles. His face is long, his teeth are small and his mouth is wide, and the combination of these features brings to mind a crocodile in long-term captivity. His expression tends towards resigned.

'Well, well, well, if it isn't Ms Kavanagh from

the fancy penthouse. Looking foxy as always, Kat.'

I say, 'Hello, Nicolas.'

'Where's Farmer Tom? I haven't seen him recently.'

'Thomas isn't a farmer. He just tells people he is.'

'Whatevs. Where is he?'

'Gone away.' I allow a trace of melancholy into my tone. Perhaps I'm after a bit of drama after my quiet few days.

Nicolas sweeps me up and down with his eyes. He always does this. I'd say he'd make a great eye-witness in a courtroom drama. He takes it all in. His eyes settle on the bags I'm carrying, straining with junk. 'Let me help you.' And before I can tell him to piss off, he's wrestled the two bags out of my hands and he's jabbing the lift call button with his index finger. Inside the lift, he puts the bags down and they clink and crinkle in a most revelatory manner. Nicolas looks inside. Cheeky rat. He says, 'Having a bit of par-tay, are we?' I ignore him, which does nothing to deflate him. He hunkers down and does a quick inventory. 'Tub of Ben & Jerry's, two bottles of Sancerre, family-size pepperoni, Kettle Chips, large bar of Cadbury's mint crisp and . . . ' he rummages around at the bottom of the bag, ' . . . ah yes, forty Silk Cut Blue.' He looks up and grins. 'How do you get to be so gorgeous on a diet like this?'

I don't know why I let him into the apartment in the end.

He's in sales. And I need a distraction from

the deadline and the quiet. A pushy salesman and a woman in need of distraction. That's a pretty deadly combination. But of course, I could have taken my bags of junk and shut the door in his face. I've done that before.

We eat the family-size pepperoni with one of the bottles of Sancerre to wash it down. Dessert is the gigantic bar of mint crisp and I resent breaking it into bits. We don't bother with coffee. We just go right ahead and open the second bottle of wine.

Nicolas becomes less sleazy as the afternoon wanes into evening. And there is something attractive about him. I just never noticed it before. He starts calling me pussy-cat, which I find not unamusing.

We have decanted from the couch to the floor and are lying on cushions, halfway down another bottle, and we're watching *Judge Judy* on the telly and roaring laughing at a woman who's suing her ex-boyfriend for stealing her hair straighteners and the pair of FitFlops that, she said, were the main cause of the tautness of her calf muscles.

That's when Thomas arrives.

I realise he's in the apartment only when he's at the door of the sitting room. He's in his farm gear. A woolly jumper with a hole in the elbow. The trousers of an old suit, tucked into mud-spattered wellington boots. The wellingtons are the ones that I bought him. As a joke. They're bright pink with yellow buttercups here and there. I never thought he'd actually go ahead and wear them.

Because it's a bit of an awkward situation, I start to laugh. It's not that I find anything funny, exactly. It's just . . . I don't know.

Thomas doesn't laugh. In fact, I get the impression he's pretty ticked off. The wine has anaesthetised me, but, still, that's the impression I'm getting.

He says, 'I thought you were working.'

I say, 'I thought *you* were working.'

'I was. But I got worried about you. When you didn't phone. And I couldn't get through to your mobile or landline. And you didn't respond to any of my emails.'

I look at Nicolas and I giggle and I say, 'I'm fine. There's no need to worry. I'm having a lovely time, so I am.'

For a moment, nobody says anything and it gets pretty quiet in the apartment, and I'd say, if I were sober, it'd be a damned awkward type of silence.

Then Thomas says, 'I'm going to go.'

'But you just got here,' I laugh after I say that, as if I happen to think that's pretty funny.

Thomas doesn't think it's funny because he just looks at me like he has no idea who I am. Then he looks at Nicolas, who stands up and holds out his hands as if he's expecting Thomas to slap cuffs on him. Nicolas opens his mouth as if he's going to recite a poem and that's when Thomas says, 'Goodbye,' in a very serious, final sort of a voice and, before I can think of anything funny to add to that, he's gone. Just like that.

Gone.

It's as if he was never here.

I look at Nicolas and snigger, the way drunk people do when they can't think of anything to say.

Nicolas says, 'I should split.'

Split. The state of him.

He doesn't try to kiss me or anything. I think he may have kissed me at one stage during the afternoon. I remember thinking: Christ, that's a long tongue. But I have no recollection of an actual kiss.

It doesn't matter now.

It doesn't matter anymore.

Three months later . . .

I check the calendar. It's the sixteenth of October, which means it's ten weeks exactly till my tenth birthday, which is also Christmas Day and, who knows, it might even end up being the new baby's birthday, if it comes three days late.

That's a lot of things for one day.

I wasn't supposed to come until the twenty-fifth of January. Mam says I was the best Christmas present she ever got. I got a dog for Christmas when I was a kid. I taught him to jump through Faith's hula hoop. His name was Setanta, after Fionn MacCumhaill's dog. He died about six months after Dad went to Scotland. The vet said it was something to do with his kidneys but I think Setanta's heart was sort of broken, because Dad was the one who took him for walks and fed him and let him sit on his lap, even though Setanta was a really big dog who moulted a lot and was a bit smelly, to be honest. For ages after Dad left, Setanta sat in the porch every day at half six, waiting for him to come home.

I was mad about Fionn MacCumhaill and the Fianna stories when I was a kid. The Fianna were this cool band of Irish warriors and Fionn was the leader. They were always fighting with other gangs but the Fianna mostly won. They were pretty legend. Mam read the stories to me. Sometimes Faith did, if Mam had to work late at the Funky Banana or go to her book club or something. Faith was pretty good at reading them but she wasn't as good as Mam at the voices. And she kept stopping at the exciting bits to play her violin. She said every story needs a soundtrack but I prefer just getting on with things.

My favourite story is the one with Fionn and the Scottish giant. Mam took me to the Giant's Causeway when I was a kid. I saw the stepping stones the Scottish giant used to cross the sea to Ireland. I held Mam's hand when I saw them but I wasn't scared. Sometimes adults make up stories and they're not true. Like Santa. He's not true. Sully told me and Damo. Sully is Damo's big brother. He's in the army and he tells me and Damo loads of stuff.

Sully isn't his real name. His real name is Jacob, I think, but everyone calls him Sully, on account of his surname which happens to be Sullivan.

It's Sunday, which means we have to go to the graveyard. Faith likes going there on Sundays. I don't know why. I don't like going. It's always really cold there, even if it's warm everywhere else. Faith says, 'Wear an extra jumper.' She's in the attic, looking for Mam's rosary beads. She says she wants to put them on the grave. Mam got the rosary beads from her grandmother, who lived to be a hundred and one. I swear to God. She got a hundred pounds from the President of Ireland because she was so old.

I don't think the beads are in the attic but Faith says she's looked everywhere else.

I asked Mam if Santa would still come to you if you didn't believe in him. She said she thought he might. She said even if you didn't believe in him, he'd still believe in you. Adults say weird things.

Last year, Dad came to the house for a couple of

hours on Christmas Day but I reckon he won't be able to make it this year, because of the baby. Dad says he has to be there for that. I will be a half-brother. A half-brother means that Celia is not my mam.

Faith says that Mam can hear me and see me and when the sun shines, that's Mam, smiling. Faith is my sister but she's an adult. That's because she was born a long time ago.

There's a bit of cobweb in Faith's hair when she climbs down from the attic. She's got papers in her hand. I ask her if she found the rosary beads but she shakes her head and says, 'Go and tidy your room or something.' She doesn't even look inside my room to see if it's messy.

I pick up the clothes on my bedroom floor and put them all in the linen basket. Then I go and call for Damo.

He says, 'Look at this,' when he opens his front door. He sticks his tongue out and pushes the tip of it into his nose. He can make his eyeballs shoot up inside his head too.

I wish it were Wednesday. I'd be going to lifesaving class after school, if it were Wednesday. I might be getting my brown badge next week, if I know all the answers.

I check the calendar. It's 16 October. Four months. Four months since the accident. Four and a half, I suppose. And only three months since Thomas left. It seems a lot longer than that.

Not seeing Thomas is like giving up cigarettes. I've never given up cigarettes but I imagine it would feel like this. There are triggers. Triggers that make me think about Thomas, and maybe even wish he was here. Like I'd wish for a cigarette if I hadn't had one for an hour or so.

Stress. That's a trigger. When I feel stressed, I think about Thomas. That's probably why I've been thinking about him so much lately.

Or, oddly, when I'm happy. When something makes me smile. Or even laugh. Something funny, I mean. Or weird. Or one of those strange road signs. Like BEWARE — BLIND PEDES-TRIANS. Something that makes me feel sure that when I look at Thomas, he will be smiling too.

Four months.

That's all it takes,.

Four months for everything to fall apart.

I'll be forty soon. January. That's when. And Christmas to get through before that.

I'm nearly forty and I should be dead.

I should have died in a pile-up. The newsreader would have described me as a thirty-nine-year-old woman. A thirty-nine-year-old woman was killed this afternoon in an accident on the M1.

A thirty-nine-year-old woman. That would have got people's attention. Would have given them pause. Might have prompted them to look up from their dinners, shake their heads, say something like 'Tragic', or 'Such a waste', or 'You just never know, do you? When your time is up?'

That didn't happen. Instead, I'm a nearly-forty-year-old woman who has been the victim, it seems, of a miracle. That's what everyone called it. I'm supposed to be grateful, apparently.

Instead, I'm alone and I haven't written one word in four months.

And I'm nearly forty. It sits on my horizon, wobbling like one of those horrible jellies Mrs Higginbotham used to make for our birthday parties when we were between the ages of four and eight. Nine, according to Mrs Higginbotham, was too old for jelly-on-a-plate. Thank Christ.

I say, 'I hate being nearly forty.'

Minnie says, 'Consider the alternative.'

'At least I'd make a nice corpse.'

'A forty-year-old corpse. You'd still be forty, dead or alive.'

'Nearly forty,' but Minnie's not listening anymore.

I'm going to be forty.

Soon.

I suppose the other stuff is bad too. The stuff about the writing and Thomas and the fact that I could have died. Everyone said I could have died. Thomas said it most of all. He said it was a miracle I walked away with hardly a scratch. I said there's no such thing as miracles. He said it didn't matter if I believed it or not.

One bloody miracle and everything falls apart.

'We want different things.' That's what Thomas said the day he came back for his stuff. I suppose that's true. We were very different, me and Thomas. I didn't mind how different we were. I even miss it, sometimes. Like the other day, when I was doing my impersonation of the weather girl on the telly (I can do a near-perfect imitation of her accent, even though she's from Longford, which is one of the trickier ones), I smiled at the place on the couch where Thomas used to sit. As if he were still sitting there. As if I thought he was still sitting there.

I get nervous when that happens, so I find something to do. Like scrub the burned milk off the inside of the microwave. Ed likes hot chocolate but he hates cleaning. And I'm not betraying confidences by saying that. It's there for everyone to read on his Facebook page.

It's four o'clock in the afternoon. I hate afternoons. Cigarettes don't taste as good in the afternoons. It's too early for a drink but you've had too many teas and coffees and water would make you cry with the boredom of it. Consider its properties: tasteless, odourless, colourless.

I told Brona about the writer's block. I was a bit excited about it, really. I'd heard of it, of course. There was a programme on the telly. But I'd never had it before.

Brona said, 'Oh that. That happens to all writers. It won't last long. You'll be fine.'

I say, 'No, it's serious. I mean, I've had a life-changing experience.'

'A life-affirming experience.'

'I could have died.'

'But you didn't,' she reminds me.

I produce Thomas, the ace up my sleeve.

'He left me, remember? Right after the accident. My ribs were shattered, remember?'

'Fractured,' she says, but in her gentle voice so I can't take umbrage. 'One rib, wasn't it? One rib had a hairline fracture.'

I say, 'It was agony.'

Brona makes soothing noises down the line.

'He left me.' I say it again. No matter how many times I say it I still can't quite believe it. I am in charge of leaving. Her tone strains a little here. She says, 'Only because you didn't want to marry him and bear his child.' I can't blame her, I suppose. She's been on a quest for 'The One' since the early nineties. In her eyes, I've committed the ultimate betrayal. I said no to a genuine offer of marriage and the chance of having my womb filled with the offspring of a man with no obvious physical defects (unless you count his feet, which differ in length by a monumental two shoe sizes), a grand head of hair, his own teeth and a job that doesn't involve anything illegal (like drug-trafficking) or poncy (like interior design).

I phone Ed.

He says, 'I can't talk. I'm working.' He's not fond of talking on the telephone. Especially when he's working.

'I thought you wouldn't be busy at this hour. It's in between lunch and dinner.'

'Yes, Kat, but we have to clean up after lunch and get ready for the dinner crowd. Chef is showing me how to make croque-monsieurs.'

'They're just ham and cheese toasties. I showed you how to make them years ago.'

'No, they're not. They're fancier.'

I say, 'Do you want to go to the movies?'

'I can't. Chef is showing me how to make croque-monsieurs.'

I say, 'I don't mean right now.' Although I would have gone right now if he had said yes. 'I mean later on. When you finish your shift. Later.'

'Are you coming too, Kat?'

'Yes.'

'OK.' And even though this is a telephone conversation, I can feel him nodding and smiling and, in spite of everything — being nearly forty, Thomas, the bloody miracle, the pain of shattered ribs — OK, OK, one hairline-fractured rib — I smile back.

I say, 'I haven't seen you in ages.' This is not true. It just feels true.

He says, 'I'm sorry, Kat,' and the way he says it causes a swelling sensation inside my nose and eyes and throat. I tighten my grip on the phone and swallow.

'You have nothing to be sorry for, you big eejit,' I tell him and I am relieved that my voice sounds like it always does: bored, disinterested, unemotional.

'Will you pick me up?' he asks.

'I'll pick you up at seven, OK? We could go to the Leaning Tower of Pizza first.'

He sighs and says, 'OK, Kat,' and that's when I feel a bit bad because there's a chance I've been monopolising his time since the near-death-and-Thomas-desertion situations. He hangs up before I can say, 'Thank you, Ed.'

People say he is Down's Syndrome. That's not true. He is Edward Kavanagh. Ed. He is gentle and loving and funny and spontaneous. He is moody and clumsy. He is a great swimmer, an avid watcher of soaps, a teller of terrible jokes. He loves going to the cinema and eating pizza. He has Down's Syndrome. Down's Syndrome is not what he is; it's what he has. There's a difference.

Ed was born in the spring of 1977. My mother never got over it. I was five and had my heart set on a girl. In a pink dress with blonde curly hair and a matching set of dimples. Instead, I got Ed, who had no hair, one dimple and a hole in his heart. In spite of these discrepancies, I loved Ed from the start and I was not a child given to gratuitous expressions of love.

Dad said he was 'special'. Mum called him 'different'. To me, he was just Ed. My little brother. It was only later, when he came home from school with his shirt torn and muck on the knees of his trousers or his lunchbox gone, I realised that the other children didn't like these differences. They didn't want anyone to be special.

I don't think Dad really noticed, bent as he was across his workbench in the lab where he worked all hours, examining intimate pieces of people he never met. Mum was often away on book tours, and, when she wasn't, she wrote in the attic room and we were not allowed to make any noise. Mrs Higginbotham brought Ed for his checkups and mended his shirts and washed the muck off the knees of his trousers and bought him new lunchboxes. She told him not to worry. Said it would make a man of him. I didn't think Ed was ready to be a man.

It is in the middle of the night that I can admit that perhaps it is Thomas, the absence of Thomas, that is the hardest thing. I wake at four. It's always four. If Thomas were where he is supposed to be, he would wake too and reach out one of his ridiculously long arms until his hand gets a grip on my shoulder, or my leg, or my elbow. 'You OK, baby?' he would say and I would let him get away with it. There is something about four o'clock in the morning that lowers my resistance to affection.

'You OK, baby?'

I'm not saying that I do anything as crass as move my hands along his side of his bed, now cold. Or wrap myself in the shirt he left, like those women in the rom-coms Ed loves, with their noses buried in the soft fabric, looking tiny and vulnerable and ridiculous.

In fact, what I did with that shirt the other day was cut it up into about a hundred pieces, put it

70

into a Jiffy bag and post it to him. Registered post, just to be sure. He called me when he got it.

He said, 'Nice touch.'

I said, 'I thought so.'

'Should I expect more parcels of this nature?'

'I shouldn't think so,' I said. 'Although you left those cords behind. The yellow ones, remember? They deserve a good hacking.'

He said, 'They're beige.'

'Anyway, I can't get the scissors through them. The material is too thick.'

A pause. And then, 'How is your rib?'

'It hurts,' I said, even though it doesn't. Not anymore.

'And everything else?'

'Fine,' I told him.

Another pause. I could hear him gearing up to say goodbye. 'You could come over and collect the cords,' I said, holding my breath in the pause that followed.

He knew what I meant. We've had post-break-up sex much more often than would be considered appropriate in a break-up guide book, I'd say.

'I don't think that's a good idea anymore,' he said.

'I never thought it was a good idea. Yellow cords.'

'They're beige.' He laughed. I always loved his laugh. The sound of it. Girlish. Almost a giggle. And the fact that I could still make him laugh.

'So are you coming?' I kept my voice light, unconcerned. The pause was the worst one yet.

71

The one that told me we were nearly there, Thomas and I. Despite the dragging of my feet all the way, it was nearly done.

Then he told me. 'Kat,' he said. 'I . . . I've been meaning to tell you . . . '

Still I said nothing. But I knew. I knew what he was going to say. Minnie saw them. She mentioned it. She said, 'It's probably nothing but . . . '

Thomas said, 'I'm sort of seeing someone.'

I said, 'How do you sort of see someone?'

'I mean, I am. I'm seeing someone.'

'Who?'

'Her name is Sarah.'

'Sarah? Sarah Keeling? From the *Farmers Journal?*'

'Yes. I didn't think you knew her.'

'I met her once. Tall. Bony. Pointy tits.'

'Where did you meet her?'

'When you forced me to go to the cattle mart, remember?'

'I didn't force you to go.'

'It doesn't seem like the type of thing I'd attend of my own free will.'

Thomas didn't say anything to that. It sounded like he was rubbing his forehead. He does that when he's tired.

'You went out with her before, didn't you?'

'That was years ago.'

'She told me. When we were at the trough. You'd gone to examine hooves or something.'

'Anyway . . . I wanted to tell you, you know, just in case . . . '

'In case what?' I said. I was impressed by my

72

voice. It sounded like the voice of somebody who was thinking about what to have for dinner.

'In case . . . you know . . . look, I just didn't want you hearing about it from anybody else, OK?'

'Fine.'

'Really?'

'Of course. Why wouldn't it be fine?'

We haven't spoken since then. It's just as well, really. The past is better left behind. It's time to move on. That's what Minnie says. And in the daytime, it's fine. It really is. I have Ed and Minnie and my writer's block and being nearly forty and the faint, lingering pain in my one hairline-fractured rib to distract me.

It's only at night.

Four o'clock in the morning, in particular. Your resources are depleted at this hour. Your resolve is not what it should be. I let myself out onto the balcony and rummage in my dressing-gown pocket for a pack of cigarettes. My hands shake and it takes a while to get one of them lit.

'You OK, baby?'

I look round. There is no one here but me.

It's Friday night. Ant and Adrian are home for the weekend. They come home a lot now. They are twins, which means that they look the same and talk the same and they used to do a magic disappearing act when they were kids. Everyone believed it, including me. They're even more identical than Fred and George Weasley. They are studying science in London, which happens to be the capital of the UK and England. Ten million people live in London. Ten million and two, now that Ant and Adrian are there.

Damo thinks Ant and Adrian are cool. Probably because they have long hair and they don't live at home anymore. Damo says that when he doesn't have to live at home anymore, he'll stay up all night and he'll eat his dessert before his dinner and he'll never eat one single green. That's what he calls vegetables. Greens. Even carrots and cauliflowers.

Tonight we are having beans on toast for our dinner. I don't like beans so I am having toast. Adrian makes my favourite drink, which happens to be hot chocolate with two marshmallows on the top. If Mam was here she would make me eat the beans. Or she would make something else, like spaghetti Bolognese. I love spaghetti Bolognese. Spaghetti is made from flour and water. Miss Williams has a machine that can make spaghetti. I'd love a machine like that. Today, she asked us to write a story about anything we like so

74

long as it had the words adventure and holiday and storm in it. She likes getting us to write long stories so she can text her boyfriend during the class. Damo says he's read her messages and there's lots of sexy talk in them, but I don't know if that's true.

I wrote about me and Mam going on holiday to Spain. That bit is true. We really did go on holiday to Spain last year. In the story, I said we sailed there and there was a big storm one night and we got tossed overboard and we would have drowned if it hadn't been for my lifesaving, because I was able to rescue everybody, even Mam. That's not true. We went to Spain in an aeroplane. There was no storm but it rained one day and the waves were huge and Mam wouldn't let me go swimming. Miss Williams liked my story. She says I'm going to be a writer when I grow up but I don't want to be a writer. How boring is that? She also says that I might be a computer programmer on account of being the person she always asks to fix the computers at school whenever there's a problem with one of them. She points at me and says, 'Fix it, Bill.' I like computers but I'm still not going to be a computer programmer, even if Bill Gates happens to be the richest man in the galaxy.

No, what I'm going to be is a lifesaver. Maybe on a beach or in the swimming pool. So is Damo, even though he doesn't go to lifesaving like me. I said I'll teach him everything I know next summer, if Faith brings us to the pool. Or the beach, maybe.

Faith and Ant and Adrian are drinking wine with their dinner. Adrian's not really supposed to drink wine because of what happened when Dad told Mam about Celia. Adrian drank loads of wine that night and Dad couldn't see out of his left eye for about a week afterwards, on account of the swelling.

I drank wine once but I had to spit it out. It looks like blood. When you cut a worm in two, it doesn't die. It just grows into two worms. Me and Damo cut one but nothing happened. It just lay on the path and didn't move, and then we got bored waiting so we went and climbed the tree in Damo's back garden. I can get to the middle bit but Damo goes all the way to the top. I checked on my way home and the worms were gone.

After dinner, I go into the sitting room but the only movie that's on is *Up* and I've seen it loads of times. Mam loves that movie but she always cries when Carl looks at the pictures of Ellie in his photo album.

I pick up the zapper and change the channel. Some boring programme about women who make stuff out of lace. Who cares? Ads, ads, ads. Some show about men going bald. Football. People talking about football. Another football match. Film reviews. This is better. The latest Declan Darker movie. Faith says I'm not allowed to watch those movies until I'm fifteen, which probably means there's loads of blood and guts and kissing in them. She says I can't read the books either till I'm older. Sully reads them. And Rob. And Dad. Dad loves all thrillers but he says Killian Kobain is his favourite thriller writer. Damo says he's read them all too but I don't think he has because he hates reading. They show the trailer and it looks deadly and there's not too much blood and guts in it. If I wasn't going to be a lifeguard, I'd probably be a policeman in New York, just like Declan Darker.

Now they're talking about another film. I think it's in French because the people in the film are saying 'wee, wee, wee', which is French for 'yes'.

I switch back to *Up*. It's the bit with the balloons. I'd love to attach balloons to our house and then we could fly away. Maybe to Ireland, where Mam is from.

I wonder if you went up high enough in the sky, would you get to heaven?

I'm only half Irish but Mam still makes me call her Mam, like Irish people do. She says her mother would turn in her grave if I called her mum, like Damo calls his. I didn't think dead people could move. Only if they're zombies. Damo dressed up like a zombie at Halloween. When we met Carla, he did that thing he does with his eyes and tried to chase her. But she wouldn't run away. She's probably the only girl in our class who doesn't run away from Damo when he does the thing with his eyes.

I go into the kitchen to get some more Coke. Faith's face is all blotchy and red. She looks like Stan in my class when Damo and Alex are picking football teams in the yard.

Adrian puts his hands on Faith's shoulders and says, 'Not being a blood relative of Hamish McIntyre has to be a good thing, right?' Sometimes, Adrian calls Dad 'Hamish' instead of 'Dad'.

I'm not very good at football but I get picked for the team because I'm the fastest runner. That's because of all the muscles in my legs from the lifesaving. I have to pass the ball when I get near the goal. I pass it to Damo. He says, 'HE SHOOTS . . . HE SCORES . . . ' just before he puts it in the net. He pulls his shirt over his head and runs around. Once he ran into the trunk of the chestnut tree and had to get four stitches in his forehead. He says he was knocked out but I saw his eyes moving.

The phone rings and nobody answers it so I have to

go out to the hall and pick it up. It's Dad. He nearly always rings on Friday night. 'How's tricks, me wee man?' he asks, like I'm a little kid.

'Fine.'

'What are you up to?'

'I'm watching *Up*.'

'How's school?'

I say, 'Grand,' the way Mam does.

'Will you put Faith on?' He never asks about lifesaving. Maybe it's because I only started doing it after he went to Scotland to do sex with Celia, which is what you have to do to get a baby. Sully told me and Damo all about it. He says you don't get a baby if you use a johnny. He gave us a johnny but it burst after we filled it with water and threw it out of Damo's bedroom window.

I say, 'Faith is in the kitchen with Ant and Adrian.'

He says, 'Go and get her for me, like a good wee man.'

I say, 'OK, but . . . '

He says, 'What?' His voice sounds like Miss Williams's when Damo tells her why he hasn't got his homework done. 'I'm running out of patience, Mr Sullivan.' Her lips get very thin when she says that.

I say, 'Faith is crying.' I don't say 'again'. I don't say she's been crying a lot since last Sunday when she found the papers in the attic, instead of the rosary beads.

'What?'

'She's crying. In the kitchen.'

He says, 'What's wrong with her?'

I say, 'I don't know.' That's true. I don't know. Every time I go into the kitchen, Faith looks away so I won't notice that she's crying. And they stop talking. The

78

way adults do when they're talking about something that's not suitable for kids.

Dad says, 'It's probably boy trouble, eh son?' I don't think so. I saw Rob kiss Faith this morning before he went to his job at the shop where they fix guitars. A proper kiss. On the lips, I mean. They closed their eyes and kissed for ages. Over a minute, I reckon.

'Hang on.' I go into the kitchen.

Adrian is saying, 'I swear, Faith. We didn't know. Tell her, Ant.'

Ant says, 'He's telling the truth, Faith. We hadn't a clue until you rang us the other day.'

I look at Faith and say, 'Dad's on the phone.' I don't tell her that I told Dad that she's been crying. I shouldn't have told him. I don't know why I did. Sometimes adults know what to do about things but I don't know if Dad will, to be honest.

Faith says, 'Christ,' and wipes her nose with the sleeve of her jumper like she's always telling me not to do.

Ant hands her a tissue and tells her to take it easy. He says, 'Maybe there's an explanation.'

Faith laughs like someone who doesn't think anything is funny. Then she blows her nose. It sounds like Damo's trumpet. He got it for his birthday but he still can't play it. He just blows into it.

Faith says, 'Bedtime, Milo,' before she leaves the kitchen. I have a feeling Faith is mad with me except I don't know why. I even tidied my room yesterday without anyone asking me to, but I don't think she noticed.

Adrian says, 'I'll bring you up.' He picks up his glass of wine and finishes it. It's probably just as well Dad's not here tonight. 'I just have to go for a piss first.'

If Mam was here, she'd say, 'Mind your manners,' and Adrian would say, 'I'm eighteen, Ma,' and she'd say, 'You're never too old for a clip round the ear,' even though she never gave anyone a clip round the ear. She just said you were never too old for one.

I say, 'I don't need anyone to bring me to bed. I'm not a little kid.'

Adrian grins and puts up his fists like a boxer, which means that he wants to mess fight me but I'm not in the mood for a mess fight. I know that's weird but I'm not.

I walk past Faith, who is sitting on the floor in the hall. She doesn't notice me when I walk past. She must be gripping the phone really hard cos her knuckles are dead white. It's dark at the top of the stairs but when I flick the light switch, nothing happens. Someone needs to put in a new bulb. I can't do it. I can't reach. I sit on the top step.

Faith says, 'Why did you never tell me?' She's not crying any more. She sounds mad now, like the time I went to the Funky Banana after school without telling her. I love the smell of the café. It smells like coffee beans and banana and peanut-butter muffins. I always used to go there after school. I just forgot that day. I forgot I wasn't supposed to go there anymore.

She sounds like that now. Really mad. 'Last week. Sunday. I was looking for her grandmother's rosary beads. I found the papers in the bloody attic.'

She doesn't say anything for a while so I suppose Dad must be talking. Probably saying, 'How's tricks?' and, 'What are you up to?' and, 'How's school?' Faith doesn't even go to school anymore. She goes to music college. She started there two years ago, after she was finished travelling round the world. And she's in a band. Damo said, 'So?' when I told him that but I could tell he was impressed.

'No, no, that's bullshit,' says Faith. 'You could have told me. I mean, Jason Bond was adopted and everyone knew about that. I came home from school and told you all about it. You could have told me then. Why didn't you tell me then?'

Another silence. I put my thumb in my mouth. I'm not supposed to do that anymore. Mam brought me to Legoland after I gave up.

'I remember Mam being pregnant with Ant and Adrian and Milo. So it was just me, right? I'm the only one. Why?'

Jessica in year seven in my school is adopted. When I was a little kid, I used to think babies came out of their mam's bellybutton. How stupid is that?

'In an orphanage? Jesus, what? Did you pick me out of a line of cots? Was I the cutest baby there? Christ almighty, Dad, you should have told me. I had a right to know.'

Another silence. I lean my head against the railings and close my eyes. It's weird how tired you can get, doing nothing.

'So let me get this straight. You thought you couldn't have kids so you adopted me. And then, BAM! Along comes Ant, Adrian and Milo, and you decide maybe you'd better not tell me cos I might feel a bit . . . what? Left out? Jesus!'

Another silence so I guess Dad is saying something about Faith feeling left out or not feeling left out. Something like that.

'So where does that leave me, then? You know nothing about where I come from and I'm here in Brighton, looking after a nine-year-old boy, studying,

81

doing the odd shift at the café when Jack needs time off. While you're swanning round Edinburgh with that slip of a girl, talking about colours for the bloody nursery.'

Ant comes into the hall and sees me at the top of the stairs. He nods towards me and Faith turns round, and that's when she sees me and she says, 'Christ,' and then she hangs up.

She looks at me again. 'What are you doing, Milo? I told you to go to bed.'

I say, 'We need a new light bulb.' I know I'm too old to be afraid of the dark. I'm not afraid of the dark, exactly. I'm just not mad about it, y'know?

Faith sighs and says nothing. Ant goes and gets a new bulb. He walks up the stairs and goes into Mam's room so he can get the stool. She keeps her library books on the stool. The ones she's read. So she won't have to go looking for them when it's time to take them back. Ant lifts the books off the stool. Someone should have taken them back ages ago. The fine is going to be gigantic.

When Ant has finished putting the bulb in, he puts the stool back and puts the library books on the stool again. Then he walks over to me and holds out his hand. I take it and he pulls me up and then he ducks down and puts me across his back like a sack of potatoes.

I don't laugh.

Or try to get down.

I just let him.

I don't know why.

I think it's because I'm tired.

Ed says, 'It's your turn, Kat.'

I say, 'No, it's your turn.'

'I made it the last time.'

'Yes, but I made the hot chocolates, remember?'

'Yes, but I'm your guest.'

'Fine.' I drag myself off the couch and haul myself to the kitchen to put more popcorn in the microwave.

It's Saturday night. Another bloody Saturday night. Luckily, Sophie — his on-again-off-again girlfriend — has gone to visit her granny in Cork so Ed is free. Mum is at some writing thing and Dad is working late at the lab so Ed is staying over. I'm glad. The apartment is so quiet now. Living with Thomas was like living with a large group of people, in terms of noise and mess.

Mum rings, which is unusual. I say, 'Everything all right?'

She says, 'I did ask you to look after Edward, didn't I?'

'Yes, of course you did. He's here. He's fine.'

'Oh good. Sorry, Katherine, I . . . I got a bit distracted and I couldn't quite remember if . . . '

'It's all right. Don't worry.'

'Good. Thank you.'

I say, 'How's the symposium going?'

83

She says, 'It's a writing retreat.'

'Oh. Sorry.'

'Did you hear from your father?'

'He's still at work. I invited him over for takeaway, but you know him, he likes being in the lab when it's quiet.'

She says, 'Good. That's good.' If I asked her to repeat what I'd just said, she wouldn't be able to. She's retreated. I can hear it in her voice.

Ed and I have assumed what I like to call 'the Position'. I've never liked going out on a Saturday night. If I have to go out, I do it on a weeknight, when there's no crush. No queues. Less noise. Fewer people.

The Position is horizontal. You need a couch and a remote control that you can reach without having to move. You need sustenance, for example dark chocolate and red wine. You need Box Sets. Tonight, it's *Planet Earth*. Once you have these props, you're pretty much good to go.

We're watching a penguin huddle when the intercom buzzes, which is odd. This is not the kind of place where people arrive at the door and say things like 'I was in the neighbourhood'. I check my phone. No messages.

Ed says, 'It might be Thomas, Kat. Thomas might be at the door.' I've told Ed about me and Thomas. I've told him loads of times. He keeps saying we'll make up. Like him and Sophie.

There's no point looking out of the window because you can't see the gates from the top floor. I pick up the intercom phone.

I say, 'Who is it?' in the voice I reserve for door-to-door salesmen and scientologists.

For a moment, I think Ed's right. I think it's Thomas. This has been happening a bit recently. I think I see him. Or hear him. When I'm in the supermarket or at the pick 'n' mix in the foyer of the cinema, I think I see him out of the corner of my eye. But when I turn round, it's someone else. Or nobody at all. Just a shadow. A figment of my imagination.

'Who's there?' All I can hear is the crackle of some static on the line. I hang up. There have been some phone calls like that lately. When I answer, no one's there.

Ed is behind me, biting his nails. I paste a smile on my face and say, 'It's probably just kids messing.'

Ed says, 'It could be burglars.'

'It's not burglars. They don't buzz the apartment before they break in, generally.'

'I wish Thomas was here.'

'I told you, Ed. Thomas isn't going to be here anymore. Remember?'

'I wouldn't feel scared if Thomas was here.'

I didn't introduce Thomas to Ed for ages. I hate the way some people talk slower when they're talking to Ed. Or louder. Or they just talk about stuff that they'd never usually talk about. Boring stuff. I hate that. When they finally met, it was by accident, really. It was St Stephen's Day and Ed and I were in the Position on my couch.

Ed said, 'It's your turn, Kat.'

I said, 'No, it's your turn.'

'I made them the last time.'

'Yes but I made the hot chocolates, remember?'

'Yes, but I'm your guest.'

'Fine.' I dragged myself off the couch and hauled myself to the kitchen to make another platter of turkey-and-stuffing-and-cranberry-sauce sandwiches.

That's when the intercom buzzed, which was strange because I wasn't expecting anyone. I checked my phone. No messages. I picked up the intercom. 'Who is it?'

'It's me.' I recognised the accent immediately. Riddled with Monaghan. The voice itself, halting and low and reminiscent of Wispa bars.

I said, 'I wasn't expecting you,' my tone sharp. See what he made of that.

Thomas said, 'I know.' Unperturbed by my sharp tone.

I said, 'Well?' I hated the way I sucked in my belly and ran my fingers through the briars in my hair.

'Are you going to let me in?'

'I . . . I wasn't expecting you.'

'You already said that.'

'But it's true.'

'Well?'

'I'm just saying.'

'Are you going to let me in?'

Perhaps that was the moment it all began to unravel. Because I did. I let Thomas Cunningham in.

I pressed the door release. I had sixty seconds. That's how long it would take him to call the lift, exchange pleasantries with every single person he met and arrive at the top floor.

Not enough time to do anything with my hair

so I just gathered it up in my hands and twisted it round and round and pierced it with a pencil until it sort of looked a bit like a bun.

Forty-five seconds.

Not enough time to wash myself but just enough time to tear off the tracksuit bottoms and T-shirt with the cranberry-sauce stain on the front of it and throw them into the laundry basket. I rubbed deodorant under my arms and checked my legs. Stubble. No way he was staying over. I squeezed into jeans and reefed a top over my head, one that very charitably hid my bum, my stomach and a good bit of thigh.

Thirty seconds.

Not enough time for foundation. I made do with lipstick and a quick flick of the blusher brush round my face. Thomas had never seen me without make-up and Christmas was definitely not the time to reveal myself. People aren't themselves at Christmas.

Six seconds. I glanced in the mirror. Long black hair, trapped in a makeshift bun with bits already falling out of it. White face, in spite of my heavy hand with the blusher brush. Green eyes, strained from all the telly watching. Not great but — with three seconds left — it was the best I could do.

I positioned myself beside the door. Exhaled. I couldn't believe it had come to this.

I opened the door of my apartment and there he was. As always, the hallway seemed to narrow, the ceiling lowered, the walls contracted. From habit, he bent his head when he walked through the door. Years of smacking your forehead on architraves will do that to a man.

In the end, there was no need to worry about Thomas meeting Ed. I probably should have known that.

Thomas said, 'You must be Ed,' when he strode into the living room.

Ed stood up and brushed turkey-and-stuffing-and-cranberry-sauce sandwich crumbs off his trousers. He said, 'Are you Kat's boyfriend?'

Thomas said, 'Kat's too old to have a boyfriend.'

Ed said, 'She's not that old. She's only thirty-eight.'

I said, 'Ed!' Thomas and I hadn't discussed our ages. Well, OK, he'd told me he was forty-five but my age hadn't come up. Well, maybe it came up once and I might have said I was thirty-five or something like that. I can't remember every little detail, can I?

Thomas looked at the telly and said, 'That's *Miracle on 34th Street*, isn't it?'

'Is it? I'm not sure . . . we haven't really been . . . ' When Ed took it out of his overnight bag I had presumed it was one of those films I'd hate.

Thomas said, 'I love that film.'

'Oh.'

'Do you mind if I stay and watch it with ye?'

'Well, I suppose . . . '

'And are there any of those lovely-looking sandwiches going a-beggin'?'

In the end, we managed to fit on the couch, all three of us. We ate the mince pies that Thomas had brought. 'The mammy made them,' he said after Ed gave them — an over-generous, I felt — eleven out of ten. I was sandwiched between them. They talked across me. They talked about football; they both supported Chelsea. They talked about films; Thomas admitted to a passionate interest in all things vampire, which Ed approved of. They talked about their jobs; Ed explained how he made the perfect scrambled eggs in the café where he worked while Thomas countered with a step-by-step account of the best way to milk a goat.

I felt a couple of things. A bit drowsy, from the overeating and the heat of being sandwiched between them. Perhaps a little tired. There may have been some shame. That I ever thought that Thomas would treat Ed differently instead of with his usual gruff charm and curiosity. He was never afraid of Ed's disability. He just accepted it, like he accepted most things, even me.

Later, when Ed went to bed, I sat beside Thomas on the couch and, without really planning it, I kissed him. If he was surprised, he didn't show it. I went all out then and wrapped his arm round me and tucked my head under the massive awning of his shoulder.

After a while, he said, 'You'd better be mighty careful, Katherine Kavanagh.'

'Why?'

'Because I think you're falling for me.' His tone was matter-of-fact, his eyes trained on the telly.

I said, 'Don't be ridiculous.'

He said, 'It's worse than I thought.'

'What could be worse than that, you dirty-looking eejit?'

He said, 'You love me.' His voice was dead-pan. He might have been talking about the weather. It was infuriating.

'You're deluded.'

'I'm right.'

Despite myself, I was curious. He sounded so . . . certain.

I cleared my throat. 'Let's just suppose — just for a moment — that you're correct. What would it mean? Hypothetically, I mean.'

He smiled. Ran his fingers down his face. They made a scratchy sound across his stubble. He said, 'I would have to admit to harbouring similar feelings.'

'Harbouring?'

'Harbouring.'

I let that sink in for a while. It felt . . . well, nice, I suppose. Warm and sort of touching, if you're into that kind of thing.

'But would anything change?'

'No.' And the strange thing was, I believed him. I did. For a while, anyway. I allowed myself to be lulled by his confidence. Despite all the evidence to the contrary, in spite of the fact that there were things about me that Thomas did not know and never would.

I believed him.

That's where I went wrong.

★ ★ ★

Now I put my arm round Ed's shoulders. I say, 'There's nothing to be scared of, Ed. Besides, I'm here. We managed before, didn't we? When it was just us?'

Ed nods but a shadow of uncertainty falls across his face. This is what happens when you throw caution to the wind. It's not as easy as you'd think to get back to the way things were. Before.

Faith takes me with her because Mrs Barber is in the hospital again. I think it's her other hip this time. I don't mind. I don't like going to Mrs Barber's house after school. It looks the same as our house but it smells funny. Like the cloakroom in school after it's been raining. And she makes me eat gingerbread men with Smarties stuck on them. Like I'm a little kid. And cups of tea. Even though I don't drink tea. She still makes tea. She never remembers.

I'm sorry about Mrs Barber's other hip but at least I don't have to go to school. Damo doesn't think it's fair that I'm going to London on a school day. 'You could go to school and then come home with me afterwards,' he says. Damo is lucky. He has his own key to the front door. And his mam works in the factory where they make the biscuits with the chocolate on the top. There're always bags of biscuits in Damo's house. Some of them are broken but they taste just as nice. I don't tell Damo that I'm not allowed to go to his house anymore when his mam or his big sister, Imelda, aren't there.

Me and Faith are on the bus. It takes a long time. I like sitting on the top deck, right at the front. Faith says it makes her feel sick but she comes up with me anyway. She sits beside me, texting. Probably Rob. He plays the guitar in the band and he has long hair. Damo says that Rob thinks he's so cool, but Rob has shown me how to play a G on the guitar and he says he'll show me a C next time. He says once you know G, C and D, you can be a guitar player in a band. I don't want to be a guitar player in a band, on account of the lifesaving. But maybe I could play in a band on my day off. Rob is left-handed like me, so his guitar is easier for me to play. It's still hard, though. Playing the G. It hurts the tips of my fingers.

I say, 'Are you texting Rob?'

Faith says, 'Mind your beeswax.'

She puts loads of XXXXXs at the end of the text. They're mad about kissing, Rob and Faith. I don't know how they can breathe when they kiss for that long. French-kissing is when you put your tongue in and lick the other person's teeth. Damo says he French-kissed Cathy in our class. Cathy has braces. Sometimes bits of her sandwich get caught in the wires. I don't think you could French-kiss someone who has braces on their teeth.

I look out of the window of the bus. London gets busier and busier the closer you get. Much busier than Brighton. Mam said she liked Brighton because it was beside the sea and it reminded her of home. She still called Ireland home, even though we've lived in Brighton for years. Since I was a baby.

We are on a road with lots of traffic. I read all the ads at each bus stop, to pass the time. Faith is still texting.

I say, 'Are we there yet?'

She says, 'Do we look like we're there yet?' Faith's accent gets really Irish when she's cross. It's because she was born when Mam and Dad still lived in Ireland.

Faith doesn't look like me, or Ant or Adrian either. Damo looks exactly like Imelda but don't ever say that to him because he'll give you a dead arm and a wedgie if you do. Faith has black hair and green eyes and white skin. Mrs Barber says she looks a bit like Diana, who happens to be Mrs Barber's cat. She calls her Diana after Princess Diana, who got killed in a car crash too. The cat is huge and very old. Faith doesn't look anything like Diana, except for her green eyes and black hair. Rob thinks Faith is beautiful. He's always saying stuff like that to her. He tells her she looks amazing, right in front of people.

Reading the ads at the bus stops is starting to make me feel a bit sick so I have to stop.

I say, 'When will we be there?'

Faith says, 'Soon.'

'You said that the last time.'

'Knock it off, Milo.'

'I'm hungry.'

'Here, have a banana.'

'I don't want a banana.'

'If you were hungry enough, you'd have a banana.'
Sometimes Faith sounds exactly like Mam.

I blow on the window of the bus until it clouds up. Then I draw a picture with my finger. Me with my life jacket on. I don't have a life jacket, but next summer — if Faith lets me — my class is going to do some training on the beach instead of at the pool and Coach says you have to wear a life jacket. Life jackets make you look a lot bigger than you really are.

'Where are we going anyway?'

'I already told you.'

'You said an office.'

'Yes.'

'Whose office?'

'No one you know.'

94

'Why are we going to an office?'

Faith throws her phone into her bag and zips it up, really quickly. I can't see her face anymore because her hands are covering it.

'I'm sorry, Faith. I won't ask you any more questions, I swear.' It's horrible when girls cry. Boys aren't supposed to cry but sometimes it's hard not to. Even Ant and Adrian cried. So did Dad.

I pull one of her hands away from her face. Actually, she's not crying. She's just tired, I think. But her hand is freezing. I put it between mine and rub, the way Mam used to do. She said Faith had cold hands because of the cigarettes. She said that Faith had poor circulation and that she shouldn't smoke, because people who have poor circulation die if they smoke too many cigarettes.

Faith smiles. Her teeth are white but Mam said they will turn as yellow as mustard if she doesn't stop smoking.

She'll be dead and she'll have yellow teeth and I'll probably have to go to Scotland and live with Dad, and Celia will make me call her 'Mum', and they'll be too busy with the brand-new baby to bring me to a lifesaving class and I'll never see Damo or Carla again.

Faith says, 'Thanks.'

I say, 'It says 'Smokers Die Younger' on your cigarette pack. Did you know that?'

'I'm not going to die, Milo.'

'Are we nearly there?'

This time, she says, 'Nearly.'

The office is in a gigantic building that is like a skyscraper in a movie. There is a man in it and his name is Jonathon. He crouches in front of me and asks if I would like a colouring book and some crayons. I

95

shake my head and Faith gives me her iPod. I listen to her band. They're called 'Four Men and a Woman'. The woman is Faith.

Faith and Jonathon talk for ages. Jonathon has a big folder on his desk with lots of papers in it. He lifts the lid of his laptop. Types his username with two fingers. Presses Tab. Then types his password with two fingers. Presses Enter.

Faith takes some pages out and she keeps shaking her head. Reading and shaking her head. I turn the volume down on the iPod in case she says anything about me.

'It's a lot to take in, Faith,' Jonathon is saying. He is one of those people who stare into your eyes all the time when they're talking to you.

'It's a big shock, Faith,' Jonathon is saying. He is one of those people who say your name all the time.

'It's not uncommon, Faith,' Jonathon is saying.

'It happens quite a lot.' Jonathon is one of those people who always have to be saying something. Staring into people's eyes and saying their names and talking, talking, talking nonstop.

Faith looks at the pages in the folder and shakes her head.

'And you and your . . . adoptive mother . . . ' says Jonathon, staring at Faith's eyes. 'Were you . . . close?'

Faith looks up and she looks mad, like when she was on the bus and I kept asking her if we were there yet. Adults don't mind long journeys but I like to know when things are going to end.

'Apparently not as close as I thought.' Her face is turning pink. Mam used to say, 'Watch out,' when Faith's face turned pink. Mam called it her 'peevish' face.

Jonathon has flecks of dandruff on his jacket. It looks a bit like snow. He takes a huge hanky from his pocket and blows his nose into it. 'Sorry,' he says to Faith. He doesn't say sorry to me. I bet he'd like to French-kiss Faith.

I cough, so he knows I'm here and he won't try any funny business. He looks at me then. 'Would you like a glass of water, young man?' I pretend not to hear him because of the iPod. He gets up from his chair and walks round to the side of the desk where Faith is. He sits on the edge.

'OK, Faith, all right,' he says, as if he's agreeing with something Faith has said. 'Yes, we can make some enquiries. Yes, we can send out a letter, Faith. Yes, we can probably find your birth mother.' I can tell by her face that Faith hates the way Jonathon keeps on saying her name, over and over again. 'But the question you need to ask yourself is why.'

'Why?' Faith says. I'm glad because that's what I would have said.

Jonathon sighs and smiles and presses his hands together like he's saying his prayers.

'Yes, Faith. Why? Why do you want to find her? What is it you are looking for? Have you asked yourself any of these questions, Faith?'

Faith stands up and moves as far away from Jonathon as she can get without leaving the room.

'I would have thought that was pretty obvious,' she says.

Jonathon is still smiling but now he is nodding too. 'Humour me, Faith,' he says. 'Tell me why.'

'Because . . . because . . . I just . . . I want to see her. I want to know what happened. I want to know why.' Faith glances at me but I close my eyes and tap

97

my foot against the floor, as if to the beat of 'Dreams in the Daytime', which is my favourite song. It's the one that Faith sings the best. She looks at Jonathon again. 'This is going to sound weird but . . . '

Jonathon nods. 'Go on, Faith.' He can't keep his gob shut for longer than two seconds, I swear.

Faith says, 'I find it really hard to believe.'

Even though Jonathon is nodding, he says, 'What do you mean?'

'I mean . . . Dad said it was true. I saw the paperwork myself. The adoption certificate or whatever it's called. You've even got a file on me, for Christ's sake.'

Jonathon nods away.

'But . . . I don't know . . . it's . . . it doesn't seem real.'

Jonathon smiles and nods and nods and smiles. He looks like the dogs in the back window of Mrs Barber's car. They start nodding the minute the car starts moving.

Faith says, 'That's why I have to see her. To make sure.' Faith looks at Jonathon but she doesn't nod or smile. She looks pretty cool for an adult. She wears boots that are called Doc Martens. They're new but they look old because she got Rob to run over them a few times in his van.

Jonathon smiles and nods and then he says, 'OK.'

And before he can say anything else, Faith says, 'How long will it take?'

Jonathon says, 'It depends.'

Faith says, 'On what?'

Jonathon says, 'On when she responds to my letter. Or if she responds to my letter.'

Faith says, 'How many letters do you send?'

98

Jonathon says, 'Usually three. The third one is registered.'

Faith nods but she doesn't smile.

Jonathon tries to ruffle my hair when I'm leaving the office but I duck and he misses.

The phone rings and I pick it up and say, 'Yes?' like I usually do, except there's nobody there. I can't hear anyone but I can sense someone. I don't say anything. I just wait. But the person who I can sense says nothing and I hang up. I'm still standing beside the phone when it rings again. This time, I pick it up and say nothing.

It's Brona. She says, 'Hello?'

I say, 'Hi, Brona.'

'What would you like for your birthday?'

'It's not my birthday till January.' I'm hanging onto thirty-nine with my fingernails, which I happen to bite most of the time.

'Well, Christmas, then. What would you like for Christmas?'

'Don't mention the C-word.'

'Someone sounds like they need a little cheering up.'

'Did you just phone here?'

'Yes, of course I did.'

'No, I mean before. Just a minute ago.'

'No. Why?'

'Someone phoned.'

'Who?'

'I don't know.'

'I don't understand.'

'It's probably nothing. I was just wondering

'. . . has anyone been asking about me recently?'

Brona laughs and says, 'My precious girl, everyone asks about you. You're the darling of the publishing world, you know that.'

'No, I mean anything . . . unusual. Lately. Anything a bit . . . I don't know, out of the ordinary.'

'No, nothing strange. What's going on, Kat? You're starting to worry me.'

'Is your office door locked? Right now? While you're on the phone to me?'

'Of course it is. I always lock it before I ring you, you know that.'

'And when you're not in the office . . . do you still lock your office door when you're not there?'

'Kat, you know how cautious myself and Jeremy are when it comes to you. What's this about?'

'It's probably nothing, it's just I've had a few calls lately. You know, when you pick up and no one's there? Except there is someone there. I'm sure of it.'

'You think someone's found out?'

'No. But last week, I picked up the phone and a man said, 'Is Killian there?' and I said, 'No,' and he just hung up.'

'Well, that sounds like it was just a wrong number.'

'Yes, but the name.'

'Lots of people are called Killian.'

'Yes, but it's a bit of a coincidence, isn't it?'

'I'm sure that's all it is, Kat. A coincidence.'

'What about the dropped calls?'

'It's probably kids.'

'I don't know.'

'Nothing to worry yourself about.'

'Maybe not . . . '

Brona says, 'So . . . '

I say nothing. I know what's coming.

After a while, Brona says, 'What's the gorgeous Declan Darker up to these days?'

'You know I don't like talking about him over the phone.'

'Come on, Kat, it's just me. You're being paranoid.'

'Just because you're paranoid doesn't mean your phone's not bugged.'

'Look, the last thing I want to do is put you under pressure but, as you know, there's a heck of a lot of interest in this one. More than usual, I mean.'

Brona is the only person I know who can get away with saying 'heck'. For a publishing phenomenon — that's how they described her in *Hello!* — there's something a little old fashioned about her. Like, if she wore a gingham apron in her kitchen and went ahead and made bread and butter pudding, nobody'd bat an eyelid. It could be her hair. It never moves. It looks like it's been set, like a trifle.

I say, 'Why?' I know why but I'm buying time.

'The tenth Darker novel? DreamWorks are already chomping at the bit for a preview. Clooney has refuted allegations that he's too old to play Darker. Looks like the studio'll have a catfight on their hands between himself and Matt Damon for the job. Either way, it's a winning combination for us, am I right? Gallons of other stuff too. There's an app in development. Merchandising is going to town. There's talk of a special-edition packet of Durex.'

'Declan Darker doesn't use condoms.'

'That's not the point.'

I wait for her to tell me what the point is.

'The point is, it's ready, steady, go here and I'm just wondering . . . you know . . . when we can expect delivery.'

This is not the usual kind of conversation I have with Brona. For starters, she hardly ever rings me. I ring her. From payphones, mostly. Just in case. And if she ever does ring me, it's never to ask about delivery. There's never been any need. Before now.

I ring her. I tell her when the manuscript will be ready. Set up the drop. That's what Brona calls it. The drop. She thinks it's funny. Over the top. Not that she'd say it. But I know she thinks it all the same.

Because nobody knows who I am, there's no need for her to ring me to talk about launches or press releases or interviews or magazine articles or appearances on cheesy chat shows, thank Christ.

When I don't answer immediately, Brona presses on.

'We've been thinking . . . '

'We?'

'Relax. Just me and Jeremy.' Jeremy is Brona's boss and the only other person in the publishing house who knows. Jeremy partly owns the company. Mostly owns it now, I suppose, since his father died. People say 'died' but the truth is he was killed by a Wii. Collapsed when he was doing a Wii Fit slalom jump. Which adds further weight to my hypothesis about the dangers of physical exercise.

He left Jeremy everything. Even the Wii. Brona says he never uses it.

I say, 'I don't like the sound of this.'

'At least hear me out.'

'No.'

Brona ignores me. 'This is the tenth book. It's time for the fans to meet the writer. It's time to unveil Killian Kobain.'

I didn't come up with that name, obviously. Killian Kobain. Brona calls it her 'brainchild'. Publishers are mad about alliteration.

I say, 'No.'

Brona says, 'Why not?'

'For starters, Killian Kobain is a recluse, remember?'

'Yes, but maybe he feels differently now.'

'He doesn't.'

'The tenth book, Kat. We could have a ball. Spill the beans. The journos would lap it up. The publicity would be gigantic.'

'There's enough publicity.'

'There's no such thing as enough publicity.'

'No. I'm not doing it.'

'Come on. It'll cheer up Jeremy.'

'What's wrong with Jeremy?'

'Harold broke up with him.'

'Harold's always breaking up with him.'

'No, he means it this time. He moved out. Just before Jeremy's birthday. He'd promised Jeremy a trip to Tuscany. They were going to do this

Italian cookery course. Now Jeremy's on his own, having Findus Crispy Pancakes for his breakfast, lunch and dinner, from the looks of his recycling bin.'

'Poor Jeremy.'

Brona pounces on my moment of empathy. 'Yes, Kat, that's precisely why we need to go all out for this launch. It would give darling Jeremy such a lift.'

'I'll send him flowers.'

'At least say you'll think about it?'

'Roses. Yellow ones. They'll do the trick.'

'Listen, I'll call you next week and see where you are with the manuscript and we can talk some more about the launch, OK?'

'Can we talk about something else?' I haven't written anything in months but I'm not ready to let Brona know that yet.

'Of course. How are you?'

'Grand.'

But she knows me too well. She says, 'Tell Brona what's the matter. Is it Thomas? Has he been in touch at all?'

'He has a new girlfriend,' I say and I am appalled to hear a crack in my voice. A sliver of a crack but a crack all the same.

Brona says, 'Gosh. That's terrible news. Are you all right?'

'Of course I'm all right. I just . . . it's weird thinking about him with someone else, that's all.'

Brona says, 'I'm sure Thomas and this woman aren't serious. It's just a rebound thing. I'm certain of it. He was mad about you.' And there it is. The past tense. It still sounds strange.

'She's young, of course.'

'How young?'

'Thirty-six.'

'That's only four years younger than you.'

'Three and three-quarters.' I'm not forty yet, dammit.

'Exactly. That's nothing.'

'He went out with her before.'

'Oh.'

'For three years.'

'Oh.'

'Why do you keep saying, 'Oh'?'

'Do I? Gosh, I'm sorry, I'm just ... I'm listening. Go on.'

'You think it's bad, don't you? That he went out with her before? For three years?'

'No. Of course not.'

'She's at that very susceptible child-bearing age,' I say.

'Physiologically speaking,' begins Brona, 'the optimal child-bearing age is eighteen.'

I'm not sure if Thomas is aware of this fact. Or if he cares. All I know is that he'd love a child. If he had one. He's that type.

'Anyway,' I tell Brona, 'it's a moot point and, even if it weren't, I'm too old to have children now.'

Brona produces the trump up her sleeve. Her sister. 'Lorna had her first baby when she was forty-two, remember?'

How could I forget? Lorna is like a lighthouse in Brona's stormy seas, shining a soft light on the dark waters of Brona's single, childless life, of which she is not a big fan.

Brona rushes on. 'And she's overweight — well, it's that gland problem, really, isn't it? Then there's the diabetes. And the alopecia two years ago.'

I know there's more so I wait.

'And psoriasis,' she adds, after a while.

I've never met Lorna but I think I'd be able to pick her out of a crowd at the O2. Not just because of the various ailments, but also because of the child that she bears in a sling about her person, in spite of the fact that the child is now two — or twenty-four months, as Brona calls it. Back-pain. There's another one we can add to the list. Chronic backpain.

'It's not just the age thing,' I say. 'There're lots of reasons I shouldn't have babies.'

There is a pause and I know for a fact that Brona is thinking about Ed.

'How did we end up talking about this?' I say, almost to myself.

'We were talking about Thomas,' Brona says and I know she thinks she is being helpful.

I say, 'Parenthood is an ego trip for men.'

Brona says, 'Thomas would make a lovely father,' as if she is thinking aloud.

I say, 'This is not helping.'

'Sorry,' she replies and there is an apology in her tone but I think her sorrow is directed at Thomas. She loved Thomas. She met him only twice but she decided she loved him anyway.

A lot of people loved him, I suppose. He was just that type of bloke. Easy-going, some people said. Undemanding. He didn't want much. And

I gave him none of it. That's the story doing the rounds.

I say, 'I'd better go.'

Brona says, 'Don't forget to watch *The Review Show* tonight.'

'Why?'

'They're discussing post-feminism in Killian Kobain's novels.'

'What on earth does Killian Kobain have to do with post-feminism?'

'I have no idea.'

'And what the hell is post-feminism anyway?'

'I'm drawing a blank there too.'

'They're crime novels, for Christ's sake.'

'I prefer to think of them as thrillers.'

'Pillocks.'

There's a pause then before Brona slips in a sly, 'So, you'll think about it?'

'About what?'

'About the tenth book. Unveiling Killian Kobain. You know it's the right time.'

I say, 'OK.'

'OK?'

'OK.'

'You'll really think about it? You're not just fobbing me off like before?'

I say, 'No,' even though I am just fobbing her off like before. But I only do it because it works. She doesn't mention it again.

Instead, she says, 'Bye, bye, bye, bye, bye, bye, bye . . . ' until the line — eventually — goes dead.

I get into a fight with Damo at school. Miss Williams makes me go to Mr Pilkington's office. She says it in a high, thin voice. Capital letters. MISTER-PILKINGTON'S-OFFICE. I pick up my bag and my library book, *The Faceless Ones*, which, in my opinion, is the best Skullduggery book so far. I got it from the library yesterday. I had to reserve it, of course. Three weeks it took. I'm on page seventy-two already.

I walk towards the door. I don't look at Miss Williams and I definitely don't look at Damo, who has to sit at the desk right beside Miss Williams's desk, which is bad but not as bad as being sent to Mr Pilkington's office.

Mr Pilkington is not there. His secretary, Denise, tells me to sit on one of the blue wooden chairs outside his office. When you see someone sitting on one of those chairs, you know they're in for it. Denise is eating a chocolate éclair. She's always eating chocolate éclairs. She says it's because she has a baby in her belly and he loves chocolate, especially éclairs. She knows the baby is a boy because she saw a picture of him on the screen at the hospital. She looks over at me a few times before she offers me the rest of her éclair. I say, 'No thank you,' but she pushes it into my hand and if I don't eat it, the chocolate will melt and the cream will squirt between my fingers.

I say, 'Thank you.'

I eat it really quickly. You're not supposed to be eating when you're sitting on the blue wooden chairs. Or reading. Or anything fun. You just have to sit there and think about what you've done.

I won't say Damo started it. I'll just say Damien and I had a disagreement. If I call Damo 'Damo' and say 'Damo and me', Mr Pilkington will make me do a hundred lines with the proper grammar. Anyway, I don't mind saying Damien and I in Mr Pilkington's office. There's nobody else in there. Mr Pilkington breathes funny when he walks. As if he's running. He has hairs growing out of his nose and his ears. He takes ages to get into the chair behind his desk and when he looks at me, he looks sad, like I was the one who started it. He looks like he might say that he's disappointed in me. That's what they say when they want you to cry. I sit up straight.

I'm not going to cry.

'Go on, then,' he says, like we're in the middle of a conversation. He holds his head in his hands and his eyes are nearly closed. He looks really bored, like Ant and Adrian do when Faith asks them if they're going to all their classes and managing their money and eating things like vegetables and being careful.

I say, 'Damien and I had a disagreement.'

Mr Pilkington says, 'You chipped his front tooth.' I know that. My knuckles hurt like mad. 'And you gave him a nosebleed.'

I say, 'I didn't mean to.' Sometimes that works.

'You said that last week. When you were caught fighting in the yard — ' he leafs through pages in the notebook on his desk ' — with George Pullman. Last Wednesday, in fact. A week ago today.'

That could be true. I might have said that. Adults remember stuff like that. Like what people said ages ago. Mr Pilkington sighs. I think he'd prefer if it were Damo in the office instead of me. He's more used to having Damo in the office.

Mr Pilkington says, 'Anyway, I thought Damien Sullivan was your best friend?'

I say, 'He is.'

Mr Pilkington says, 'Well, that's a funny way of treating your best friend.'

I'm missing PE, which happens to be my favourite class of the week. I make sure and do all the exercises properly so my muscles will get bigger. It's important to have big muscles when you're a lifesaver. Especially in your arms so you can swim with one arm and lifesave with the other.

Still, if Mr Pilkington keeps me here much longer, there's a chance I'll miss the class after PE. The one I have to go to on a Wednesday. You only have to go to the class if your mam and dad don't live together anymore. Or if your granny dies. Lots of people go to the class but I'm the only one who goes on Wednesdays. I have to sit there and listen to Mrs Appleby. All her clothes are purple and she has a lisp. She says 'thadneth' and 'loth'. She gives me two Jelly Babies when she's finished. Like the doctor does when you're a little kid.

'Teacher's pet'. That's what George Pullman called me last Wednesday when Miss Williams said I didn't have to do the history homework on account of missing the first bit of the history lesson on account of being at Miss Appleby's class. Damo arranged the fight in the yard. He dragged me over to George and started shouting, 'FIGHT! FIGHT! FIGHT!' until there was a crowd around us, waiting for it to start. Damo always wants something to happen.

Mrs Appleby asks a lot of questions about Mam. She calls her Mum. Mam would have hated that. I say everything is fine. Faith tells me to say everything is fine. 'The last thing we need is the bloody social breathing down our necks.'

I don't know what the social is. I say, 'Why don't we need the social breathing down our necks?'

She says, 'Because if they think I'm doing a rubbish job, they won't let me mind you, will they?'

So I tell Mrs Appleby that everything is 'fine' when she asks how we're managing.

Everything is fine, mostly. Everything is the same, really. Except that I don't go to the Funky Banana after school anymore. And I don't know what dinner I'm going to have when I get home. And it's nice having a surprise for your dinner. Like pizza. Faith loves pizza. And chips. And potato waffles. She puts a fried egg on the top to make them healthy.

And there are never any apples in the bowl anymore. Mam says that an apple a day keeps the doctor away. Maybe a potato waffle a day keeps the doctor away too because I haven't been sick for ages.

Mr Pilkington says, 'I've called your sister. She should be — '

I say, 'No. No. Please, sir. I won't do it again, I — ' Faith will kill me if she finds out I was in a fight. She won't let me go to lifesaving class. I know she won't. And we're doing CPR. Only on dolls, but still.

Mr Pilkington puts up his hand, like he's stopping traffic. 'It's too late, McIntyre. I've already called her. I had no choice.'

Adults always say they have no choice. I feel the

stinging behind my eyes and my nose. I blink and blink. Sometimes that helps.

The thing is, me and Damo never fight. Yeah, Damo gets into scraps. He doesn't ignore people, like his mam tells him to. He fights them instead. Even if they're in year eight. He doesn't care. I mean, he's big for his age but he's not that big. I think that's pretty brave. Faith says it's just stupid.

The fight happens in the classroom. Miss Williams goes to the staffroom to get our spelling tests. The last thing she says before she leaves is, 'Stay in your chairs.'

As soon as she's gone, Damo gets out of his chair.

He writes 'I LUV SPURS' on the whiteboard, even though Miss Williams will know it was him because he's the only Tottenham Hotspur fan in the class.

Then he puts his hands in his pockets and wanders down to my desk, near the back of the class.

I say, 'Miss Williams will be back in a minute.'

Damo says, 'Look at this.' He takes something out of his pocket and puts it on my English copybook, on the table.

I say, 'Is that the scab?'

Damo nods. 'I'm keeping it to show Sully.' Sully is in Afghanistan. He's at the war there, because that's where Osama Bin Laden was from. He's dead now but Sully is still there. I think there are other people he has to kill before he can come home.

Damo says, 'Do you want to touch it?'

I say, 'OK.' It feels hard and rough and it's the colour of dried-up blood. Damo got it when he skateboarded down the hill at the end of our road with his eyes blindfolded. He asked me to dare him to do it and I wouldn't but he did it anyway.

113

Damo says, 'Do you want to come over after school? I found a magazine in Sully's wardrobe. It's got pictures of girls with no clothes on.'

I shake my head. 'I can't. Faith says I have to go straight home today. She wants me to tidy my room.' That's not actually true. Faith never says anything about my room. But she didn't go to college today. And Rob is in London. And she hasn't played her violin in ages.

Damo says, 'You don't have to go home if you don't want to. She's not your sister anymore.'

'She is so my sister.'

'No she's not. You said she was adopted. That means she's not your sister so you don't have to do what she tells you.' Damo puts his scab back into his pocket, careful not to break it. 'You're lucky,' he says. 'You don't have a mum to nag you, and Faith can't boss you around anymore cos she's not your sister.'

Damo is a lot bigger than me. When I stand up, I come up to his shoulder. The one he picked the scab off. 'Take that back.' I must have shouted because the classroom goes dead quiet all of a sudden and everyone turns to look at us.

Damo stops smiling. 'No. I won't. It's true. You said so yourself.'

'Take it back.'

The chant starts at table two. Flapper starts it, I think. He turns his chair round so he can see better. Then everyone joins in. 'Fight, fight, fight, fight, fight.'

Carla says, 'Shuddup, will ya? Miss Williams will be back in a minute.' Nobody pays any attention.

Everyone looks at us and the chant gets louder.

I don't want to fight. And it's not just because

Damo's bigger than me and has a brother who's in the army and teaches him proper fighting techniques.

I say, 'Take it back or I'll hit you.' Damo looks like he does when Miss Williams gets him to do a sum in his head. Before she moved us, I used to write the answers down for him.

'No. I won't,' he says and I see his hands curl themselves into fists.

All round me, the others chant.

'Fight, fight, fight, fight, fight.'

I swing my fist and when it lands, on his front tooth, the pain is as much of a surprise as the noise. The sharp crack of it. My knuckle is bleeding and a bit of his tooth is on the floor, beside Horrid Henry's lunchbox.

'Milo McIntyre!' Miss Williams is standing at the door of the classroom, holding our corrected spelling tests in both arms, like a baby. Mine is on the top of the pile. I can see it. Twelve out of twelve, circled in red pen, with a smiley face beside the mark. My knuckle throbs. Damo holds his hands against his mouth and curses at me but the curses are muffled so he doesn't get in trouble. Miss Williams says, 'Oh my goodness,' and then she runs to her desk and puts the papers on it and stands there with her hand cupped around her mouth. I didn't mean to chip his tooth. His mam might ask Faith for money for braces or something. Braces cost a lot. When Faith had them, Mam said we couldn't go on holiday for two years. But we did. We went to a caravan in Blackpool and I swam in the sea every day.

Faith barges into Mr Pilkington's office without knocking like you're supposed to. She looks at me and shakes her head. She looks disappointed. The burning, stinging sensation is back behind my eyes and nose, and this time, tears run down my face. They feel hot. I make fists of my hands again and push them against my eyes but I can't stop now. I can't stop.

She stands beside my chair and rubs her hand up and down my arm, as if Mr Pilkington isn't even here and I'm not in dead trouble.

She says, 'Hey? You OK?'

She says, 'What happened?'

She says, 'Stop crying now,' and her voice is sharper than before. She sounds like Mam when I say a bad word. She always gave out to me when I said a bad word. 'You've some mouth on ya, boyo.' That's what she used to say.

I stop crying. I wipe my nose with the sleeve of my jumper. Faith says you shouldn't do that because the snots harden and they're a divil to get out. Divil is one of Mam's words. A divil is something that isn't easy.

Faith doesn't say anything about the snots and the sleeve of the jumper. Instead, she looks at Mr Pilkington. He covers his belly with his jacket. He smiles at Faith but he's looking at her like he's checking the buttons on her shirt are closed or something. He gestures her to a chair and then sits on the corner of his desk, right in front of her. She moves her chair back and curls her feet up underneath her, even though you're supposed to sit up straight when you're in the office. Mr Pilkington doesn't tell her not to. Instead, he folds his arms and crosses his legs and tells her all about me hitting Damo. When he bends towards her, I can smell his breath: cold coffee and Polo mints. I think Faith can too because she leans farther back in her chair.

When he stops talking, Faith says nothing. Instead,

116

she looks at me like she's trying to remember my name.

Mr Pilkington says, 'So, you agree, this is a very serious matter?'

Faith looks at him again. 'It's out of character.'

'But serious, nonetheless.'

'He's never done anything like this before.'

'Well, there was the incident last week. With George Pullman. Remember?'

I didn't think Faith knew about that. But she nods again when he says it, as if she knows all about it.

She nods. 'I'll speak to him.'

Mr Pilkington frowns. 'You said you'd speak to him last week.'

Faith never said anything to me last week. Not about George Pullman anyway. She said she wanted to talk to me and took me to Eddie Rocket's, because the tuna melts happen to be my favourite sandwiches in the world. She gave me fifty pence to put in the jukebox. I played 'Oliver's Army', which is one of Faith's favourite Elvis Costello songs. And when I asked her what she wanted to talk to me about, she said it was my lifesaving class. How great I was doing. And how Coach thinks I'll definitely pass my exams. Maybe even come top of the class.

I think it's true. I might pass all my exams. Maybe even come top of the class. And it's not because I'm big-headed or a know-it-all or anything like that. It's just that I train really, really hard. Even when Faith brings me to the pool just for fun, I make sure I do my laps and my different strokes. Sometimes I can swim nearly two lengths under the water. In one go, I mean.

Faith and Mr Pilkington are still talking. I look out of the window. I feel really tired all of a sudden. Mam always made lasagne on Wednesday. She took a half day from the café, just so she could go home and make lasagne. It's her favourite dinner, lasagne. She said Wednesday was a nothing kind of a day. Right slap bang in the middle of the week with nothing going for it anymore, since they stopped showing *Coronation Street*. She loves *Coronation Street*. Becky is her favourite. Becky and Steve. She'll be pretty upset when she finds out they've split up.

Mr Pilkington says, 'Mrs Sullivan will have to be told, of course.'

Faith says, 'I'll pay for any damage done. Any dental expenses.'

'I'm not sure if that's going to placate Mrs Sullivan.'

'She's a family friend. She'll understand.'

'Hmmm.' Mr Pilkington doesn't seem convinced.

'And Milo will apologise, won't you, Milo?' Faith looks at me but only briefly. I don't have time to say anything. 'He'll apologise to Damo. Damien. And Miss Williams, of course. He won't do it again, will you, Milo?' Again, the flash of her face towards me, then back to Mr Pilkington, lots of smiling, and then she stands up and pulls at my elbow until I am standing up too. 'I think it's best if I take him home now.'

Mr Pilkington says, 'Well . . . ' He looks at his watch. I put my hand in my pocket and cross my fingers. I won't have to go to Mrs Appleby's class. I can't believe it.

Faith says, 'Thank you for being so understanding. I really appreciate it.' Now she's giving him one of those smiles she gives Rob when she wants him to do something, like take out the rubbish or dance with her.

Mr Pilkington goes the colour of the tomatoes Miss Williams is growing in a pot on the windowsill of the classroom. He opens his mouth but no words come out and Faith turns, grabs me again and steers us out through the door.

She waits until we're in the car. 'Jesus, Milo, what the fuck are you at?' She bangs her fist against the steering wheel. I reckon it hurt because she doesn't do it a second time.

'You never used to say the F-word in front of me.'

Faith looks at me. 'I know. I'm sorry, Milo. I'm making a bloody dog's dinner of this.'

'Well, it's not easy bringing up a nine-year-old boy, going to college, being in a band and looking after the café.' I'm glad I said that because she sort of smiles. It's a pale kind of smile, like when you don't mix enough Ribena in the water.

'Where did you hear that?'

'You said it to Dad. On the phone.'

She says nothing for a moment. Then she nods. 'I didn't mean for you to hear that stuff.'

'I'm sorry.'

'No, I'm sorry, Milo.'

' 'S'all right.'

'I was just . . . I was upset.'

'Because Mam's not your real mam?'

'I suppose.'

'I heard you talking. To Dad. And that man in the office. Jonathon. I'm not stupid, you know.'

'I know you're not stupid. I just . . . I should have told you all this myself, I've been . . . Christ!'

'I'm sorry. I couldn't help overhearing. I wasn't spying.'

'No, it's not . . . I'm sorry, Milo. Shit. I'm sorry. I'm crap at this.'

'You're not that bad.'

'Then why do you keep hitting people?'

'I don't.'

'George Pullman last week. And now Damo.'

'That's only two people.'

'But Damo. He's your best mate. You never fight, you two. What were you fighting about?'

I look away. Out of the window. The school looks empty when it's not home-time. 'Can I tell you later?' If she goes to band practice later, I'll be in bed when she gets back — Mrs Barber always makes me go to bed dead early — and I'll pretend to be asleep and she'll forget to ask me in the morning.

She mightn't go though. She hasn't been to band practice for ages.

Faith nods and turns the key in the ignition. It doesn't always start first time round. It's Dad's old car, the one he taught her to drive in. He says he'll teach me to drive too, when I'm seventeen, but it'll be pretty tricky, seeing as he lives in Scotland with Celia and I live in Brighton with Faith.

Damo is right, I suppose. About Faith not being my sister anymore. I don't even think she's my half-sister. Not really. I wish she was still my sister. She says she's crap but she's not. Not really. It's just hard to be good at things when you're sad a lot of the time.

Faith lets me sit in the front so I don't think she's too mad with me. She even lets me put the car in gear and take the handbrake off. She yells, 'Clutch!' and I put the car in second, then third, then fourth, but we never get to fifth. The traffic is too slow for that.

The great thing about having my bedroom all to myself again is the space. For example, I can use both bedside lockers now, if I want to. For books, say. I could put books on top of the bedside locker that was on Thomas's side. There's nothing on it at the moment. But the point is that there could be things on it. If I wanted to put things on it. If, say, I ran out of room on my bedside locker. There's the extra space now.

It's Thursday night. I hate Thursday nights. They remind me of Thomas. I hardly think about him at all and then Thursday night comes round again and he advances like floodwater. I suppose you could say that Thursday night was sort of like 'our night'. I know, I hate couples who have their own special night of the week but it's not like we ever told anyone. We'd just say, 'Sorry, I've made other plans,' to anyone who asked us to do anything on a Thursday night. It was never usually a problem for me because Minnie knew about our Thursday-night arrangement and Ed usually worked late in the café on Thursday nights. But Thomas was often invited to book launches and film premieres and what have you but if it happened to be on a Thursday night, he'd say, 'Sorry, I've made other plans,' and that would be that. We never discussed it, this Thursday-night thing. It just sort of happened that way, I suppose. Not long after he moved into the apartment, as far as I remember.

In fact it was a Thursday. The day that Thomas moved in. But really, he'd been moving in for a long time. Long before he ever brought up the subject of his moving in. He did it by stealth. He was so good that I hardly noticed myself until it was mostly too late.

It started off with a toothbrush. I let this pass, being a bit of a stickler for oral hygiene. Soon, other items appeared. A disposable razor, a book of blades, a travel pack of shaving cream, aftershave and shower gel. Citrus-smelling. I opened the little bottles when he was out and inhaled them. Lemons. That bittersweet smell.

Clothes began to appear in the wardrobe. I found his gym bag in the utility room. Shoes under the bed. When he arrived one night with a towel — a small, frayed scrap of material that would have difficulty covering one cheek of his arse — I began to experience disquiet.

'You don't mind, do you?' he asked, stuffing the towel into the drawer in the bathroom that is home to sanitary towels and tampons and painkillers and a hot water bottle and a couple of copies of *Now* magazine. It is — unofficially, at least — my time-of-the-month drawer. I have never put a towel into this drawer.

'Well, I . . . '

'It's just that your towels are so soft.'

'Towels are supposed to be soft,' I told him,

grazing my fingers against the thing masquerading as Thomas's towel.

'Yes, but they're a bit too soft. It's taking me ages to dry myself.'

I said, 'If, by drying, you mean peeling the top layer of skin off yourself, then this towel is perfect.'

Thomas smiled. 'I love it when you're stern.'

I said, 'And that drawer is not for towels.' If you were to go ahead and describe my tone, you could do worse than call it 'prim'.

And then he said, 'Let's go to bed,' as if there were nothing prim about my tone.

'But it's only — ' I looked at my watch ' — nine o'clock.'

'Great,' he said. 'That gives us two hours. Plenty of time for a spot of *Grey's Anatomy*. Bagsy being the patient this time.'

'Subtle,' I told him. But I forgot about the discoloured dishcloth of a towel and followed him into the bedroom.

When I am writing, I have to be asleep by eleven so I can get up at six, shower, dress and drink a lot of coffee and be at my desk by seven.

The next morning, he got up at the same time as me, went for a jog, came back, dropped his clothes on the bathroom floor and used up all the hot water in the shower. Then he strolled into the kitchen wearing nothing round his waist but the tiny, frayed towel that barely covered one cheek, even though his bottom was of the two-eggs-in-a-hanky type.

Thomas opened the fridge. 'There's never any

food in here.' By food, he meant potatoes and steak and turnips.

I say nothing.

'I could go shopping.' There was something about the way he said it that made me stop doing what I was doing — making more coffee — and look up.

'I've got everything I need.'

He stuck his head back inside the fridge. 'You've got two eggs, three low-fat natural yoghurts, a lettuce that is two days past its sell-by date and an empty bag of mini Kit Kats.' He closed the fridge door. 'I'll go shopping,' he said again.

'No!' I said. It came out a bit panicky. 'I mean, there's no need; it'll just go to waste.'

'No, it won't. I'll eat it.'

'But you don't live here.'

'I've been here every night for the last week.'

When I thought about it, I was shocked to discover that it was true.

He said, 'I'm starved and I'm tired of eating out.'

'Then why don't you go home and boil up a pot of those spuds you're always talking about?'

'The Golden Wonders?' he asked, a smile spreading like fertiliser across his face.

'Yes.'

'They're not ideally suited for boiling. You'd be better off baking or roasting those ones, Kat.'

'Then you could go home and bake them. Or roast them,' I said. 'How about that?'

'Or,' he said, closing the fridge door and moving to the kitchen table. 'I could move in.'

Silence fell like fog. Thomas pulled out a chair and sat down. It creaked under the weight of him. After a while, he said, 'It makes sense, Kat. I'm here most of the time already.'

'You said nothing would change,' I said, eventually. 'You promised.' I sounded petulant, like a child being pulled from a playground.

Thomas looked confused. He said, 'What do you mean?'

'On St Stephen's Day that time. When you said that thing . . . '

'When I told you that you loved me?'

'You said nothing would change.'

'That was ages ago. And anyway, nothing is changing, Kat. I just want to move on a bit.' He reached for my hand across the table. 'At least think about it, will you?'

After a while, I nodded my head. I said I would. I said I'd think about it.

Now it's Thursday again. I keep meaning to make a Thursday arrangement with Minnie. Take her to see a play or something. She's cracked about the theatre. But then I forget and — BAM! — it's Thursday again. I don't know where the weeks go, I really don't.

I take three books from the pile on my bedside locker and put them on Thomas's bedside locker. There. That's much better.

It's really great having all the extra space again.

It makes such a difference.

Me and Damo are at the Funky Banana. I didn't say sorry for hitting him but Damo got me in a headlock in the playground the next day at school and ran around for a bit and then let me go and laughed, so I knew we were friends again.

Jack asks about Faith. He says, 'How's the lovely Faith these days?' He always calls her the lovely Faith and wants to know how she's doing. I don't know why he doesn't ask her himself when she's here.

I say, 'She's fine.'

'Has she heard from Jonathon yet?'

Faith rings Jonathon nearly every day and he never has any news for her. But I don't tell Jack that. I just shrug as if I don't know. I'm not mad about talking to people about it, to be honest.

Jack is great. Damo thinks so too. He has a motorbike and he always gives us the biggest slice of banoffi with ice cream on the side, even though you're not supposed to have ice cream on the side because of all the cream on the top of the banoffi. It's hard to pick a very favourite dessert but banoffi is definitely one of my favourites. I'm not allowed to pick up the bowl and lick it in the café so I just use my finger instead. Damo puts a blob of ice cream on the end of his nose with his finger and then licks it off with his tongue.

Earwigs are the only thing Damo is afraid of, on

account of the way they crawl inside your ear and lay eggs and then you have millions of baby earwigs inside your brain. He's always putting his fingers in his ears, checking. When he takes them out, they've got yellow wax on them and then he chases me around the Funky Banana, like he's going to wipe the wax on my T-shirt with his fingers. Jack doesn't mind. He is cleaning up. He says this is his favourite time in the cafe. When there're no customers. I prefer it when there're lots of people. I like guessing what they'll order. That's easy with the regulars, although it depends on what time they come in at. The banana and peanut-butter muffins are the most popular. Jack says they're our signature bun. He makes them now. They're nearly as good as Mam's.

Jack says he'll take me and Damo to the cinema, just as soon as he gets his paperwork done. He does it on the computer. He types in his username and password. His username is Jack2276, because his name is Jack and the last four digits of the cafe's telephone number are 2276. His password is cinnamon, which happens to be the name of his cat. He's had the same password for ages. I've told him he should change it regularly but he never bothers.

We're going to see *The Three Musketeers*. We are going to take it in turns to be d'Artagnan. We use the cardboard holders inside the rolls of tinfoil, for swords. We point them at each other and shout, 'ALL FOR ONE AND ONE FOR ALL.'

We were late getting to the café because Faith and Rob were fighting again, in our house, before we got into Rob's van to drive over to the Funky Banana. Jack said that me and Damo could have a sleepover in his house because Four Men and a Woman are doing a gig in London. A gig is like a concert except you don't get paid.

But Faith said no. She said she'd come straight home after the gig and pick us up, which is a pity because that means we won't get a really long go of Jack's Xbox. Jack lets us play Batman: Arkham City, even though you're not supposed to until you're fifteen.

That's when the fight started, because Rob said, 'Ah come on, Faith. We haven't been out in ages. We can stay with Kegs. It'll be a laugh.' Kegs is Rob's older brother. He wears a suit and works in an office. I'm pretty sure Kegs isn't his real name.

Faith shook her head. 'I can't. I want to have a clear head for tomorrow. I'm going into the café to do the books.' The books aren't really books at all. It's just sums. Like the amount of money the customers pay for a Sweet Funky Monkey sandwich (that's a banana and honey sandwich, which happens to be the most popular one for the customers who are about my age), minus the cost of the bread and bananas and honey you use to make the sandwiches. Ant and Adrian are the best at the books but they are in London. Dad used to like doing the books. He said it relaxed him. Mam said there were better ways to relax. She said it in a funny sort of voice and looked at him weird and then they'd go for a nap, which is when you go to sleep in the middle of the day with no pyjamas on. But that was ages ago. Way before he went to Scotland to live with Celia.

Faith said, 'I'm not going to just palm him off on any Tom, Dick or Harry.'

Rob said, 'You're not palming him off. You're going out. For one night. One measly night. And this gig is important. That scout could be there tonight. He might want to talk to us afterwards. We don't want to be rushing off.'

They were standing in the hall, talking in really loud whispers that sounded like Mrs Barber's cat hissing.

'Oh, I'm sorry if his mother dying has inconvenienced you.' Faith doesn't sound sorry. She sounds mad. Really mad, like the time her appendix burst and she missed the Raconteurs at the Hammersmith Apollo.

'Faith, stop. You know I didn't mean it like that. It's just — '

'Let's see, what else? Oh yes. And I can see how you've overlooked this tiny detail, but let's not forget that I've just found out that my whole life is a lie. Everything I thought was true is in fact the opposite of true.'

'False' I think, but I don't say it out loud. Miss Williams loves opposites. She makes us play this game. She calls it 'Word Buzz', when she shouts out a word and points at one of us and we have to shout back, except we have to say the exact opposite of the word she has said. It's better than mathematical patterns, I suppose. And we don't get in trouble for shouting.

Rob says, 'That's a little melodramatic, don't you think?'

Faith says, 'No. I don't.'

That's when Faith looks at Rob like she's about to give him a Chinese burn. She opens the hall door and walks out to the van. Rob shakes his head. He says, 'Come on, Milo and Damo. It looks like we're going.'

Later, at the café, Faith says, 'I'll bring you back something from London. What would you like?'

I say, 'Nothing. I'm fine.'

Faith says, 'I'll get you some sweets, yeah? And I'll pick you up from Jack's house after the gig, yeah? Around midnight, all right? I'll ring if I'm going to be a bit later, OK?' She doesn't kiss me because Damo is here.

I say, 'You know, I could have a sleepover at Jack's. I don't mind. I want to.' This is not exactly one hundred per cent true. I mean, Jack's great and everything. It's just, when it gets dark, I like being in my own house. Faith doesn't mind me leaving the landing light on when I go to bed.

Faith hugs me but I don't think Damo notices. He's too busy telling Jack what happens in the movie, even though Jack keeps telling him not to. Jack doesn't like knowing what's going to happen next.

'And you have to start thinking about what you want for Christmas, yeah?' She doesn't say anything about Santa. That's one good thing about your sister minding you instead of your mam. Even if she's not really your sister. You don't have to pretend to believe in Santa.

I say, 'It's only November.' But I'm glad she mentioned Christmas, all the same. I was a little bit worried about it this year.

Rob is standing at the door of the café, jangling the keys to the van. Faith's violin case is tucked under his arm. He says, 'Come on, if you're coming.'

Faith nods and they walk outside. I run out of the door and catch Rob before he gets back into the van, and tell him what the speed limit is on the A23, which is the main road to London. I Googled it.

He says, 'Don't worry, Milo. I won't drive fast. Faith won't let me, will you?' He tugs her hair and she punches his arm, which means they're friends again. Just like me and Damo.

I ring Ed.

'Whatcha doin'?'

'Whatcha' doesn't sound as needy.

'I'm working.'

'Oh.'

Ed waits for me to say something else.

'Whatcha doin' after work?'

'I have a date. With Sophie.'

'Oh.'

'A letter came for you this morning. To our house.'

'Really?' Sometimes the secretarial college I went to a million years ago sends letters to my parents' address. Trying to sell me refresher courses and whatnot. Upselling, Minnie calls it. It's probably from them.

'You working tomorrow?'

'Nope.'

'Wanna do something?'

'Wanna' is good too. People feel they can say 'no' if you use the word 'wanna' rather than 'Do you want to . . . ?'

'Yep.'

'I'll pick you up,' and I hang up before he remembers something he needs to do tomorrow instead of coming out with me.

I ring Minnie.

132

'Whatcha doin'?' Whatcha. Casual. Carefree.

'It's Monday morning. I'm working.'

'It's Monday?'

Minnie doesn't answer. I can hear her furious fingers thumping a keyboard.

'I'm just ringing to make absolutely certain that you're not planning on organising a surprise birthday party for me.'

'It's only November.'

'Yes, but if you were organising a surprise party for January, you'd probably start planning in November, wouldn't you?'

'I'm not.'

'You sure? Because I would hate that. I would really hate that.'

'I know.'

'So you're not planning anything.'

'Definitely not.'

'Great.'

'Anything else I can help you with?' Her tone is not as sincere as it could be.

'You busy?'

She sighs. If there were papers on her desk, there's a good chance they're on the floor now.

Minnie is an accountant. I can't believe she ended up being an accountant. She could have done any course she wanted. She got eight As in her Leaving Certificate. In those days, the As and Bs weren't divided up like they are now. But I'd say that if they re-examined her papers, the As would have been A1s. I'm positive. She did her best to mask her smarts, and because she was so good-looking and wild, she mostly got away with it. She joined a small, strictly

133

nonprofit theatre troupe and toured with them for a while. It drove her old pair mental, which I think might have been the point. She sometimes acted, sometimes directed, all the while experimenting with the kind of meds you can't get over the counter, drinking complicated Martinis and judging Battle of the Band competitions up and down the country. I'm not sure how she got that gig. She may have slept with Fiachna Ó Braonáin at one time or other.

Anyway, that's not the point. The point is that she spent six months doing that. And then she met Maurice, who happened to be an accountant. Just met him in a random sort of a way. In a café, I think. Or a Spar. Somewhere like that. They got to talking, I suppose, and that was it. Accountancy was like an infection that Maurice passed to Minnie. Like German measles. Soon she was covered in it and before you could say tax fecking return, she had herself enrolled in an accountancy course at Trinity College for the following September. It happened so quickly. There was nothing I could do.

Minnie says some people are born to be accountants. I swear to God, she said that once, and, even though the two of us were most of the way down a bottle of wine, I think she meant every word. She said that if she hadn't met Maurice and discovered her love of accountancy (and accountants, let's face it: Maurice is an accountant and she's cracked about him), then she might have ended up a junkie. Or — knowing her — an A-list actor. She shuddered when she said that, as if she was dead and a junkie, or an A-list actor, was jumping on her grave in heavy boots.

She couldn't look at me the morning after she told me that she was cracked about Maurice and had signed up for an accountancy course. Too ashamed, I suppose. We were on holiday together at the time. I told her there were worse things to be but when she asked me to be specific, it took me a while.

Back then, I was writing the second draft of the first Declan Darker novel and had three publishers interested. That was Minnie's fault. Read and destroy was the deal. Read the manuscript, destroy the evidence in the bottom of an industrial bin at the industrial estate where her father's business was. She swore. I should have known better. After she'd read the first draft, she put the whole lot into a brown envelope and used up pretty much an entire week's cigarette money posting it to Hodder & Stoughton in London. She said Dublin wasn't big enough for Declan Darker when I asked her why she didn't send it to an Irish publisher. She also told me that I owed her five pounds and twenty-two pence.

I kept writing and pretended — to my father and sometimes to my mother, whenever she enquired — that I was attending the private secretarial course that my father had paid a fortune for and which was about all I was fit for, once the Leaving Cert, results came out.

The publishers found my insistence on a male pseudonym amusing. I know that, because Jeremy said, 'How amusing.'

135

At first, it was just about Mum finding out. Crime fiction was up there with breaking and entering, as far as she was concerned. It was most certainly not an art. It wasn't even a craft. It was like painting by numbers. She said that once. In a television interview.

So I told Dad that I'd graduated from my secretarial course with first-class honours — that never happened — and was now gainfully employed as a trainee technical writer for a software company based in Cork. This is a handy job for someone who needs a cover. In fact, be wary of the man you meet on the shady side of a bar on a Thursday night who confesses to being a technical writer. Dodgy as all hell.

Cork was where I said I was whenever I needed to be somewhere like, for example, London, meeting Brona, or what have you.

Of course, I always meant to tell them. Someday. Confess, Minnie calls it. But things got out of hand. It really started when *Dirty Little Secret* featured on Oprah's Book Club. One word from Oprah (the word happened to be 'compelling') and the book started selling like Nicorette patches on New Year's Day. Then there was the bidding war for the third book. I think there were five publishing houses involved, in the end. Minnie fielded the offers, from a payphone outside the Raheny public library. Then, the media campaign to find out who Killian Kobain was. You wouldn't believe some of the stuff the papers made up about the man. Outrageous. Then Scorsese made the first Declan Darker film and it won a truckload of Oscars and Golden

Globes that year. After that, everybody wanted a piece of Killian Kobain. The problem was, he didn't exist. Brona and Jeremy begged me to 'come out', as it were. But by then, it was too late. And in a way it was kind of nice. Being someone else. Someone other than me.

Minnie finally agrees to meet me for lunch. It's the only way she can get me off the phone.

Harry's Bar on Dawson Street is often full to the brim of snazzy-looking people. Important-looking people. Glamorous-looking people. But when Minnie Driver (the accountant, not the actress) rocks up, obscurity gets a dust-sheet and drapes it over everyone else in the room. Minnie is just one of those people. It's not enough to say she lights up a room. It would be more apt to announce that she detonates it. She walks in and everybody else — men, women, children, even really small babies — just cash in their chips. Fold like deck chairs after a long, hot summer. Throw in their towels. Raise their hands. Admit defeat. Walk away. Minnie does that to people. She doesn't mean to. And she'll deny it if challenged. But that's what she does all the same. It could be her thinness (we called her Skinny Minnie in school), or her height (which seems greater because of her thinness), or her blonde hair (which is actually, genuinely, blonde and not dyed off her head like that of most women her age). It could be her ice-blue eyes that look enormous in her tiny, heart-shaped face. Or the remarkable clothes she wears, which you will never find in any shop, no matter how much you look. They look like clothes that have been designed especially for her.

But, to be honest, I don't think it's anything to do with the way Minnie looks. Loads of women are gorgeous, but who cares? No, it could be more to do with the way Minnie presents herself in a room. In the world! As if it belongs to her. As if she owns it. There is a certainty about Minnie. A sureness of step. An aura that even sceptical people can see. She looks like one of those people who are familiar with the customs of Benin, speak conversational Russian and can fillet a fish in under a minute. In truth, she couldn't point to Benin on a map of the world, has no Russian, conversational or otherwise, and can't walk down the pier in Howth, what with the fishy-guts smell.

People either love her or hate her. Immediately. They decide the minute they meet her. They can't help it.

My first memory of Minnie is my sixth birthday. Mrs Higginbotham had made bucketfuls of her cold shivery jelly, and I was in the back garden, looking for a big bush to scrape the jelly into. Through the thick wall of hedge separating our gardens, I heard Minnie and one of her five sisters.

Minnie: No, she doesn't exist. It's Mam and Dad. Or just Mam, I'd say.

One-of-five-sisters: Why would Mam want my teeth?

Minnie: She doesn't, you big eejit. She throws them away. In the bin. Or out of the window, probably.

One-of-five-sisters: You're telling fibs. I'm telling on you.

Minnie: If Mam hears about this, she won't put any more money under your pillow and . . . let me have a look . . . open your gob, for God's sake . . . yeah, you've got about two pounds' worth still in there. I'd wait if I were you. Before you start bleating.

There is the sound of crying during which Minnie says not a word. Then:

One-of-five-sisters (in teary, jerky voice): Wha . . . wha . . . what abou . . . about S-S-S-Santa?

A pause. A long, long pause. I begin to wonder if Minnie has left the garden. Eventually:

Minnie (sighing): He's true.

One-of-five-sisters: Are you sure?

Minnie: I said so, didn't I?

To be honest, I doubt Minnie ever believed in Santa.

She bangs her stopwatch thingy on the table between us. It's like one of those contraptions professional chess players use. She presses a button and the thing starts ticking, as loud as a bomb. 'I have forty-two minutes so make it matter,' she says, peeling her suit jacket off and hanging it on the back of her chair. She sits down and looks at me, drumming her fingers on the table.

Ignoring the crowd, who will leave this place with cricks in their necks, trying to get a better view of her, she says, 'Well?'

I say, 'Well what?' as if I haven't a clue what she's on about.

'Why did you want to see me?'

139

'Why do I need a specific reason to meet you for lunch? I never did before.'

'You never had time to meet for lunch before. You were busy before. Remember? Writing books? Doing strange things with Thomas? And Ed? Any of this ringing a bell?'

She has a point.

'Well, yes, maybe I do have a little more time on my hands these days. That could be true. But it still doesn't mean I have to have something to discuss before I'm allowed to meet my best friend for lunch.'

'Just because I'm your only friend does not mean I'm your best friend.'

'You are not my only friend.'

'Name two other friends.'

I open my mouth.

'And you can't say Ed. Or Brona.'

I shut my mouth.

I say, 'I got another one of those calls.'

'A dropped call?'

'Yes.'

'Have you reported them?'

'No. It's not against the law to ring someone and not say anything, is it?'

'It's harassment. It could be a stalker.'

'Why would someone be stalking me?'

'Not you, dimwit.' Minnie leans forward and whispers, 'Killian Kobain. Maybe somebody's found out.'

I look round. Nobody is paying any attention to me although some customers are still gazing at Minnie.

I shake my head. 'No. I've been so careful.

And I checked with Brona. There've been the usual enquiries from journalists but nothing out of the ordinary.'

Minnie says, 'I can't believe you've managed to keep it a secret for this long.'

I pick up my napkin. Unfold it. Fold it again. Unfold it.

'Spit it out, Kat.'

I look at her. 'You've never said anything to Maurice, have you?' I know I shouldn't ask. It's Minnie. I can trust Minnie. But she's been part of a couple for years now. Some couples tell each other everything. Don't they?

Minnie says, 'I'm not even going to answer that. And I'm going to have to insist that you pay for lunch.'

'I'm sorry . . . the calls . . . they've left me a bit . . . paranoid, I suppose.'

'You've always been paranoid.'

'I mean more paranoid than usual.'

'Call the cop-shop.'

'No.'

'Call the service provider. Change your number. Change your provider.'

'No.' I never, ever communicate with call centres. That's non-negotiable. It's the way they play mind games with you, getting you to press this button, then that button, then hash, then star, then another button until you're so confused, you can't even remember why you rang in the first place. Then, when a human finally speaks to you and you go ahead and tell your sad story, they say that, in fact, the person you need to tell your sad story to is in

141

such-and-such a department and they put you on hold for half an hour and make you listen to 'Greensleeves' over and over — or, worse, Lyric FM — and then you speak to someone in such-and-such a department who doesn't even know your name, never mind the gist of your sad story so you have to start all over again.

'Ring the number back. After they hang up.'

'I can't. It's a withheld number.'

'Then don't bother answering the phone.'

'But it could be Ed. He sometimes rings from Sophie's landline if he wants a lift and he's run out of credit. Her number is withheld.'

Minnie throws her hands up in the air. She says, 'That's all I've got.'

'OK.'

'You have thirty-four minutes left.'

The waitress arrives. I'm not hungry. Not that I'm complaining. I've been subsisting mostly on coffee and cigarettes and red wine and the weight is tumbling off me. This must be the silver lining. In fact, had I known, I would have broken up with Thomas ages ago. OK, yes, technically, he was the one who broke up with me.

Minnie takes ages to decide. She and Maurice became foodies during the boom. A lot of people did. They know about things like celeriac and truffles. The old Minnie would have beaten any talk of celeriac and truffles out of anyone, especially an accountant like Maurice. And I mean actually physically beaten it out of him. With the branch of a tree.

I haven't looked at the menu yet, so I just ask

the waitress what today's special is and she tells me, but I can't hear her because Minnie is talking at the top of her voice about some hostile takeover or other she's working on, and the waitress has the low voice of someone who has been told to SHUT UP all her life. So I nod and return the menu to her and take a huge slug of wine out of the carafe I've ordered and watch Minnie sip her sparkling water, and I wish that Minnie didn't have to go back to the office and work on a boring bloody acquisition because then the two of us could go to Lincoln's and get properly pissed, like we used to. Back when we laughed so hard, sometimes a tiny little drop of piddle would slip out and wet my knickers.

She says, 'Twenty-two minutes left.'

I say, 'Fuck.'

She says, 'What?' She's trying her best to sound impatient but I hear a sliver of concern in her voice.

'Everything. It's . . . everything. Everything is just so . . . flat.'

'You're just bored.'

'I shouldn't be. I've loads to do.'

'Yes, but you're not doing any of it. Just start doing the stuff that you're supposed to be doing and then you won't be bored and everything won't seem so flat and I might get this acquisition sorted out and even manage to dodge the latest redundancy cull.'

'They'd never make you redundant. They wouldn't dare.'

That's when I see the blackboard where the specials are written and realise that today's special is beef and Guinness stew and that if there's one thing I hate it's beef and Guinness stew; and that's when the waitress whooshes out of the swingy door from the kitchen holding two plates, one of which is overflowing with beef and Guinness stew. I pick up my glass of wine. I don't drain it but I nearly do.

Minnie says, 'You could go to your house in Italy. Have sex with your gardener, whatshisface? Pedro? Or Antonio? He's a grand-looking fella. Strong as an ox. He'd keep you going, take your mind off things.'

'It's Stefano. And I can't just rock up and have sex with him. What if it didn't work out? Where would the garden be then? Those lemon trees aren't going to prune themselves.'

Minnie spears a piece of asparagus with the prongs of her fork, even before the waitress has guided the plate to the table. She's like that, Minnie. Impatient. I look at the timer. I've twelve minutes left. With no plans for the afternoon. And beef and Guinness stew over-flowing on a plate in front of me. It's enough to make anyone have a nervous breakdown. God knows, I've time for one.

Minnie bends her head to her plate and ingests at least a third of her lunch before she comes up for air, while the rest of the restaurant looks on and tries to work out exactly where she puts it or to see if she will belt to the bathroom immediately afterwards for a quick barf. She is smiling now. Food is the only thing that has a tangible effect — for the good, I mean — on Minnie. Food and maths. When she eats, or does maths-related things, there is a subtle shift and something slips into place; so, when Minnie looks at me, I know that she cares about me, even though she would never say such a thing out loud.

It's the same when she's at a restaurant with a big group of people and the bill comes at the end. Minnie says, 'I'll do it,' and her voice suggests she would rather be dipped in bloody fish guts and lowered into the Great White Shark-ridden waters off the Cape of Good Hope.

But the truth is, she loves it. There's no splitting the bill's total plus tip by the number of people at the table. Not with Minnie around. No. Instead, she will work out — to the last penny farthing — how much everyone owes. Who had the early bird? Who said they were having the early bird but then went for the fillet steak with its sneaky little fifteen per cent supplement in tiny lettering underneath? Who didn't have any wine? Who had more than their fair share? Who had two starters instead of the traditional starter and a main? Who insisted on dessert? Who ate some of the dessert that someone else ordered? The list of possibilities are endless at such a table but Minnie will tap-tap-tap at the calculator she carries in her bag at all times (the way most women carry a compact and a stick of mascara — although, of course, Minnie carries these weapons in her arsenal too). There is a carefully crafted 'weighting' system. Minnie will take into account things like age (students and OAPs get a 'Minnie-calculated' discount). Ed has to pay full whack; there is no disability discount in Minnie's calculations and for this — and many things — I love her. If people are 'between jobs', as many people are at the moment, there's a discount for that too. Everything — and everyone — is taken into account. Is given due consideration. She works it out while the rest of us are scraping the froth from the bottoms of our coffee cups. It takes her about five minutes. Less, probably. She tells everyone what they owe and if there is a problem with change, she will sort it out. That's what Minnie does. She sorts things out.

I say, 'You were right about Thomas, by the way.'

She says, 'What? That's he's a skyscraping muck savage with Monaghan silage-breath?' And the funny thing is that Thomas is one of the few people that Minnie genuinely likes.

I say, 'No, the bit about him seeing someone. He's seeing someone.'

'So?'

'Nothing. I just . . . I thought I'd tell you. Confirm it.'

Minnie says, 'No need.' And then she scoops couscous out of a clam shell. When it's all scraped out and tipped into her mouth, chewed, swallowed and washed down with water, she continues, 'A creature like Thomas doesn't get to sit in the swamp licking his balls for any length of time. Especially in a recession, when people are desperate. I'm just surprised he managed to hold out this long.'

If I say, 'I miss him,' Minnie will laugh and say, 'Catch yourself on, girl.'

146

So I don't say that. I don't say anything.

Minnie says, 'Anyway, it's just as well.'

I say, 'What's just as well?'

Minnie has two settings on her optimism metre: none and bizarre. If nothing else, her response will distract me from the beef and Guinness stew.

'You and Thomas. It's good that you realised you weren't suitable. When he got all domestic. It's good that he played his hand so early. You've wasted less time.' Minnie looks at me like I'm a balance sheet that doesn't add up. 'It's not too late. You're still fairly . . . viable' she says eventually.

'Good to know.' I pierce a chunk of beef with my fork and scrape the Guinnessy sauce off it before putting it in my mouth. I manage to get it down by drinking most of my glass of wine. The carafe is nearly empty now.

We order dessert. Carageen for Minnie, which is, at the end of the day, nothing but seaweed. And Baileys cheesecake for me. Baileys cheesecake makes you feel really good and really bad, at exactly the same time.

I say, 'I'm done.'

Minnie looks at my plate. 'Can I have the rest of your cheesecake?'

'No, I don't mean . . . I mean I'm done with dating. All that malarkey.'

'What about sex? Are you done with that?'

'Do forty-year-olds still have sex?'

'Well, my parents are in their sixties and they're still at it. I rang them yesterday afternoon and Mam said they were in bed and that's why her voice sounded post-coital.'

'She actually said post-coital?'

'Swear to God.'

'Let's face it, sex is overrated.' This may not be true of *Grey's Anatomy* but nobody knows about that.

Minnie says, 'Hmmm,' and I know immediately that she's probably having terrific sex, even if it's only with Maurice, and she doesn't want to tell me because she feels sorry for me since Thomas dumped me and I'm about to turn forty. In less than two months. A matter of weeks, really. I'll be forty and I'll probably be a virgin again because I won't have had sex in so long.

And I can't even write anymore. Which is the only thing I was ever any good at. My English teacher would be horrified if she knew that. She'd give us a three-page essay to write and I'd stop at the bottom of the third page. Even if I was in the middle of the story. Even if I was in the middle of a sentence. She said she'd never witnessed such indolence.

Minnie looks at her stopwatch thingamajig. 'I should go, I'm out of time.' Which really means that I'm out of time. In fairness, we're at minus six minutes and forty seconds.

'How about coffee?'

'Kat, I really should . . . '

'Espressos.' This is pathetic. I know it is. I don't even like espressos. That sharp, bitter taste and the way I have to squash my finger into the handle of the cup. If I had my mother's fingers, I could drink espressos to a band playing.

Minnie nods and puts her handbag back on the floor. In my head, I hear the conversation she will have with Maurice, later: ' . . . letting herself go . . . drinking at lunchtime . . . not touching her dinner . . . yes, it wasn't bad actually. I had the couscous with the clams and jus de blahblahblah . . . ' I can hear it all as clearly as if Minnie and Maurice were standing on either side of me, talking over my head. Couples always talk about their single friends. I overhear them, when I'm sitting in a restaurant, or a café.

We drink the espressos. Minnie stands up, puts her time-ometer into her bag and slips on her coat, which is actually a cape, on closer inspection. Everyone in the restaurant gazes at her as she does this, some with open hostility and some with hopeless adoration. It's always been the same where Minnie is concerned.

Minnie says, 'I'll call you.'

I nod.

Minnie bites her lip and shakes her head, like she's having an argument with herself. 'I feel like a heel, abandoning you like this.'

This is unusual territory for Minnie. I must look really miserable. I try to maintain the expression. 'Does this mean you'll come to Lincoln's with me and get pissed?' I say, taking advantage.

'No.' But she leans across the table and kisses me — briefly — on my cheek. Her lips are warm from the espresso.

She straightens and wipes her mouth with the back of her hand.

She says, 'Are you going to be OK?'

149

I say, 'Yes.'

Minnie nods but she's looking at me funny. She reminds me of her mother when she looks at me like that. Like her mother looked at me afterwards. Back when I was fifteen. All worry and concern. I don't like it.

She looks away but she doesn't move. Instead, she stands there. A bit shifty.

I say, 'What?'

Minnie takes a breath, the way people do when they're gearing up to say something that may be like a lead balloon, in terms of the way it'll go down.

I say, 'What?' again. I'm worried now. I'm thinking the worst. I'm thinking tumours. Big, malignant ones.

'I'm pregnant.'

'Wow.'

'I know, I know. I said I'd never have one and I'm too old and we're too set in our ways and there'd be no more hopping to Bilbao to visit the Guggenheim at a moment's notice. But that doesn't mean we'll never be able to go again. Besides, you can bring buggies into the Guggenheim. I Googled it.'

I begin to say something that goes like, 'Minnie . . . I think that's . . . '

'You don't have to pretend to be delighted or anything. I know how you feel about babies.'

Sometimes I hate her. I hate the way she knows everything about me.

'Of course I'm delighted. That's fantastic news.' And it is. Fantastic news. I just wish it wasn't Minnie's fantastic news. I hate myself for

150

thinking this thought but there it is. It's done now. Stuck in my head like a piece of spinach gripped by front teeth. Everything changed when she met Maurice. Changed a little more when they moved into their monstrosity in Ballsbridge. Then the wedding. Then the foodie holidays. And now this. I know this is the way things are supposed to go. It's just . . . it feels like she's slipping away from me. Like I'm being left behind.

'How many weeks are you?'

'Only eight so don't say a word to anyone. Maurice is superstitious about not telling anyone till I'm twelve weeks. It took us a while. To conceive, I mean.'

'You never said you were trying.'

'We've been trying for a few months now. I didn't want to tell anyone in case nothing came of it.'

I want to say, 'I'm not anyone,' but I don't say that.

'So we just kept ourselves busy, having sex and eating anchovies.'

'Anchovies?'

Minnie explains about anchovies then. About how they're a superfood when it comes to sperm speed and agility.

I say, 'How are you feeling?'

'Puking around the clock and gorging myself in between the puking.'

'You don't look sick.' My tone seems accusatory so I add, 'You look great' in a more ordinary voice.

Minnie beams then and I recoil a little. It's the

shock. She's never beamed before. 'I feel great. It's the weirdest thing.'

I say, 'You'll make a great mother.'

Minnie rummages in her handbag for her keys. I don't know why I said that. That's what Thomas said to me, back when he was trying to change everything. After the accident. The bloody miracle. Why do people say that? What do they think they know?

'I'm a terrible mother,' I told Thomas.

He was confused. 'What do you mean?'

I changed the tense. The tense made no sense. 'I mean I'd be a terrible mother. That's what I mean.' And that's what he couldn't understand.

How I knew.

For sure.

Faith says, 'Have you seen my cigarettes, Milo?'

I say, 'No.' Which is not really a lie. I haven't seen them. Not today anyway. I put them in the cupboard under the stairs at Mrs Barber's house. She never goes near that cupboard because of her hip. I don't think it can bend, even though it's brand new.

Faith's voice is muffled because she is under my bed, which is where I put them the last time. She slides out and sits up.

I say, 'There's chewing gum you can buy. Whenever you want a cigarette, you just chew a piece of gum instead. Damo's mam chews them and she hardly ever smokes anymore.'

She says, 'Milo . . . '

Her voice is sort of sad but she doesn't look annoyed, so I ask her, 'Will I go and stay with Ant and Adrian when you're not here?'

Mam always said that she didn't know how Ant and Adrian would look after themselves in London. They couldn't even use a tin opener. But you can buy tins now that you can open without a tin opener. I saw them in Damo's house.

Faith says, 'Why wouldn't I be here?' She opens the drawer on my bedside locker but there's nothing in there except my post office book and the football cards that come with the Hubba Bubba. The apple ones are my favourite. They make your tongue green. But not green enough so your mam thinks you're too sick to go to school. Damo already tried that.

'I don't know.'

Faith closes the drawer and looks at me. 'I'm not going anywhere, Milo.' She sneezes. She's allergic to dust and there's a lot of it around.

'What about the tour?'

She stands up. Then sits down again. 'Nothing's been decided yet.'

Rob is excited about the tour. He talks about it nearly as much as Damo talks about girls and Sully.

Rob says, 'Supporting the Crowns. That's something, Faith. That's really something.'

'I know, but . . . '

'And it's in the summer. So you won't miss any college.'

'Yes, but what about Milo?'

I don't hear what they say after that because Faith closes the door into the kitchen.

She probably said something like a tour's no place for a nine-year-old boy. She's always saying stuff like that. There are loads of places that aren't suitable for nine-year-old boys, according to Faith. Like Damo's house when his mam or Imelda aren't there. Or the bit of the park that's near the river, where all the squashed beer cans are.

I say, 'So, will you try them?'

Faith says, 'Try what?'

'The chewing gum.'

Faith looks out of the window. You can see Damo's house from my bedroom window. We signal each other with torches when we have batteries.

She says, 'Come here.' I sit on the bed beside her.

154

She says, 'I'm not going anywhere, Milo. And I'm not going to die from cigarettes. I only smoke about seven a day. When I can find them.' She reaches over and takes my fringe out of my eyes. 'We have to get that mop cut.'

Dad says my hair is just like his, except he doesn't have hair anymore. His head is very shiny and there are freckles all over it.

I hear the sound of someone walking down the driveway. Then the plop of something through the letterbox. Faith jumps up and runs out of the door and down the stairs.

I stand at the top of the stairs. Faith grabs the post. Two brown envelopes, which means they're bills. And another takeaway menu for the curry shop on the high street. She puts the menu in the recycling bin and puts the brown envelopes on the hall table, without opening them.

She sees me then and says, 'Milo, make your lunch and go to school.' She walks down the hallway, towards the kitchen.

If the lady writes to Faith, she'll probably have to go and live with her. And then I'll have to go and stay with Ant and Adrian in their student flat in London and make sure I buy cans you can open without a tin opener. I don't want to live with Dad. He's nice and everything, but I'm supposed to be doing my lifesaving exam in the spring. How could I do a lifesaving exam if I was in Scotland? And Damo wouldn't be able to visit because Scotland is miles away. Me and Mam drove there once and it took us about a hundred hours. Anyway, the new baby is coming and everyone knows that babies are noisy. Imelda was supposed to be getting one but she isn't anymore. Damo's mam hates noise.

London's not so far. Perhaps Ant and Adrian would bring me to Brighton once a week. On Wednesdays, maybe, so I could go to lifesaving and see Damo.

Brona rings. She says, 'I don't want to put any pressure on you but . . . '

This means she's about to put pressure on me. I'm not going to make it easy for her. I say, 'What?'

She says, 'Oh sorry, Kat, I'm probably disturbing you, am I?'

'I'm in the middle of a pretty tricky chapter, to be honest.' When I say 'to be honest' at the end of a sentence, that often means I'm lying through my teeth, but Brona doesn't know that because she takes everyone at face value, which is both her greatest gift and her biggest failing, if you ask me.

'Oh gosh, I'm terribly sorry. Should I ring back later?'

The choice is to have pressure applied now and thereby get it over and done with, or later, which would allow me to continue what I am doing, which is, in fact, nothing at all.

I say, 'No, it's fine, now is fine.'

'I'm just wondering about the book. Did you have a date in mind?'

'A date?'

'Yes. For the drop.'

Brona can't understand why I can't just email the manuscript. Or put it in a Jiffy bag. She insists that none of her colleagues would open a Jiffy envelope that is addressed to her. I've never worked in an office but I've seen them on the telly. Everyone wants to know everything about everyone. You can't be careful enough.

The drop never takes place at or anywhere near the publishing house. In fact, I've never been to the publishing house. Instead, I meet Brona at various train stations around London. I ring her when my plane lands at Heathrow and give her the name of the train station. I vary it. We've never met in the same place twice. We often meet in bookshops at the stations, although never in the crime/thriller section.

Brona says, 'Hello? You still there, Kat?'

I say, 'Sorry. I was miles away.'

'Penny for them?'

It's true. I am miles away. I'm in Paddington station. The Mind, Body and Spirit section of WHSmith, to be precise. I remember every drop, but this one in particular. Brona was there when I arrived, leafing through a book entitled *Soulmates and How to Get One*. Beside her, on the floor, was a black leather briefcase, with a combination lock.

I moved towards her.

We didn't speak to each other. Or even look at each other. We never do. I stood near her and set my briefcase — a black leather one with a combination lock — on the floor, then picked up a random book, which happened to be *Love in the Time of Cauliflowers*, and which Brona would later deem to be a sign. It was a cookbook for food-lovers in search of aphrodisiacs.

Brona replaced her book on the shelf and reached down, careful to bend at the knees. Her back can sometimes 'go out', she told me once.

She picked up my briefcase — with the manuscript of the seventh Declan Darker book — and slipped away. After an appropriate lapse of time — long enough to read a recipe for 'star-crossed lentil-lovers soup', I too replaced the book, picked up the other briefcase — containing nothing other than a congratulations card and a wilting bunch of lilies — and left the bookshop.

I headed to the Savoy. I always booked into the Savoy after each drop. I bought the usual supplies — a family-pack of Jelly Babies, a split of champagne and two Cuban cigars — and stayed for the afternoon.

I love hotel rooms. The anonymity of them. Sometimes, after I've eaten and drunk and smoked everything, I kick off my shoes, put on some music and tango through the room with my arms wrapped round an imaginary partner. And why not? Who would know? The walls of the Savoy hotel are as solid as a shelf of hardbacks.

All the drops have been pretty much identical. They've all gone to plan apart from Drop Number Five, when a baseball-cap-wearing pimply youth tried to steal Brona's briefcase. She gave chase, caught up with him outside Dunkin' Donuts, wrestled him to the ground and beat him about the head with the heel of her shoe. The manager of Dunkin' Donuts phoned 999 and Brona remained in a seated position on the flat of the man's back until the police arrived.

159

She may be small but she's pretty solid.

'Kat?'

'Yes?'

'My goodness, you really are in a daze today. I should let you get back to the writing.'

'Yes, I . . . '

'You're thinking about the drop in Paddington station. WHSmith. Aren't you?'

'Why on earth would I be thinking about that?' Brona claims she's got 'the sight' ever since she had a premonition that Jeremy would sustain a grievous bodily injury, and the very next day, Jeremy's boyfriend, Harold, rang in to say that Jeremy was incapacitated following an incident with a lawn mower and some WD40.

'Because . . . you know . . . you met Thomas after. On the plane home, remember? It was a Friday. It poured with rain.'

'You've some memory.'

Brona is a details woman. And she's also an incurable romantic — her description, obviously. She thought it was romantic, the way me and Thomas met. She thinks lots of things are romantic but there's nothing romantic about a suspicious package in the men's toilet in Terminal Two.

But now I'm thinking about the magic show in the Button Factory and I hate the way memory does this. Goes from one thing to the next, like a line of dominoes falling one by one.

Oddly, it wasn't as bad as I thought it would be, the magic show. It was better than I expected, actually. A lot better, in fact.

Brona says, 'What do you mean?'

I say, 'What?'

'You said, 'a lot better'.'

'Did I?' My thoughts are seeping out of me. Probably all the time I'm spending on my own.

Brona persists. 'What's a lot better?'

'Oh you know, everything really. Now that everything's, you know, pretty much back to normal.'

'That's marvellous, Kat.' A lengthy pause ensues. Then Brona says, 'So, the manuscript. I'm simply dying to read it. May I?'

'May you what?'

'Read it.'

'Oh . . . yes. Of course. But I'm . . . it's not finished yet.'

'No, no, of course not. Don't overdo it now, will you?'

I look around. The apartment looks like it's been burgled. And the burglars ate a fair amount of fast food, judging by the empty boxes and cartons lying about. And they got through a fair bit of wine. I haven't seen my laptop in weeks. It might be under my bed. There's some kids' programme on the telly. The main character is a yellow sponge, as far as I can tell.

I say, 'No, I'll try not to overdo it.'

'Good luck.'

'Thanks.'

'I'm so excited about this one, Kat.'

'Me too.'

'Ta ra, then.'

'Yeah. Ta ra.'

'So you'll call me?'

'Hmmm?'

'When it's done? You'll let me know?'

'Of course.'

When she starts into her usual recital line of 'Byebyebyebyebye . . . ' the relief is gigantic. And when the line, eventually, goes dead, I lie on the couch for a long, long time as if I've been exerting myself. Overdoing it.

But I haven't been overdoing it. I haven't been doing anything. I don't know what's wrong with me.

Rob and Faith have a meeting with somebody called Lewis Lennon, who is in charge of the Crowns. Rob bought a new-second-hand leather jacket that looks the same as his old one except there's no hole in the shoulder from Faith's cigarette. He is wearing sunglasses. The windscreen wipers on his van make a screeching sound every time they move across the window.

I'm in the back seat. Sometimes Rob lets me sit in the front even though you're supposed to be twelve years old or a hundred and thirty-five centimetres. I'm short for my age but Faith says that Ant and Adrian were midgets till they were eighteen and now they're even taller than Dad.

I'll be ten next month. Double digits, Mam said. She said Damo could have a sleepover when I was ten. Not on my actual birthday. Maybe on Boxing Day or the day after that. She said she'd take us to the cinema and for a proper meal afterwards, one with cutlery that's not plastic and fish and chips that aren't wrapped in paper. I don't know if Faith knows about the sleepover. I'll tell her about it when she's happy again.

Rob lights a cigarette and Faith tells him to put it out. He pulls down the window and blows the smoke outside. Faith shakes her head and Rob says, 'For fuck's sake,' and Faith says, 'Can you stop cursing?'

and Rob shakes his head and Faith sighs and Rob throws his cigarette out of the window and they don't say anything to each other for ages.

Faith forgot about the parent-teacher meeting at school today. We got a half day because of all the parents coming. Good job I got home when I did. Two minutes later and Faith would have been gone. When I arrive, she's climbing into Rob's van. Faith gave me a key for the front door. Just for emergencies, she said. That means if Mrs Barber is not at home when I get back from school. It's on a keyring that has a picture of a lifeboat on it. I don't mind being in the house on my own. I usually sit at the window in the sitting room because you can see people on the street so you know what's going on. The house is very quiet when it's just me, though. Apart from the floorboards upstairs, which creak a lot, as if someone is walking on them.

Faith says, 'What the hell are you doing here, Milo?'

She bites her lip when I tell her and looks at Rob, who shrugs and says, 'It's just a parent-teacher meeting. No biggie. My parents never went to those things. Waste of time.'

Faith looks at me and says, 'Do you mind if I don't go to it? It's just . . . this meeting is important for the band and I want to call in to Jonathon too.'

I say, 'I don't mind at all.'

It takes ages to get to London on account of the traffic. When we get to the street where Jonathon's office is, Rob pulls over and a car behind beeps because he didn't put his indicator on, like you're supposed to.

He turns off the engine. It ticks like a clock.

He picks up Faith's hand and says, 'Look, I'm sorry

about this morning. I'm just nervous about the meeting, y'know?'

Faith says, 'I know. And I will come with you. I just want to check in with Jonathon first. See if there've been any developments.'

Rob takes his hand away from Faith's. Puts it back on the steering wheel. 'If there were any developments, he would have rung you. You know that.'

Faith picks up her bag. She looks at me. 'Are you right, Milo?'

I take off my seatbelt and slide over to the door beside the pavement.

Faith says, 'Will you wait here for me?'

Rob says, 'Yeah, unless I get moved along by a warden.'

'I have my phone.'

'Don't be long. We can't be late for Lewis.'

'Wish me luck.'

'Luck.'

She opens the door and Rob grabs her hand and pulls her towards him so he can kiss her. I get out of the van but they're still kissing so I bend down and untie the lace of my trainer and then tie it up again. I do it really slowly, so that they'll be finished by the time I stand up.

He says, 'Twenty minutes. Max. Otherwise we'll be late for the meeting. OK?'

Faith nods and gets out of the van. She stands on the pavement for a moment, looking up at the building. Then she says, 'Right,' and moves towards the revolving doors. If you close your eyes and go round and round and then jump out, you stagger like Sully does when he drinks beer really quickly out of a can.

165

If Faith is in a good mood on the way out, I might do it.

Jonathon says, 'Well, this is a pleasant surprise,' when Faith pokes her head round the door of his office. He doesn't look surprised. He looks happy. Then he sees me and he doesn't look as happy as before.

Faith says, 'I was just wondering if there have been any developments?'

Jonathon looks at his watch before he stands up and says, 'Come in, come in. Would you like a coffee? Or a glass of water? It's too late for lunch, I suppose?'

Faith moves inside the office. I follow her. Jonathon doesn't ask me if I'd like a coffee or a glass of water or some lunch if it isn't too late. I don't like coffee. If he had a can of Coke, I'd drink that. Damo can drink a can of Coke in one gulp and then do the loudest belches you ever heard. He can talk when he belches so his voice sounds like a robot or something.

On the desk is a paper plate with a half-eaten ham sandwich on it. Jonathon wipes his hands on the back of his trousers before he holds out his arm towards Faith. She shakes hands the way Mam told us to. A short shake with a firm grip. Faith sits down on a chair that is just like the one on the other side of Mr Pilkington's desk, and, after a while, Jonathon sits down too. I sit on the couch again.

Jonathon looks at Faith and says, 'To what do I owe this unexpected pleasure?' and then he smiles like he's said something really funny. Faith says, 'It's just ... it's been three weeks and I've heard

166

nothing from you and I just wondered . . . '

Jonathon taps at his keyboard, peers at the monitor, shakes his head. 'There haven't been any developments, I'm afraid.'

Faith doesn't say anything. Jonathon squirms in his chair, as if he's trying to hold in a fart. 'I told you that we'd write to you. If we have any news. You have my word on that.'

Faith says, 'How many letters have you sent?'

Jonathon peers at the computer screen again. He squints his eyes when he does this, as if he should be wearing glasses. 'The registered one is due to go out this week. That'll be the third one.'

Faith stands up, walks to the window, looks down. I hope Rob hasn't been moved on by a warden.

'What happens if you don't get any response?'

Jonathon makes a bridge out of his hands and puts his chin on it. He takes a deep breath before he answers, as if he has a lot of things on his mind.

He says, 'There's only so much we can do, I'm afraid. There are regulations. Very strict guidelines and — '

'Couldn't you just give me her name and address and I can follow it up myself?'

Jonathon shakes his head. 'That's against regulations.'

'I don't see why. This is my information. I'm entitled to it, surely?'

Jonathon shakes his head again. 'There are two people involved here. It has to be mutual.'

'What? Like the decision that was made twenty-four years ago? That was hardly mutual.'

Jonathon rubs his hand down his face. He looks tired. 'That was different.'

Faith turns round. Sits on the windowsill. She looks at Jonathon and he picks up the mouse and moves it round on the pad beside the keyboard. She stands up. 'So you'll contact me if . . . '

Jonathon lets go of the mouse and looks at her. He is smiling again. 'Of course. In fact, you could give me your mobile number and I could — '

'I don't feel well.'

Jonathon stops talking. He looks at me. So does Faith.

Then he stands up. Looks at the couch where I'm sitting. Then looks at Faith. 'He's not going to be sick, is he?'

I say, 'I feel a bit . . . faint. I might just be hungry. I didn't have any lunch.'

'You did have lunch.' Faith looks at Jonathon and says, 'He did. At school. I made him cheese sandwiches.'

'No, I didn't. I had to run an errand for Miss Williams at break so I didn't eat my lunch. And now I feel sick. I think it might be hunger pains.'

Faith looks at me the way adults look at their kids when they're going to kill them later. Not right away. 'Jonathon, sorry, I . . . I'd better go and get him something to eat.'

I say, 'I need something now. Maybe some toast and a hot chocolate?'

Faith says, 'Milo!' Her face is red.

Jonathon says, 'No, it's no problem. The boy does look a little peaky. Maybe I could — '

Faith says, 'No, no, it's all right, I'll take him out and . . . '

Jonathon says, 'There's bread in the kitchen. I'll get

168

him a slice. No toaster, I'm afraid. I don't think there's any hot chocolate but there should be some milk in the fridge.' He moves beside Faith, touches her arm. 'I'll be back in a few minutes, OK?'

When he leaves, Faith hisses at me. 'For the love of God, Milo, what are you at? You're making a holy show of me.'

I close the office door, run behind Jonathon's desk and grab the mouse. The password prompt appears. I type in 'jonath001', which, if you ask me, is the stupidest password you could have, if your name is Jonathon. A hacker is going to tap into that in two minutes flat. And Jonathon doesn't even cover the keyboard with the mouse pad when he types it in, like I do when anyone's around. He just enters it as if no one is watching.

'Milo, for fuck's sake! Stop it.' Faith is beside me, pulling at my arm. I point at the screen and she bends down to see. There's Faith's name and our address. Some stuff about Faith. Her date of birth and a copy of the birth certificate she gave Jonathon the first time we came here. The one with Mam and Dad's name at the top.

Faith looks at the door, still closed, and whispers, 'Click on the correspondence tab.'

The mouse on the screen turns into an egg timer and the screen goes blank. For a moment, I think the computer has frozen, the way our one at home sometimes does when I'm playing Sims.

'Jesus, hurry up.' I know Faith is talking to the computer. Not me. I get the mouse in my hand and bang it on the desk a couple of times.

'Ssshhhhh.' Faith straightens and stares at the door again. 'Someone's coming.'

169

We listen. I hear footsteps. Heavy ones. Getting closer.

Faith grabs my arm, tries to pull me out of the chair. 'Close it, Milo, close it now. He's coming.'

I hook my feet round the legs of the chair so I don't budge. The egg timer flashes. Faster now. There is a beep. And then the correspondence tab opens.

I scroll down.

Three letters.

One name.

One address.

I hear voices in the corridor. Two voices. One of them is Jonathon's.

'Jesus, quick. Close that tab. Hurry up. Get over to the couch.' Faith waits until I've pressed the X before she hauls me out of the chair. When the door opens, we are standing at the edge of the desk. I duck my head between my legs.

Faith says, 'I was just going to open the window. Milo is feeling a bit . . . '

'He's not going to barf, is he?' Jonathon is one of those adults who talk about you like you're not there. His shoes match but his laces don't.

I stand up straight. 'Actually, I feel a lot better now.'

Faith says, 'Good. Great. We should go.'

Jonathon says, 'But what about . . . ' He nods at the two slices of bread on a plate in one hand. The glass in the other, half full of milk.

I take one slice of the bread. 'Thanks. I'll eat it on the way out.' I move towards the door, pulling Faith along behind me.

Faith says, 'Sorry, Jonathon. And thanks. For everything.'

He stands in the middle of the office, with his shoes that match and his laces that don't. He looks like he wants to say something but can't think what. I bet he'll eat the bread when we're gone. Probably drink the milk too. He looks like the type.

Declan Darker opened the door and stepped inside, his hand resting on the gun tucked into the waistband of his faded 501s. The house was quiet. Dark. He closed the door, making no sound, and began to move up the stairs. He knew Spencer was here. Hiding in the dark like the rat he was.

I select the paragraph and stamp on the Delete button with my fist.
Blank screen. Page one of one.
I begin again.

Darker stopped at the foot of the stairs. Every muscle in his body was taut, straining in the silence for a sound. The hand gripping the banister was as steady as a rock. He began to climb. He knew this was how it had to end. Him and Spencer. The two of them. There could be no other way.

This time, I use the backspace. BACKSPACE-BACKSPACEBACKSPACE.
Blank screen. Page one of one.
Dialogue. I'm not bad at dialogue. Even the

reviewers have to admit it. I'll kick-start the chapter with dialogue.

'I thought you'd retired, Darker.'

'With scumbags like you roaming the streets, Spencer? I don't think so.'

'I heard you'd lost your nerve. Since Razor Bill. I heard he cut you pretty bad.'

Darker tightened his grip on the gun. 'I'm lookin' for a reason to pull this trigger, Spencer. Go ahead. It won't take much.'

CHRIST! DELETEDELETEDELETE.

And there it was again. The blank screen. Page one of one. I bang the lid of the laptop down. Again. Shove it into the bag and push the bag under the desk until I can't see it anymore.

I get up. Put on my coat. Outside, the cold is shocking. So are the fairy lights. And the stars. And the lit-up Santas. It shouldn't be Christmas. It's only November.

And yet somehow it is.

I get in my car. My beautiful car. I love everything about it. It even smells the same as the last one. I bought the exact same air freshener. I turn the key and the engine engages with its low hum. I check the mirrors and get going. I love driving. People said I would be nervous, getting back behind the wheel. I forced myself not to think about it.

In the supermarket, I'm back in the express lane. Ten items or less. A net of satsumas. One large tub of low-fat natural yoghurt. A packet of

Jacob's Cream Crackers. A triangle of Brie. One bag of porridge oats. A bottle of red wine. A family-size pepperoni pizza and a frozen stick of garlic bread.

Music pours like rain into the lift back to the car park. Christmas music. 'Joy to the World'. Some marketing person came up with that idea. Told the MD that playing Christmas songs in the shop and the lift and the car park and the toilets would make people buy more tinsel and baubles and ribbons and wrapping paper. I'd love to take to the speaker with something hard. The garlic bread, maybe.

Minnie is going to her Yoga for Pregnancy class, then home to cook dinner with Maurice. They got a new fish kettle that they're pretty excited about.

Ed said I could go to see *Harry Potter and the Deathly Hallows Part Two* with him and Sophie but I said no. Things will have to get much worse before I agree to tag along on a date with my brother and his girlfriend. He said, 'There's another letter for you. It looks the same as the first one.' It's unusual for the college to do mailshots at this time of the year. They usually wait till the new year, when people are desperate for a change. I make a mental note to ring the college on Monday morning and tell them to stop writing to me. I don't know why I bother making a mental note because, even as I make it, I know I'll never do it. Minnie says it's because I'm disorganised and slovenly. She doesn't mean it as an insult. Just as a matter of fact. I couldn't agree more.

Thomas is probably playing *Grey's Anatomy* with Sarah or Sandra or Sorcha or whateverhernameis.

I turn on all the lights in the apartment. Even the lamp in the spare room, which is really Ed's room. I turn on the oven. Switch on the telly. Nothing on. I mute it. Put on the radio. A Christmas song. 'All I Want for Christmas is You'. I switch the station. 'Joy to the Fecking World'. I turn off the radio.

I don't quite make it to the end of the family-size pepperoni, but I nearly do. Enough to do a fair bit of damage on the scales tomorrow. I manage to finish the wine, though. I realise this as I lift the bottle to pour another glass. I light a cigarette. I'm not supposed to smoke in the apartment. I made up that rule myself. It seems silly now. I'll catch my death out on the balcony, I tell myself. Besides, it's Friday night, I tell myself. And it's only me here. Not like the pot plants are going to die of second-hand cigarette smoke, are they? Although they don't look at their best, to be honest. Thomas bought them all. He said, 'Aloe vera — ' when I touched an odd, spiky-looking one ' — great for sunburn and pimples.'

I said, 'I don't have pimples.'

He broke the top off one of the stems, poured a sticky substance onto his fingers, rubbed them together and put them under my nose. I stepped back.

'Smell,' he said. I sniffed perfunctorily.

Thomas said, 'See?'

I nodded and allowed him to smear a bit on

175

my neck. It didn't feel sticky. In fact, it wasn't all that unpleasant, to be honest. It even smelled a bit like the aloe vera cream in the bathroom. Thomas undid the buttons on my shirt. Expertly. With the fingers of one hand. Like he'd done it a hundred times before he met me. And perhaps he had. We never told each other our tales.

I said, 'Eh, excuse me. What are you doing?'

He didn't look up. Just continued unbuttoning and then he unhooked my bra. One of those ones that opened at the front, which he called 'handy'. He didn't do anything for a moment. Just looked at them. My nipples were like football studs. Then he said, 'Aloe vera is especially effective on sunburn.' He said it as if he were reading it out from the *Farmers Journal*. Matter-of-fact.

'But I'm not sunburned.'

'I'm merely demonstrating.'

Anyway, the aloe vera plant is dead now. And it's not the only one. The one that used to have pale purple flowers has the decayed look of the long, long departed. Ditto the herbs on the windowsill. Basil and something that begins with a C. Coriander, maybe.

The phone rings.

The noise is huge in the quiet of the apartment. I walk into the hall. I might have drunk too much. My shoulders glance off the walls.

It takes ages to reach the phone. The hall seems longer than usual. The phone keeps ringing. I pick it up. 'Hello?'

Nothing.

176

'Who's there?'

I hear someone breathing. This is when I'm supposed to hang up. But the wine has me cosseted like a suit of armour.

I say, 'I know who you are.' See what he makes of that.

It works, because he speaks. After weeks of ringing up and saying nothing, he finally speaks. It is a man. A man with an English accent. His voice is low-pitched. He enunciates each word, like an elocution lesson.

'And I know who you are, Kat Kavanagh.'

My heart hammers in my chest. The kitchen door creaks in a draught and I jump. The hallway seems darker than before. I press the phone against my ear until it hurts.

'What do you mean?' I try to keep a grip on my voice but it sounds shaky. Like I'm afraid.

'But then again, everybody knows who you are, don't they, Kat? Or should I say, Killian?' His voice is lower now. Almost a whisper.

'I don't know what you're talking about.'

'I think you do.'

'Don't ring this number again.'

'How's book ten coming along, Kat?'

I hang up. My legs shake. Everything shakes. I sit on the floor. I sit there for a long time. Thomas was right about the tiles. They are cold. I sit there until it passes. The need to phone Thomas is huge. It's been there before but never like this.

I sit on my hands.

I don't ring Minnie. She won't be surprised.

177

She'll say, 'You can't hide forever, Kat.' She's said that before.

'I know who you are.' The voice was sure of itself. There was no doubt. Only conviction. I check the Caller ID. This time, the number comes up as 'blocked'. I replace the phone on the cradle. Pull the lead out of the wall. Tuck my hands back under my legs.

I've been so careful. Nobody could have been more careful than me.

I'm sober now. An entire bottle of wine and I'm sober already. That's bad value. I get up slowly. My legs are stiff. I hobble to the kitchen and lift the blind to look out of the window. The streetlamp gutters and in the flickering orange light I can see it's been raining. The street is empty.

I get into bed with my clothes on and a full face of makeup. The electric blanket is on but it takes ages to warm up. I turn the light off and the darkness advances like something solid, surrounding me on all sides.

'I know who you are.' I believed him when he said it. He sounds like someone who knows things. He sounds like someone who knows everything.

I sit up and switch on the light.

I open my laptop. Press the button. Open the document. There it is again. The blank screen. Page one of one.

It was difficult to see. The dark was thick. Penetrating. Darker couldn't even make out shadows. Outlines. Nothing. It was the kind of dark that suggested it may never be light again.

This time I don't read it before I press Delete.
Delete.
Delete.
Delete.

Faith says, 'No, Milo. You can't come to Ireland with me. You just can't.' She's organising her clothes into piles on her bed. She says she's only going for two days but from all the piles of clothes you'd think she was going for two weeks. Her dress is on the top of the 'to be washed' pile. Faith calls it her all-weather dress because you can wear it in spring, summer, autumn and winter. She never goes anywhere without it.

I say, 'Why can't I come?'

Faith says, 'Because . . . well, there's school for a start.'

'I won't be missing much. And I can catch up when I get back. And besides, I'm doing really well in all my subjects.' This is not exactly true. We did fractions last week. I got seven-and-a-half out of ten. Dividing an apple tart into sixteen bits is harder than you'd think.

Faith takes her favourite jeans out of the wardrobe.

I say, 'You can't take those. They're too big on you now.'

Faith says, 'I'll wear a belt.' She folds them. Mam ironed our clothes, but Faith says folding is just as good.

I say, 'I'm not going to Dad's.'

'You don't have to. Dad's coming here.'

'He can't. The baby might come when he's not there.'

180

'The baby's not due till the end of December, for God's sake.' Adults have an answer for everything.

'When are you going?'

'I've booked a flight for the day after tomorrow.' She tousles my hair. 'I'll be back before you know it.'

'That's a lot of clothes for two days.'

Faith smiles. 'It's Ireland. You never know what the weather's going to do.'

'I don't want you to go to Ireland.'

'Nothing bad is going to happen to me, I promise.'

Mam promised too, but I don't say that to Faith.

'Your birth mother mightn't live at that address anymore. Maybe she moved.'

'I have to go, Milo. I've explained why.'

When I was a kid, I could make myself cry. If I wanted to go somewhere. Or I wanted a chocolate mint Cornetto, which happens to be my favourite type of Cornetto. Damo says it's weird to like mint, on account of it being a green. His mam put a mint leaf into a salad once. Damo hates salad.

I can't make myself cry now. And even if I could, I don't think it would work. Faith would just laugh and call me a cry-baby.

I'll have to think of something else.

181

Minnie's not two steps into the apartment when she says, 'There's a guy.'

'No.'

'He's the financial controller of this company we're working with at the moment.'

'The company you're taking over? In a hostile manner?'

'Yes.'

'Well, he mustn't be very good at his job.'

'Not the point.' Minnie's in the living room now, looking at the couch. There's a pizza box on it. Lines of cards; I've taken to Solitaire recently. Last Sunday's papers. A pair of shoes. Minnie moves the pizza box to the table and sits down. She says, 'I don't know how you can live like this.'

'It's great. There's virtually no cleaning up to be done.'

She withers me with one of her looks. It's a good one. I'm thinking about getting the Hoover out when she's gone. The thought is slight. Remote. But it's there, which is an improvement.

Minnie says, 'Anyway, the guy. He's set to make a mint out of this transaction. Plus, he's attractive. Divorced. No kids. Good head of hair.'

'No.'

'I'm ringing him.' She grabs her phone out of her bag.

I think about grabbing it and running away but then dismiss the thought. There's no point. Not with Minnie.

She punches in a number. Lifts the phone to her ear. Says, 'It's ringing.'

'Hang up. Right now.'

'Dammit. Voicemail.' She hangs up.

I breathe out. 'Do you want something to drink?' and she gives me daggers so I say, 'I meant tea. Or coffee. A cold drink?'

'Coffee is giving me heartburn.'

'Tea, then?'

'It's giving me the trots.'

'I have Coke and 7UP.'

'I can't drink fizzy anymore. It's giving me nightmares.'

'How about some water.'

'Sparkling or still?'

'Whichever.'

'Well, I can't have sparkling because . . . '

'Still, then.' I beat a retreat into the kitchen.

Minnie follows me. She says, 'How's the book coming along?'

'Did Brona put you up to this?'

'No.'

'The book is coming along fine.'

'Liar.'

'Do you want ice in your water?'

'Yes, and a sprig of mint.' I love that about Minnie. That she thinks this is the type of apartment where one might chance upon a sprig of mint. Although one might, if Thomas still lived here. He had a little herb garden going on, out on the balcony, back in the day.

I make myself tea and hand Minnie her water. I spill a packet of Jammie Dodgers onto a plate. We sit down.

Minnie says, 'It's time, Kat.'

'It's not time.'

'Yes it is. You can't stay here, pretending to write a book, for the rest of your life.'

'I'm not pretending. I'm busy, as it happens. Very busy. That's why the place is a little . . . messy.'

Minnie says, 'A little messy? I've seen playrooms that are tidier than your apartment.'

All her analogies involve kids now. In some form or another.

Minnie says, 'You need to start dating again.'

'I hate dating.'

'Not every man rates bog snorkelling as a date, you know.'

That makes me smile. 'We never went bog snorkelling, in the end.'

'A lucky escape.'

'I got sick. I couldn't go.'

'Proper sick? Or pretending sick?'

'Proper sick.'

'I can't believe you were even thinking about going bog snorkelling.'

That was the thing about Thomas. He made everything sound easy. Feasible. Even the idea of me squeezing my way into a smelly wetsuit and forcing myself down a hole in the ground in a bog in Athlone didn't sound as crazy as it should. Not when Thomas said it.

184

Minnie looks at her watch. 'I have to go. I'm meeting Maurice in town. There's some seminar on breastfeeding he wants us to go to. I said I didn't think he had the tits for it, but there you go.'

When Minnie's gone, I sit on the space on the couch where the pizza box used to be. I'm not thinking about hoovering anymore. I'm thinking about that day. The bog snorkelling day.

I didn't even ring him to cancel. That's how sick I was. It was only when he rang the buzzer that I remembered. I crawled out of bed and answered the phone. I said, 'I can't go bog snorkelling. I'm sick.'

'Ah, you cray-thur. Let me up till I get a look at you.' Thomas had a way of talking about me as if I was a heifer that he was thinking about buying at a mart.

'I'm probably contagious.'

'I haven't been sick since 1972. I'll take my chances.'

'What did you have in 1972?'

'Let me up and I'll tell you.'

I pressed the buzzer and, for the first time since I'd known him, I didn't do my usual dash around the apartment, kicking plates under the couch and hiding my face under a ton of make-up. That was how sick I was. Instead, I leaned against the door and waited the sixty seconds.

'What did you have in 1972?' I asked when he arrived.

'Anaphylactic shock.'

'Impressive,' I said. 'What are you allergic to?'

'Bee stings.'

'That's pretty serious,' I couldn't help saying.

'You look worried,' he said, chuffed with himself.

'I'm not, it's just . . . '

'Don't worry,' he said, even though I wasn't worried. 'I've an antidote in the car. Besides, bees sting only if they feel threatened.'

He bent to examine my face. 'So what's wrong with you?'

'Tummy bug.' It sounded pretty lame when you compared it to anaphylactic shock.

'You've got a temperature,' he told me, clamping one of his massive hands across my forehead. The coolness of his skin was delicious. I allowed myself to sag a little, against the door.

'Come here to me,' he said, and before I could say, 'Diarrhoea and vomit,' he had me up in his arms, like I was a doll.

He put me in bed and made me weak tea and dry toast. He even emptied the bucket beside my bed. He drew the curtains and checked on me every ten minutes or so.

I said, 'You don't have to stay.'

He said, 'I know.' But he stayed anyway.

Later, I lay on the couch. I felt much better but I didn't tell Thomas that. I was reluctant to relinquish the feeling I had. It felt like I'd spent the last twelve months running and running and then, just for that day, just because I was sick, I stopped. I surrendered. I was appalled at how good it felt.

You're not yourself when you're sick.

Thomas sat on the couch. He picked up one

of my feet and began to knead it with his fingers. I tried to pull it out of his hands. 'I haven't had a shower today,' I said.

'I've been elbow-deep in ewes in the lambing season,' he told me proudly. 'I can handle smelly feet.'

'I didn't say they were smelly.'

'You didn't have to.'

'Besides, you only have one ewe. You can hardly call that a lambing season.'

'She's a pretty fertile ewe — I can call it what I like.'

'Tell me something I don't know,' he asked later, when we were supposed to be watching the telly.

I said, 'There are nine planets in the Solar System.'

He said, 'Eight, actually. Pluto is only a dwarf planet now.'

'Since when?'

'Since 2006.'

'That seems unfair.'

Thomas said, 'I meant tell me something I don't know. About yourself.'

I said, 'Oh,' even though I knew that's what he'd meant.

And then I told him. Up till then, I told him what I tell everybody who wants to know. I said I was a technical writer for a software company.

I didn't make a conscious decision to tell him. I just told him. Without really giving it any thought.

I said, 'I'm a writer.'

He said, 'I already know that.'

'No, I mean a fiction writer. I write fiction.'

'Oh.'

'I have a pseudonym.'

'Like John Banville?'

'Sort of.'

'What's your pseudonym?'

It was strange. Telling him. A bit like the first time I took off my clothes in front of him in the middle of the day so he could see everything, and I ran out of breath in the end and couldn't suck my belly in anymore. He didn't seem to notice. He said I was beautiful. Ha!

'It's . . . it's Killian Kobain.'

Thomas didn't just read the Declan Darker books. He was friends with him on Facebook. He followed him on Twitter. He subscribed to Declan Darker's blog. I'd seen all the Declan Darker books on his bookcase in Monaghan. The box set on top of his DVD player. Thomas happened to be a fan. He happened to be my fan.

Thomas shook his head. 'I can't believe it.'

I got my laptop. Showed him the files. The stories. All the various drafts of them.

Still, he shook his head.

In the end I had to bring him to my office, open the safe and drag out various documents that happened to have the names of the books written on the top of them.

Eventually he believed me. He said, 'You really are Killian Kobain?'

I nodded.

He grinned and said, 'I knew there was something fierce womanly about that bloke.'

Afterwards, he looked a little shy, like he'd just met me and he was trying to think of something interesting to say. I got a kick out of it, to be honest.

He said, 'You dreamed up Razor Bill.'

'He's basically a male version of Minnie.'

He laughed and that broke the ice and we were back to being us again. Kat and Thomas. Thomas and Kat. He said, 'That's pretty weird.' But I could tell he was impressed too. And I liked it. A lot. I felt like I was fifteen again. Before everything went wrong. The good side of fifteen.

'Why don't you write under your own name?'

'I like the anonymity, to be honest.'

He nodded. He got it.

I said, 'What about you?'

He said, 'Well, I really am a farmer.'

'You're not, you're a journalist.'

'I'm a farmer who happens to be a journalist as well.'

'You're a journalist who happens to have a farm. A very small farm.'

'It's not that small.'

'It's five fields of stony grey soil in Monaghan.'

'Five grand big fields,' he said.

Then he said, 'I was married.' I felt like someone had slapped my face. Hard.

'It was a long time ago. We were young. In our twenties.'

I said, 'What happened?' Even though part of me didn't want to know. This was messy territory.

'She died.' He said it in a way that suggested

189

he didn't say it often. 'In a car crash. She was five months pregnant. So I suppose they both died. That's the way it felt to me anyway. At the time.'

At first, I was kind of mad with him. Why couldn't he have been like everyone else and just been married and then got divorced? Why did it have to be such a tragedy? How could anyone compete with that? The least he could have given me was a much-hated ex-wife who had left him for his best friend and was now screwing him for maintenance. That would have been a helluva lot easier to take.

Another part of me was glad to know. I told him something. He told me something. This was what people did. People in a relationship.

Out of the blue, I said, 'I don't want to have children.' I don't know why I said it like that. Just blurted it out like that.

'Oh,' is all he said.

'I mean, I know we're not serious or anything. But I just want you to know. I don't want any misunderstandings.'

I dived into the space in the conversation where he was supposed to say something but didn't. 'Just because I've got a womb doesn't mean I have to fill it to the brim, does it? I mean look at you.'

'What about me?'

'Well, you've got those three nipples and you never use any of them.'

'That's a birthmark, I keep telling you.'

'It's a nipple.'

'It's a birthmark.'

190

'It's a nipple.'

'Anyway. I am serious.'

'About what?'

'About you.'

And in the space in the conversation where I was supposed to say something, he leaned towards me and kissed me and, even though my mouth might have tasted of vomit, I kissed him back.

And there it was.

I suppose, if you want to be soppy about it, I could say that was the moment when I knew that he was right. What he had said. That day. 'You'd better be mighty careful, Katherine Kavanagh.'

But I wasn't careful. My door was open wide and here he was, traipsing all over my lovely cream carpet in his steel toe-capped, mucky boots. And instead of telling him to get out, or at least have the decency to take off his shoes, and getting busy with the Shake n' Vac, I just let it go. I let everything go. I might as well have gone to the roof garden at the top of the apartment block and roared at the top of my voice, 'I LOVE YOU.'

That's how bad it was.

# 1

The next day, Faith says, 'Where are you going?'

I say, 'To the library.'

'Is Damo going with you?'

'Yeah.' Which is pretty funny when you think about it, because Damo isn't a member of the library. I don't think he's ever been inside it.

But Faith won't let me go to the library on my own on account of the two roads, even though there's a zebra crossing on one of them and traffic lights on the other.

I run out of the door in case Faith thinks of something else to ask me.

The post office isn't that far from the library and you still have to cross two roads but neither of them has a zebra crossing. I stand beside a mam and a dad and their two kids. One of them is strapped in a buggy, all wrapped up. You can't really see the kid but I reckon it's a girl because everything is pink. The other kid is holding her mam's hand. They're both wearing mittens, the same colour, so it looks like a pair of hands except one of them is really big and one of them is really small. The dad is carrying the shopping bags. I wait until they're crossing and then I cross too. People probably think we're a family.

There's a long queue in the post office and the man behind the glass screen keeps looking down the line and then looking at his watch and shaking his head.

Mam used to love it when there was a queue at the Funky Banana. She'd rub her hands and say, 'We'll eat like kings tonight, my son.' I don't think the man behind the counter loves queues as much as Mam.

It takes ages to get to the top of the queue. The man behind the screen looks at me like I've called him a name or picked my nose right in front of his face. 'You want to clear your account?'

'No. Thank you.' Sometimes, if you say please and thank you, it makes adults smile, but not all the time. Not this time. 'I just want to take out one hundred and fifty-three pounds and forty-one pence, please.'

'But that's all you have in your account.'

I say, 'I know.' I point to my post office book, which I have slipped under the glass between us so he can see it too. See the number at the bottom. One hundred and fifty-three pounds and forty-one pence.

The man rubs his eyes as if he hasn't slept for a really long time. Maybe he hasn't. Maybe that's what's wrong with him.

He says, 'So you do want to clear your account, then?'

'Does that mean the account will be closed?'

'No.'

'I don't want to close it because I'll be saving up again. Half my pocket money every — '

'Your account won't be closed.'

'OK. So can I have my money? Please? One hundred and fifty-three pounds and forty-one pence?'

He sighs. 'Does your mother know you're here?'

I nod. 'Yeah. I mean yes. She does.'

He sighs again. He opens a drawer with a key. He counts out the money. Three fifty-pound notes. Three pound coins. Two twenty-pence pieces. One penny.

It's all there. He pushes it under the glass, towards me.

I say, 'Thank you.'

He says, 'NEXT.'

I don't go outside until I have the money inside the pocket of my jeans. Just in case. I've never actually seen a mugger but I've heard about them.

I can always start saving again for a PlayStation 3 when I get back. Sully has one and, when he's in a good mood, he lets me and Damo have a go. If a girl lets him kiss her, Sully gets in a good mood. He says he's done sex with girls. Loads of times. When he's away at the war, he locks his PlayStation 3 inside his wardrobe.

One hundred and fifty-three pounds and forty-one pence. That's worth more than half a PlayStation 3.

I got more than that for my First Holy Communion but I spent some of it on a new snorkel and facemask. Mam said I should put the rest in the post office because you never know when you might be glad of a few bob. Your First Holy Communion is when you eat the bread, except it's supposed to be the body of Jesus. And the wine is the blood, but we didn't get to drink the wine. Only the priest got to do that.

My jeans are in the laundry basket on the landing so I take them out and put them into the bag. They don't smell bad. They just have the grass stains on them from the game of Bulldog Takedown we played at school the other day. I have three clean pairs of boxers.

The socks I find don't match and have holes in the toes. They feel dead uncomfortable. Mam cut my toenails every Saturday night after my bath. I told her I didn't need a bath on Saturday nights on account of going to my lifesaving class once a week and then a regular swim as well. That's like having a bath. Twice. In one week. She'd tickle my toes when she was cutting my nails and, even though I'm too old for tickles, I'd laugh anyway. You can't help it. Not when it's your toes.

I do it myself now. Cut my toenails. Except that I keep forgetting. That might be why most of my socks have holes in the toes.

In the end, I find four socks. They're all too big. I think they're Ant's. Or Adrian's. And they don't match or anything like that. But there're no holes in them. Not yet anyway.

Faith is talking to Dad on the phone. He says he'll be here in an hour. I hope he's not talking on the phone and driving at the same time because that's a pretty dangerous thing to do when you think about it.

I check the bus timetable. The bus into London goes from the top of our road so it's not too far to walk. I could get the train but the station is ages away and the bus is way cheaper and I'll be able to sit on the top deck at the front. The last one leaves at 00.14, which means fourteen minutes past midnight. Then I'll take another bus to Gatwick. Faith's flight is at eleven o'clock tomorrow morning. I'll be there way before then.

I find my passport in Mam's room. I run in, take it out of the drawer and run back out. I used to love going into Mam's room. When I was little, I bounced on the bed. It's a very bouncy bed. When I got too big to bounce, I lay across it and read my books. Mam sat on the end of the bed and put make-up on her face or brushed her hair or painted her nails, and I'd read and she'd say, 'Tell me something,' and I'd tell her about a new dive we were learning at lifesaving or a new star that had been discovered or something like that.

I shut the door behind me when I get out of the room.

I put my passport into my bag. I'll probably be able to buy a ticket to Ireland at the airport. Faith won't be able to say, 'No,' once I've got a ticket.

I end up hoping the birth mother turns out to be a horrible person because then Faith will come back to Brighton with me. I know that's mean but you can't stop your thoughts from thinking stuff, even if it's bad stuff.

I hide the bag under my bed. It's small enough so it fits. I hide it behind the box with the costumes. I'm too old for dressing up now but some of them are still in pretty good condition, like the Power Ranger and the Death Eater. There's a cowboy outfit too. I could give them away, I suppose. To a charity shop, maybe. There's one in town.

I'll do it when I get back.

When everything gets back to normal.

On Sunday, I visit my parents' house. There is nothing unusual about that. I often visit their house on Sunday. I've been doing it for years.

It's cold inside. Dad doesn't like it too warm because of the orchids, in various stages of development, that occupy most windowsills. He's supposed to grow them in the orchard but he brings some of them inside. The ones that need special attention, he says. I've come across him doing all sorts with them. Talking to them, playing 'Things Can Only Get Better' by D:Ream to them, painting their pots (although he says this is a last resort, not being gifted with a brush and a palette). I think it was their second date when Mum expressed a liking for the flower. Dad never forgot it.

Ed says, 'Where's Thomas, Kat?'

Maybe this is the worst part about me and Thomas. About Thomas and I.

Ed.

From the moment he met Thomas, Ed has declared himself to be Thomas's best friend. And who could blame him, the way Thomas carried on? Bringing him everywhere. Like to the film premiere of *Pirates of the Caribbean*, a Skullduggery Pleasant book launch, a trip to the set of *Fair City*, just because he knows that *Fair*

*City* is Ed's favourite soap.

'Ed doesn't need a chaperone, you know,' I often said in the voice Thomas called my 'testy' voice.

'Sure, don't I want to go too?' he'd say. 'Isn't yer woman, what's her face, Penelope Crows in it?'

'Cruz.'

'Exactly. And there'll be a bit of a feed and maybe some goodie bags. We'll have a blast, won't we, Ed?'

And they always did. Have a blast. They went to football matches at Croke Park, the opening night of *The Sound of Music* at the Grand Canal Theatre, a journalists-only trip to the zoo when the baby elephants were born.

'There's no need for you to take Ed on every jolly you go on,' I told Thomas, more than once.

'I know,' Thomas said. 'Do you want to come with us?'

'To the smelly zoo to see some smelly elephants lifting their tails and excreting the contents of their bowels right in front of me?'

'Yes,' said Thomas.

'OK,' I said, enjoying his surprise. And my own, if I'm honest. And the elephants weren't even that smelly. In fact, what I remember is the heavy sweetness of jasmine in the air and the smell of summer when Thomas bent and kissed the corner of my mouth in public, before I could tell him not to.

No matter how many times I try to tell Ed about me and Thomas — Thomas and I — he still asks. Especially on Sundays. In the months before we broke up — before he left me — Thomas had infiltrated the tradition of our family Sunday lunches the same way he had infiltrated everything else: without my noticing until it was too late. So there he was, squashing himself into my father's chair at the head of the dining-room table. BAM!

Today, I just don't have the stomach for it. I say, 'He's at work.'

This catches Mum's attention and she looks up from her notebook. She says, 'I thought you two broke up?'

I look at Ed, but he's gone back to reading *Soap Watch* and isn't listening.

I say, 'Yes, but that doesn't mean he's not at work.'

She nods and returns to her notebook. I don't mind. Not really. She can be vague, is all. It takes her longer than normal people to focus on the real world as opposed to the fictional one in her head.

Ed puts down his magazine. He says, 'Thomas can come next Sunday, if he doesn't have to work on the farm, can't he, Kat?'

I say, 'Who's for wine? I got a lovely bottle of Côtes du Rhône in Fiztpatrick's yesterday.' I stick my head into the sideboard and rummage around for the biggest wine glasses I can find.

When I return to the table. Ed is waiting for me. 'Thomas can come next Sunday, if he doesn't have to work on the farm, can't he, Kat?'

I look at Mum, who is scribbling something in her notebook. Then at Dad, who looks at the leg of lamb on the plate in front of him with distrust, as if it is about to jump up and reattach itself to its previous owner at any moment.

I look at Ed. 'I don't think so, Ed. I'm sorry.'

'Why not?'

'Thomas and I broke up. After the accident, remember?'

Ed nods and smiles. 'Yeah, but you can get back together, Kat,' he tells me. 'That's what me and Sophie do. We get back together. All the time.'

Mum says, 'It's Sophie and I.'

It's like a reflex with Mum. I don't think she's even aware of it. Today, I can't let it go. 'Jesus, can you just stop correcting him? For once? What difference does it make? Me and Sophie? Sophie and I? Who cares? You get the picture. You know what he means. Don't you?'

She doesn't respond.

'Is there anything else to eat?' I say. 'Apart from the lamb, I mean.' It's not that I'm hungry. I just want to get the meal over and done with so I can get out of here.

Mum looks up from her notebook. 'Of course there're other things to eat,' she says, looking around. 'Aren't there, Kenneth?'

My father's name is not Kenneth. It's Leonard. But when he first introduced himself to my mother, she thought he said Kenneth. Of course, he was too polite to correct her. And a little awestruck, to be honest. He presumed that a woman like Mum would never be interested in a man like him, so the mistake was inconsequential. When she decided that she wanted to see him again, he agreed. She only found out, by

200

accident, months later that his name was actually Leonard. And by then it was too late. She said it was too late. It would feel odd, she said. To call him anything other than Kenneth. In fact, lots of people call him Kenneth now. He says he doesn't mind.

I get up from the table and walk into the kitchen. In the oven there is a dish of roast vegetables and a bowl of mashed potatoes. I get oven gloves, carry the dishes into the dining room, set them on the table. In that time, Dad has managed to carve two slices of meat. Mum is still scribbling in her notebook and Ed takes a sip of wine from a glass and tries not to wince. He doesn't really like wine. He likes the idea of liking wine.

I keep up a kind of chatter that could best be described as idle.

'You'll have two scoops of spud, Ed.'

'And there's some roast pumpkin for you, Mum. I know you're partial to roast pumpkin.'

'Don't worry, Dad, none of your vegetables have been anywhere near the aubergine. I made sure.' Dad doesn't like aubergine. I don't know if I'd go so far as to say he hates it but his displeasure at the leathery purple skin of the vegetable is fairly acute. And because he so rarely voices an opinion, especially a negative one, everybody goes out of their way to ensure that aubergine never crosses his path, Monday to Saturday. An exception is made on Sunday because of Ed and Mum, who love it. As for me, I'm pretty non-committal.

I sit down. Mum closes her notebook, pats the

bun of hair at the back of her head, like she's making sure it's still there. Ed pours milk into a wine glass. Dad puts a slice of meat on everybody's plate and tucks a napkin into the collar of his shirt.

We eat.

The silence isn't strained but it's there. It's always been there. We are not a family who sit together for meals, Monday to Saturday. But, for some reason, Mum insists on the Sunday dinner tradition. As if perhaps she read somewhere that this was the kind of thing that families did.

We eat.

Mum cuts her vegetables and meat into tiny pieces, then spears one tiny morsel of everything — potato, pumpkin, a sliver of lamb and, of course, the controversial aubergine — with her fork and steers the food into her mouth, which opens only at the very last second, and even then it's only a slit of an opening, barely wide enough to get the food through, but she manages, nonetheless. Then the mouth closes and the chewing begins. At least ten careful chews before she allows herself to swallow. She is pedantic about chewing. 'Eat slowly,' she always told me and Ed.

'Don't speak with your mouth full.'

'Chew carefully.'

Some people have a fear of flying. Or spiders. Or lollipop ladies. Mum was afraid of choking. Of me or Ed choking. That's how I knew she loved us.

I say, 'So . . . how's the new book coming along?' Mum waits until she has chewed her ten

202

chews and taken a huge gulp of water — just to be sure — before she speaks.

She says, 'Difficult.' She shakes her head. 'Difficult.'

I say, 'Oh.'

She says, 'As you know, the story is told through a series of letters from the Archbishop to the Diocesan manager and so the narrative tone must be quite constrained, which makes it . . . ' She stops.

I say, 'Difficult?'

She says, 'Yes.'

We eat.

Dessert is home-made. Dad has several sweet teeth and Ed got him *Nigella Does Dessert* for his last birthday. I don't know why, as Dad has never expressed an interest in either baking or in Nigella Lawson, who is like the polar opposite of the women he usually favours: Mum; Judi Dench; Margaret Thatcher, circa 1980. I think it's because the book was fifty cents in the local charity shop. The price is written in pencil inside the cover. Ed loves charity shops. His room is full of other people's rubbish.

Since he got the book, Ed and Dad meet in the kitchen on Sunday mornings and bake something. They do it chronologically. Today, they've done page forty-three, which is a chocolate fudge cake. They serve it warm with a generous scoop of vanilla ice cream on the side. I usually have a coffee and a cigarette for dessert but not on Sundays. Not since Nigella. She has made them surpass themselves, Ed and Dad. That's what I tell them most Sundays. That they've surpassed themselves. Even Mum, who has the appetite of a tiny bird, concedes to a sliver of cake. For a while, all you can hear is the scrape of forks against plates. Forks aren't great implements to eat ice cream with. You really need a spoon. At times like these, you can understand why children lick plates, you really can.

I make coffee. A decaf espresso for Mum, a cappuccino for Dad and Ed — with cocoa powder sprinkled on the top — and a black coffee for me. I grind the beans and I set up the machine and I sit on the worktop, as I always do, and wait. I love the noise of the machine. The gurgle and the splutter of it. And the smell. That strong, earthy smell.

The tray is not in its usual spot: in the cupboard beside the fridge. Mum says it might be in the utility room when I ask her. And it is. It's on the counter, covered in papers and bills. She insists on taking care of the household paperwork, even though, if Dad did it, there'd be less chance of the electricity getting cut off twice a year. I think she feels like it's her link to the real world. To how the real world works. It's a fairly tenuous link.

On the tray are flyers for the local supermarket, unopened bills, a handwritten letter from a fan — three foolscap pages — and a couple of coupons for the local taxi company. I tilt the tray and they tumble onto the counter, and that's when I see them. The envelopes. Three envelopes. Identical. Cream envelopes with a window. A British stamp. A registered post sticker on one of them. They're not from the college. Printed in the window is my name. Ms Katherine Kavanagh. My parents' address. I haven't lived at this address for twenty years.

Somewhere in my head, a pulse begins to beat.

I pick them up, the three envelopes, and walk into the dining room.

'Mum?' She looks up from her notebook. Sees me. Sees the envelopes in my hand.

'Oh, yes, I'm sorry, Katherine. I meant to forward them to you.'

'When did these arrive?'

Ed says, 'Who are they from, Kat?'

Mum says, 'Oh, I'm not sure. Recently, I think. The last few weeks, definitely. I've been so busy with the book, you see. It's been . . . '

'Difficult. Yes. We know. You said.'

Dad steps in. 'Well, you have them now, Kat. No harm done, eh?' This is the role he has always played. The middleman. The referee. The facilitator. The one who rings the bell. The one who says, 'Enough'.

I'm at my chair now. The envelopes are in my hand.

Ed says, 'Who are they from, Kat?'

I sit down. Pick up my glass. Drain it. Pour more wine.

Mum says, 'Aren't you driving?'

Dad says, 'I'll take her home.'

Ed says, 'That's an English stamp, isn't it, Kat? Look, it's got the Queen on it.'

I look at the envelopes. A cream queen on a pink background. The postmark is London. I don't know anyone in London. Except Brona, of course, and she posts everything to the PO Box number I gave her.

I open the first envelope. Take out the letter. One page. I turn it over. One side of one page. It is written the way I like things to be written. No fancy language. Precise. To the point.

Ed says, 'Who's it from, Kat?'

Mum says, 'Edward, don't put your elbows on the table. And please don't speak with your mouth full. How many times have I told you that?'

'Stop it.'

Mum looks at me and says, 'I beg your pardon?'

'Leave him alone.'

She picks up her fork. Puts it onto her plate. 'I'm merely trying to instil some manners in the boy.'

Dad says, 'Janet!' Which is the closest he'll come to telling her off. He puts his hand on Ed's shoulder and wanders out of the room, into the kitchen.

I say, 'He's thirty-four years old. He's not a boy.' Anger is not something I feel all that often. I'm more inclined towards peevishness. That's what Thomas used to say anyway. Anger has its two hands round my throat now. It's strangling me. 'And he's not speaking with his mouth full,' I say. 'He's finished.'

Dad comes back into the room and says, 'Here's the coffee.' He looks at us as if we are an audience and he a reluctant after-dinner speaker. Everything about my father is small. His voice, his size, the portions he eats, his expectations of other people.

I say, 'The first letter is dated nearly a month ago.'

There's one morsel of cake left on Mum's plate. She spears it with her fork, dips it in a puddle of melted ice cream, lifts the fork to her mouth, opens, closes, chews her ten chews, swallows, drinks water followed by the merest sip of wine. Then she looks at me and shakes her head. 'I forgot about them.' And if this were a normal Sunday, one of the hundreds of Sundays I have sat round this table and watched my mother chewing and swallowing and forgetting about things, that would be that. I would shrug and remind her, or not remind her, depending.

I don't do either. I look right at her. 'The letter is from an adoption agency.'

'An adoption agency?' She sets her fork down. I nod. My breathing is funny. Jerky. Mum looks at me and it's like she's just arrived. She is present. I have her attention.

I say, 'Did you know it was a girl?'

Ed says, 'Who was a girl?'

Mum says nothing. Her lips have retreated into a single, thin line.

I say it again. Louder this time. 'Did you? Did you know it was a girl?'

Dad says, 'Katherine?'

Ed says, 'Who was a girl?'

Mum looks at her plate. She nods.

'Why did you never tell me?'

'I assumed you knew.' Her voice is low, almost a whisper.

Ed says, 'Who was a girl?'

I look at Ed and shake my head. There are things I need to tell him but I don't know where to start.

The thing is, we never discussed it. Afterwards. Maybe it was the shock of the thing. She thought I was in Minnie's house, revising for a history test on the Normans. I was her only daughter. A fifteen-year-old girl. I remember her arriving at Minnie's house. Out of breath, like she'd been running, her hair escaping from the bun that she wore, even then. I remember how I felt when I saw her. Relief. That she would sort it out. Make sense of it.

And she did, I suppose.

'It's for the best, Katherine.' That's what my mother said. Afterwards.

'Do you want to hold your baby?' the nurse asked. The one with the country accent and the big hands. Her name badge said 'Ingrid'. Capital letters. 'INGRID'. I shook my head and they took it away and I signed the document in the places that Mum had marked with an x. 'It's for the best, Katherine,' she said and I nodded and she brought me home and we never talked about it again.

I open the second envelope. The third one. All from the same person. All saying the same thing. I put them on the table. I push them towards her.

I say, 'Read them.'

She looks at the thin little pile of letters but doesn't pick them up.

She says, 'I think we should talk about this

later, Katherine.' She nods towards Ed as if he can't see us.

Ed says, 'Talk about what?' He abandons his fork and uses his finger to mop up the last traces of ice cream from his plate. Mum does not tell him not to.

Dad clears his throat and I know he's going to say something and I know that once he says the thing he's going to say, nothing will ever be the same again. Everything will be different. I know it.

He clears his throat and then he says, 'Kat had a baby, Ed.' His voice is like the rest of him: quiet and small. His words are like a blow to the head. I look at him. At his kind, familiar face. It is the bluish-white of shock. He looks old. Properly old. For the first time. There is a shake in his voice. Still, he goes on. 'She'd be twenty-four by now.'

Ed looks at me. 'Why is she writing to you? Does she not have your phone number?'

'She asked the adoption agency to write to me. She wants to see me.'

Ed says, 'Does she not want to see me?'

No one says anything.

'Will she be my little sister?'

Dad says, 'You're her uncle.'

'She can sleep in my bottom bunk.' Ed stands, heads for the door. 'I'd better go and tidy my room.' Ed has never tidied his room in his life. Mrs Higginbotham did it. Or me. Or Dad. He tears up the stairs, stopping at the top.

'Uncle Ed!' he shouts.

Dad stretches out his hand and puts it on

mine. Just for a moment. Mum looks at the gesture, then opens her mouth as if she is about to say something. Closes it.

'Did you hear what I said?' Ed shouts from the top of the stairs.

'UNCLE ED.'

Dad is asleep in Ant and Adrian's room. I was worried he might sleep in Mam's room. He doesn't snore anymore. He says Celia doesn't let him.

I wait till Faith goes to bed and the house goes quiet and the floors start to creak. She goes earlier than usual. Probably because Rob didn't come over. She told him not to bother, when he rang.

'Get someone else to sing your song. It's shite anyway, so it is.'

Faith and Rob sound like Mam and Dad now. Before Dad went to live with Celia in Scotland. I reckon they'll break up soon, which is a shame because Rob is all right, for an adult. He never tells you that things are good for you and he hates cauliflower and celery as much as I do.

I put two pillows on the bed and cover them with my duvet, which is made of the same material as the uniform Sully wears when he's going to the war. I take out the bag from under my bed. It's got everything I need, even my toothbrush.

I stop outside Faith's bedroom door. There's no sound so I keep going. The stairs are tricky, on account of the creaks. I make it to the sixth one before I drop my bag. When I bend to pick it up, the step creaks. It sounds like an old woman moaning. I nearly drop my bag again.

I don't move. I crouch on the sixth step and I listen.

211

Nothing.

Still, I force myself to wait for one minute. I count up to sixty, as slow as I can.

Nothing.

I creep down the rest of the stairs.

The kitchen looks different in the dark. The clock in the shape of Ireland ticks much louder at night-time. When I open the fridge door, the light nearly blinds me.

I take four EasiSingles, a packet of ham and three strawberry yoghurts. I take two slices of bread out of the breadbin and wrap them in tinfoil. A packet of crackers. A Kit Kat from Faith's secret chocolate stash that she thinks I don't know about. I leave the Flake. She's mad about Flakes.

I fill my flask with orange juice from the carton, except that I spill some on the floor and then I walk in it by accident. There's no kitchen roll and the only tea towel I can find is Mam's favourite one. The one with the recipe for Funky Banana Bread. That's where she got the idea for the name. I sneak out to the hall and get toilet paper from the downstairs loo and I wipe the kitchen floor and the sole of my shoe with that.

I haven't told anyone. Not even Damo. That way, when they ask him, he won't have to lie and say, 'I don't know.' He can just say, 'I don't know,' and it'll actually be true.

Outside, it's raining. I suppose I should have packed my raincoat. It's pretty cold too. My anorak probably would have been better than this jacket. I have a torch but I don't turn it on. I don't want to run out of batteries.

Dad's going to drive Faith to the airport in the morning. He says he's going to drive me to school and then drive Faith to the airport. That's why I have to go now. Otherwise, Dad will drive me to school, and I don't think I'd make it to the airport on time.

I check my wallet, which is in the pocket of my jeans. It's actually Mam's purse; I don't have a wallet. I might buy one in Ireland. The money is still there. Three fifty-pound notes and three pound coins and two twenty-pence pieces and the penny. It's all there.

The bus stop is at the end of our road. There's no one there. And there's no sign of the bus coming. I look at the watch Ant gave me for my ninth birthday. It's not a kid's watch, like the Spiderman one that George Pullman has. It's a proper watch, except the hands light up in the dark, which is good because the torch isn't working. I think the batteries are dead.

It's 00.10, which means the bus should be coming in four minutes. But when I look at the timetable at the bus stop, the time of the last bus is 23.55, which was fifteen minutes ago.

Coach says you should always have a Plan B. I should have remembered that.

I sit down on the kerb. I think better when I'm sitting down. It's probably because the blood doesn't have as far to go to get to my brain.

The taximan says, 'Where do you think you're going?' when I put out my hand and he pulls over.

I say, 'The airport, please.'

He turns off the engine. Leans his head out of the window. Examines me like Miss Williams does before the school inspectors come.

'The airport?'

'Yes, please. The one in London.'

'There're a few airports in London town, my son. Did you have a particular one in mind?'

'Eh, Gatwick.'

'Which terminal?'

That's the problem when you're talking to adults. They always end up asking you a question you don't know the answer to.

The taximan lights up a cigarette. Blows smoke out of the window. It comes out of his nose as well as his mouth. Sully can do that too. And make smoke rings.

'Goin' someplace nice, is ya? Spain, maybe. Benny-dorm, eh?'

Damo's been to Benny-dorm. He said it was too hot and nobody spoke any English.

I shake my head. I say, 'I'm going to Ireland.'

'You don't wanna be doin' that, mate. Too bloody cold over there. And the beer is black. Suspect, mate.'

'I'm going with my sister. She's twenty-four. I'm meeting her. At the airport. The one in London.'

He takes another drag, looks at his watch and, for a moment, I think my Plan B is working, but then he shakes his head and looks at me. 'It's a bit late to be going to London, mate. Why don't I take you home? Your mother's probably wondering where you've got to.'

I step back from the car and give it one last go. I say, 'I have to go tonight. I have money.' I take out Mam's purse and show him the three fifty-pound notes, the three pound coins, the two twenty-pence pieces, the penny.

'Let's see that.' When the taximan smiles, I see his teeth. They're crooked and yellow. They look like they haven't been brushed all day. Or yesterday either. I put the money back into the purse. Stuff the purse into my bag. But now the man is struggling with the seatbelt. Trying to get out of the car. It's not easy, on account

214

of how fat he is. The bottom of the steering wheel sticks into his belly. He takes another drag of his cigarette. Throws it out of the window, even though the butt will take twelve years to decompose. He opens the door. Puts one hand on the roof and uses it to hoist himself out. The streetlamp throws a light across his face. His face is huge and red and sweaty. If he was in a film on the telly, he'd be a baddie, I reckon.

He says, 'Come 'ere, my son. Let's have another look at that money. Make sure it's all there.'

That's when I run. I'm not as good at running as I am at swimming but I still came second in the hundred metres at school last year. Only Carla beat me and her mam did the London marathon two years in a row and Carla says she's going to do it too, when she's old.

Stranger danger. We learned about that in school. You're supposed to run away. And scream to attract attention.

I don't scream. I don't want to attract attention. I just run. I don't look back till I'm at the top of the road. I can't see him. But I see his car moving towards me, making hardly a sound.

Damo's house is round the block. I jump over the gate and run to the side entrance. The door is locked but easy enough to climb over. I run down the narrow passage to the tree at the end of the garden, where the tree house is. It's really just a big slab of wood with sheets on either side, pretending to be walls. I climb past the middle bit, which is usually where I stop. But this time I go all the way to the very top of the tree. Damo probably won't believe me when I tell him.

There are no leaves, on account of it being winter,

but it's dark so I don't think he'll see me unless he's got a torch with batteries in it.

I hear the car coming down the road. Dead slow. When it reaches Damo's house, it slows down even more. The lights are off but I can see the tip of a cigarette, glowing red in the dark. And I can see the man. He looks like he's staring right at me.

I'm thinking about screaming now. Opening my mouth as wide as it will go and screaming my head off. Loud enough to wake Damo's mam and Imelda. Sully's at the war and I probably wouldn't wake Damo. His mam says if a bomb exploded right beside him, he still wouldn't wake up.

I open my mouth.

And then I think about all the trouble I'll be in if I scream loud enough to wake Damo's mam and she goes and wakes Faith and Faith finds out about me going to the post office on my own instead of going to the library with Damo. I bet I'd be grounded for about a month. Maybe even longer. And I probably wouldn't be allowed to go to lifesaving or buy a PlayStation 3, even if I had the money for one.

My breathing sounds funny. Really loud, for starters. I press my hand across my mouth but the breath comes out through my nose instead, just as loud. The taximan is still there, still sitting in his car with the lights off and the window down. Still smoking, even though I don't think you're allowed to smoke in taxicabs.

Just when I'm so cold that I think I can't hold onto the branch anymore, the lights of the car turn on and the engine starts and the car disappears up the road. I make myself wait ten minutes after the man drives away. To make sure. Then I climb down to the tree house, and it's a good job I'm pretty good at tree-climbing now, because, if I wasn't, I'd definitely fall out on account of my hands and feet being so numb with the cold.

It's hard to think about a Plan C. I drink the orange juice in my flask and wish I'd made hot chocolate instead. I look up at Damo's window and try not to think about him snoring his head off in his warm, cosy bed. I pretend he's here too and I have a conversation with him. Not out loud or anything stupid like that. Just in my head. Just to pass the time. When I'm finished, I'll get cracking on a Plan C.

Not much happens.

I think about ringing Thomas.

I don't ring Thomas.

This might be how smokers feel when they think about cigarettes but don't light up.

It gives me a twitchy feeling.

I smoke a lot.

Brona rings. I tell her I can't talk. I'm in the middle of a chapter.

I don't write anything.

I examine my face in the mirror. My almost-forty-year-old face. Every day I look a bit older. The lines lengthen and deepen. If I watch long enough, I can almost see it happen.

Minnie rings to tell me she has stopped vomiting in the afternoon, evening and night. She says, 'It's just the morning sickness now. Proper morning sickness.' She sounds delighted.

I don't tell her. Even though Minnie is the only one in the world who knows everything, I don't tell her. About the letters. The three letters.

I pick up the phone and put it down and pick it up again. Then I put it down.

I don't ring. I don't ring Thomas.

So when he does find out, it's quite by accident.

He comes to Ed's swimming gala.

He remembers.

Of course he remembers.

I arrive late so he's already there, in the best seat in the house. He turns his head, looks behind him, smiles when he sees me. A benign sort of a smile. As if nothing had ever happened between us. Nothing good. Nothing bad. I don't smile back. All of a sudden, I am seething with resentment. We were so close. He's the one who said that, not me. That day on the farm. Only a couple of weeks before the accident. The bloody miracle. I was wearing a pair of one of his sisters' wellington boots. Three sizes too big. They all have massive feet, the Cunninghams. Massive hands too. Even the tiny one, God help her.

I was in a field. We were making hay. Thomas said it would be 'fun'. Later, he said, 'Do you fancy a roll in the hay?' And I said, 'All right.' So we rolled in the hay and I made sure that I was on top because hay turns out to be prickly and not as pliable as you might think, and afterwards I sat on Thomas's jacket and leaned against a stack of hay — a hayrick, he calls it — and smoked a cigarette. Thomas said, 'You shouldn't smoke around the hay,' and I said, 'Shut your mouth,' and he said, 'I love this time of the year when everything's at full tilt,' and I slapped at a mosquito and said, 'I fucking well hate it,' and he took my hand and held it and I pulled it away and then I put it back into his hand and we sat there like that for a while and then he kissed my mouth, even though I tasted like cigarettes and he hates cigarettes, and I kissed him back and my eyes were closed and I could feel the heat of

219

the day in my bones and the softness of his mouth on mine and, for a moment, I was so happy I thought I might cry. So I stopped kissing him and I looked away, and that's when he said, 'You'll get used to it eventually,' and I said, 'What?' and he said, 'Us. Being all coupled up, like Minnie and Maurice.'

'We are nothing like Minnie and Maurice.' The very idea.

He said, 'We are. We're close. I'm sorry but that's the way it is.' He spread his hands in front of him and shook his head as if he were sorry, but there was nothing he could do about it.

I punched him in the arm. I said, 'You dirty-looking eejit.' And we sat there, with our backs against the hayrick, and we watched the sun spill her gold into his five stony fields in Monaghan and we didn't say much. We didn't say anything. There was no need.

Now Thomas smiles a benign sort of a smile, as if we are two people who might have known each other a long time ago.

He stands up and people in the rows behind click their tongues and crane their necks. He shuffles along the row saying, 'Sorryexcuseme-sorryexcuseme . . . ' as he goes. He is careful not to stand on anyone's toe. The last time he did that, it cost him three hundred and twenty-four euro in surgeon's fees and a four-and-a-half-hour wait with a peevish woman in A&E.

He looks . . . the same as always. Casual. Smiley. Easy. There's something so easy about Thomas Cunningham. If he were a sum, he'd be two plus two. I'm more like algebra.

His clothes are terrible, but that's to be expected. And there's a bit of a dog smell on him. Or goat, maybe. And his hair could do with a cut. But apart from that, he looks . . . well. Healthy. He looks like someone who never smoked but would just say, 'No, thanks,' when you offered him a cigarette and never 'I don't smoke,' in that smug way that non-smokers have. Or reformed smokers. Thank Christ, I'm never going to be one of those. They'd do your head in with the smugness.

The hair is the same; the grey curls are more knots now where the weather has twisted and tossed them. I always told him his eyes were the colour of the mud in his five fields in Monaghan. But that's not true. They are grey from a distance but they change to green the closer you get. Or blue sometimes, depending on the light.

Today, they are grey.

He says, 'Hello, Kat.'

I say, 'Hello.'

He says, 'Ed's on in five minutes, I think.' He looks at the pool. Ed sees him and waves. Thomas smiles and waves back. When he turns to me, his smile has faded, like wallpaper in a house where nobody lives anymore.

The thing is, I never said sorry. I wanted to. Lots of times. But I just couldn't say it. And time rolled on, the way it does, and now, if I say anything, it'll come under the category of 'picking the scab off an old wound'. I'm pretty sure there is such a category, although it might be called something different.

It was just one of those things, I suppose. What

happened to us. After the accident. The bloody miracle. Things were fine before that. But Thomas wanted to change everything. All the talk of marriage. And children. Although he didn't say 'children'. He referred to 'a child', as if this child already existed and it was just a question of us going somewhere to pick it up.

It's true what I said. It was Thomas who ended the relationship. But he said he had no choice. That I left him with no choice. After the lies I told. How I avoided him. And the Nicolas incident. Thomas, standing in the doorway, looking at me. Never even glancing at Nicolas. Throwing his keys on the table. 'This is what you want, Kat? Fine! I'm done here.'

The silence after he left. The hollow depth of it.

I'd say sorry now. If I could go back. I'd make Nicolas from number thirteen leave. No, I'd never invite him in, in the first place.

I'd say sorry.

If it hadn't been for the accident — the stupid, bloody miracle — we'd be fine, me and Thomas. Thomas and me. I believe that. There's no reason not to. Everything just got out of hand in the end.

And I never said sorry. I should have. But it's like Mum calling Dad Kenneth. It's too late now.

The heat from the pool rises and collects between us. I pull at the neck of my jumper.

I say, 'I didn't realise you'd be here.' It sounds like an accusation, the way I say it. I try to smile, to show that it is not.

He says, 'I promised Ed, remember?'

I nod. Thomas happens to be one of those people who mean the things they say.

'Would you like to . . .' He points towards his empty seat in the middle of the row.

'Oh. No. Thank you, I'll just . . .' I nod and smile and point towards the pool.

He nods and then contorts himself into a sort of squat and shuffles back along the row to his seat, with the 'sorryexcusemesorryexcuseme' and the sound of tutting and shifting all around as he goes.

I think Ed comes second. I'm nearly sure he does. I cheer as if he does. I hurry from the balcony when it's over. I don't catch Thomas's eye. Don't want him to think that I expect him to stay and congratulate Ed, like he would have done, before.

In the car park, Ed spots him immediately. Inconspicuousness is not something that Thomas is good at.

It takes a while for him and Thomas to dispense with their formalities, which include a long and complicated system of hand slaps and shakes.

I am freezing. Thomas does not take my fingers and put the tips of them into his mouth, like he used to when they went a bloodless yellow in the cold. I told him not to do that. 'That's disgusting,' I said. 'Do you have any idea how many germs are in that cake-hole of yours?' I never told him that I liked it. The warm wet of his mouth on my skin. The pleasure of the pain, as he coaxed the blood back into my fingers.

I make fists out of my hands and shove them

223

inside the pockets of my coat.

'Did Kat tell you?' Ed smiles at Thomas.

Thomas looks at Ed and smiles because Ed's smile is contagious and that's just a fact. Even John Banville's face would crack if Ed smiled at him.

Just as it dawns on me what Ed is about to say — the cold has given me brain-freeze, in much the same way a bowl of Chunky Monkey would — Ed comes right out and says it.

He says, 'I'm going to be an uncle. Uncle Ed. I'm going to be Uncle Ed. Did Kat tell you? Is that what Kat was telling you? When I was doing my swimming race?'

And, just like that, it's out there, and for the first time since I opened the envelopes, it seems real.

Ed will be an uncle. He is an uncle. Uncle Ed.

And I am a mother.

The baby was a girl. Her name is Faith and she's twenty-four years old and she wants to meet me because I'm her mother.

Realisation grabs me from behind like a mugger. I feel like I might fall with the force of it, but I don't. Of course I don't. I stand there and concentrate on Ed. He is smiling at Thomas, waiting for Thomas to say something. The world seems strangely quiet, as if we are not standing in the middle of a car park with engines revving all around us.

Ed nudges Thomas. 'Did you hear me? I'm going to be an uncle, I said. Uncle Ed. Her name is Faith and when she comes to Dublin I'm going to meet her. She's going to sleep in the bottom bunk and I'm going to bring her to Arch club and everything. Isn't that right, Kat?'

Ed taps my arm with the tip of his index finger. He is smiling but there is confusion around the edges. I nod. 'That's right, Ed.'

'Ed!' I recognise Sophie's voice and look up. She's standing on the back seat of her father's car, her head and shoulders poking through the sunroof. She waves at Ed with one hand and holds her medal with the other. Ed picks up the medal round his neck and holds it up as he runs towards her. Thomas and I watch his progress across the car park. Ed opens the back door of Sophie's car and crawls in, pushing himself up through the sunroof until he is standing beside her. They both look at us — Thomas and I — holding their medals and waving at us. We wave back. It's a relief to have something to do. When we have to stop waving, I fumble in my bag for my cigarettes.

Thomas lifts the cuff of his jacket until he can see the wristwatch I bought him for his forty-fourth birthday. I went into nearly every jeweller's shop in the city before I settled on that one. Thomas is not the sort of man you could buy just any old watch for. It has to be particular. It has to be waterproof and manure proof and goat-droppings proof and silage proof and all sorts. Durable, I suppose. But aesthetic too, you know? Thomas has lovely forearms, I'll give him that. They're pretty tanned. From being outside so much, probably. Strong enough too, what with all the pulling and hauling around the farm. You couldn't just buy him any old watch.

225

He pulls the cuff back down. 'I'd better go.'

I inhale and nod. He is not going to refer to Ed's news. The relief feels strange. It feels like disappointment.

I say, 'Yes, you'd better. Get back to — Sandra, isn't it?'

'Sarah.'

I can't make out any expression on Thomas's face. You could call it impassive. Or indifferent. I blow smoke towards him until I can't see the indifference anymore.

He turns away as if he is about to leave, then seems to change his mind and turns back. 'And you'd better get back to your daughter,' he says. 'Faith? Isn't that what Ed said?' This time when he turns away, he doesn't turn back. He walks towards his car.

'Thomas.' I check to see that Ed is still standing on the back seat of Sophie's car before I run after Thomas. I'm not sure what I'm going to say. I reach for his arm. The warmth of it through the sleeve of his jacket is shocking in the rawness of the day.

He pulls his arm away from me, as if he has been stung. 'Don't,' he says, and there is something like contempt in his voice and it doesn't seem possible because I'm sure he is speaking to me and he has never spoken to me like that before. Not ever. Not even when he let himself into the apartment. That day with Nicolas.

'Thomas, I . . . '

Now he is opening the door of his car, shrugging off his jacket despite the icy

226

temperatures. I find myself thinking about the heat of him. How can one person be that warm?

'Thomas, please . . . '

He gets into the car and throws his jacket on the passenger seat. He puts his hand on the door handle as if he, is about to slam the door, but then he looks at me. 'What is it?'

I hadn't thought of what I might say after that. I just presumed he'd drive away. I take a drag from my cigarette, buying some time. 'I just . . . I didn't want you to find out like this. I . . . I should have told you.'

Thomas shakes his head. 'No,' he says. 'You didn't have to tell me anything. We were only going out for a few months, weren't we?'

I say, 'Twenty-three months,' the way Thomas used to.

He shrugs. 'I have to go.'

'Wait.' Suddenly I want to tell him everything. I want to go back. Start at the very beginning. Start again. Why didn't I tell him? I know now, with the certainty that comes with hindsight, that Thomas would be a good person to tell. A great person to tell. He listens. He doesn't just nod and say, 'Yes . . . yes . . . yes.' He listens. He doesn't move. He doesn't interrupt. He listens. Afterwards, he would say something. Something sensible. I'm nearly certain of it. He might have some questions. He wouldn't dispense advice. But he might make a suggestion. I want to know what that suggestion is. I am desperate to know.

Thomas says, 'What?' He seems tired now, his features rigid and drawn.

'I should have said something. I should have

227

told you. Ages ago.'

He looks at me and then he says, 'It's all right,' and when he says it, the features of his face relax and he looks like himself again and, for a moment, I think maybe it will be all right.

Then he says, 'It doesn't matter now,' and there is nothing to do but step back from the car and watch him pull away. He beeps the horn so that he catches Ed's attention and waves at him.

Ed waves back.

The phone booth smells bad. Like one of Damo's farts after he's been eating pickled-onion flavour crisps. He's mad about pickled onions.

'Milo? Milo? Is that you? Oh thank God. I thought you were . . . I didn't know what . . . Are you all right? . . . WHERE THE HELL ARE YOU?'

I can't answer right away because Faith is crying really loudly. Even if I tell her, she won't be able to hear me. I hate it when she cries. She usually does it quietly, in her room, so she thinks I can't hear her.

I say, 'I'm sorry.'

'Don't you DARE say you're sorry. If anything had happened to you, I'd . . . I don't know what I'd do. Aren't things bad enough already without you pulling a crazy stunt like this?'

I say, 'I'm sorry,' before I remember that I'm not supposed to say that. But I can't think of anything else to say. I think it's because I haven't had much sleep.

'Jesus Christ, Milo.' She stops for a moment and I can hear her taking a puff of her cigarette, which is actually good because she might calm down a bit.

Her voice is quieter the next time she says something but I don't know if it's because of the cigarette or maybe she's a bit hoarse after all the shouting. She says, 'Where are you? I've been worried sick.'

'I don't want you to go to Ireland on your own.'

'What are you talking about? We've been through this. I have to go on my own. You know that.'

'Why?'

'Because . . . because . . . look, this is beside the point. Where the hell are you?'

'You could take me with you. I won't be any bother.'

'Stop it, Milo. You're not coming and that's that. Now tell me where you are so Dad and I can come and get you.'

'I promise I won't be hungry all the time. I won't eat anything. I won't even go into your birth mother's house. I'll wait in the front garden. I promise.'

'Jesus, Milo.'

'And if you want to stay in Ireland with her, I'll fly back on my own. I'm old enough, I reckon. You probably just have to sign a form or something.'

'Milo, what are you — '

'I could go and live with Ant and Adrian in London. I don't want to live with Dad and Celia because they'll be busy with the baby and Scotland is about a hundred miles away and I'll miss my life-saving exams and I won't get into the intermediate class.'

'Nobody is going anywhere, OK?'

'But she might turn out to be really nice? The lady in Dublin. You'd want to go and live with her then, wouldn't you?'

'No. I wouldn't. I'm staying with you.'

'But you might change your mind.'

'I WON'T.'

I have to hold the receiver far away when she shouts like that. When I put it back against my ear, there's silence. Then she says, 'Milo . . . look, it's complicated. You're only nine. It's hard for you to understand. I haven't explained it very well. I'm sorry.'

'I'll be ten soon.'

'Milo?'

'Yes?'

'Where are you?'

'I'm not going to tell you.'

'What do you mean?'

'I'm not telling you unless you say I can come to Ireland with you.'

I can't hear what she says then because of the announcement. Something about a flight to Buenos Aires that's leaving from Gate 32. The gate is closing in five minutes.

Faith says, 'Oh my God. You're at the airport. Are you at the airport?'

'No.' I cup my hands round the receiver so she won't hear anything else.

'Christ, how did you get to the airport?'

I've already decided that I'm never going to tell her about the taximan. When we're on the plane, I'll tell her about getting the first bus this morning from the bottom of our road into the main bus station. Then the airport express, which costs more than the normal bus but the poster said it was way quicker. It's weird being on a bus on your own. There's no one to ask if you're there yet.

'Is it Gatwick? Are you in Gatwick?'

I say, 'I'll tell you, Faith. But you have to tell me first.'

Silence then. I think that's good. I think that means she's thinking about it.

Then, 'I'll be back in a few days, Milo. You'll hardly notice I'm gone.'

I say, 'Mam said she'd be back in a few days.' I don't

231

know I'm going to cry until I start to cry. The thing about Mam was that she always did what she said. If she said she'd be there to pick you up at three o'clock, then she would be. The only time she didn't do what she said she was going to do was when she went to Ireland, because she never came back. Not really. It doesn't count if you come back and you're dead.

Now I'm sort of crying and shouting at the same time, as if I'm not in the middle of an airport with millions of people all around. I say, 'I will notice you've gone. I always notice when people are gone.'

After a while, I get myself to stop crying but now I think that maybe I've pressed a button by accident because I can't hear anything down the phone. I say, 'Faith? Hello? Are you there?'

Faith says, 'I'm here.' Her voice is a whisper, like she's telling me a secret.

I say, 'Can I come with you? Please?' I cross my fingers because Carla says it brings you luck. I cross my toes too, except I'm not sure if that brings you as much luck.

And then she says, 'OK.'

'OK?'

'OK.'

'OK, I can come to Ireland with you?'

'Yes.'

'I promise I'll be good.'

'You'd better be better than good.'

I'm not sure how you can be better than good but I say, 'I will,' just in case she changes her mind.

# March 1987

I'm seven months pregnant and I don't even know. Fifteen years old and seven months pregnant. I haven't got a clue.

Minnie works it out, in the changing rooms of O'Connor's Jeans in the Ilac Centre. I can't get the Levi's over my belly.

I say, 'Coconut snowballs,' by way of explanation. I laugh when I say it. Minnie doesn't laugh. She looks at my belly so I look at it too. I say, 'I'm a bit bloated after the Big Mac.' Minnie puts down the jeans she's holding. She stretches her arm towards me. Puts her hand on my belly.

She says, 'It's hard.' She pokes it like she did with the frog we dissected in biology yesterday. Then she drops her hand and moves away from me.

I say, 'What?' Minnie doesn't scare easy.

She says, 'It moved.' She points at my belly and when I look down, I think I see something. A ripple along the skin.

I say, 'Oh shit,' and I back up until I bump against the mirror of the changing room.

Minnie says, 'You're up the duff.' That's what Minnie says about her mother when she's pregnant. Up the duff. Minnie's mother is always up the duff. Minnie hates how up the duff her mother always is.

The minute she says it, I know it's true.

Minnie says, 'You did it. You had sex and you never told me. We're supposed to be best friends. We're supposed to tell each other everything.' Her face is flushed with shock and I don't know if it's because of me being up the duff or me not telling her that I'd done it.

'I only did it twice.' It doesn't seem real. Even now.

'Twice?' She's livid. We always assumed Minnie would be the first one to go.

'Jesus.' I sit on the stool in the corner of the changing room. All of a sudden. As if my legs have forgotten what to do with themselves. 'What am I going to do?'

Minnie shakes her head but hunkers in front of me. I realise how serious this is when she touches my hand and squeezes it. But then she shakes her head again. 'How the hell can you be this up the duff and not know?'

I shake my head. 'I don't know.'

'And who the hell was it? You haven't gone out with anyone since . . . ' She stops talking and looks at me. I nod.

Minnie says, 'Elliot Porter?'

I say, 'Yes.'

Saying his name is enough to bring me right back to that sick, heady, dizzy, delirious feeling. It is like a hollow, the feeling. Right inside you. A hunger pain that no amount of food can ease.

Elliot. Elliot Porter. Right from the start, Mrs Higginbotham calls him 'an unsuitable boy'. He doesn't introduce himself at the front door. Nor does he take his hands out of his pockets. She has a thing about men's hands and their pockets. Elliot Porter walks up to my front door, knocks on it and, when Mrs Higginbotham opens it, he says, 'Is Kat in?' like he's been at the front door millions of times, except he hasn't. He's never been at the front door before. He's never said, 'Will you go with me?' so I'm not sure what the story is. He kisses me. Twice. Behind the changing rooms at school, where we smoke at lunchtime. A couple of days after our first conversation, which happened to be about the Smiths. He liked that I liked them too. He wasn't even talking to me. Not really. He was talking to one of his gang. His herd, Minnie calls them. About a bootleg recording of a Smiths gig in the SFX the previous May. I say, 'I was at that gig.'

He looks at me, and I know for a fact that, up till now, he was not aware that I was there.

He says, 'You?'

'Me and Minnie.' I don't tell him that we went with Minnie's dad, who was given tickets because he happened to be the insurance broker for the SFX at the time. Instead I say, 'We went backstage. Morrissey signed my ticket.'

He says, 'FUCK OFF!' before he walks over to me and offers me his cigarette. I take a drag, give it back to him.

I'm in.

I make him laugh. I can't remember how but I remember the sharpness of his Adam's apple, jutting against the pale skin of his throat, as if it might cut through. He says, 'You're funny.' The next thing you know, we're walking through St

Anne's Park and then he's got his arm round my shoulder and somehow — I don't know how — we end up kissing in the Rose Garden. The next day, at school, there's a new rumour doing the rounds and it's about me and Elliot Porter. We're going out.

No one can believe it. Especially me.

I doodle his name in the margins of my homework notebook. Surround it with lovehearts and cupid's arrows and wedding bells and bubbles of champagne spilling from the tops of long, narrow flutes. I write my name too. Underneath. But only in the faintest pencil, which I rub out immediately.

Mrs Katherine Porter. Ms Kat Kavanagh-Porter.

Of course, I don't tell him any of that. I'm in love. But I'm careful. You have to be careful with a boy like Elliot Porter.

I don't tell Ed. Ed is not good at keeping secrets. 'Kat's in love,' he would have told my father. 'But she made me promise not to tell anyone so don't tell anyone, OK?'

Instead, when Ed asks what's wrong with me, I shake my head and say, 'Nothing,' and he asks me to play Snakes and Ladders and I let him win and then Mrs Higginbotham makes us mugs of chicken soup and we watch *Gidget* on the telly — with the sound down low if Mum is working in the attic — and I stir the soup round and round with a spoon and think about Elliot Porter.

Elliot Porter is not an easy boy to be in love with. He is moody. Unpredictable. He mitches off school. He smokes cigarettes lifted from packets of blue Rothmans his father leaves lying around. He fills SodaStream bottles with mixtures of brandy and gin and vodka and whiskey, filched from the drinks cabinet in his parents' front room. He washes it down with cans of Coke, in the fields behind his house. He steals things from shops. Things he doesn't need and will never use. He has long black hair and wild navy eyes that never settle on any one thing for long.

And then there's the sex. Elliot Porter is keen to have sex. He's done it before. Loads of times, I'd say. He assumes I have done it too. I don't tell him the truth. I think he won't be interested in me if he realises the extent of my experience, which is Bressy Dolan putting his hand up my T-shirt and — fleetingly — cupping one breast through my bra last summer.

The sex turns out to be brief and messy. The first time, in his house, when his mother goes to the tennis club. Her white tennis skirt strains against her waist. She says, 'You two behave yourselves, OK?' She winks at us. Blows Elliot a kiss. His father is away again. Malta, I think. Or Tunisia, maybe. A business trip. There are no brothers or sisters to worry about. We do it in the room they call the sunroom, which is a small room at the back of the house. He lowers the blinds. Turns off the telly. Pulls me by the hand onto the couch. We are still in our school uniforms when it's finished. I pull my skirt down, say I have to go to the bathroom. Wipe at the cold white dribbles running down my legs with a piece of toilet paper.

The second time is a few days later in my house, during the fifteen minutes between Mrs Higginbotham leaving the house and my father arriving home from the lab. Elliot sends Ed to his room. Tells him he's hidden a surprise in his room. Sweets. Tells him not to come down until he finds them.

'That's not nice,' I say. 'You haven't hidden any sweets up there. Have you?'

Elliot says, 'Don't worry. We won't be long.' He smiles his beautiful smile. He pulls my T-shirt up, undoes my bra. He calls my breasts tits. He says, 'Your tits are gorgeous.' He takes a nip out of each of them. Then undoes the button on my jeans, pulls the zip down. He is right. It doesn't take long.

I say, 'We have to use johnnies the next time, OK?' I don't care about the next time. I'm glad the sex bit is out of the way. Now I can concentrate. On being in love. This is where the good stuff is.

But there is no next time. The next day at school he looks away when I catch his eye in history. The day after, in the canteen, I say, 'Hi!' as I walk past the table where he is sitting with his friends. He ignores me and his friends snigger, as if I have something on my face. Ketchup, maybe. Or mayonnaise. I go into the toilets. Check myself in the mirror. There is nothing. Nothing on my face.

After school, I walk home with Minnie. She says, 'Nicola Moriarty told me that Porter's after dumping you. True or false?'

If Nicola Moriarty said it, then it must be true. I nod my head. 'I think so.'

Minnie punches the top of my arm with her fist in a rare public display of affection. 'At least you didn't do it with him, right?'

Humiliation burns like acid. I think of Elliot Porter telling his friends. Telling them everything. Laughing at me. I wish I were dead.

I say, 'No, of course not.' I want to tell her. But I can't. She'll feel sorry for me. I know she will. And if Minnie Driver feels sorry for you, things are bad.

Two weeks later, he's going out with Melissa Hegarty, a sixth-year doing a roaring trade in fourth-years, and a reputation for being 'fast'.

Minnie says, 'How could you not know you're up the duff?'

I sit on the stool in the cubicle in O'Connor's Jeans in the Ilac Centre. I shake my head. I have no idea.

In my bedroom, I play the Scorpion's 'Still Loving You' from their *Love at First Sting* album, over and over and over again, the needle scratching deeper and deeper into the groove until you can nearly see the tip of it poking out the other side. I wear baggy Frankie T-shirts that fall to my knees and hide the safety pin that now strains across the waistband of my Levi's.

Sometimes, in the gap between Marillion's *Misplaced Childhood* and Dire Straits' *Brothers in Arms*, Minnie asks the question: 'What are we going to do?' She says 'we'. I am pathetic with gratitude. I am not alone.

We don't say much during those two months,

Minnie and I. We spend a lot of time together. Even more than usual, I mean. We listen to music, we smoke out of my bedroom window, we play Snakes and Ladders with Ed.

Ed notices. He says, 'You're fat, Kat. You're really fat.'

And Mum, not looking up from her notebook, says, 'Edward, that's rude. You don't tell ladies they are fat.'

Ed says, 'But what if they are?'

She doesn't answer. Just sighs and returns to her office. Dad sits in his study. I pop corn in a hot, oily pot and me and Ed sit on the couch like puddings, with the bowl of popcorn between us, watching *Mork and Mindy.*

Ed says, 'You're going to get even fatter now, Kat,' nodding at my hand on its way to my mouth with its cargo of warm, buttery popcorn. I nod and Ed smiles. He is not rude. He is right.

I skip school, citing innocuous ailments that need no formal medical intervention: sore throats, period pains, a cold, headaches. I vary them, so nobody notices.

Mum is away again. A book tour in America and Canada. Her book is called *The Ten-thirty from Heuston.* Short stories.

When Dad gets home from work, he says, 'How are you feeling?'

I say, 'Better, thanks,' and he nods and says, 'Good, good,' before picking up his briefcase and walking, in his vague, distracted way, into the study.

Mrs Higginbotham scrapes half my dinner

into the bin. She says, 'You're off your food, Kat-Nap,' which is what she called me when I was a kid and sometimes still does. 'What's the matter?'

I say, 'Sore throat,' or 'Cramps in my tummy,' or 'I had something to eat at Minnie's house,' and Mrs Higginbotham fixes me with her steely stare and then, for a moment, I think: she knows. She knows everything. And I feel a magnificent surge of relief, as if everything will be all right now. Mrs Higginbotham knows and she'll fix it. She'll make it right. But then she nods and returns to the sink and says, 'Gargle with hot water and salt,' or 'Fill a hot water bottle and have an early night,' or 'I told you not to eat between meals.'

Two months to go.

My belly is hard. And the deep well of my bellybutton is gone. It's stretched across my stomach. There is movement. I don't look down when that happens. I don't put my hand on my belly when that happens. I put a tape in my Walkman. Turn the volume up and up. If I'm in my room and Mum is not in the house, I sing along. I'm really bad at singing. I close my eyes and sing along at the top of my voice.

Two months till the exams. The Intermediate Examination. We talk about fourth year. We'll be seniors then. We'll wear blue jumpers and we'll be allowed on the blue stairs that are currently off limits to third years like us.

We don't talk about it, Minnie and me. I think it's because we don't know what to say. We don't know what to do.

Instead, we slag each other.

'Is that a face on your spot?'

'Givvus a match.'

'My arse and your face.'

'Fat bitch.'

'Spotty cow.'

'Givvus a fag.'

'Kenny Everett.'

We laugh. We laugh all the time. Sometimes we laugh so hard that we cry. That's the only time I cry. When I laugh so hard.

Faith says, 'I liked your note.'

I say, 'I didn't want you to worry.'

Faith says, 'You spelled responsibilities wrong.'

I say, 'Miss Williams hasn't done that word with us yet.'

We are on the plane. It hasn't taken off yet, which is good because taking off happens to be my favourite bit. The stewardess is showing us how to fasten the seatbelt. I check mine. It's fastened. I tighten it as much as it will go but it's still loose. I look at Faith, wondering if I should tell her, but she is looking out of the window.

My second favourite bit is when the plane goes into the clouds and then out the other side, where the sky is blue and the clouds below look like snow. Proper snow. Not like the stuff a week ago. Me and Damo made a snowman but it was really small. There's no such things as leprechauns but Americans think there are. They're really small. And green. Our snowman was like that, except he wasn't green. More like a dirty white.

I feel under the seat with my hand but I can't find the life jacket. Maybe there are two under Faith's seat. The stewardess says that adults have to attend to their own life jacket first, before the kids'. I expect I'd be able to put on my own one. If I had one. I don't know about Faith, though. She's still looking out of the window. She hasn't listened to a single word the stewardess has said. I hope we don't crash. I really do.

I don't think the woman knows we are coming to see her. I don't think Faith has a plan. Having a plan saves lives. That's what Coach says.

Now the stewardess is walking down the plane. She's checking to see everybody has their seatbelt on and I pull up my jacket so she can see my belt, which is fastened as tight as it will go but is still a bit loose. She stops at our row and smiles at me. She doesn't even check my seatbelt.

She says, 'Hello, there.' Her teeth are very long and very white and she is wearing a necklace that says 'Angela'. I bet that's her name.

She moves past our row, without even glancing at my belt. I pull on the strap again but it's definitely as tight as it will go.

After the runway bit and the going up through the clouds bit, I'm bored. I forgot to pack *Dark Days*, the fourth Skulduggery Pleasant book, which is actually turning out to be just as good as the third one. Damo says reading's for nerds but Ant is always reading and he's not a nerd. He's had about a hundred girlfriends and he never studies.

George Pullman said he flew to America once and everyone on the plane had their own telly and you could watch whatever you liked. I don't believe him. He said his dad was an astronaut but me and Damo saw him with his dad in Pizza Hut once and his dad was wearing a dark suit, like an undertaker. Undertakers are people who sell coffins. They wear dark suits.

Faith says, 'What's wrong with you?'

I say, 'Nothing.'

She says, 'You haven't asked me if we're there yet.'
I shrug, as if it's nothing.

Faith says, 'Well, we are there. Nearly there.' She nods towards the window and I look out. Faith has the window seat. I thought it might cheer her up.

Below, I see the sea. It's called the Irish Sea, the one between England and Ireland. We did that in Mrs O'Reilly's class, last year. She taught us lots of things about Ireland because that's where she's from. She didn't let us say, 'Londonderry'. If you did, she'd make you stand by the wall with your back to the class so you couldn't see anything.

I see an island with a round tower. There's no roof on the tower. I reckon if I parachuted down right now, I'd land inside it, no problem.

The fields look really small. Green.

'The Emerald Isle' Mam called it. Emeralds are like diamonds except they're green. From up here, everything looks green, even the sea. Not many people know that the sea is actually green. Most people think it's blue.

I say, 'Faith?'

She says, 'Ummm?' the way adults do when they're not listening. I tap her elbow and this makes her turn away from the window and look at me.

'What?'

'Nothing.'

'What were you going to say?'

'Nothing.'

'I swear to God, Milo . . . '

'OK, OK, I was just wondering if we're going to see your birth mother as soon as we get off the plane.'

Faith shakes her head. 'Will you keep your voice down?' Her whisper sounds like a hiss. She looks around but no one is listening. Most of them are looking at the sea and the fields and the island and the tower. She puts her elbows on the table top in front of her. It's still down but it's supposed to be up by now. She pushes her hands into her hair.

I say, 'I thought that's why we were here. So you could talk to her.'

She says, 'It is, but . . . Milo, look, it's . . . it's complicated. You're just nine. You don't understand.'

Adults always tell kids they don't understand instead of saying that they don't know how to explain it. Miss Williams doesn't let us say, 'I don't know'. She says you have to make a stab at it.

I only want to know if we're going to visit the lady when we land. And if we're not, then I just want to know what we're going to do instead. I like having a plan. When you have a plan, you know what's coming. When you're a little kid, you don't think about what's coming. But I'll be ten soon. Double digits. Damo says I'll be a pre-teen, like him. A pre-teen is like being a teenager except you don't need to shave and you don't have spots yet. Damo has three hairs under each arm now. He says he got them two days after he turned ten. He's always wearing tops with no sleeves. He hangs off the monkey bars at the park, so that everyone can see them.

I say, 'So?'

Faith says, 'What?'

And I say, 'So what?' and that makes her smile and I love when Faith smiles so I don't ask her again.

The landing is really bouncy, which is pretty exciting. The lady in the seat in front of Faith doesn't like it.

She says, 'Jesus, Mary and holy St Joseph, preserve

246

us.' Then she blesses herself loads of times. I think Ireland is a pretty holy place. Mrs O'Reilly was Irish and she was dead holy. She went to mass on Sundays and gave out to us if we had a ham sandwich on Fridays. You're not supposed to eat meat on Fridays if you're holy. Not even chicken nuggets, which have hardly any meat in them at all.

I've only been to mass four times, I think. When I got christened and when I made my First Holy Communion, and then the two masses after the accident. Faith didn't want me to go to the first one. Dad and Faith had a big fight about it.

Dad said, 'He needs to be there. He needs to understand.'

Faith said, 'He's only nine years old.'

Dad said, 'I know what age my own son is, thank you very much.'

By then Faith was crying and Dad said something like, 'Your mother would have wanted him there.' And that's when Faith started shouting at Dad. 'What the hell would you know about what Mam wanted?' Dad didn't even tell her to stop shouting and saying hell.

Later, when Damo asked me why my eyes were red, I said, 'I ate a chilli pepper,' and he said, 'A whole one?' and I said, 'Yeah,' and he said, 'A raw one?' and I said, 'Yeah,' and he said, 'Awesome,' and that made me stop thinking about Dad and Faith shouting, and Mam not being here anymore.

I see Faith's bag on the carousel and I drag it off. It's pretty heavy for just a couple of days but that's because Faith is a girl and girls need more clothes than boys. Sometimes Imelda wears three different outfits in one day but Carla always wears the same jeans, even if there're grass stains on the knees.

When we get outside, Faith lights a cigarette and checks the bus timetable. Afterwards, she says, 'Let's go,' and I pick up my bag and follow her, even though I don't know where we're going to or how long it's going to take to get there.

And I don't ask.

It's probably because I'm nearly ten now. Double digits. A preteen. I'm going to check my armpits when we get to wherever we're going, because you just never know, do you?

Not much happens.

I think about Thomas. About ringing him. I don't ring him.

I smoke. A lot.

Brona rings. I tell her I've just started a chapter. I can't talk.

I don't write anything.

I examine my face in the mirror. My almost-forty-year-old face.

Minnie rings and tells me about her teeth. Apparently, they're falling into disrepair due to all the calcium in her body bypassing her mouth and going directly to the baby. She doesn't seem put out by this turn of events, even though she's particular about her teeth, having worn train tracks for much of the eighties.

I tell her I can't talk, I've got Brona holding on the other line. She wants to discuss the chapter I'm writing. Minnie tells me to ring her back. I don't.

I avoid Ed. I tell him I can't come over to play Super Mario Galaxy with him.

'We could play Super Mario Galaxy 2, if you prefer.'

'I can't.'

'Why not, Kat?'

'Because . . . '

'Is it because you're getting things ready for when Faith comes to visit us?'

'Something like that.'

Later, the phone rings. I check the screen. Withheld.

But it could be Ed phoning from Sophie's, looking for a lift somewhere. Maybe he's out of credit. I don't think it's Ed. But it could be.

'Hello?' My voice sounds sharp. Caustic. I don't sound like someone who is afraid.

'You were wrong.' The voice is the same as before. A man's voice. Low-pitched. English accent. The enunciation of each word like an elocution lesson.

'Who is this?'

'Last time we spoke, you said you know who I am. But you don't, do you? You haven't got a clue.'

'I know you're a coward.'

'I'm a businessman.'

'What do you want?'

'An investment in my business.'

'What business?'

'The business of not giving an exclusive to one of our lovely tabloids about Killian Kobain and who he really is.'

'I don't know what you're talking about.'

'Everybody wants to know this story.'

'What story?'

'The Killian Kobain story.'

'That's got nothing to do with me.'

'The clock is ticking on this deal, Kat. I'm not looking for a big investment. A modest six-figure sum should be sufficient. I don't think that will pose much of a problem for someone with a net worth of about . . . what did the *Bookseller* report say? Oh yes, twenty-two million, wasn't it? Now is that euro or sterling?' He laughs, like he's said something funny.

I know I should hang up. I know I should.

I don't.

He says, 'Let's hope you have no other secrets to hide, Kat.'

Something twists in my gut, like a knife. 'What are you talking about?'

'Once the press gets hold of this story, they'll go through you for a shortcut. No stone will be left unturned. I wouldn't want that for you, of course. But by then the matter will be out of my hands.'

'Fuck you.'

'Now, now, Kat, that's not very polite.'

'You're blackmailing me.'

'I'm not fond of that word.'

'That's what you're doing.'

The edge returns to his voice. 'This story will either get told or it won't. It's up to you, Katherine.'

'Don't ring this number again.'

'We'll talk again. When you've had a chance to think about things.'

'There's nothing to think about.'

'There's always something to think about.' This time, he hangs up first.

I throw the phone at the wall but it doesn't break. The back cover comes off, that's all. I put it back and dial the number, but I hang up before it gets a chance to ring. I end up doing it a couple of times. Dialling and hanging up. I don't know why. I'll be glad in the morning, I'd say. That I didn't ring Thomas.

I open a Word document. Look at the blank screen. Page one of one. I type 'Chapter One'. Then I close the lid of the laptop, put it into the bag and put it under the stairs, behind a case of wine.

I go out. Sit in the cinema. I can't remember the name of the film. Subtitles. German, maybe. I go to a sushi bar. The food goes round and round on a conveyer belt. I drink a glass of wine. Then I go home.

As soon as I open the hall door, I see it. A light, flashing on my answering machine. A red light. In the darkness of the hall, it looks sinister. It looks like bad news.

It's probably nothing. Someone selling broadband. Or asking me questions about the telly programmes I like. For a survey. My viewing habits they call it, when they ring.

The car keys are in my hand, my coat is on, so I turn, away from the light, the red flashing light, close the door and back down the hallway. I don't wait for the lift. Instead, I take the stairs two at a time and don't stop running until I reach my car. I get in and turn on the radio — loud — and light a cigarette, even though I am not supposed to smoke in the car.

Rain lashes against the window and blurs my view as if I've been crying, which I haven't because I don't, as a rule.

My breath is coming hard and shallow now. If I didn't know myself better, I might think I'm having a panic attack. I roll down the window and pitch my cigarette out. Sheets of driving rain sting my eyes and my cheeks but the coldness of the air feels good. I stick my head out of the window and drink it in, like it's a good stiff Merlot. I start the car and begin to drive.

Here's what I love about driving. Even when your mind is someplace else, you can drive. You don't have to think about it. Not really. I don't make a conscious decision to go to Minnie's. All of a sudden, I'm just there. Pulled up outside her and Maurice's huge pile in Ballsbridge. That's the only good thing about accountants coupling up. Money is no object.

I smoke one more cigarette before I ring the bell, taking care to hide the butt in the hanging basket. I push it deep into the soil at the back. Minnie has an eye for butts.

Minnie says, 'Oh shit. What's happened?'

I say, 'Charming,' although it's true that I rarely call at their house, mostly because Maurice is often there. And I never come without ringing first. From Minnie's point of view, I can see how this looks.

Minnie says, 'Sorry, sorry, it's just . . . come in, come in.'

I say, 'Is Maurice here?'

She shakes her head. 'He's gone to his Mensa meeting.' And there you have it. Maurice, it seems, is a genius. The only thing Maurice has ever done that might denote a modicum of genius is get Minnie to marry him. Lots of people wanted to — men and women alike — but Maurice was the man who managed it.

253

God knows, you'd have to have some — grudg-
ing — respect for that kind of achievement.

Minnie leads the way to the kitchen, which is
like a kitchen in a restaurant with its gleaming
stainless steel and its football-stadium propor-
tions. The radio is on. *Front Row* on BBC Radio
4. I look at Minnie, who shrugs. 'There was a
programme about famous recluses. I thought it
might amuse me.'

'Recluses are usually just famous for being
recluses. Take Howard Hughes, for instance. I
bet you can't name one of the films he
produced.'

Minnie ignores the question, which means she
doesn't know the answer.

'They compared Killian Kobain to JD
Salinger.'

'About time.'

'No. Not the writing. Just the fact that a
couple of killers were found with copies of
*Catcher in the Rye*, either on their person or in
their houses. And a copy of one of your books
— *The Secrets You Keep* — was found in
Catherine Nevin's walk-in wardrobe.'

'Is she the one who's in the slammer for
paying a bloke to polish off her husband?'

'Black Widow Nevin. Apparently, she had
passages marked in your book. Murdery-bits. In
pink highlighter pen.'

I shake my head. 'Murderers just don't have
the same edge anymore, do they?'

Minnie sighs. 'She's no Jack the Ripper, that's
for sure.'

She switches off the radio and says, 'Sit down,'

and I do. The fact is, my legs feel funny. Like I'd just done a spinning class. I took one once. I can't believe anybody goes a second time.

Minnie puts on the kettle. When she reaches up to the press for cups, you can see the beginnings of a slight swell of her belly against her top.

'Could I have a drink instead?'

'You're driving.'

'Just the one?'

'You're driving.'

I don't argue because there's no point. Not with Minnie. If you're driving, you're not drinking and if you're drinking, you're not driving. There's no grey area. No middle ground. She'd be desperate in a peace-talks capacity.

I want coffee. Minnie makes me a peppermint tea. 'No coffee after three p.m.,' she says, as if this were a bald fact rather than a random opinion she happens to hold. She puts a sprig of mint into the tea. I unwrap the chocolate brownie she gives me. From Avoca. Minnie never buys brownies anywhere else because, she says, the Avoca ones are the best. She doesn't do things by halves, Minnie. That's the really great and the really terrible thing about her.

She hands me my drink and says, 'I'm eleven weeks pregnant today.' Then she sits down in a chair opposite mine. 'I still can't get my head around it. Me and Maurice. Having a baby.' Minnie's eyes look bluer than usual. The whites whiter. There is something shiny about them, like a child's eyes.

I say, 'I'm so happy for you.' BAM! There's a

255

humdinger. Once the baby comes, there's no way I'll be able to drop in like this. Can you imagine the noise? And the mess? The distractions. Neither of us would get a word in edgeways, with all the squawking.

Minnie says, 'Don't worry. I'm not going to ask you to be godmother or anything like that.' But the way she says it suggests that perhaps she would ask me. She'd like to ask me. If I were different. A different person. A better person.

She says, 'Well? What's your story?'

'Me? Not much.'

'Don't fuck around, Kavanagh. The last time you called out here without letting me know was on your way home from the hospital. When Ed was sick that time.'

'I was worried. I thought he was having a bloody heart attack.'

'I know. I'm not saying you shouldn't have called in. I'm merely illustrating the point that you don't call in unless it's some kind of an emergency. Now, what is it?'

I take a breath. It goes straight to my head. It feels like the first one I've taken in ages. 'I met Thomas the other day.' I thought I was going to tell her about the man on the phone, but it looks like I'm not.

Minnie opens her mouth.

I head her off at the pass. 'And don't say, 'So?''

Minnie swallows the word like it's one of those gigantic vitamin pills that are hard to get down, no matter how much water you drink.

'Am I allowed to say, 'And?''

'That's pretty much the same as 'So?'.'

Minnie makes her lips as narrow as they will go, like she's trying to prevent words getting past them that might be considered offensive. Then she says, 'OK, then, what else? Did you talk? What did he say?'

'He's still going out with Sandra.'

'Sarah.' Minnie tries not to sound impatient. 'Kat, I don't understand. I really don't. He would have taken you back. All you had to do was apologise. For all that carry-on after the accident. And that ridiculous thing with Nicolas . . . '

'It wasn't ridiculous.' Except it was. And not just because Nicolas is quite a bit younger than me. There were loads of other reasons.

'It was ridiculous. You said he wore a T-shirt under his shirt. A Celine Dion T-shirt.'

'I said I thought it was Celine Dion. I wasn't sure.'

'If you thought it was Celine Dion, then it was definitely Celine Dion. There's no mistaking that woman.'

'I was telling you about meeting Thomas. The other day.'

'Go on.'

It's tricky to know where to begin so I begin at the end.

'Ed told him about Faith.'

'Faith?'

'Remember when I got pregnant when I was fifteen and I went into labour on the couch in your mother's front room and then I had a baby later on that evening — at twelve minutes past seven — in Holles Street?'

I don't look at Minnie when I say any of that. I look at the floor. I recite it like it's a poem I learned a long time ago but never forgot. Like Shelley's 'Ozymandias'. 'My name is Ozymandias, king of kings: Look on my works, ye Mighty, and despair!' No one forgets that one, do they? It's nice and short, for a start. And bleak. That was one pretty bleak poem. I did it in third year. Again. I had to stay back because I missed the Inter. Cert, the first time round. Minnie got to wear the blue jumper and walk up and down the blue stairs that year. The year I had to repeat third year. I spent most of that year in the library, reading Stephen King. *It*. That was my favourite one. I've never been able to go to the circus since. The clowns bring back the dark corners of that book. The dark corners of third year, when you're supposed to be in fourth year. On the blue stairs. Wearing a blue jumper.

That's when I started to write. In the library. I'd forgotten that. Pages and pages of horror. Awful stuff. I don't know what I did with it. I must have thrown it away. I really can't remember.

Minnie says, 'Yes.' Her voice is quiet. Much quieter than usual.

The thing is, we never talked about it, me and Minnie. Not afterwards. Not really. I mean, yes, Minnie called round when I came home, said she was glad she didn't have to hang around with a fatso anymore and asked me if it was true about hospital doctors being rides? We talked about school and the Inter. Cert, and what she thought she got, which had no bearing on what she actually got (it was an easy result to remember because she got As in every subject), and the fact that I would have to repeat the year and how I was going to manage without her (badly, as it turned out), and how she was going to manage without me (very well, as it turned out).

But we didn't talk about the baby. Not once. Maybe some adult — my mother or her mother, perhaps — told Minnie not to say anything. I never asked. I was just grateful that I didn't have to talk about it. It made everything more bearable. Not talking about it. And after a while of not talking about it and just going about my ordinary, dull, boring life, it was almost as if it had never happened. Not really. It didn't seem real anymore. Perhaps I had imagined it. A bad dream I had that woke me in the night once, a long time ago.

Minnie waits.

I say, 'Well, the baby was a girl. A baby girl. Faith. That's her name. And now she's twenty-four and she wants to meet me. I got a letter. I got three letters, actually. From an adoption agency in London. It said that her name is Faith and she's twenty-four and she wants to meet me.' I pick up my cup and put it down again.

Minnie opens her mouth and then closes it. She pushes her hair off her face. She gets up. She says, 'Christ.' She goes to the cupboard where the serious drink is kept and takes out a bottle of whiskey that has dust all over it, like a shroud.

She pours a measure into a heavy, cut-glass crystal tumbler.

Minnie-if-you're-drinking-you're-not-driving Minnie. That Minnie. She hands me the glass and I toss it down. It burns.

Minnie says, 'Christ,' again.

I say, 'Anything else?'

She shakes her head. She looks different when she doesn't know the answer. She looks like someone else.

After a while, she says, 'Did you respond to the letters?'

'No.'

Minnie seems unsurprised by this.

'Does your mother know?'

I nod.

'What did she say?'

'Nothing, really.' Minnie nods, again unsurprised.

For a while, we sit there, the pair of us. In two easy chairs in front of an enormous flat screen that is turned off. For a while, all you can hear is a clock ticking somewhere. It sounds like a timer, counting down the seconds until something big happens.

Minnie arranges herself straighter in her chair and I can almost hear her changing gears. 'So,' she says, back to brisk. 'What are you going to do?'

I shrug. Shake my head. Minnie leans towards me, puts her hands on my arms. I'd say she'd like to shake me a little bit but she doesn't.

'What is it you want, Kat?'

That's easy. 'I want none of this to have happened.'

Minnie nods, sits back in her seat, crosses her legs. 'Let's just suppose for a moment that that's not possible.'

'Well, you asked me what I wanted. I was just saying . . . '

'What else?'

I open my mouth.

'Something realistic.'

I close my mouth.

'Come on, Kat, you must have some sort of a plan.' In Minnie's world, people have plans. In my world, people have hiding places.

I look at my watch. 'It's getting late. I'd better go.' I don't stand up. I sit on the chair in Minnie's gigantic kitchen and think about the red flashing light. I'll have to press the button when I get home. No way I can just leave it.

Minnie stands up. 'Wait.' Something about her tone, her stance, her new shininess, makes me suspect that she is thinking about hugging me. Minnie and I don't hug. It's like an unspoken pact we made a long time ago. If she hugs me now, I think I'll come undone. I really do.

Into the kitchen at that precise moment walks Maurice, back from Mensa. I don't think I've ever been so glad to see him.

Maurice hugs me. He's terribly tactile. His anorak makes a swishing noise when he moves. He smells of anchovies. Minnie was right about them.

Maurice takes down the hood of his anorak

and says, 'So, Kat, how's life in the technical writing world?'

I picked technical writing because it's such a safe haven. Normal people don't know anything about technical writing. But Maurice knows. Probably because he's a genius.

And he's interested in it.

He says, 'What project are you working on at the moment?' He always asks that. It's fine, though. I know a hell of a lot about technical writing when you consider that I've never done a day's work in it in my life. I subscribe to a dreadfully dull blog about technical writing issues. It's called *Technical Writing Issues.*

Other than that, I make it up. And because I'm a fiction writer I'm pretty good at that too. I tell him about some obscure Java product that hasn't come to market yet. He's heard of it.

'Is that the New Field Communications Library?' he wants to know.

'No, it's more for the Augmented Reality stuff on mobile,' I tell him.

He whistles. 'Impressive,' he says and I take a step back because of his breath, which is atrociously anchovy. Minnie doesn't notice. In fact, she puts her face right in front of his and kisses him, as if there is nothing anchovy about his breath at all.

'I told Kat our news.'

'I thought we weren't telling people until week twelve?' Maurice smiles when he says this but it is a bit of an effort of a smile, as if he wishes that there was no one else in the kitchen — or perhaps the world — only him and Minnie and

262

Mensa and the baby in Minnie's belly.

Minnie says, 'I just told Kat. She not people. Besides, it's practically twelve weeks. And Kat won't tell anyone. Sure you won't?' Minnie's smile is directed at me and edged with menace, like a warning of the things Minnie will do to me if I decide to spill the beans.

I shake my head and say, 'Congratulations,' which gives Maurice an excuse to hug me again and I hold my breath so I don't inhale the anchovies, and Minnie is saying something but I can't hear what it is because of the swishing of Maurice's anorak.

I say, 'I'll go.'

Maurice looks at Minnie, then back at me. 'What's up with you two?' Wary now, as if he finally senses something awry. Genius, my arse.

'Nothing.'

I move towards the kitchen door. 'I was leaving anyway.'

Minnie follows me. 'I'll see you out.'

'No, no don't, it's too cold, I'll see myself out.'

Minnie sees me out. At the door, she says, 'What are you going to do?'

'I'm not sure yet.' As if, at some stage in the not-too-distant future, I will be sure. Just not right now.

'I think you should meet her.'

And now Minnie's hallway feels as dark as mine. I think about going back. Going back to my hallway with the red flashing light. I don't want to.

I open the hall door. 'I'll call you tomorrow.'

'I really do, Kat. I think you should meet her.

I think it would be good for you.'

I don't ask her why. Why she thinks it would be good for me. Instead, I say, 'Go on, you'll catch your death.' Already the rain is advancing into the hall.

'I'll come with you, if you like.' Minnie's hand is on the slight swell of her belly. I don't think she is aware of the gesture. There is something intimate about it. Like an overheard conversation between lovers. It warms you and, at the same time, leaves you with a feeling of loss, even though nothing has been given. Nothing has been taken away.

I nod and wave and run towards my car.

This is what I am good at.

Running.

This is where I excel.

Auntie May looks almost exactly the same as Mam, especially when she smiles or cries. Not that Mam ever really cried. Just at movies, mostly. Like *Up*. And *Toy Story 3*. *Toy Story 3* nearly broke her heart clean in two. That's what she said. Clean in two.

Auntie May is crying. So is Faith. They're hugging each other and crying. I don't know why we're here. Faith said we were going to a hotel. But then, on the bus from the airport into the city centre, she decides we're going to Auntie May's house. She just decides. All of a sudden. She doesn't even phone to let anyone know we're coming. She just decides, and the next thing is, we're on a train.

I stand beside the tank and watch the fish. They're all goldfish. May says she loves the colour of them. Goldfish have really bad memories. That's why they swim round and round all the time. Because they forget they've done it before. Like about a million times already.

Auntie May stops hugging Faith and says, 'You look frozen, the pair of you. Why didn't you tell me you were coming? I would have met you at the airport, you know that.'

Faith nods. 'I'm sorry, I just . . . I've a hotel booked. For me and Milo. We're just staying the one night.'

'Nonsense. You'll stay here. With us.'

'No, really, it's — '

'Where's this hotel?'

'I don't know. Marlborough Street, I think.'

'Jesus, Mary and Holy St Joseph, is it raped and murdered and dumped in the Liffey in a suitcase you're after?'

I look at Faith. I really want to stay here. In May's house. And it's not just because I don't want to be dumped in the Liffey in a suitcase. It's because . . . well, it's nice in May's house. Like, it's dead clean and the kitchen smells like lunch or dinner or something. Shepherd's pie, maybe. I love Mam's shepherd's pie because she doesn't put peas in it. I wonder if Auntie May puts peas in her one?

I didn't tell Faith about being starving because I promised.

May looks at me. 'You'd like to stay, wouldn't you, Milo?' She puts her hands round my face and shakes her head. 'Cut out of your mother, so you are.' Then she kisses my cheek and it feels dead gooey, but I have to wait till she turns back to Faith before I can wipe it off. Lipstick, I reckon. Ladies are mad about lipstick.

'You can't be dragging the boy to a place like Marlborough Street. Your mother'd lambast you, God rest her.'

Faith doesn't say anything for a while and then she says, 'I know, May. I know about Mam. About me and Mam.'

May lowers the kettle back onto the counter. She looks at Faith. She says, 'What do you mean?'

Faith looks at me and then May looks at me too. I can see them both, in the reflection of the fish tank. Behind me, May picks up my bag. 'Milo, love, you can sleep in Finn's room. He won't be back from college till

266

Friday. Come on. I'll show you where it is. You can see the sea from there.'

Faith says, 'May, there's no — '

May says, 'I won't hear another word about it, Faith.' She sounds exactly like Mam when she says that. Her voice is quiet and soft but you know for a fact that there's no point arguing.

I've stayed in Auntie May and Uncle Niall's house before. But not in Finn's room. I slept in the attic on a sofa bed and you can't see the sea from there. You can only see the sky.

May says, 'I'll put fresh sheets on that bed later, Milo. The Lord knows when that dirty pup changed them.' She puts my bag on the bed and looks inside a cupboard. 'There are a few books in there. *Treasure Island*. Have you read that one yet? Your mam always said you're a great one for the reading.'

I shake my head. I say, 'No, not yet.'

'And there's a chess board, I think. You can play chess with your Uncle Niall later.'

I know how to play chess. Dad taught me the last time he came down. He says it's the thinking man's game.

'Good boy, Milo.' May stops at the door. 'I'll . . . I'll call you down in a bit, all right? I'll make lunch. Something nice. Pasta, maybe. Carbonara. You like that one, don't you?'

My mouth waters. Auntie May is nearly as good at cooking as Mam. And I ate everything I had in Damo's tree house. The Easi-Singles and the packet of ham and the three strawberry yoghurts and the two slices of bread and the packet of crackers and the Kit Kat. I tried to keep the Kit Kat for last, like you're supposed to, but it was too hard in the end. I stayed there until the first bus, which came at 06.35, which is twenty-five to seven. I was so stiff and cold, I nearly fell off the rope ladder. Once, I threw a pebble up at Damo's window but nothing happened. Damo's mam says that Damo is as lazy as sin and not even a nuclear bomb landing on his head would get him out of his pit. I didn't think he'd wake up. Not really. I just did it to pass the time.

The bus driver looked suspicious when he saw me but he didn't say anything. Not even 'hello'. He just gave me my ticket and my change and went back to looking at his newspaper, at a picture of a woman in her togs, and he didn't drive off till nearly twenty to.

I say, 'Yes, I love carbonara.'

May says, 'And do you like garlic bread?'

I nod.

May says, 'And I'm guessing you wouldn't say no to a bit of chocolate cake?'

I shake my head.

'With a blob of ice cream on the top?'

I nod.

'Vanilla do you?'

I nod again, even though the truth is that I'd prefer chocolate ice cream.

May claps her hands together and rubs them. 'We're in business, so.' I know she's going to hug me. I just know it. And then she does. She has a different smell to Mam. Not a bad smell. Just different. But she feels pretty much the same. Sort of warm and squashy. Her hair tickles my face. She has a tight hold on me. She says, 'You're a great boy, Milo,' when she stops the hug and stands up straight. Her eyes are really bright. The same blue as Mam's. I hope she doesn't cry. Then she ruffles my hair and then she leaves. She doesn't cry.

Donabate is still in Dublin but it looks like the countryside, on account of the fields. There's a caravan park beside Auntie May's house. That'd be legend. To live in a caravan. When you get bored, you can just hop in your caravan and drive away.

We pass an ice-cream parlour when we come out of the train station but Faith says, 'No,' because we're going to get a taxi to the house and there's no way the driver will let a messer like me into the car, with ice cream dripping everywhere. We end up walking all the way to Auntie May's house from the train station and not one single taxi passes us by, only three normal cars and one man walking a really skinny dog.

It's freezing and the wind would cut you in two. That's what Mam used to say. But then she'd say, 'At least it's dry.' Before Dad went away, he called her his weather girl because she was always talking about the weather and looking at the sky to see what would happen next.

The farther I walk, the heavier my bag gets. Faith's bag has wheels but she has to lift it over tree roots that cut through the path every so often. I'm glad when Faith stops to light a cigarette. I cup my hands round my mouth and blow into them a couple of times.

Faith says, 'Are you cold?'

I say, 'No,' because I promised I wouldn't complain.

'Do you want me to put your bag on my back for a while?'

'No, thanks.' You don't get girls to carry your bag, no matter how tired you are. No way.

The road to Auntie May's house is the longest road

I've ever been on. Dead straight with no end in sight. It just goes on and on. Then, all of a sudden, it ends. Right in front of the sea and then we're at the house. It takes about five hours to get there, I reckon.

After dinner, Uncle Niall plays chess with me. He's the type of adult that lets kids win. He pretends to be dead annoyed when I say, 'Check,' or 'Checkmate'. He clutches his head as if he's got a really bad pain in it and he says things like, 'You jammy little git,' except he's smiling so I'll know he's only messing.

Auntie May and Faith are looking through photo albums. I've seen them before, those photographs. There's loads of Mam in there. Mam and May. On the beach. Mam and May in bumper cars. Mam and May at the Tower of London. Mam and May on a boat. With their arms round each other and scarves wound round their heads. They're always laughing. I say, 'No, thank you,' when May asks if I'd like to look at the photographs. I'm glad I'm playing chess with Niall, even though he's the type of adult that lets kids win.

Faith says, 'I'm just . . . I'm so angry with her. I don't even feel sad anymore. I'm just . . . I'm furious.' It's weird because Faith doesn't sound angry. Her voice is really low. She sounds tired. She probably is tired. I'm tired too. Sleeping in a tree house is not as legend as you'd think.

May nods and says, 'Anger is all part of it, you know. Part of the grieving process.'

'No, I'm angry with her for not telling me.'

May puts her hand on Faith's shoulder. Squeezes it. 'She called you her lucky charm. The doctor told her she'd never be able to carry a baby to full term. But after they adopted you, your mother got pregnant twice. She couldn't believe it.'

May turns to the next page of the album. 'Lookit!' she says, nodding at a picture. 'Look at the pair of you there.' She's smiling at the picture and Faith smiles too.

It's Niall's turn and he takes ages to make a move so I walk over to the couch and look at the picture that May is pointing to. I've seen that one loads of times. Mam has it in a frame in her bedroom. Her and Faith. On the beach in Donabate. I know it's Donabate and not Brighton because of the sand. They have their backs to the camera, walking away. Faith is carrying a bucket full of shells and she comes up to Mam's knees. Mam has to bend to reach her hand. Faith is wearing nothing except a nappy. Mam's in her bare feet and has one of Dad's shirts on over her togs. They're both smiling. You can see the smiles in the sides of their faces because they're looking at each other.

May puts her finger on Mam's face. Slides it across like she's taking the hair out of her eyes. She says, 'That was taken a week after you arrived. One week. I never saw her so happy.' She looks at Faith. 'She didn't tell you because she loved you. She never wanted you to feel any different to the boys.'

Uncle Niall says, 'Beat that!'

That means it's my go and May looks up then and notices me, standing behind her, peering over her shoulder.

'I've a picture like that of you and your mam too, Milo. Taken on Donabate beach. I'm sure of it.' She starts flipping through the pages. I hope she doesn't find it. I really do. Imagine what Damo would say if he saw a picture of me in a nappy?

After I beat Niall four times in a row, he says he

271

can't take it anymore and he goes into the kitchen to get himself a stiff drink, which turns out to be a can of Coke. 'I suppose you want one too?' I nod. I know he's only pretending to be mad.

Auntie May insists on tucking me into bed. She tucks the covers around me so tightly, I'm like a sausage in a roll and I can barely breathe. She says, 'Promise me you'll never run away again, Milo.' Which means that Faith has told her everything. I was really hoping she wouldn't. I say, 'I didn't run away. Not really.' May pulls the blanket under my chin as if it's a napkin. She says, 'I'd be worried sick if I thought you were going to run away again, d'ya hear me?' There's no point saying anything so I just nod.

She clears her throat, which means she's going to say more stuff. I wait. She says, 'So . . . you and Faith . . . you're going off tomorrow to meet this . . . this woman . . . Katherine Kavanagh.' She picks up a thread that's sticking out of a bit of the blanket and rubs it between her fingers.

I say, 'I'm not sure. Faith hasn't said anything about tomorrow yet. And I'm not supposed to ask. I promised.'

May smiles and nods. She doesn't say anything else. She looks like she's trying to work out a really hard sum in her head.

I say, 'Do you think Mam would mind?'

May looks at me. 'Mind?'

'About us. Being in Ireland. Looking for Faith's real mother.'

'Your mother was Faith's real mother.' She sounds a bit mad now so I just nod. After a while, May sighs and says, 'I'm sorry, Milo. It's just . . . things haven't been great lately, have they?'

I shake my head.

She puts her hand on my shoulder. 'Maybe you'll come and spend a week with us in the summertime? Niall and Finn could take you fishing. You'd like that. Wouldn't you?'

I nod, except that I don't want to come here for a week in the summertime. I think it might be something to do with Auntie May. I mean, she's nice and everything. It's just . . . it might be something to do with her looking like Mam except that she isn't Mam, and I know it's weird but it makes me feel a bit funny. Like . . . I don't know. Just funny. Mrs Appleby says it's OK to feel sad and mostly I do my best not to think about it in Brighton. But in Dublin, I keep thinking about it. I don't know why. Usually, I think about great stuff. Like lifesaving. And hanging around with Damo and Carla. Or playing alien-chasing in the playground at breaktime.

I say, 'Do you know what time we're leaving tomorrow?'

May says, 'After breakfast. I'll make pancakes.'

I say, 'Is there a train into the city centre then?'

May nods her head. 'Don't worry, Milo. There're lots of trains. Or I can drive you. Wherever you're going, all right? Don't worry, love.'

I turn on my side and close my eyes. May tiptoes out of the room and whispers, 'Night night.' She closes the door and I hear the creak of the stairs. When she's gone, I get up and open the door. Just a tiny bit. A thin line of light falls in from the landing. Not much but just enough to sleep by. I'm really tired but it takes ages to fall asleep. Downstairs I hear the low murmur of voices. I expect they're talking about the woman. Katherine Kavanagh. I wonder what she looks like. I wonder what she'll say to Faith when she sees her tomorrow? I hope it's something nice, I really do.

I think Faith could do with someone to cheer her up.

I don't think I'm doing a very good job of it.

The red flashing light turns out to be a message from Thomas. His voice fills the cold and dark of the hallway, instantly familiar and strange, all at the same time.

There is relief. That it isn't the man. The one looking for Killian Kobain.

Or someone looking for me.

The girl in the letters.

Faith.

And there's apprehension. What does he want? Thomas is not a phone person. He doesn't ring for conversation. He rings for a reason. A specific reason. Like news to impart. Phone conversations with Thomas never last long. Not even in our heyday. Twenty seconds. Thirty, tops. Long enough to say 'who' and 'what' and 'when' and 'why' and 'where'. The five Ws. Once a journalist, always a journalist, I suppose.

The first W he covers is 'why'. Why he's ringing on the landline. 'I didn't want to ring your mobile because I wanted to make sure you were at home when I talk to you.'

Relief seeps away and apprehension is all that's left now.

Then comes the 'what'.

'I wanted to tell you the other day. At Ed's swimming gala.'

Brief diversion here: 'Ed was great, wasn't he? He's really coming on. He used to be nervous competing, remember? He looked like such a natural in that pool, didn't he?'

There are a few features in Thomas's voice that I recognise. There's pride. There's definitely pride. I recognise that. I've heard that before, when he's spoken about Ed. As if it's true. What Ed says. About Thomas being his best friend.

And there's hesitation. A dragging of heels along the floor of this one-sided conversation.

He launches into a 'why not'.

'I just . . . when Ed told me your news, I didn't feel that it was appropriate then to talk about my news.'

His news?

The 'what' again.

'It's just . . . I wanted to tell you myself. I mean, I didn't want anyone else telling you . . . '

Tell me what?

'It's not like it'll come as a huge surprise to you. Or even that you'll care all that much and why should you? But still . . . I wanted it to be me to tell you and there might be a small mention of it in tomorrow's paper so that's why I'm leaving this message . . . sorry it's so bloody garbled. I hate these machines.'

Tomorrow's paper?

I hear Thomas take a breath. A really long one.

Then another pause.

'I'm getting married.'

Nothing. No dramatic reaction from me. No leaning my back against the wall and sliding down and down until I am sitting on the floor.

No escaping moan. No gasp. Nothing. I'm just a woman, standing in the cold and dark of her own hallway, with her coat on, listening to a message — a garbled message — on her answering machine, from somebody she used to know.

'Engaged, really. I'm getting engaged. I am engaged. To Sandra. I mean, Sarah. Christ, you have me doing it now. I got engaged to Sarah.'

A short pause here as if he thinks I might laugh at this and is waiting for me to finish. Polite. To a fault. I have to give him that.

'So, that's it. That's all. I just wanted you to know.'

Another pause. Then an addendum that doesn't come under any of the five W headings.

'And your news. I'm sorry I reacted the way I did. I think it was shock, really. The idea of you being a mother. I don't mean . . . it's just you always said . . . Anyway, just, sorry.'

A pause. A really awkward one.

'And, you know, you can . . . give me a buzz. If you want to have a chat, or . . . a talk or something, I don't know. I mean . . . I'd say we can still talk to each other, if you'd like to. You know?'

And in the cold, dark of my hallway, I find myself nodding. I do know. And I did know. Even back then, when it was all to play for. I knew. And I did nothing about it.

'OK then, I'll . . . I'll hang up now. I just . . . OK, see you. Goodbye.'

A click. A beep. And then nothing.

The worst thing in a situation like this is that there's no one else to blame.

277

The house is on the Howth Road in Raheny. Auntie May drives us into the city centre. She wanted to bring us all the way to the house but Faith said she preferred to go at her own pace and May nodded and said she understood. She dropped us at Busaras, which is the big bus station in the city. The bus to the airport goes from here. We put our bags in a locker and Faith asks me to mind the key because she doesn't trust herself today, and for extra safety I put it into the pocket that's halfway down my jeans, because it has a zip.

Auntie May says, 'You'll ring. Won't you?'

Faith nods.

May says, 'Remember what we talked about last night, won't you?'

Faith nods again.

May says, 'I won't say goodbye.' She blows me a kiss and waves at Faith and then she checks her mirrors and drives away.

Faith has the address written in her notebook. I remember it in my head. I'm pretty good at remembering things like that. Without writing them down, I mean. That's why I usually get ten out of ten in my spelling tests. We take the bus and I don't ask Faith if we can sit upstairs. She looks as white as Damo did that time he ate the custard powder. He was trying to make custard in his stomach. He swallowed four tablespoons of powder, then drank about a pint of milk and then jumped up and down so it would get all mixed up inside him. When he got sick, it really did look like custard.

When we get to the house in Raheny, Faith walks right past it.

I say, 'Faith, it's here. We're here.' The house is like a mansion. I reckon there're about ten bedrooms. Probably a playroom too. George Pullman has a playroom. He's always talking about it. He has an Xbox too.

'Faith.'

Faith keeps on going. She can walk really fast, on account of her legs being so long. I run after her.

'Faith, wait. The house is back there. You've walked straight past it. It's a mansion. Your real mam, I mean your birth mam, must be loaded.'

Faith doesn't stop until we reach the end of the road. From here, you can see the Irish Sea. The tide is out so far, it's almost in England, I reckon. I put my hands on my knees. Try to get my breath back. Faith takes a packet of cigarettes out of her pocket. Lights one. After a while, she looks at me and says, 'I'm sorry, Milo.'

I try to remember if Faith has done something mean to me but I don't think she has. 'Why do you keep saying that?' She doesn't answer me. I look out at the sea.

'Do you know how many miles between here and England?'

Faith says, 'No.'

'Fifty-six nautical miles, which is seventy-five miles. And do you know how deep the Irish Sea is?'

'No.'

'Three hundred metres, at its deepest point.'

'Where do you get this stuff?'

'From Mrs O'Reilly. She knew everything there was to know about Ireland, remember?'

Behind us is a low wall and Faith sits on it. I follow her.

She says, 'Tell me something else.'

'Well . . . ' I close my eyes. I find it easier to remember stuff when I close my eyes. I could tell her some stuff about astronomy. Carla's mad about astronomy. 'Did you know that stars are suns?'

'They don't look like suns.'

'They are. They're just really, really far away.'

'How far?'

'They're so far, you don't measure in miles. You measure in years.'

'Light years.'

'Yeah.'

'What about black holes?'

'What about them?'

'What do they do?'

'Nothing, really. They just suck everything inside them, even the light.'

'That sounds horrible.'

I look at Faith. Her face looks sort of sad.

I say, 'Yes, but before suns burn out and turn into black holes, they're called supernovas and that's when they shine the very brightest that they've ever shone in their whole lives.'

'So a supernova is a dying sun.'

'Sort of. But it's better than it ever was before. That's why it's super, see?'

Faith nods but I don't think she's all that interested anymore. That's the thing about adults. They're only interested in the actual universe for a little while and then they go back to talking about their kids or their houses or someone they saw in the shop who was the spitting image of Tony Blair, who used to be the boss of England but isn't now. I think he got fired or something.

Faith throws away her cigarette. She cups her hands round her mouth and blows into them.

I say, 'Why did you walk past the house?'

'I don't know. I just . . . I need to think about what I'm going to say.'

'I thought you were doing that on the plane.'

'Doing what?'

'Thinking about what you were going to say.'

'I couldn't think of anything.'

We look towards the sea for a while. I think it's cold enough to snow. Ireland's climate is mild, moist and changeable. Mrs O'Reilly told us that. It doesn't feel mild today. I stuff my hands inside the sleeves of my jacket. I have ski gloves at home. I don't use them for skiing but they're great for building snowmen because they don't get wet, like woolly gloves do.

I jump off the wall. 'You could write a note.'

'What?'

'You could write a note and we'll leave it in the letterbox. There's one attached to the pillar at the start of the driveway. I saw it. A green one with a lock so no one can get the post out of it except the person who lives in the house.'

Faith slithers off the wall. She's still looking at me but I don't think she's seeing me exactly. She's thinking. You can see it in her eyes.

She says, 'That's not a bad idea, Milo.'

I'm glad she likes the idea. Maybe now we can go

someplace where it's warm. I could change my money. Buy some gloves for Faith and me. Her hands are blue on account of the cigarettes and the cold.

'You could write your mobile number on the note. Then, we could go to a café where it'll be warm, and we can have a muffin and I'll think of things that you can talk to the woman about. There's tonnes of stuff you could talk about.' Girls are always talking. Like Imelda and her mam. They never stop talking. Sometimes it's fighting but mostly it's talking.

Faith opens her bag. Takes out a notebook. The one she writes her songs in. The last one she wrote was called 'All About You'. It's a love song but it's not bad. She wrote it a long time ago. Before Mam was in the accident.

Faith holds her pen between her fingers but she doesn't write anything down. She looks like she's thinking again and not coming up with any ideas.

She glances up. 'I don't know what to write.'

You're supposed to know loads of stuff when you're an adult, but I'm not so sure about that anymore.

'Just put your name and your mobile number. And say you're in Dublin and you'd like to meet her. That's all.'

After a while, Faith says, 'OK.' She blows into her hands again and then begins to write.

I say, 'Don't mention me, whatever you do.'

Faith says, 'Why not?'

'Some adults aren't mad about kids.' This is true. Like Mr Swinton at our school. The caretaker. He says, 'What's it got to do with you?' if you ask him when the leak will be fixed in the hall so we can play dodgeball again.

When Faith gets mad, her face turns sort of pink

and her eyes go into a sort of narrow line. She unfolds the page and adds a line at the bottom of the note.

*PS. I am with my brother Milo, who is ten.*

I say, 'I'm not ten yet. I'm only nearly ten.'

Faith draws an arrow in the gap between 'is' and 'ten' and writes, at the top of the arrow, 'nearly'. 'Happy now?'

I nod. If people think you're ten, they might expect you to be bigger than you really are. There's a pretty big difference between nine and ten. Even Damo doesn't pick his nose in front of people anymore. Not since he turned ten. He wants girls to fancy him. None of them do yet, apart from Tracey in Miss Roberts's class, and she fancies just about every boy in the school, even Donald Battersby, who tells on everyone and cries when you say you don't want to play with him on account of him being a telltale.

We walk back. The buses in Dublin are blue and yellow instead of red. The postboxes are green. The national emblem of Ireland is a shamrock. That's green too. Irish people are mad about green. There's green in the flag, which is called the Tricolour. It's flown at half-mast when a patriot like James Connolly dies. Mrs O'Reilly said the Brits tied him to a chair and shot him in the head. I asked Mam if that were true. Mam said it was a Rising, which was a bit like a war and that it all happened a long time ago. I didn't tell Damo about it because he might worry about Sully getting tied to a chair and shot in the head when he's at the war.

Apart from the buses and the postboxes, things look pretty much the same. The sweets in the shops are the same as the ones we get in Brighton. I checked when Faith was buying cigarettes in the Spar in the city centre. They have Mars Duo, which happens to be my favourite chocolate bar on account of it being bigger than an ordinary Mars bar. I also like the Mars Duo ice cream, but I didn't get to check the freezer to see if they had those.

Outside the house, Faith hands me the note that she has folded and folded until it's about the size of a stamp. I unfold most of it and push it through the letterbox. It doesn't make any sound when it lands.

I say, 'There,' instead of saying, 'What are we going to do now?' which is what I really want to say.

Faith says, 'Thanks.'

I say, 'For what?'

When Faith smiles, she doesn't look as thin and worried as before. Rob tells Faith not to smile at him because it makes him do things he doesn't want to do, like the dishes, or watching a film that's not in English.

She punches my arm and says, 'I'm glad you're here.'

I don't punch her back. Mam said you should never hit a girl. Besides, I might hurt her by accident.

Not many people know this but I'm a lot stronger than I look.

# May 1987

Me and Ed and Minnie are watching *Top of the Pops*. It must be Thursday.

Minnie says, 'Mel and Kim are still at number eight.' We love Mel and Kim. We have Mel and Kim hats. We put them on and do the Mel and Kim dance. I am Mel. Minnie is Kim. I am a better dancer but the hat looks better on Minnie.

Something happens. I'm not sure what. I look down and am surprised to see the top of my jeans darkening with wet. It feels warm.

'Jesus, Kat, did you piss yourself?' Minnie says. Ed laughs, because Minnie said, 'piss'. He loves bad language. All ten-year-old boys love the word 'piss'.

I've been feeling strange all day. There have been pains. Tight clutches of pain that are gone as suddenly as they arrive. I ate a McDonald's for lunch. I put it down to that. Now, with the water gushing from me, I'm not so sure. I sit on the couch.

Minnie says, 'Be quiet.' I don't realise I have made any sound. She closes the door. 'My mother will hear you.'

Ed sits on the couch beside me. 'Is Kat OK?' he asks Minnie.

Minnie says, 'Don't worry, Ed.' She grabs my hand and tries to pull me up. 'Kat's just got a pain in her tummy. I'll take her to my room.'

Ed says, 'I'll go and tell my mammy,' and Minnie runs after him while I wrestle with another pain. It hurts more than the last one.

Minnie says, 'Shut up, would you?' She's got Ed in a headlock. He's struggling but he doesn't say anything, which means he's scared.

I say, 'Let him go,' when the pain loosens its grip.

Minnie says, 'He'll tell your mam.' Ed begins to cry. He doesn't cry often but when he does, he lifts the roof of the house. I feel a kind of relief. Resignation. Ed will tell Mum and she will come and she'll know what to do.

The next pain terrifies me. Up to now, the most painful thing that ever happened to me was getting my finger caught in the hinge of the hood of my doll's pram.

'Help me, Minnie.' I think I shout it.

Ed looks as scared as I feel. He struggles out of Minnie's grip and runs out of the room. For once, Minnie looks unsure.

I say, 'What will I do?'

Minnie shakes her head. 'I don't know,' she says. That's the first time she's ever said that.

I hear the sound of footsteps coming down the hall. I know it is Minnie's mother. It's the plink-plink of her stilettos against the floor that gives her away. No matter how many babies she holds in her arms, she insists on high heels. She says they're all she has left, whatever that means.

'Girls?' she calls as she approaches. 'Minnie?

Kat? What's going o — ' I look up. She stands in the doorway, looking at me. Her mouth is a circle of shock. Her hands fly to her face.

'Jesus, Mary and Joseph,' she whispers.

I begin to cry.

We're in a café that's called the Cream Bun, which is a pretty good name for a café but not as good as the Funky Banana. The Christmas tree is a silver, artificial one with flashing lights. If you're going to put a Christmas tree up this early, you'd better make sure it's artificial. Otherwise, it'll be long dead by the time Christmas comes around.

They don't have banana muffins so I just get an apple and cinnamon one, which happens to be my second favourite. It's good, but there's icing on the top. Muffins aren't supposed to have icing on the top.

I don't order the hot chocolate with the marshmallows because it's three euro and twenty cents. I haven't changed my one hundred and thirty-six pounds and fifteen pence into euro yet and I don't know how much money Faith brought with her. I know she's in a band and everything, but I don't think she makes very much money. It's not that they're no good or anything. It's just that no one's ever heard of them and their songs aren't on the radio yet. When their songs are on the radio, I expect Faith will have more money for hot chocolates. I ask for a glass of water and when the man says, 'Sparkling or still?' I just say, 'From the tap, please.'

Right about now I'm missing maths, which is fine by me, but in twenty minutes, I'm supposed to be in the library with Carla. It's our turn to help Miss

Rintoole tidy up and put the books where they're supposed to be. The library is just a classroom really. And Miss Rintoole is not a real librarian. She's a teacher who happens to be in charge of the library. Miss Williams always gets me and Carla to do jobs together, like bringing books to the office to get photocopies. Carla's got one of those laughs that make no sound, which is probably why she never gets in trouble. Her hair is very long. She can sit on the ends of it when it's not in plaits. She looks a bit like Pocahontas, when her hair's in plaits. And she never wears anything but jeans. She was the only girl wearing jeans at Stephanie Nugent's party. Stephanie's mam said it wasn't fair to leave people out so she had to invite everyone. Even George Pullman.

Faith says, 'You're miles away. What are you thinking about?'

I say, 'Nothing.' If I tell her about Carla, Faith will think that Carla is my girlfriend, because that's what adults say when a boy happens to be friends with a girl who happens to be in his class.

Faith says, 'You never tell me anything anymore.' She's sort of smiling but I think she's being pretty serious too.

I say, 'I do so,' even though I don't. Not really. Not anymore. Because Faith is sort of a bit like Mam now. Like, she's supposed to make me my dinner and make sure I brush my teeth and check that there's no dirt under my fingernails and that I say 'please' and 'thank you' when I'm talking to adults. Stuff like that.

Before, I might have told her about Carla. Not that there's anything to tell, exactly. I might have said something about me liking Carla, not because she's a girl or anything but because she happens to be a pretty interesting person when you think about it. She knows a lot about the Big Bang.

Faith looks at her phone again. It hasn't rung or beeped since she left the note in the letterbox but she keeps checking it as if it has.

So I say, 'I was thinking about school.'

'What about it?'

'Me and Carla usually help in the library on Tuesdays. Just before break.'

'Carla?'

'Yeah.'

'Is she your friend?'

'She's in my class.'

'Is she your girlfriend?' See what I mean?

I shake my head.

Faith checks her phone.

Before Faith goes to the loo — she calls it the Ladies — she checks her phone again. It hasn't made one single sound since the last time she checked it.

Then, the minute she's gone, her phone starts to ring. If Mam were here, she'd say, 'Typical!'

Ed says, 'Kat, do you think the baby will mind that I have Down's?'

I say, 'She's not a baby. She's twenty-four.'

Ed says, 'Is she ten years younger than me, Kat?'

'Yes.'

'So that means I was ten when she was born.'

'Yes.'

'I don't remember seeing her when I was ten.'

'You didn't see her.'

'Did you see her?'

'Not really.'

'That must have made you sad.'

Ed and I are ice-skating in Smithfield. Well, Ed is ice-skating. I stand outside the rink, on the green felt that is reserved for anxious parents so that they can watch their offspring wobble round the rink.

I am not anxious. Not about Ed ice-skating, at any rate. He loves falling as much as he loves skating. He has no fear of falling, which sets him apart from any of the other adults on the ice. He falls in a tumble of arms and legs and ends up skidding, on his knees, sending up ice like a flurry of snow. This sets him off. He laughs like a group of people laughing. It's loud. And pretty traditional. He actually uses

291

the words: 'Hahahahahahaha!' When you hear him laugh, you'll laugh. Even if you're like me and not given to outbursts of laughter. And it's not because I'm humourless. It's just that things are rarely all that funny.

This is our December tradition. We always come here as soon as it opens on the first of December, to avoid the Christmas crowds. We've been doing it for years. Just me and Ed. Ed has never invited Sophie. I have never asked Minnie. Although, last year, Ed suggested that Thomas might come. And last year, Thomas asked me if he could come. I told Ed that Thomas couldn't come because he was working. And I told Thomas that he couldn't come because Ed would prefer if it was just the two of us. Just me and Ed.

Ed said, 'That's a shame.'

Thomas said, 'I see,' looking at me like he knew everything. Then he said, 'Maybe next year.' And for a moment back then, I thought: yeah. Maybe. Why not? Why not next year? And I shrugged my shoulders as if I wasn't thinking that and I said, 'Maybe,' and then I stopped walking and I grabbed his arm so he had to stop too. We were on Dollymount Strand that day doing one of those unbelievably long walks that Thomas was so fond of. I suppose I got used to them in the end. I might even have enjoyed some of them. And he said, 'What?' And I said, 'Nothing.' But I think he sort of knew what was going on inside my head because he bent down and stuck his face in front of mine and kissed me in that offhand way he had. Without touching me. He had no form whatsoever. No style at all. I don't know why I liked it so much. The way he kissed me. Then, only because he knew I wasn't a sand-dune kind of woman, he suggested we go straight to my apartment for a matinee performance of *Grey's Anatomy*. I said, 'OK.'

Ed says, 'Did it, Kat?'

I say, 'What?'

'Did it make you sad? When you didn't get to see Faith?'

I don't answer quickly enough because Ed shoots off, shouting, 'Time me,' over his shoulder as he scorches his way up one side of the rink and down the other.

I say, 'Twenty seconds.'

He says, 'That's my fastest time, Kat.'

'No it's not. You did it in nineteen the year before last.'

The woman standing beside me looks at me. She has a white face and a long narrow nose with a red tip — a testament to the bitterness of the day. If her face wasn't so frozen solid with the cold, it would have an expression that I have seen before. A 'have a bit of compassion' expression. A 'give the mentally handicapped man a break' expression.

I see off her look with a matching one of my own, except that mine is more of a 'mind your own bloody patronising business' kind of an expression. She looks away.

Ed is sulking. I know he is because his bottom lip sticks out.

I say, 'Go on, try again. If you did it in nineteen seconds the year before last, you can do

293

it in nineteen seconds now.'

Ed says, 'I can't do it any faster.'

I say, 'You can.'

He pushes himself off the wall and goes again. Nineteen seconds around the rink.

I say, 'See? I told you you could do it.'

Ed can't respond because he is bent over the wall, panting hard.

I put my hand round his arm. 'Ed?'

He shakes his head.

'Ed? Are you all right? Do you want to sit down?' I bend so I can see his face, which is brick red. His eyes are shut. Maybe Thomas was right. But the tests from the hospital were good the last time. So long as he keeps taking the medication.

'Ed?'

When he straightens, his bottom lip is not sticking out anymore. It is curved in a smile. 'I did it!' he says, when he catches his breath.

I smile. 'I told you you could do it. Come on.' When he steps off the ice, I take his hand. He's great on the ice but inexplicably unsteady on level, non-slippy ground when he's got the skates on. 'Let's go and get some lunch.' I want red wine and a packet of cigarettes but Ed will want a main course and dessert. The doctor told him to watch his weight but it's like telling Gordon Ramsay not to shout in a kitchen.

We take a cab to the Guinness Storehouse, which is one of Ed's favourite places. He loves the glass lift that goes to the top. He says it's like the lift in *Charlie and the Chocolate Factory*, which is one of his favourite books-made-into-films films. I love the views of the city from the bar. The pigeon houses, sturdy and dependable, in their candy stripe, lording it over Dublin Bay.

Already, the lights are coming on around the city, like cats' eyes, getting brighter as the pale light of afternoon drains away. I drink red wine, which is frowned on at the Guinness Storehouse, but not forbidden. I like the aesthetics of a pint of Guinness. The intricacy of the pour. The angle of the glass below the tap. The pause near the top to allow the stout to settle. The ceremony. I like that. It's the taste of it I object to. Ed drinks a glass of it, sweetened with blackcurrant.

In the restaurant, Ed eats Guinness and beef stew. He orders the same thing everywhere we go. The chicken wings in Elephant and Castle. The mussels in the Winding Stair. The profiteroles in the Talbot 101. And, of course, the lean-on-me pizza in the Leaning Tower of Pizza. He never deviates. He is a comforting restaurant companion. For a week after payday, Ed insists on paying. He says, 'I'll get this,' when the waitress brings the bill in a leather wallet and hands it to me. He reaches across the table with his big smile and takes the wallet and says, 'I'll get this.' He pays in cash. He has a laser card but he likes the heft of his wallet when there are notes inside. He leaves a tip. A big one. He winks at the waitress and says, 'Keep the change,' when she returns to the table.

Adults don't look at Ed. Not really. Children do. They look and they listen and then they turn to their mothers or fathers or childminders and they say, 'Why is that man talking like that?' And they are pulled away by their thin little arms and told to ssshhhh or be quiet or stop staring and they don't know why, and so they grow into adults who don't look at people like Ed.

Thomas says, 'Not everyone is like that.' He likes to see the good in people.

Ed says, 'I got Faith a present.'

When I don't answer, he says, 'Do you want to see it?' He unzips the pocket of his anorak, digs his hand in and pulls out a square blue box, a little creased and dented at the edges. He undoes the pale pink ribbon that is tied round the box and lifts the lid. His movements are slow, careful. His tongue, trapped between his front teeth, pokes out of his mouth in concentration.

The necklace is a silver one with a plaque that reads 'Faith', in old Irish script. When you see necklaces like these, dangling from a stand in a tourist shop with every name you can think of engraved along their plaques, you think nothing of them. Or if you do, you think they are cheap and tacky.

Perhaps it is the box. The careful way that Ed handles the box. Or the way the necklace nestles inside the box, on a cloud of cotton wool. Or perhaps it is because the necklace is on its own and not jostling for position, dangling from a stand in a tourist shop with all the others. Maybe it's the engraving on the other side of the plaque. The one that says 'Love from Uncle Ed'.

After a while, I say, 'It's lovely.' My tone is brisk. Economical.

Ed says, 'I know.'

I put my glass down and cover his hand with mine.

'What's wrong, Kat?'

'I'm scared.' I didn't know I was going to say that.

Ed looks around the restaurant. He turns back to me. 'There's nothing there, Kat. Nothing to be scared of.'

I nod. 'I know.'

'You're being silly.'

'I know.'

'Why are you crying?'

'I'm not.'

'You are.'

I grab a napkin and press it against my eyes. 'I think I'm getting a cold.' My voice sounds like someone is squeezing their hands round my throat. Ed looks worried and the doctor said he wasn't to worry. No worry. No stress. No fried foods. Things like that are bad for his condition. I clear my throat. Put the napkin down. Straighten in my seat.

Ed says, 'Do you think Faith won't like you? Is that what you're scared of? Because you don't have a present for her?'

I nod.

Ed says, 'She will like you, Kat. You're the best.'

I stand up. 'We should go.'

Afterwards, when I drop him home, Ed runs round to my side of the car and knocks on the window so I have to lower it. It's cold enough to snow. He leans in and hugs me. I'm not mad about hugging but Ed is pretty good at it.

Especially when it's cold. He's always warm.

He pulls away then and looks at me. He looks at me like I am someone good. When he looks at me like that, I nearly believe it. Just for a moment. And then he smiles and turns. I stay like I always do. I stay until he opens the door and gives me one more wave and disappears into the house.

I'm most of the way home when the phone rings. 'Hello?'

'Kat? It's Dad.' Which is strange because he never rings.

'Is Ed OK?'

'You need to come back here. Straight away.'

I pick up Faith's phone. A number flashes on the screen. A landline number. It's not a number that I recognise. It doesn't look like it's from Brighton, the number. It's only got about three more rings before it goes onto voicemail. Not enough time to run into the girls' toilets and get her. If I was allowed to go into the girls' toilets, which I'm not.

Two more rings.

Faith will probably kill me if I answer it. But then she might be mad if I don't answer it. It might be important. It could be her real mam. Her birth mam. Ringing to say that she got Faith's note and that she's sorry about before but she'd like to meet up and bring us to a dead fancy restaurant for our dinner. She'll probably try to get us to eat lobster. That's the kind of stuff they serve in fancy restaurants. I hate lobster, even though I've never eaten one. It looks like it might still be alive.

One more ring.

Maybe it's Rob? Maybe he followed us to Dublin and he's ringing from a public phone box because his mobile ran out of battery or something? He's ringing to say he's sorry for fighting again and he wants Faith to come on the tour with the Crowns. I think Rob is wrong about Faith. I don't think she's changed. She just has to do stuff now that she didn't have to do before, but, apart from that, she's pretty much the same. She still watches *EastEnders* and practises her violin and listens to music on her iPod.

I pick up the phone.

I say, 'Hello?'

'Oh . . . hello. I was . . . I was looking for Faith. Faith McIntyre?'

'Who are you?' It doesn't sound like a birth mother. Or Rob.

'I'm, er . . . My name is Kenneth. I mean Leonard.'

That's a pretty weird answer, when you stop and think about it. I should probably hang up.

'You must be Milo.'

'How do you know that?'

'It was in the note.'

'Oh.'

There's silence for a while. I think he's thinking about what he's going to say next.

I say, 'Are you Faith's birth father?' I don't know if that's a proper word, to be honest.

'No, I'm her . . . her birth grandfather.'

'Oh.' It must be a proper word, after all.

He says, 'I was wondering . . . if I could speak with Faith. Is she there?'

I say, 'No, she's not.'

'Oh. I see.'

'She's in the toi — in the Ladies.'

'Oh. I see.'

'But she's been in there for ages so I don't think she'll be too much longer.'

'I could phone back.'

'I expect she'll be out in a second. She's probably just putting her make-up on again.'

'Er, fine then. I'll . . . I'll wait. Are you . . . are you still in the area?'

'What area?'

'Near our house. Faith left a note. In the letterbox.'

I say, 'We're in a café.' I don't say the name of it. I don't say, 'We're in the Cream Bun.'

Faith comes out of the toilet. She has brushed her hair and put on more lipstick. I know because there's a little bit on her front tooth. I think it would taste awful, if you had to kiss a girl who was wearing lipstick.

I say, 'She's here now.'

The man says, 'Oh. Good. Good,' even though his voice doesn't sound like the voice of someone who thinks things are good.

Faith says, 'What are you doing with my phone?'

I say, 'It's your birth grandfather.'

Faith doesn't say anything. She sits down.

The grandfather says, 'Is she OK? Will she talk to me? Could you put her on?'

I hold out the phone to Faith but she shakes her head. I press the phone against my ear again. There is silence down the phone and then the grandfather says, 'I could come and pick you both up. Bring you up to the house. Would that be an idea?'

I say, 'Hold on a minute.' I put the phone on the table beside us and say, in a whisper, 'He wants to come and collect us. In his car, I think. He wants to take us to his house.'

Faith doesn't nod or shake her head. She just sits there. She might be thinking about something but it's hard to tell.

I pick up the phone again but I'm not sure what to say so I just ask, 'What kind of a car do you have?'

Faith gives me one of her looks. It means that question is not appropriate. I don't see why not.

301

'Er, it's a Lexus. Past its sell-by date now, I'm afraid. Like myself, I suppose.' He sort of laughs as if he's said something funny.

Then he says, 'So, what does Faith think? Should I come and pick you up?'

I look at Faith. She's stirring her spoon round and round the cup.

I say, 'I don't know.'

He says, 'That's all right. You're in a café, you said?'

'Yes. I'm having an apple and cinnamon muffin because they don't have any banana muffins, which happen to be my favourite ones.'

'I like banana ones too.'

'They're dead easy to make.'

'Oh. Do you bake?'

'Not really anymore. I used to. My mam showed me. It's not that hard. You just have to be dead careful with the measurements and the oven temperature.'

Now Faith is looking at me. She is shaking her head. She takes the phone out of my hand. Holds it to her ear. Says, 'Who is this?'

After a while, she says, 'Look, I'm sorry, I shouldn't have come. I just . . . I shouldn't have come.'

And then she hangs up.

I say, 'Are we going back to his house?'

She shakes her head.

'What are we going to do then?'

She shrugs her shoulders. We sit there. I lick my finger and use it to pick crumbs off my plate until there are none left. I look at my watch. We've been here for forty-five minutes. The waitress comes and picks up the plate. She asks Faith if she's finished with her coffee and Faith nods, even though it's nearly half full. Mam said that if you're an optimist, you'd say,

302

half full. I think Faith would call it half empty now.

I wonder if something will happen. I think it's going to turn into the kind of day where nothing much happens.

And then, all of a sudden, something does happen.

A car pulls up outside the café. A big car. It's dead shiny and clean. I bet the boot opens by itself. George Pullman's dad has a car like that and the boot opens by itself. I think you have to press a button first and then it opens, all by itself.

The driver's door opens and a man gets out and I get this feeling inside me. I know, nearly for sure, that it's the man from the phone. The grandfather. For starters, he looks like a grandfather. He's probably around eighty or something and his hair is grey and he's wearing one of those caps that grandfathers wear. Damo's granddad has one. He stands outside, on the pavement, and stares into the café like he's looking for someone. Us, probably. And he looks kind of expensive, like the sort of man who would live in a mansion with maybe ten bedrooms. I don't know why. I think it's because he wears his scarf like a tie round his neck and he has a coat that goes right down past his knees instead of a jacket with a hood.

I look at Faith to see if she's noticed but she's still fiddling with her phone. I think she's texting Ant, maybe. Or Adrian.

I look back at the man and now he's looking straight at us, and he walks to the door and he opens it and now he's inside the café, still looking straight at us.

The waitress sees him and says, 'Howeya, Ken.'

The man says, 'Hello, Eileen.' His voice is serious,

like a newsreader on the telly. He's at our table now. Faith looks up.

He says, 'Excuse me.'

Faith says, 'Yes?'

He says, 'I'm Leonard. Leonard Kavanagh.' He holds out his hand but Faith doesn't shake it like you're supposed to. She stares at him.

He looks at me and says, 'You must be Milo.' He reaches out his hand to me and I shake it like you're supposed to. Firm and brief. His hand is huge.

I open my mouth to say something except I don't know what and that's when the man looks at Faith and says, 'And you're Faith. I'd know you anywhere.'

If.

If I hadn't answered the phone.

Or if I'd left my phone at home.

Or if the phone had been in the bottom of my handbag instead of on the hands-free set.

If I hadn't heard it.

If I'd turned it off.

If I could go back.

Not just to the phone ringing and me answering it.

But back.

All the way back.

Everything would be different.

Nothing would be the same.

And this conversation would never have happened.

Dad says, 'No, don't worry, Ed is fine. He's in the house. He's . . . he's in great form. He's playing Super Mario.'

I say, 'He must be winning, so. Who's he playing with? Sophie?'

Dad says, 'Well, no. That's what I'm ringing about, actually.'

Maybe there's something the matter with Sophie? 'Is Sophie OK?'

'Yes, yes, she's fine. At least, I'm sure Sophie is fine. I haven't seen her today.'

This is why my father never rings me. Never rings anyone. He is unable to communicate on the phone. You have to be direct with him. In the end, I have to say, 'Why are you ringing me?'

'Faith is here.'

I'm stopped at a red light. It's like the whole world is stopped at the red light. Nothing moves. Everything dims round the edges. Quietens.

'Kat? . . . Kat, are you there? . . . Say something, for God's sake.'

I jump when the car horns blare. The lights have turned green.

'Kat?'

A car swerves out from behind. Overtakes. The driver shouts at me. I know he is shouting because of his face. The colour of it. The wild gesture of his hand. The shape of his mouth.

I sit there.

'Kat? Are you there?'

I put on my hazard lights. The line of cars behind overtake, one by one.

'For God's sake, Kat, bloody say something.' My father's whisper is like a shout. It would be a shout except someone is there. He can't shout in front of visitors. Nice people don't shout in front of visitors.

The lights change from green to amber. Now they're red again.

'Dad?'

'Look, Kat, I know this is a shock.'

The pedestrian lights are green now. A woman crosses the road, wheeling a pram. The hood is up. You can't see the baby.

He says, 'Are you in the car?'

'Yes.'

'Good. That's good. You can drive. You can drive over to the house.'

'Why?'

'What do you mean, why? Because they're here. They're in the house. You need to come over.'

'No.'

'No?'

'No.'

'Kat?'

'I can't.'

'You can. Of course you can.'

The lights turn green again. The horns blare and the cars overtake.

I don't look at them as they pass by so I can't be sure about their hands. Gesturing. That's what I'd do.

The hazard lights blink.

On.

Off.

On.

Off.

'Kat?'

The hands gripping the wheel don't feel like my hands. I can't feel them. I can't feel anything.

'Listen to me, love. That young girl has come all the way from Brighton to meet you. You have to come.'

'I can't. I just can't. I'm sorry. I have to go.'

'Kat, please, don't hang up.'

I hang up.

The lights turn red.

Faith's birth grandfather's house is legend. I don't know if it has ten bedrooms because I haven't counted all of them but I bet it does. I reckon Faith's granny and granddad are bookworms because there're bookshelves in every room I've been in so far, which is four. Some of the books are really old and look like they might fall apart if you touch them. If Mam were here, she'd say, 'Don't even think about it, Milo.' It's too cold to go into the back garden, which is a pity because there are two orchards out there. Ed says his dad grows tomatoes and apples and pears in one of them but the other one has nothing but orchids. He says his mam loves orchids but they're really hard to grow and sometimes they die. But the tomatoes are dead easy. Ed says some of them grow as big as baseballs. I've never played baseball. He says his dad makes tomato juice because Kat loves Bloody Marys. Whatever they are.

There's a room called a den and that's where me and Ed are. We're playing Mario Kart. He's got a Wii. I tell him I'm saving up for a PlayStation 3. Ed lets me be Mario. He says he doesn't mind being Luigi. He's winning but it's only because he practises every single day. He said so.

When I finish the third lap of Luigi's Mansion, I say, 'How old are you?'

Ed says, 'Thirty-four.'

I don't think Ed is thirty-four because that's middle-aged.

We look at the results and then Ed presses Start again. He says, 'How old are you?'

I say, 'I'm nine but I'll be ten really soon.'

Ed says, 'What's your mam going to buy you?'

I say, 'WATCH OUT!' because Bowser is about to overtake him.

Ed moves his whole body when he's playing. Like he's right inside the game. That would be cool. To be right inside the game.

After a while, I say, 'I go to lifesaving class. Back in Brighton, I mean.'

Ed says, 'What's that?'

'It's like swimming only you get to rescue people who are drowning. And you get to do CPR on them.'

'What's CPR?'

'It's like the kiss of life.'

Ed laughs. I think it's because I said 'kiss'. Damo laughs too, when I say that. He says it would be legend to do CPR on a girl but he'd never do it to a boy. I say, 'What about if a boy was drowning?' but Damo just says, 'Tough nuts.'

Ed says, 'I go to swimming classes too. Kat brings me. I'm great at swimming. I came second last time.'

'Is Kat your sister?'

'Yeah. She's brilliant. She brings me swimming and loads of other places too.'

'Why'd you call her Kat?'

'Because that's her name.'

'Oh.'

'Kat is Faith's mother.'

'Her birth mother.'

'What's that?'

'I'm not sure.'

The walls of the den are covered in framed photographs. Ed is in most of them.

'Who's that?' I point to a picture of Ed, holding up a medal. He's standing between a man and a woman beside a swimming pool. The woman looks like Faith, except she's old. She's got the same black hair and the same green eyes and the same white skin. She's smiling like Faith used to. She's got her arms round Ed.

Ed says, 'That's Kat and me and Thomas. I only came third that time. I had a cold.'

'Is Thomas Kat's husband?'

Ed says. 'He's Kat's friend. Except they're not friends anymore. They had a fight. I'd say they'll make up soon. That's what me and Sophie do, when we fight.'

'Who's Sophie?' Faith calls me 'Twenty Questions' sometimes but I don't think Ed minds. He points to a photograph of a girl wearing tiny round glasses and a tracksuit. She is holding a medal in her hands but I can't see if it's gold, silver or bronze because the photograph is in black and white. Ed says, 'She's my girlfriend,' but I don't ask if he French-kisses her, like Damo would.

Ed says, 'She's got Down's Syndrome too.'

I say, 'What's Down's Syndrome?'

Ed says, 'I'm not sure.'

The grandfather says, 'Boys, come down for something to eat.'

I'm starving. We forgot to have lunch, me and Faith. Well, I had an apple and cinnamon muffin with icing on the top but that doesn't count.

The table is like a table in a restaurant. It's really long so you keep having to ask people to pass this and

310

pass that. There are napkins that are not kitchen roll. And there's a glass beside my plate. A proper glass, that will break if I drop it.

Faith is sitting across from Leonard and his wife, whose name is Janet. I know because she said, 'Call me Janet,' when I arrived.

The grandfather says, 'And what genre of music does your band play, Faith?'

'Well, I suppose you could call it garage rock.'

'Oh. Is that a bit like rock and roll?'

'Sort of.'

Ed sits down and looks at his plate. 'I don't like fish.'

The grandfather says, 'It's good for your heart.'

Janet turns to Faith. 'Do you write your own songs?'

Faith nods. 'Some of them.'

Janet picks up her knife and fork. 'I write too.'

The grandfather says, 'Ah, yes, so does Kat, as a matter of fact. She's a technical writer, you know. For a company in Cork.'

Faith says, 'A technical writer?' like she's never heard of it, which is good because I've never heard of it either.

Janet cuts a green bean in four even pieces and spears one of the pieces with her fork. 'Yes, well, we're not entirely sure what that means, exactly, but it's something to do with instruction manuals for appliances. Dishwashers and tumble-dryers. That sort of thing.'

The grandfather gets up. 'I'll try her again quickly. Before we eat.' He leaves the room.

I don't like fish either, unless you count fish fingers. Mam always said they were more finger than fish.

Janet looks sort of like a ballerina. She's got a bun

311

and she's dead skinny for a granny. I don't have any grannies but I've seen other people's grannies and they're usually pretty fat, no offence.

You never see fat ballerinas on the telly. They're like matchstick people that kids draw. A line for their bodies. Janet is like that. She's quiet too. Even when she talks, she's quiet.

She says, 'So, er, Milo. What class are you in?'

'Year five,' and I get ready to tell her what my favourite subject is (science) and who my best friend is (Damo), except I won't say 'Damo', I'll say 'Damien Sullivan'. That's usually the kind of stuff adults want to know.

But she doesn't ask me any of that. She takes a drink of water. The bones in her neck stick out when she swallows. I know I'm not supposed to stare but it's hard sometimes.

The grandfather comes back. Sits down. Janet asks Ed to say Grace and he says, 'GRACE!' and roars laughing, and so do I because it's pretty funny when you think about it. Faith gives me daggers and Janet says, 'EDWARD!' and then everybody starts eating their dinner and nobody says anything for a while.

Then, the grandfather says, 'I've left another message for Kat. I'd say she's . . . ' He looks at his watch. 'Well, she should be home by now but she could have been delayed. The traffic . . . it can be bad at this time of the day. Any time of the day, really.'

I think he's talking to Faith. She puts her knife and fork on her plate the way people do when they've finished eating, except I don't think she's eaten anything yet. I'm nearly finished. The fish isn't all that bad.

He pours wine into Faith's glass. She shakes her

head and says, 'No, thank you.'

He stops pouring. Puts the bottle down. He says, 'Are you all right, my dear?'

Faith nods her head.

He says, 'Look, I know this isn't easy but when Kat gets here . . . '

Faith says, 'She's not coming. I know she's not coming. She didn't make contact with me before. Why should she bother now?'

I don't know the answers to any of those questions so I don't say anything. I don't think anybody else knows either. It's pretty quiet round the table.

Faith says, 'If my . . . my adoptive mother hadn't died, I would never have known. About Kat. Katherine. Whatever you call her. I would never have known. Would I?'

Then she changes her mind about the wine because she picks up the bottle and pours it into her glass. Right up to the top. She takes a big, long drink out of it. When she puts her glass back on the table, she has wine stains at the top of her mouth, like fangs.

The grandfather picks up his napkin. Wipes his mouth, even though there are no wine fangs at the top of his. He says, 'I . . . I don't know, Faith. I'm sorry. I can't speak for Kat. But I know that she will regret not coming here today. She's just . . . ' He looks at his wife but she keeps chewing and chewing and chewing and not looking back at him. I've never seen anyone chew as much as she does. I really haven't.

The grandfather looks at Faith again. 'She just needs a bit of time, that's all. It's been a bit of a shock for her, I suppose.'

Faith says, 'It's been a bit of a shock for me too.' Her voice sounds funny. High and tight. I cross my fingers and toes. I know Faith wouldn't want to cry. Especially not in front of strangers.

Leonard says, 'Of course, of course, I'm sorry, I didn't mean . . . I'm sorry.'

No one says anything. There's just silence. Even Janet has stopped chewing. Ed has finished his dinner and has left the table. I don't know where he's gone. I want to finish my dinner so I can leave the table too but I don't want to make any noise. That's how quiet everything is. Even my breathing sounds loud.

After a while, Faith looks up. She looks at Janet. She says, 'Why don't you say something?' Her voice is mostly back to normal. I keep my fingers crossed, though. Just in case.

Janet takes a long time to answer. Finally, she says, 'That's the thing, Faith. We've never really said anything. Afterwards, I mean. Katherine was fifteen years old. She was just a girl. Things were different then. I thought . . . ' She nods at the grandfather. 'We all thought . . . it was for the best.'

The grandfather puts his hand on top of Janet's.

Janet says, 'It takes Katherine a good while to come round to things. Even when she was a child. It took her ages to get over starting school. Mrs Higginbotham said she cried every morning for a year and a half. And after that, well, I suppose she just got used to it.'

I want to know who Mrs Higginbotham is, but I don't ask.

That's when Ed bursts into the room. Janet looks up and says, 'You have parsley sauce on your chin, Edward.'

My napkin is folded on the table beside me so I pick it up and shake it out and use it to wipe round my mouth. I don't think I have parsley sauce on my chin but you can never be sure.

Ed wipes his chin with his hand. His face is really red, like he's done something embarrassing, which he hasn't, as far as I can tell. He keeps on walking until he reaches Faith. He says, 'I got you a present.' He takes a squashed blue box out of his pocket and he puts it on the table. He says, 'You're not supposed to open it yet,' but he doesn't say when you are supposed to open it.

Faith looks at the box and says, 'Why did you get me a present?' instead of just saying, 'Thank you,' like you're supposed to.

Ed says, 'Because I'm your uncle. I'm your Uncle Ed.'

And then Faith remembers and she says, 'Thank you.' Her voice is so quiet it's nearly a whisper but I think Ed hears her because he smiles and Faith smiles back and, for a moment, everything feels dead nice.

I can't help thinking about dessert. It looks like the kind of house where there might be dessert. And I don't mean just biscuits or Mars bars. I mean proper dessert. Like pavlova. I love pavlova. Mam said it was because she ate buckets of it when I was in her belly, waiting to be born.

Leonard looks at me just then and there's a chance that he could be a mind-reader because he says, 'Dessert!' Just like that.

Faith says, 'No, we should go.'

Leonard says, 'Stay a little longer, Faith. I'm sure Milo would like some dessert.' He looks at me and smiles. He has one of those smiles that end up all over his face. 'Wouldn't you, lad?'

I say, 'Is it pavlova?' Faith catches my eye and glares at me, which means that I'm not supposed to ask that

315

question. It's hard to remember everything.

Ed shouts, 'Vienetta!' and he runs into the kitchen and comes back with a gigantic box of Vienetta that hasn't even been opened yet. It's not as good as pavlova but it's still pretty good because it's chocolate and ice cream, all mixed up together.

Ed gets a bit shy when he talks to Faith. He says, 'Would you like some?' in a dead polite voice.

Faith says, 'No, thank you,' but then Ed looks really disappointed so Faith says, 'Actually, I will have a slice. Just a small one, please,' and that makes Ed smile again. I don't know why. I'd be happier if no one else had any. Then there'd be more for me.

I'm much quicker eating dessert than dinner. When I'm finished, I want to lick my plate, but you're not supposed to when you're in someone else's house. I wipe the ice cream off the plate with my finger when no one is looking.

Faith says, 'No, thank you,' to coffee and tea. She catches my eye. I go and get our coats.

The grandfather says, 'I could drive you over to Kat's apartment? It's not far. You'd have time. Before your flight.'

Faith says, 'Thank you for your hospitality,' just like Mam told us to do. Janet nods her head. She's the only one who hasn't finished her dessert. I wonder if she's going to be able to eat it all. She doesn't look like someone with a huge amount of room in her stomach. Faith moves towards the door.

Ed says, 'Can't Milo stay? Just for a little bit? We haven't finished the game and he's still got one life left.'

Janet says, 'Say goodbye, Edward.'

The grandfather picks up his car keys and Faith

says, 'We don't need a lift, but thanks all the same.' He puts his car keys back on the table. He doesn't even argue. It's like he already knows that there's no point arguing with Faith.

I say, 'See ya, Ed.'

Ed says, 'See ya, Milo,' and he gives me a gigantic hug that nearly squashes me flat. I can't move my arms. After a really long time, he lets me go and holds up his palm for a high-five. We high-five.

The grandfather shakes my hand. That's twice in one day. Nobody has shaken my hand since the day in the church. Loads of people shook my hand that day. My hand hurt, with all the shaking.

Janet talks to me like I'm an adult or something. She says, 'It was lovely to meet you, Milo.'

In the hall, there's a photograph of Kat and Ed standing in front of a pond. Ed is about my age in the photo, I reckon. Kat has her arms on his shoulders, as if she's worried he might fall in.

Faith sees the photo too. She says, 'Do you have any other children?'

Janet shakes her head. 'No. Just Katherine and Edward.'

Faith says, 'Well, thanks again.' She holds out her hand so that Leonard can shake it, which is weird because he's her granddad when you think about it. Still, he shakes her hand as if he's not her granddad. As if he's just an old man she happened to meet one day.

He says, 'It was so lovely to meet you, Faith. To finally meet you.'

Janet says, 'Yes. It was.'

Leonard says, 'I'll give Kat your phone number. I'm sure she will . . . ' Janet puts her hand on his arm and he stops talking, right in the middle of his sentence.

She turns to Faith and she says, so quietly I can barely hear her, 'I'm so sorry, Faith.'

Faith nods, and I slip my hand inside hers, only because she looks like she could do with warming up. And it's true: her hand is freezing. I hold it as we walk out through the door and down the eight steps to the driveway. It'd be nice to jump them. I bet it would feel almost like flying, jumping from the top of those steps.

When we get to the end of the driveway, I turn round. Janet and the grandfather are still at the door and they wave so I wave back, but Faith doesn't turn round. She just keeps on walking.

# May 1987

The nurse says, 'Bend your knees . . . that's it
. . . Shuffle your feet up. Right up, towards your
bottom . . . that's right . . . As far up as you can
. . . OK, now let your knees fall apart . . . that's
right. Good girl.'

The nurse's head disappears between my legs.
I feel something cold.

'Relax, relax now, like a good girl.' When she
stands up, she peels a pair of latex gloves off her
hands. I see blood on the fingers.

She says, 'All done,' like the woman in
Arnott's when she's fitting me for a new school
tunic. 'That episiotomy is healing nicely.'

I don't know what an episiotomy is. I don't
care. The nurse walks around the cubicle, pulling
the curtain behind her until I'm in plain view
again. I pull the sheet up to my chin.

She says, 'How are you feeling?'

'Fine.'

She writes something on a piece of paper
stuck to a clipboard. 'Let me know if you want to
talk to someone. There are people here you can
talk to.'

'When can I go home?'

'The doctor will talk to you later.'

Three days.

That's how long I have to stay.

Three days.

Nobody comes. Nobody except Mum and Dad.

I say, 'Where's Ed?'

Mum says, 'He can't come. He won't understand.'

Dad says, 'You'll see him when you get home, love.'

I say, 'When can I go home?'

Three days.

That's how long I have to stay.

Three days.

I'm in a room on my own. It smells funny. Like dinner. It smells like dinner. I don't go out of the room, because when you go out of the room all you can hear are babies crying. It's like all the babies in the world are here. In this hospital. And they're all crying. Every single one of them.

I don't know where my clothes are. There's a wardrobe but it's empty. I'm wearing a nightdress that's not mine. It's too big for me. I don't know where it came from. It's not Mum's either. It would swim on her too.

I think about Ed. And Minnie.

Ed will wonder where I am. He cries when I'm not there. He cries like a baby, even though he's ten. He's too old for that kind of crying.

Minnie will say I'm lucky. Because I don't have to do the Inter. Cert. But I'd prefer to be doing the exams. Maths. I'd prefer to be doing the maths exam in the Inter., which is really saying something. Everyone knows I'm thick at maths and I'd fail the exam if I did it. I'd prefer that. What's the big deal anyway? It just means you get to do Lower Level for your Leaving Cert. and that's fine by me. Lower Level maths. It's no skin off my nose.

The nurse says, 'Have you been to the toilet yet?'

'Yes.'

'I mean, have you moved your bowels?'

My face is so hot, it's scorching. I shake my head. The nurse draws the curtains around the bed, pulls a clean pair of gloves on.

She says, 'This won't hurt.'

She says, 'You won't feel a thing.'

She says, 'Try to relax.'

She explains that it's a laxative. It'll make my bowels move. I nod and push my nightdress down over my knees when she's done. She snaps off the gloves.

I get under the sheet. 'When can I go home?'

'As soon as your bowels move.'

I sit on the toilet. There's a bath in here. The nurse said I should take a bath. At least once a day. With lots of salt in it. She leaves a box of salt beside my bed. I don't get in the bath. There are stains along the bottom. They're brown, like rust. Who'd sit in a rusty bath?

I say, 'My bowels moved.'

The nurse looks at me. 'Are you sure?'

'Yes.' It doesn't feel so bad. Lying.

'So can I go home now?'

'Just as soon as the doctor gives you the all-clear.'

I sit on the edge of the bed. She says, 'Are you sure you wouldn't like to talk to someone?'

I shake my head. 'Do you know when the doctor will come?'

She sighs, and rubs her eyes like she's tired. 'He'll be here soon, pet.' When she leaves, she doesn't say goodbye. She thinks I'll be here when she gets back.

The doctor says, 'You're fine.' I nod and smile, like I agree.

'You'll bleed for about six weeks. Wear pads. No tampons.'

I nod. My bag is on the bed. My toothbrush is in the bag.

'So can I go home now?'

The doctor looks at me. Nods. He says, 'After a while, it won't hurt anymore.'

It's dark now. And cold. We don't talk, me and Faith. We just walk. We walk past bus stops, a taxi rank, a train station. Faith walks really fast. She always complains about being out of proportion, because of her legs being so long and her body being so short, but Mam said it would have been worse the other way round, like Dad, for example.

We pass a chip shop. Chip shops in Ireland smell as good as the ones in Brighton and they have batter burgers on the menu too, which I'm not allowed to get on account of them being bad for you. I've had them at Damo's house. His mam doesn't know about them being bad for you.

I don't say anything. I don't ask her where we're going or how long it'll take to get there. I just try to keep up with her until I'm a bit out of breath, like I've swum nearly two lengths of the pool underwater, which I can do but not every time.

Faith stops without letting me know and I bang into the back of her. She sounds like she's swum nearly two lengths underwater too.

She sits on the wall and lights a cigarette. The smoke passes over me like a cloud and I try not to breathe it in, because if you breathe it in you could get cancer and die. I sit on the wall too. I feel dead hot. Once, I had a temperature of a hundred and three and I didn't even dip the thermometer into a mug of tea, like Damo did.

The good thing about smoking is that it calms people down. Faith's not breathing funny anymore.

She says, 'Go on.'

I say, 'What?'

She says, 'Go on and ask me. Whatever it is you want to ask me.'

'I don't have anything to ask you.'

'I won't mind.'

She doesn't sound like she'll mind if I start asking her stuff. She just sounds tired.

I say, 'I have two things to ask.'

Faith looks at me. 'Go ahead.'

I say, 'The first thing I want to know is, where are we going?'

'What's the second thing?'

'Don't you want to answer the first question first?'

'No, I want to know what I'm dealing with.'

'OK then. The second question's going to be, how long will it take us to get there?'

Faith nods and puts the cigarette in her mouth for ages, which means that even more smoke is going into her lungs. Afterwards, she throws the butt on the ground, even though it's not even half finished yet. Mam would call that a waste. I'd only call it a waste if it was a Mars Duo or something. I stamp on it until it goes out.

Faith says, 'We're going home.'

'Home home? Or back to Auntie May's?'

'Home home.' She doesn't say how long it'll take to get there. Instead, she turns away from me and she stares at the wall, as if there's something dead interesting on it. A spider, maybe. Or a cockroach. But I don't think she's looking at anything interesting. I think she's crying. Her shoulders are moving up and down. She's either crying or laughing but I think she's crying. Nothing funny has happened so far.

I look around. There's a bus stop with two old ladies standing at it, which means that a bus will be coming soon. I say, 'Wait there,' to Faith and she doesn't turn round but she nods so I know she heard me and she's going to wait there, just like I said. It feels weird being in charge. This is the way adults must feel most of the time.

I ask one of the old ladies if the bus is coming soon and if it goes to Busaras in the city centre. She's about the same size as me. I think maybe people stop growing when they are adults and then, after a while, when they get really old, they start getting smaller and smaller until they are as small as kids.

When the old lady smiles, her eyes disappear. Now her face looks like it has only a nose and a mouth and zillions of lines where her eyes used to be.

The old lady says, 'You can take any of them from this stop, young fella. They're all headin' the one way. Like the rest of us, wha'?' She whacks the other old lady on the arm with her handbag and the pair of them cackle, like the hens at the petting zoo in Brighton. I don't really get it but I laugh along because Mam always said that you should be polite to old people. I suppose it's because they're so old and they might die any minute.

I walk back to Faith and tell her about the bus. She nods and says, 'Thank you, Milo.' She leans against the wall and closes her eyes.

We wait for the bus.

Coming up the road is a woman with a boy. The boy is six or seven, I reckon. The woman is his mam.

You can tell by the way she walks ahead of him and then stops and looks back and waits for him to catch up. The boy is holding a string and the string is attached to a balloon. One of those helium balloons you sometimes get at posh kids' parties. The balloon is red and because the evening is so cold and dark you really notice it, that balloon. The way it sort of dances at the end of the string. And the colour too. A really bright red, like a fire engine. The boy is holding the string in one hand and an ice-cream cone in the other. Adults always wonder how kids can eat ice cream in the wintertime, but it tastes exactly the same as it does in the summertime.

The mam takes a tissue out of her pocket and walks back to the kid. She bends so she can wipe the melted ice cream off his hands. She wipes his face too, even though there's no ice cream on his face.

That's when he lets go of the string.

That's when the balloon floats away.

It's funny how quickly balloons can float. One minute, they're right there. Right beside you. And the next, they're gone. All you can see is a little circle of red in the dirty grey of the sky. You can hardly see the string anymore.

The kid is crying now. He cries really loudly for his size. His mouth is open and his tongue is white, on account of the ice cream.

I look away. I wouldn't want people looking at me if I was crying like that, in the middle of the street.

I look at the balloon instead. I wonder where it'll end up. England, maybe. It'll never come back here, that's for sure. Not unless the wind changes direction, and even if it does, I bet it'll be burst by then.

The kid has stopped crying now. His mam wraps a

tissue round the cone and hands it back to him. She says something. I don't know what. But it must be something nice cos the kid smiles.

If I rubbed a lamp right now and a genie appeared and granted me a wish, I'd wish that Mam were here. If she were here, I know I'd be wearing a warmer coat. She was always going on about wrapping up if it was cold out. Perishing. That's what she called it.

It's perishing outside, so it is. Wrap up warm, Milo, there's a good lad.

And Faith wouldn't be crying in the middle of the street.

And we wouldn't be in Ireland. Or, if we were, we'd be on our holiday and I'd be the one with ice cream dripping everywhere, even in the middle of winter. Mam knew about ice cream and the way it tastes the same in the winter as it does in the summer.

I look at Faith. She's still leaning against the wall and her eyes are still closed. I don't know why I'm thinking about genies and lamps. There're no such things as genies. Everybody knows that.

I zip up my jacket and I put up my hood. I push my hands deep into the pockets.

When I look at the sky again, the balloon is gone.

It's like it was never there at all.

Nothing happens.

Nothing you'd notice.

I don't ring Thomas.

I tell Brona I can't talk right now. When she rings, I say, 'I'm in the middle of a chapter.'

I listen when Minnie tells me about spinach and how it's a great provider of folic acid, which is really essential at this stage of the baby's development.

'Tell me to fuck off if I'm boring you, won't you?' This is after she's been talking about her stools — that's what she's calling them now — and how regular she is compared with before, when days could go by without so much as a whimper out of her bowel, never mind a movement.

I say, 'Of course you're not boring me,' which is a lie.

I don't tell her what happened. That Faith came to Dublin. I don't know why not.

Instead, I sit in my apartment and I field calls.

Dad calls. Nearly every day. He's started shouting into the answering machine, like they do in overblown American films. 'Pick up! Pick up, Kat. I know you're there,' even though he doesn't know I'm here. Not for certain.

Ed calls. He wants to come over. I tell him I'm

sick. He says, 'Do you have the flu?'

'Yes.'

'You should take some tablets.'

'I did.'

'You should get into bed.'

'I am.'

'Can I come over?'

'When I'm better.'

'When will you be better?'

'I don't know.'

I see nobody except delivery men. They're nearly always men. Pizza delivery men. Indian takeaway delivery men. Chinese. Thai. Even the chip shop down the road delivers. I alternate between them and say as little as possible. The last thing I need is a friend who's a fast-food delivery guy. What would that say about you? I hand over money, take the box, say, 'Keep the change,' and close the door, lock the door, put the chain across the door, close the curtains, eat the chips, the egg-fried rice, the samosas, the thin-crust pepperoni. I wash it down with red wine. Australian, Chilean, South African. I don't look at the bottles. Screw tops, the lot of them. Easier that way. Twist and pour. I have loads of bottles. Cases and cases. I won't have to get more until March, I'd say. February, at the earliest.

Just as I'm settling into a bit of a routine, the doorbell rings. At first I ignore it. I'm not expecting anyone. I haven't ordered any food yet.

But whoever is at the door is persistent, which means three possibilities: a Jehovah's Witness, someone selling cable television, or Thomas. But Thomas hasn't knocked on the door since he came to pack up his stuff.

I don't pick up the intercom. I don't open the curtains and look out of the window. In fact, I do nothing at all. The doorbell keeps ringing. One long, mournful sound. And then, all of a sudden, it stops.

When I stand up, pins and needles prickle up and down my legs and I hobble out of my bedroom and into the kitchen. I shuffle to the breadbin, where I keep the takeaway menus. Put on the kettle. Turn on the radio. I reach up my arm to the press and put my hand around a cup.

Then I stop. Look at the kitchen clock. It shows a quarter past five and my rule is, no drinking till six. But it's only forty-five minutes earlier than usual. I'll order dinner forty-five minutes earlier too. That'll even it up. I lift my hand off the cup. Pick up a glass instead.

I open the bottle. Pour myself half a glass. Swill the wine around. Put the glass down. Pick up the bottle. Fill the glass this time. Take a huge drink. Wipe the wine stain — already forming — off the corners of my mouth.

I jump when the kettle whistles.

That's when the knocking begins. On my front door. Which means one of the neighbours has broken the Golden Rule, which is never, ever, Under Any Circumstances, let someone into the building unless that person is calling specifically for you. Even if you know them. You've known them for years. Since they were born, in fact. Even if they're a member of your own family

330

who happens to be calling for somebody in the building and you know perfectly well that it's perfectly legitimate. Even then. You don't do it. You just don't.

Except now, it seems, someone has done it. The chief suspect is Mrs O'Dea on the fourth floor. She's a sucker for a sad story. There was that time last year when she let the *Big Issue* seller in. Hours, it took us. To get him out. He looked ancient but he was a dab hand on the fire-escape stairs.

'Katherine? Can you open the door? Please?'

It's not a Jehovah's Witness. Or a cable telly salesman. And it's not Thomas. Of course it's not.

I open the door. She says, 'May I come in?' and then she waits as if she's not sure what my answer might be. I nod and step aside, opening the door wider as I do.

'I wasn't expecting you.' I can count on the fingers of one hand the number of times she has been here on her own. She's always with Dad. Or Ed. Or Dad and Ed.

Mum nods and peels her black leather gloves away from her hands, gives them to me along with her coat and her hat. It seems that she is staying.

I say, 'Would you like a cup of tea?'

'I'll have what you're having.' She nods at the glass in my hand.

Mum does not drink wine except on Sundays. She says it interferes with 'the Work'.

I say, 'Go on through.' She takes a couple of steps up the hall, then turns back and points at a door with a question on her face. I say, 'Yes.'

I bundle her hat and coat and gloves into the cloakroom. In the kitchen, I get another glass and fill it with wine. I top up my own glass. I put my hands on the counter. Close my eyes. Steady myself. Try to remember the last time Mum and I were in a room together. Just the two of us. On our own. I can't. I can't remember.

I pick up the glasses. Bend and look at my reflection in the toaster. I look pretty bad but there's no time for bronzer or a hairbrush. I'll have to wing it.

I hand her a glass. 'Here you are.'

'Thank you, Katherine.' She takes the glass and views it with deep suspicion. Places it on the coffee table beside her chair. I grip the back of the chair I'm supposed to be sitting on.

I say, 'So?' in a way that I'm hoping strikes a balance between not-unwelcoming and mildly curious.

I don't think I manage it because she says, 'What do you mean, so?' Her voice is pinched. It's not coming easily. She sits on the edge of her seat, as if she's about to leave. But she doesn't leave. Instead, she looks around the room. Stops at the record player. She smiles and nods. 'Your father bought me that before we were married. I can't believe you still have it.'

The silence that follows isn't awkward as such. It's just . . . there. I pass the time by drinking wine.

She says, 'Does it still work?'

'Yes.' Even though it doesn't. Not really.

Sometimes I wish we were the type of mother

and daughter who could have the television on in the background. *Countdown*, maybe. Something interactive.

She lifts her glass, takes a drink and puts it back on the table. Then she clears her throat and I brace myself and she looks towards me, but not directly at me, and says what she came here to say, which is, 'What are you planning to do?'

'Nothing.'

She nods. There is resignation in the nod. She expected me to say that.

For a moment, I think that's it. That's all she's going to say. But then I realise there's more. I'm pretty sure she's going to say something else. I can tell by the way she shifts in her seat. Picks up her wine glass. Puts it back down again. Tucks a stray strand of hair behind her ear and pushes her finger up the bridge of her nose, as if she is wearing her glasses, which she is not.

The thing she ends up saying is this: 'Faith looks just the way I imagined her.'

I am not surprised that Mum mentions Faith. It's the fact that she imagined her that I can't get over.

'She looks like you.'

I take a drink. 'I didn't think you ever thought about her.'

'Of course I did. Didn't you?'

'No.'

'No?'

'No.'

'Well, I did. And she looks just as I imagined.'

'You never talked about it. Afterwards. You never brought it up.'

Mum picks up her glass. Takes the tiniest sip. She shakes her head. 'I thought it was for the best.'

'And even Minnie. She never mentioned it either. Not really.'

'I spoke to Mrs Driver. Afterwards. Told her I thought it was better if we didn't . . . make a fuss.'

'And Dad never said anything.'

She shrugs. 'No. Well, he wouldn't, would he?'

'It was like it never happened.'

She looks at me. 'Don't be silly.'

'Afterwards, when I came home, nobody said anything. Sometimes I wondered . . . '

'What?'

'If it had actually happened.'

'You're being fanciful, Katherine.'

Fanciful. There's a word. I've never heard anyone use it except my mother.

She puts her glass on the coffee table but the gesture is a little brisk and wine reaches for the rim, scales it, splashes onto the pale wood of the table. She doesn't notice.

Now the silence is awkward. After a while, she straightens. 'So. The reason I came . . . Well, I mean, we have to do something, don't we? We can't just do nothing. Can we?'

I don't say anything.

'About Faith, I mean.' When she says her name, I want to clamp my hands against my ears. She sounds real, when she says her name. Faith. She sounds like a real person. A person who's twenty-four. A person who has a brother called Milo. A person who lives in Brighton.

334

I don't clamp my hands against my ears. I say, 'No.'

Mum continues as if I hadn't said anything. 'Her mother died recently. Her . . . adoptive mother, I mean.'

Something twists inside. A feeling. Sympathy, perhaps. For this woman who keeps turning into a real person, no matter what I do.

'She died in that car crash. The one you were in. Isn't that strange?'

'That's . . . so strange.'

'Perhaps it's fate.'

'You don't believe in fate.'

She doesn't respond to that. Takes a drink of wine instead. Then she says, 'She found out she was adopted afterwards. By accident, really.'

'Her parents never told her?'

'No.'

'Why would they do that?'

Mum shakes her head. 'People make odd decisions every day.' I glance up but she's not looking at me. She says, 'I'm sure they had their reasons.'

I nod. I don't know what else to do.

Mum says, 'You have to contact her.'

'I thought you didn't do this.'

'Do what?'

'Interfere. You say you don't believe in interfering in people's lives. People can make a mess of their own lives without any help from you. That's what you say, isn't it?' My voice is louder than it has any need to be. I try to get a hold of it.

She says, 'This is different.'

I don't say anything.

'Faith is my granddaughter.'

She looks like a grandmother when she says that. There is something frail in her bearing. As if she might break a hip if she fell.

I say, 'Did you see her? In the hospital, I mean?'

'What do you mean?'

'The day she was born. Did you see her then?'

'Of course I saw her.'

'I didn't. I never saw her.'

'What do you mean? You must have seen her.'

'I didn't. They took her away. And then I signed the papers. And then you drove me home.'

'You must have seen her. You gave birth to her.'

'I didn't even know she was a girl.'

'You must have known.'

'Why do you keep telling me what I must have seen and must have known? I'm telling you I didn't. I told them not to tell me. And I'm not being *fanciful*. I'm merely stating a fact.'

Mum opens her mouth, then closes it. She reaches for her glass. Changes her mind. Looks at me. Says, 'Maybe if you'd seen her, you might have changed your mind.'

'I never made up my mind. You did that. You made all the arrangements, remember?'

'I only did what I thought was best.'

I say, 'When did you decide? About the adoption, I mean.'

'I . . . as soon as I found out. When Ed brought me round to Mrs Driver's house and I saw you, on the couch.'

'You were very composed.'

'Somebody had to be.' She seems angry now. She hurls the words, like stones. Throws them at me.

'I was scared. I was fifteen years old.'

'You were old enough to know better.'

'I was a child. I didn't know anything.'

'You knew enough to get yourself into that state in the first place.'

'That's charming, so it is.'

'Somebody had to take charge. Make a decision.'

'You could have discussed it with me.'

'You were in no position to discuss anything. You were hysterical.'

'I was in labour.'

'Somebody had to come up with a plan.'

'Well, you certainly did that.'

'I thought it was for the best.'

'You keep saying that.'

She glares at me but says nothing.

I take a drink. Put my glass down. Pick it up again. Take another drink. A longer one. I say, 'And now what? You're disregarding all that and you think I should make contact with her and we'll be like the Brady Bunch and live happily ever after?' My voice shakes. I think I'm angry. I feel like breaking something. Hurling something heavy against a window. There's an ashtray somewhere. A Waterford Crystal one. That would do.

For the first time since she arrived, she looks at me. Really looks at me. Looks at my face. She says, 'Yes.'

337

I say, 'No.'

She puts her head in her hands. For a moment, I think she's crying.

'I'm sorry, Mum. But I can't. I just . . . I can't. I wouldn't know what to say. Where to start. I wouldn't be able for that.'

She nods. Her head is still in her hands but I see now that she's not crying. I am glad. I can deal with anger and resentment. But sadness is a different animal altogether. Sadness can encourage you to make promises you can't keep.

She takes her hands away. Bits of her face are red where her fingers have gripped too tightly. She stands up. 'I'll go.'

I stand as well. My legs shake and I think it might be relief. She looks at me. 'You're not going to change your mind, are you?'

'No.'

I go to the cloakroom and fetch her coat and her hat and gloves. It seems like she arrived a long time ago, but when I look at my watch I see that only twenty minutes have passed.

She pauses at the door. 'It's easier to do the wrong thing, you know.'

'What's that supposed to mean?'

'Maybe I did the wrong thing.' There is something vulnerable about her expression. Lost.

I shake my head. 'You did what you thought was best. At the time.'

'Maybe I was wrong.'

There is nothing to say to that so I say nothing.

She pulls at the cuff of her glove so that the tips of her fingers strain against the leather.

When she speaks again, she sounds like her usual self. 'You should spend some time with Edward. He hasn't been himself lately.' My stomach rumbles when she says it. As if I'm starving and Ed is a portion of chicken tikka masala. Or an onion bhaji.

'I will.' And I mean it. I'll ring him tomorrow. Maybe I'll pick him up and bring him somewhere. The Christmas market at the docks, perhaps. If it's open yet. He loves Christmas and I love mulled wine. It'll suit both of us. Take our minds off things.

'I'll ring him tomorrow.'

'Will we see you on Sunday?'

'Yes. Of course.'

For a moment, I think she's going to add something but then she turns and walks down the hall. She passes the lift and opens the door that leads to the stairwell. She never takes lifts. Says they're like people: unpredictable. From the back, she looks more like herself. Her back is straight and her head is high. There is a sureness in her step. Her heels rap sharply against each step as she descends. I stand at the door and wait until the sound fades away.

Dad says, 'Are you sure you'll be able to manage?'

Faith says, 'Yes. I already told you. I'm fine. I'm fine now. It was very good of you to pick us up from Gatwick. You didn't have to wait in Brighton for us to come back.'

'I was anxious to hear how it all went.'

'You should go. I expect Celia wants you home. In case the baby comes early.'

'I can stay till tomorrow if you want to go out with Rob tonight?'

'No. No thanks.'

'OK then, I'll get ready to hit the road.'

Dad never says 'leave'. He never says, 'I'll get ready to leave.' He says 'hit the road' or 'sling his hook' or 'make like a bee and buzz off'. Something stupid like that. That time, when he left to go to Scotland to do sex with Celia, he said, 'I'm headin', buddy.' Mam was crying in the kitchen and I wanted to say, 'I'm not your buddy,' but I didn't say that. I didn't say anything in the end.

He rings Celia so he can tell her that he's leaving. He says, 'I'm outta here after lunch. How are you, pet?'

He never called Mam 'pet'. He called her 'Beth'. Sometimes, he called her 'love'. Like that time in the hospital when he was getting something taken out. His appendix or his tonsils or something. Afterwards, he said, 'Would you pour me a wee dram of that grape juice, love?' in the kind of voice Damo puts on when he's pretending to be sick so he misses art. He hates art. He says it's for girls and gays. You won't know you're gay till you're about sixteen, Damo says. I hope it doesn't happen to me.

Mam said, 'Do I look like Florence bleeding Nightingale?' but I think she was just messing because she poured him a glass anyway.

Dad spreads butter and jam on a slice of white bread. It's a good job Celia's not here because she says he's not supposed to have butter. Or white bread. And he's not supposed to eat between meals. I don't know if he's allowed to have jam. He picks up the bread and takes an enormous bite out of it. Then he washes it down with a can of Coke that's not Diet Coke like he's supposed to drink. He looks at me and smiles. 'I suppose you're hoping for a wee brother.'

I shrug. 'I don't mind.' Actually, because I already have two brothers, I was kind of hoping for a sister, to even things out. I don't say that to Dad. He thinks boys should like brothers and girls should like sisters.

'Maybe we should have a talk, son. Before I go. About, you know, the birds and the bees and all that.'

I know all about the birds and the bees. Although Damo didn't call it that. He called it screwing.

I say, 'I already know. We did it in school.'

That is kind of true. Damo told me in school at lunchtime. He drew diagrams with his finger in the muck. For someone who hates art, he's pretty good at drawing.

Dad looks at me and for a moment I think he's going to tell me anyway but then he shrugs his shoulders and says, 'OK-sey,' instead of 'OK.'

I say, 'Do you want me to help you pack?' Now that I know he's going, I sort of can't wait for him to be gone. Once he's gone, it's fine. I just don't like knowing he's going when he's still here.

He laughs and tosses my hair out of my eyes with his fingers. 'Trying to get rid of me, are you, son?'

'No, I just . . .'

'I'm not away till after lunch. There's one other thing I have to do.'

'I could make you a sandwich. Ham and eggy mix. I think there are some rolls in the breadbin.' Eggy mix is Mam's invention. It's hard-boiled eggs, mashed in a bowl, with anything you like chopped up and thrown in. Then you mix it all up with mayonnaise and maybe some mustard. My favourite mix is chives and green peppers. I don't bring eggy-mix sandwiches into school, on account of the smell.

Dad winks at me. 'We'll let Faith worry about lunch, son. That's what the ladies do best, isn't it?'

If Mam were here, she'd say, 'MCP,' which stands for Male Chauvinist Pig, and he'd laugh and say, 'I suppose you'll be burning your bra next,' and Mam would laugh and pretend to whack Dad over the head with her rolled-up newspaper. Later on, when they fought all the time, she wouldn't laugh. She'd just say something like, 'You're a great role model for a seven-year-old boy, aren't you?' Then Dad would tell me to go to my room and I don't know what they said after that, but whatever it was it was loud because I could hear them shouting from my room, even when I closed the wardrobe door.

The other thing that Dad has to do before he leaves turns out to be about Christmas. He says we have to

342

go and buy a tree. A real one, even though there's an artificial one in the attic that Mam has used every year since Dad went away.

He says, 'You have to have a real tree at Christmas, son.' But he doesn't say why.

I say, 'Don't you think it's a bit early?'

'It's never too early for Christmas, son.'

We go to a garden centre and he tells me I can pick whatever tree I want. They all look the same to me. I point at the nearest one.

He says, 'That's a sorry excuse for a tree, son.' I point to the one beside it and Dad sighs and shakes his head and then he picks a tree near the back. It's so big, he can't lift it. He has to drag it to the man, who takes the money and doesn't give him any change, on account of how big the tree is.

Dad says, 'That's highway robbery!' But he ends up sort of saying it to himself because the man has gone over to another customer, who is buying the first tree I pointed at. He gets change.

There's no roof rack on Dad's car so he has to lay the tree across the back seat with the top of it sticking out of one window and the bottom of it sticking out of the window on the other side.

I say, 'We'll have to be careful of cyclists. And pedestrians. And lamp posts.'

Dad says, 'Get in.' I have to sit in the front on account of the tree.

I sit up really straight so that I look like I'm twelve, or a hundred and thirty-five centimetres, in case we're stopped by the police because of the Christmas tree poking out of both sides of the car.

We don't get very far before Dad starts talking again.

He says, 'I presume you've written your letter to Santa?'

I say, 'I don't believe in Santa. I'm ten.'

'You're ten?'

'Well, I'll be ten on Christmas Day.'

He looks at me, which is dangerous because you should be looking at the road when you're driving, especially when you have a Christmas tree sticking out of your car.

He shakes his head. He says, 'It seems like only yesterday when you were born, son.'

Adults always say that it seems like only yesterday when things happened, even though they happened years and years ago. And they always say that time flies. I don't think that's true. I think time drags and drags, which is good because I don't want it to be Christmas Day. It won't be the same. This year, I'm not going to call it Christmas Day. I'm just going to call it Sunday.

Another thing that I'm never going to do when I'm an adult is tell the same story over and over again. Like Dad. He says, 'You had to be lifted out through the sunroof.' That means that Mam had a Caesarean section, which is when the doctor cuts a bit of your stomach and takes the baby out that way. Mam was in labour for seventeen hours before that.

Dad says, 'Your mother was in labour for seventeen hours before the doctor took you out.'

The next thing he'll say is that Mam shouted so loudly that the foundations of the hospital shook and he thought the whole place would come tumbling down.

'Your mother screeched so loudly I thought the roof would cave in.' Sometimes, he changes it.

At the traffic lights, everybody stares at us and stares at our car, with the Christmas tree poking out either side. I duck down as if I'm looking for something on the floor. I sit back up when we start moving.

Dad says, 'So?'

I say, 'What?'

'Don't say 'what', say 'pardon'.'

I don't say anything, and after a while, Dad says, 'So what would you like? For Christmas? And your birthday, of course.'

'I'd like a new pair of goggles.'

'Goggles?'

'For my lifesaving class. The ones I have still work but they get fogged up really quickly now.'

'You're still into that?'

'Yeah.'

'You must be brilliant at it by now.'

'Well, Coach thinks I'm OK.' Actually she said I was one of the best in the class, but I'm not a show-off, like George Pullman.

'That's great. What class are you in now?'

'I'm still in the beginners' class.'

'Beginners'?'

'Yeah. But I'll be doing my exam in the spring. Coach thinks I'll pass and then I'll move up to intermediate.'

'I should hope so. After all this time.'

'Lifesaving is pretty tricky, you know. Even lifesaving for beginners.'

'So that's all you want, is it? Just goggles?'

'They're the Speedsocket Mirror ones. They're dead expensive.'

'Still. That doesn't seem like a lot.'

'That's what I'd like.' The Speedsocket ones are twenty-three pounds, but I don't say that in case Dad says, 'Highway robbery!' again.

'Shouldn't you be looking for a sword? Or a bow and arrow, or something? I thought that's what nine-year-old boys were into. Stuff like that.'

I say, 'I'm into lifesaving. We learn CPR and everything.'

Dad looks at me again, but the road we're on is fairly quiet. He says, 'I hope you don't have to do mouth-to-mouth resuscitation on any of the boys in your class.' He laughs after he says this, like he's cracked a joke.

I say, 'We practise on dummies, mostly.'

He says, 'Well, we'll see what we can do about the goggles, OK?' I nod. I don't know why he's saying 'we' when it's just him. Maybe he means him and Celia. Or maybe him and Faith? I don't think Faith has done any Christmas shopping yet.

'The thing is, son . . . '

I wish he'd call me Milo.

'The thing is . . . well, we . . . Celia and me, I mean . . . we'd like you to come and stay with us for a while. After Christmas, I mean. And after the baby is born. When everything settles down. Celia was saying that — '

'No.'

'What do you mean, no? I haven't even finished what I was saying.'

'No.'

'Don't use that tone with me, boy. You'll go where you're told. You're nine years old and — '

'I'm nearly ten.'

'What?'

346

'Ten. I'm nearly ten, remember?'

Dad doesn't say anything for a while. He concentrates on driving, which I'm pretty glad about because there's a cycle lane now and he has to be careful that he doesn't hit any of the cyclists with the Christmas tree.

After a while, he sighs and says, 'That's not the end of it, Milo. We'll talk about it again. Another time. OK?'

I don't say anything so he says, 'OK?' again, louder this time, so I have to say, 'OK,' even though it's not. It's not OK.

Nothing else happens until we pull into the driveway and then one end of the tree — I think it's the top bit — gets squashed between the car door and the pillar. It's still pretty much attached to the rest of the tree but only by a couple of splinters. Dad gets out, kicks the pillar and says, 'Bloody hell!' He tugs at the squashed bit of the tree and it comes away in his hand, which is just as well because now there's a chance that the tree might fit in the sitting room.

In the end, I have to ask Sully — who's home from the war for a few days — to help Dad carry the tree inside. There are pine needles all over the floor by the time they're finished. The top of the tree is bent against the ceiling. I don't think Dad notices the bent bit at the top because he just says, 'Now that's a tree, eh son?' He looks at me and punches my arm but he's smiling so I know he's only messing.

When Faith comes downstairs, she has make-up on her face. She looks like everything is back to normal. She's even wearing the black dress that Rob bought her last Christmas. She's wearing tights and boots and she looks like she might go out later, which would be good for her because she hasn't been out in ages.

After lunch, Dad says, 'I'm going to skedaddle.'

Faith says, 'Drive carefully.'

Dad doesn't make a joke, the way he normally tries to. He nods and says, 'I will. I'll ring you when I get there, OK?' He holds out his arms and this time Faith walks right into them and he hugs her really tightly and she says something, but I can't hear what it is because of the way her face is squashed against Dad's shirt.

Dad bends down when he's talking to me. I've grown five centimetres since he last saw me but he still bends down. 'You be good for your sister, son.'

I nod.

He puts his hand on top of my head. 'I'll ring you on Friday, OK?'

I nod again.

He opens the car door but instead of getting in, he turns around to me. 'Look, Milo, you know I won't be able to come down this year. For Christmas, I mean. Because of Celia. Having the baby. You get that, don't you?' I nod a couple of times. I do get it. I really do.

Faith says, 'Go on, Dad. It'll be getting dark soon.'

He gets into the car and turns the key in the ignition. I knock on the window and point to the seatbelt and he nods and pulls the seatbelt round him. He says that haggis is the reason his stomach looks like Celia's. Haggis is the lining of a sheep's stomach and people in Scotland eat it, but I don't know why. Dad says it's because it tastes nice but that couldn't be true.

He rolls down the window and looks at Faith. He starts to say something and Faith says, 'Don't worry, Dad. It's fine. We'll be fine.'

He shakes his head, like it's not fine. 'When we brought you home, Beth worried that she wouldn't know what to do with you. That she wouldn't do a good job.'

Faith says, 'Tell Celia we said hello, won't you?'

'She was wrong. She did know what to do. She did a great job.'

'Roll up that window. You'll catch your death.'

'She loved you, Faith. It never mattered to her. She loved you just the same.'

Faith nods a tight nod, like her neck is stiff or something. Dad blows a kiss at Faith and salutes me as if I'm a soldier or something, and then he drives down the road, turns left and is gone.

Faith walks inside the house, up the stairs and into her bedroom. When I go up later with a cup of coffee, she's in her pyjamas, in bed, with her headphones on.

I say, 'Are you tired?'

'Sort of.'

'You should go out. Get some fresh air into your lungs. It would do you good.'

'You sound like Mam.'

I say, 'Well, somebody has to.'

That makes Faith laugh but not for very long.

I go downstairs to make a sandwich. The sitting room is dark now, on account of the Christmas tree. It's so big, it blocks out most of the light. Dad and me were supposed to put on the decorations before he left. Normal trees look fine without decorations but Christmas trees look kind of sad. Bare.

It takes me a lot longer than I thought it would. Mam and me usually argue about what to put at the top of the tree. She liked the red star I made from a Weetabix box when I was a little kid. She always liked the stuff I made at school, even if it was a bit ripped or not coloured in properly.

I like the angel. We've had her for years. Mam bought her the first Christmas after Faith was born. Well, after Faith came to live with Mam and Dad, I suppose. Dad said she was eighteen months when she came to stay. That's still a baby, but I think you can probably walk a bit and you can talk but it's mostly gibberish so no one knows what you're saying. The angel has black hair and green eyes, which is why Mam bought her, because she said she looked like Faith. I like her because there's a button under her dress you can press to make her light up.

Usually me and Mam can never agree. The star. Or the angel. Usually we end up tossing a coin for it.

I have to stand on my tiptoes on a kitchen chair to reach the top branch.

When I'm finished I turn off all the lights downstairs and then I plug in the fairy lights. They're all different colours and they flash like mad, and if you look at them too long your eyes go funny. You can't really see the rip in the star from here.

I text Ed. 'Do you want to do something today?'

Ed texts back. 'I am sick.'

I ring him. He tries to be huffy but he's not very good at it.

'Hi, Ed.'

He doesn't say 'Hello, Kat.' Just 'Hello.' That's how I know he's huffy.

'What's wrong?'

'I've got a cold and a cough.'

'Do you want to come over?'

He says nothing.

'I'll pick you up.'

He says nothing.

'I've got *The Wizard of Oz* on DVD.'

He says nothing but I can feel him falter. *The Wizard of Oz* is one of his favourite films. It's the lion who thinks he has no heart that does it for him. Every time.

'I'm going to order pizza and drink Coke and eat Skittles.' I'm not going to drink Coke. I'm going to drink wine. But Ed is a sucker for Coke. The fizz of it.

'Did you get a family-size bag of Skittles?' He's nibbling at the bait.

I let out more line. 'I got two.'

Another pause but not as long this time. Then, 'OK.' I reel him in.

The outside world is unchanged and yet seems unfamiliar to me. For starters, there's Christmas. It's like Santa's sack has exploded and left the debris of Christmas all over the place. Christmas looks awful in the daylight. Cheap and tacky and miserable.

It feels good to be in the car. I hold the wheel with one hand, a cigarette with the other. I pull into a garage. Get a black coffee. I like garages. Nobody has a clue who you are and, better still, they don't want to know. I hate corner shops. There's often a jolly, fat woman behind the counter and she always thinks she has the measure of you. 'Still smoking? Even after the hike in the budget? Isn't it well for you?'

In the garage, nobody says anything, apart from, 'Any petrol or diesel with that?'

I pull in at the top of the road and ring Ed. I say, 'I'm at the corner.'

He says, 'Are you not coming in?'

I say, 'I'm at the corner.'

Dad walks Ed down the road, even though he's perfectly well able to walk that far by himself. Ed gets into the front passenger seat and puts on his seatbelt. Dad opens the driver's door and says, 'Well?'

I say, 'Hi, Dad,' like nothing happened.

He says, 'I've been trying to get in touch with you.'

'Sorry. I've been busy.'

He stands there. Looks at me. He must be frozen. He's not wearing a hat or even a coat. He doesn't look cold. He looks like he's got a puncture. Like someone let the air out of him.

He says, 'I gave Faith your number.'

I look in my rear-view mirror. 'I'd better go.'

He straightens. He says, 'I forgot. You're busy.'

'Do you want a lift back up the road?'

He shakes his head. 'I like the cold.'

Ed says, 'See ya, Dad,' and Dad nods and waves and I drive away and don't look back.

For a while, neither of us speaks. I know Ed is getting ready to say something. I recognise the signs. His mouth moves (I call it 'picture but no sound'), and he's checking off things on his fingers. So far, he's checked off three things.

Then he says, 'Milo is cool, so he is. And he's good at the Wii too. He's not as good as me but I told him he just needs to practise as much as I do.'

When I don't say anything, Ed goes on: 'Is Milo a bit like my little brother now? Or my nephew or something?'

'No.'

'I'd love a little brother. I'd show him how to play the Wii and bring him swimming with me and everything.'

I say, 'You're my little brother and I never showed you how to play the Wii.'

Ed says, 'You showed me other stuff.'

'Did I?'

'Yeah, you showed me how to tie my laces, remember?'

I nod. I remember. He was ten and he still couldn't do it. It took a whole weekend to teach him. That's the thing about Ed. It takes a while. But after that, he never forgets.

In the apartment, I want to put on the film but

Ed is still talking about Milo. 'He's got loads of hair and he never brushes it because his mam is dead so he doesn't have to anymore. And his best friend is Damo and their favourite game is Bulldog Takedown. He told me how to play it and I showed it to everyone at Arch club last week. He doesn't have a girlfriend like I do but he likes a girl called Carla. She's in his class but he doesn't want to kiss her. Just hang around with her sometimes.'

'Ed?'

'And his sister is in a band. It's called . . . I can't remember what it's called but Milo said you can download their album, if you want to. Do you want to?'

'Do I want to what?' I'm lighting the fire. Well, I'm switching on the gas fire.

'Do you want to download Faith's album?'

'Maybe later.'

We watch *The Wizard of Oz*. Ed sings along with the Munchkins of Munchkinland, like he always does. He covers his face with his hands when the Wicked Witch of the West makes an appearance. And he cries when Lion sings 'If I Only Had a Heart', just like always. I sit beside him on the couch. There's a chance I'm smiling. It feels nice.

Ed hates it when the film returns to black and white, near the end. I get up to switch it off before he begins complaining. It's only when I return to the couch that I notice he's asleep. I shake his shoulder. I say, 'Ed. ED! Wake up.'

He jerks awake and looks for a moment like he has no idea where he is or how he got here.

I say, 'Ed, sorry. I didn't mean to give you a fright . . . Are you all right? It's just . . . what the hell are you doing falling asleep in the middle of *The Wizard of Oz* anyway? It's one of your favourites.'

'Was I asleep?'

When I look at him carefully, I see the skin of his face is pale. Tight. There are dark circles under his eyes. I think he's right. He is a bit tired. I put my hand across his forehead. The skin there is a bit damp. I take his temperature. It's normal.

I say, 'I'll make you a smoothie. That'll perk you up.'

Ed shakes his head. He says, 'No, Kat. Thanks a lot. I think I'll go home now.'

'I thought you were staying over? I've made up your bed and everything.' I even draped fairy lights along the top of the mirror in his room. Ed loves fairy lights.

Ed says, 'OK, Kat. I'll stay.'

I know that Ed does not want to stay.

'It's all right, Ed, you don't have to stay.'

'OK then. Can you drive me home?'

I ring the Italian restaurant and cancel our order, then turn off the fire.

I say, 'Come on, then,' as if there's nothing wrong. And there is nothing wrong. Probably nothing. People get tired. People get tired all the time. And just because Ed never complains about being tired doesn't mean that he is immune to fatigue, right? He just needs one good night's sleep and a hearty breakfast in the morning and he'll be fine. Kippers, maybe. Ed loves kippers. Despite the foul stench. And they're very good for you, I'd say. Smelly food often is. Like cabbage. Smelly as hell but a brilliant source of various bits and bobs, like vitamins and minerals and whatnot.

Ed doesn't move so I take his hand and lead him towards the door. He sways a little, as if he's dizzy. His hand feels cold. Clammy. I am carrying his overnight bag but he doesn't take it from me, as he usually would. He says ladies aren't supposed to carry baggage.

Outside, the air is solid with cold. It feels like it might stick in your throat. I hold the keys out to Ed. He likes pressing the button. The way the lights flash on and off by themselves.

Ed shakes his head.

So I press the button myself, like it's no big deal. I press the button, open the boot and turn to pick up Ed's bag, and that's when I see Ed and he's bent over and sort of clutching his chest and his breath is coming and going in gasps and he looks at me and there is confusion all over his face and I'm afraid. I'm not supposed to be the one who is afraid. I'm supposed to be Kat. The big sister. The one who knows things.

But I am afraid. I say, 'ED!' I think I shout it. I run till I reach him, put my arms round him. He leans against me like I'm a wall and then he sort of crumbles until he is sitting and then lying on the hard, cold ground. His eyes are open but I don't think he can hear me. I take off my coat, wrap it round him, throw everything out of my bag, look for the bloody mobile.

The hospital is listed under A for A&E in my

contacts. The phone rings and rings. I hang up and I scream out loud and lights snap on in various windows. I dial 999. I ask for an ambulance. I tell them it's an emergency. They say it'll be twenty minutes. I say, 'No. That's too long. Twenty minutes is too long.' They say they'll do their best.

It's hard to think.

In the end, I half lift, half drag Ed into the back seat of the car. I look at his face. He looks like he's asleep but he does not react when I shout his name. His lips are blue. There are flecks of spit on them. I wipe them away with a tissue. I try whispering now. 'Ed,' I whisper. He does not move. I push my fingers into the soft folds of skin round his neck. I can't feel his pulse.

I get into the front seat. Switch on the lights. The engine. The heater. The wipers. I turn to look at Ed one more time and then I gun the engine and the car moves.

I use the bus lanes. I speed, too. Nobody notices. Just when you're desperate for some flashing lights and sirens, the roads remain eerily empty. I put the phone on the hands-free and ring my parents' landline. No point ringing their mobiles because they're never switched on, and if they are, they're on silent. The phone rings and rings.

Minnie's phone goes direct to voicemail. 'I'm sorry but neither myself nor Maurice, my husband, can come to the phone. You could try leaving a message . . . '

In the end, there's no choice. Even though I've

deleted the number from my phone, I know it. I know it by heart. He picks up after four rings. The lights turn green. I fling a glance back at Ed, then put the phone on loudspeaker.

'Thomas, can you hear me?'

'Kat? What's the matter?'

'It's Ed.'

'Where are you?'

'I don't know. I'm on my way to the hospital. I couldn't wait for the ambulance.'

'Are you on your way to Beaumont?'

'Yes.'

'Is it his heart?'

'I don't know. I think so.'

'I'll ring the hospital. Tell them you're on your way in with Ed. I'll ring your parents. I'll meet you there.'

If Thomas is anxious about Ed, he does not reveal it. He sounds like someone who will make sure that everything turns out all right in the end. Someone who knows what they're doing.

Before he hangs up, he says, 'Drive carefully.'

I drive like a lunatic, flinging my head back much too often to look at Ed.

'Ed . . . ED . . . ED! . . . WAKE UP, ED. IT'S TIME TO WAKE UP.'

Ed does not respond. He makes no sound at all.

It's the middle of the night but adults are often up in the middle of the night, aren't they? And I can't ring at any other time or else Faith will hear me, even though she's not really listening anymore. She'll still hear. Adults always hear the stuff you don't want them to hear.

I carry the phone into the kitchen, close the door and sit on the floor. It's dark but if I turn on the light it spills into the back garden because there are no blinds on the window, and it's really bright, that light, so there's a chance that Faith might notice it because of the gap where her curtains should meet but don't.

I wait till my eyes have adjusted to the dark. I imagine my pupils getting bigger and bigger till they're as big as a cat's. That's probably how cats can see so well in the dark. Because of their gigantic pupils.

The number is really long, on account of it being an Irish number, which means you have to add the international country code as well as the area code to the beginning of the number. I know the numbers because they're the same ones Mam used to ring Auntie May. Before Dad went to Scotland, he'd give out stink about the phone bills but Mam just said, 'I need to talk to someone, don't I?'

When the phone starts to ring, I hang up. I didn't expect it to start ringing so soon.

I imagine the lady throwing off the duvet and

getting out of bed. She's probably really annoyed now.

I take a deep breath like Miss Williams tells Damo to try to do before he starts fighting. Sometimes it works, but not always. I don't think it's because of the breathing. I think it's because Damo just happens to be someone who likes fighting. He says he's going to be a boxer when he grows up and I think he'll be a pretty good one.

Anyway, I take a breath and then I hold it and then I start to let it out, dead slow like Miss Williams tells us, and by the time I've dialled the last number my breath's all out and the phone starts to ring again.

'Didn't you hear me the last time? I said, 'Fuck off.''

That's about the worst curse word you can say. Sully says there's another one that's even worse than that but he won't tell me and Damo till we're teenagers. Kids say 'fuck' all the time but it sounds way worse when an adult says it. I don't know why.

I say, 'This is Milo McIntyre. Is that Kat?' I spent ages wondering what I should call her. Mrs Kavanagh? Or Miss? Or Katherine, like her mam calls her? But, in the end, I decided to call her Kat, like Ed does.

She doesn't say anything for so long that I think maybe she's hung up or something, so I say, 'Are you still there?'

She says, 'Who is this?'

I've already told her that I'm Milo McIntyre but I say it again anyway. She might wear a hearing aid, like Mrs Barber. In a loud whisper I say, 'THIS. IS. MILO. McINTYRE.'

'Who?'

'Milo McIntyre.'

'Do you know what time it is, young man?'

Adults only ever call you 'young man' when they're

annoyed with you. Miss Williams calls Damo 'young man' all the time.

I look at my watch. 'It's oh-one-twenty.' Sully taught me and Damo the way you say the time in the army. People sound older when they say it like that.

There is a pretty long pause and I can tell she's thinking about what to say next, so to save her the trouble, I say, 'I'm ringing because of Faith. I'm Faith's brother. Well, I'm not really her brother anymore, except that I still feel like I'm her brother. And she's still taking care of me and she still sort of feels like my sister, but I'm not sure if I'm supposed to call her my half-sister now, like when Celia's baby comes along. Or half-brother, if he's a boy.'

'Jesus, slow down will you?'

I don't know why I said all that stuff about Faith. It's not anywhere on the page where I've written what I'm supposed to say so I won't forget anything.

'Sorry.' She sounds cross.

'Milo. That's your name, isn't it?'

'Yes.' I already told her that. Loads of times.

'You're Faith's brother, aren't you?'

'Yes.' I don't say any of the stuff about half-brothers or half-sisters again.

'Milo, look — '

'You sound like my mam.' Sometimes, you end up saying things you never meant to say. Like Kat sounding like Mam. That's not on my page either. But it's true. She says my name just the same. With loads of O at the end.

'Do I?'

'Yes. Mam was from Ireland. Just like you. From Galway. Do you know Galway?'

'Eh, yes.'

361

'She lived in Galway and then she went to London and she met Dad and they both lived in Galway for a while. After they got married. Six years I think. And then they got Faith. She was eighteen months old. Dad said Faith was a baby when they got her, but eighteen months is one and a half and I think that's more like a toddler, don't you?'

'Ah . . . I don't . . . I suppose . . . I haven't really given it very much thought.'

'Did you give away any other babies? Besides Faith, I mean?' Nobody else has thought about this, but Faith could have loads of other brothers and sisters she doesn't know about. Or half-brothers and half-sisters.

She doesn't say anything for a while and I'm just about to say, 'Hello? Are you still there?' when she says, 'No, I didn't. It was just . . . it was one baby. It was Faith.'

'Do you have any other children? Ones you didn't give away, I mean?' They'd still be Faith's half-brothers or half-sisters, wouldn't they?

'No.'

She sounds dead tired all of a sudden. I'm worried that she might say she has to go so I look at my notes and I begin. 'Do you think you could come over? To Brighton? That's where we live. I think Faith might be happy again if she got to see you. And if she's happy again, then Dad won't make me go to Scotland to live with him and Celia and the new baby.'

The lady says nothing so I go right on talking.

'I mean, Dad and Celia are fine and everything and I'm sure it'll be nice to have a new baby half-brother or half-sister. It's just . . . I won't get to see Damo every day. Or Carla. Or go to my lifesaving classes.'

Kat coughs, like there's something stuck in her

throat. She says, 'I'm sure there must be lifesaving classes in Scotland.'

'They wouldn't be the same.'

She says, 'I know what you mean,' and the way she says it, it's like she really does know.

'So you'll come?'

She must have been holding her breath because now she lets out the biggest, longest breath you ever heard. I bet she's got huge lungs. She can probably hold her breath underwater for at least one length.

Then she says, 'Milo, things aren't as simple as that, I'm afraid.'

'Why not?'

'Because they . . . they just aren't.'

'Is it because of the money?'

'What do you mean?'

'The flight? I know it's dead expensive but I still have pretty much all my First Holy Communion money left cos I didn't get to spend much of it in Dublin.'

The lady doesn't say anything after that. I wait for a while and then I say, 'So I have some money left over and you could borrow it and you could fly over and you wouldn't even have to stay in a hotel because you could stay here. You could stay in my mam's room. It's empty now. Faith cleared it out after she found the papers in the attic.'

'What papers?'

'The ones about being adopted.' Sometimes adults can be pretty slow on the uptake.

'Oh.'

'She was pretty upset about it because she didn't know she was adopted. Not like Jessica.'

'Who's Jessica?'

'She's just this girl in my school. She's in year

363

seven. Her parents told her she was adopted when she was a baby and everybody knew she was adopted. But Mam never told Faith. And then Faith found out by accident when she was looking for Mam's rosary beads and that's why she went to Ireland. So she could talk to you about it. But you were at the meeting.'

'What meeting?'

'I don't know which one. Your dad said you were at a meeting and it was a really important one and that's why you couldn't ring back. I think that's what he said anyway. That's why we didn't get to meet you.' I don't know why I'm telling her all this stuff. I look at my notes and see what I need to say next.

'So, anyway. You could stay with us. When you come over, I mean. And I could cook. I'm not bad for my age. Do you like pancakes?'

'Sorry?'

'Pancakes. Do you like them? I put chocolate and banana in them.'

'Ah . . .'

'You can use Nutella as well. If you don't happen to have any chocolate to melt.'

'Milo?'

'You can slice the banana chunky or thin, depending on how much you like bananas. I love them so I slice 'em dead chunky.'

'Milo?'

'Yes?'

'I can't come over.'

'You don't have to come right away.'

'I just . . . I can't.'

'Why not?'

'It's just . . . Ed hasn't been well and — '

'Ed? What's wrong with him? There's a flu going round here. Sully got it when he was home from the war so he couldn't go back when he was meant to and his mam was so happy she said I could have a sleepover next weekend, and she never lets me have a sleepover anymore on account of us setting off the smoke alarm that one time.'

'No, it's not the flu. It's . . . he had a . . . it's his heart. He needs to have an operation.'

'Did he have a heart attack?' I really hope Ed didn't have a heart attack because George Pullman's granddad had one of those and he dropped dead on the spot.

'No, they didn't say . . . they're calling it an episode. Something like that. He's always had a weak heart, from when he was a baby. That's what they said, after he was born.'

'He looked dead healthy when I met him.'

'He said it was lovely meeting you.'

'He's legend at Mario Kart, he really is.'

'He's — ' She stops right there and I wait to see if she's going to say something else but there's nothing but silence down the phone.

I say, 'Maybe Ed could come with you? When he's better, I mean? You could both come. I could take Ed to my lifesaving class. I told him all about it. He said it sounded great. He said he swims too but he doesn't do lifesaving. I could show him some of the techniques I'm learning.'

'Milo, I'm sorry.'

'What for?'

'I can't come. Not now.'

'But sometime, right? You can come over sometime? Later, I mean. Not right now. I don't mean right now.'

'I don't know. Everything is . . . up in the air at the moment. With Ed and . . .'

'But he's going to get better, right? You could come then. When he's better.'

'He's having an operation. Tomorrow. Today, I suppose. I just came home to . . . I don't know really.'

'Tell Ed I said good luck.'

'I'm sorry about . . . the way I answered the phone. It's just . . . I thought you were someone else.'

I'm glad I'm not the person she thought it was. It sounds like that person is going to be in for it whenever he does ring.

She says, 'I'd better go.'

'Me too. I'm supposed to be in bed. Asleep by now.'

'Faith doesn't know that you're ringing me?'

'No way. She'd kill me if she knew.'

She says, 'I'm sorry,' again, but I don't know what for.

'Hopefully Ed will be better soon and you can come over then.'

'Milo?'

'Yeah?'

But then she just says, 'Goodbye,' before she hangs up.

# 1

I've lost track of time. There's something about hospitals that makes time drag. Or stop altogether. I went home for a couple of hours during the night. Mum said I should get some sleep. I didn't sleep. I don't know what I did. Milo rang while I was there. He talks about Ed like he's known him for years. Ed has that effect on people. He's just that sort of man.

Now it's the next morning and Ed is having a procedure. That's what the consultant called it. A procedure. Like it was nothing.

Thomas says, 'Hey.' He is sitting on the chair beside mine. He reaches over and puts his hand on the back of my chair. When he smiles, I think, just for a moment, that everything is going to be OK.

I stand up. Start the pacing thing again.

'How long has it been now?'

'Not long. Don't worry, Kat. He'll be fine.'

'How do you know?' He sounds so sure.

'He's in good hands.' I walk past his chair and he reaches for my hand. Presses it between both of his. Coaxes the warmth back in.

'You're frozen.'

'I'm always frozen.'

'Do you want some tea?'

I nod. I don't want tea. But the getting of it.

The drinking of it. The process of it. All that helps pass the time.

When he comes back with the tea, I say, 'You don't have to stay, you know. I'll ring you. When he's out of theatre. As soon as he's out. I'll give you a ring.'

Thomas shakes his head. 'I'm better here.' I don't tell him how relieved I am. How grateful.

We drink the tea.

My parents are still in the chapel, lighting candles. For all the good that will do. They arrived at the hospital about half an hour after me and Ed. Staff in green and blue scrubs were waiting for us when I skidded to a stop at the door. They had a stretcher, an oxygen mask. Blankets. They looked like a group of people who knew what they were doing. Reliable. That's the word that comes to mind when you look at such a bunch of people. I felt relief. When they lifted Ed out of the car with their efficient, reliable hands. When they placed him — so gently — onto the stretcher. Covered him in blankets. Put the oxygen mask over his face. Stepped back. Smiled at him. Smiled at me. I thought — just for a minute — that everything was going to be all right. Then someone pulled a lever and someone pushed the stretcher away from me. It went down a corridor and there were double doors at the end and the doors swung open and the trolley was wheeled through, then a nurse put her hand on my arm and said, 'Don't worry. Your brother is in good hands.' And the double doors swung shut and the relief drained away and fear was all that was left.

Thomas says, 'Kat? You OK?'

I shake my head. 'I should have known something was up with him. I wasn't paying enough attention.'

'You got him here as quickly as you could.' When Thomas smiles, his eyes change from grey to green. He is wearing wellingtons and an ancient wax jacket. There's a bit of hay in his hair. He was mucking out the stable — where he keeps his one goat, two pigs, three hens, the garrulous goose and the lamb-bearing ewe — when I rang him.

I reach up and pull the hay out of Thomas's hair. Habit, I suppose. I hand it to him and he takes it and I look around the room, even though there's nothing much to look at. Just some faded linoleum and three hard-backed armchairs that don't belong together.

We wait. My parents return from the chapel.

Dad says, 'Any news?'

I shake my head. Thomas says, 'Not yet.'

The consultant said it was a routine procedure but that didn't stop him getting us to sign forms with lists as long as your arm as to what could go wrong. Transparency. That's what he called it. Covering your arse, more like.

Mum says, 'Tea?' Everybody nods, and she looks relieved. That she has something to do. Something to fill the space between the start of Ed's procedure and the end.

After she's got the tea, Mum retreats to the corridor to pace it. Dad stands as close as he can to the operating theatre without being in the way.

Thomas and I stay where we are.

We don't say much. Having him here, in the room, squashed into the narrow chair beside mine, isn't strange. I suppose it should be, when you consider everything. But it isn't. It's a comfort. Like the embers of a fire on a hard day in November. It's almost as though I think that, once Thomas is here, nothing bad will happen. Nothing bad will happen to Ed.

Time somehow passes. I don't know if it's a lot of time or a little but it passes all the same. I don't think about anything in particular. If pressed, I'd say I'm thinking about Ed but I couldn't tell you for sure.

Thomas sits so still, you'd be forgiven for thinking he is asleep. He has a capacity for stillness that is rare, especially in someone so long. His legs stick out in front of him, providing an impediment — and almost certainly a tripping hazard — to anyone entering the room. I used to trip over them in the beginning. Then I got wise and commanded him to 'call them home' before he got a chance to fling them around the place.

Later, Thomas gets me a coffee. Not one from the machine. He goes to the deli on the corner to get it. A decaf-cappuccino with skimmed milk, one and a half sachets of Demerara sugar and a light dusting of chocolate powder on the top. It's perfect. It's definitely the best thing that's happened all day. Maybe even longer than that.

I don't tell him that. Instead I say, 'Thank you.'

This part of the hospital is quiet. There is

something unnatural about the quiet. As if the world is holding its breath. Waiting for the bad news. Or the good, I suppose.

I think about bargaining. And then I dismiss the idea as ridiculous. And then I go right ahead and bargain anyway.

With whom, I couldn't say.

'If you make sure Ed is OK, I won't drink for a month.'

Nothing.

'OK, two months, then ... Fine. Three ... What the hell, I won't touch a drop for the whole bloody year. I'll be a ... whatdyacallem ... a teetotaller. For a year. Twelve months. So long as Ed is perfectly fine. He has to be one hundred per cent perfect or the deal's off.'

Thomas looks at me. 'What did you say?'

'Nothing.'

'You did. You said something.'

'No, I didn't.'

'You did. Something about a deal.'

'I didn't.'

We go back to being quiet again.

A face appears round the door and I jump. It's not a particularly horrific face. It's a perfectly acceptable, round little face, with spectacles and worry lines where spectacles and worry lines have every right to be. It's just that, curled as it is round the door, it looks a little disembodied.

'Katherine? Katherine Kavanagh?'

'Yes.'

'I'm Dr Collins, the cardiologist. I've just spoken to your parents. They're in with Edward. They asked me to come and find you.'

371

'He's out of theatre?' I stand up so fast the chair topples backwards. Thomas stands up too, puts his hand on my shoulder and says, 'Steady,' in the same tone he uses on his goat when the goose gets her goat up and she goes on one of her sunflower-fuelled rampages.

I put both hands on my face. The tips of my fingers are cold, despite the dense heat of the waiting room.

I say, 'How is he?' Thomas stands beside me.

'Edward presented with an acute arrhythmia, very probably brought on by his congenital heart condition, which doubtless was the cause of his collapse and loss of consciousness.'

I say, 'How is he? Is he OK?'

'We performed a procedure whereby we inserted a catheter in through the leg and up into his heart, through his vascular supply, and in this way we've been able to put a patch over the orifice that appears to have . . . '

I study the man's face but I can tell nothing from it. It is the most impassive face I have ever seen. I say, 'Just tell me how he is, for the love of God.'

He nods and allows a curt smile to glance across his face. He is obviously used to dealing with unpleasant people. 'Given the severity of the arrhythmia, we felt it prudent to insert a pacemaker into Ed's heart, but this is a precautionary measure. On the whole, I believe that the procedure went well. There were no complications and . . . '

I look at his mouth and it's still moving so he's still talking but I'm not listening anymore.

He said 'well'.

He said, 'The procedure went well.'

I have the most curious sensation. As if the world has stopped. The world has stopped and everything is still and silent, and I get a sense of how ridiculous things are. Saying 'God bless you' when someone sneezes. Keeping a snake as a pet. Fascinators. And pseudonyms for crime novels. Crime novels, for fuck's sake.

'OhmyGodOhmyGodOhJesusOhmyGod.'

'Let her sit down. Open a window. Kat?' It might be Thomas. The voice is muffled. Faint.

He said 'well'.

He said, 'The procedure went well.'

All of a sudden, I'm George Bailey in *It's a Wonderful Life* and Clarence has just shown me what life would be without Ed and it takes my breath away. It does.

'I'd say she's having a panic attack.' That's Dr Collins. He sounds vaguely uninterested. I'd be offended if I didn't feel so . . . peculiar.

'Kat?' Thomas again. I want to say something. There are things I need to say. Hands push against my shoulders and I'm sitting in a chair now and suddenly there's a sharp crack and lovely cold air comes gushing into my mouth and down my throat, like water down a mountain after a thaw. I gulp it in, blow it out, gulp it in. It feels delicious to be alive. I've never noticed it before. How delicious it is. And it's only then, after a few gulps and exhalations, that I realise that Thomas has hit me, with his open palm, right across the face.

Afterwards, he denies it. 'I smacked you, is all.'

373

My red, throbbing cheek pays testament to the truth.

Apparently, you're not supposed to hit people when they are having a panic attack. Dr Collins told Thomas that. Afterwards.

In spite of this sage-if-untimely piece of free medical advice, it works. Thomas hitting me.

I stop hyperventilating.

Now I'm crying. Not discreet, delicate crying that people reserve for public places. It's the real thing. There's mascara. There're secretions. There's blotchy skin. Red, swollen eyelids. Minnie told me once that I wasn't a pretty crier and she was right. It's bad. It's about as bad as it can be. I'm crying in public. Right in front of Thomas. And Dr Collins.

I don't think I can stop.

Thomas puts his arms around me and says, 'It's all right, Kat. Ed is fine. The doctor said Ed is going to be fine. The procedure went well.'

This has no impact on the weeping. It's like I'm fifteen again. I'm in the changing room of O'Connor's Jeans. Minnie has just told me. And instead of standing there and saying nothing, I'm crying. I'm weeping. I'm wailing. Like I'm fifteen all over again. Dr Collins says, 'I'm afraid I'm going to have to go now.'

Neither of us responds so he leaves.

I'm crying so hard now, I can't catch my breath. There's a chance I might suffocate, which I suppose isn't as bad as it could be, considering I'm at a hospital. If you're going to suffocate anywhere, a hospital isn't a bad place to go about it.

It's only afterwards I realise that I'm clinging to Thomas like a limpet on a rock. One entire section of his shirt is saturated with my tears. Later, I will notice a deep circular indentation on my forehead caused — I assume — by the gigantic wooden button on the lapel of his jacket. Buttons don't usually appear on lapels of jackets but he insists on buying shop-soiled clothes. Seconds, he calls them. He has a thing about waste. He says somebody has to buy them. 'Why does it have to be you?' I often asked him.

As suddenly as I began, I stop. I stop crying. Thomas, God love him, looks a little dazed. I suppose I can't blame him. He's never seen me crying. He has no idea what an ugly crier I am. Well, he knows now. I reach into my pockets for tissues but there are none. Why would there be? Thomas takes a gigantic piece of material out of his pocket and I hope it's a clean handkerchief because he goes right ahead and wipes my face with it. He pats it. When he spreads his fingers, one of his hands can span my entire face. I remember that.

And, just like that, I reach for him with my hand and sort of touch his cheek with my fingers. If I were writing it down in a romance novel, I might call the gesture 'tender'. I can't believe it. But instead of jerking my hand away like it's been bitten by a dog, I hold my fingers there. Against his face. Here I am, standing in this barren room, touching Thomas's face with my fingers, as if it's nothing. As if it's normal.

The stubble scratches against my skin. Everything is so familiar. The angle of his cheekbone. The lines that stretch from the corners of his eyes. The dark thicket of his eyebrows. And his mouth. You could say a lot of things about a mouth like that.

I think Thomas is as shocked as I am because he looks at me as if he has absolutely no idea who I am. I decide to let my hand drop and not mention it. Pretend it never happened. Start a conversation about something else entirely.

I let my hand drop.

And then I start having a conversation, but it's not the one I planned. It's this one, right here.

'I'm not crying about Ed.' It takes about a minute to get this sentence out because, while I have stopped crying, my body and my voice are still twitching and heaving and juddering.

Thomas nods. He waits for me.

'I've made a mess of everything.'

Thomas nods again. The cheek.

'After the accident, I . . . I freaked out. All that stuff you were saying . . . about getting married, having a baby . . . '

'I didn't know about — '

'Don't say anything, Thomas. Please. Let me . . . '

He nods.

'I never said sorry. But I am. I'm sorry. I'm really sorry. I'm so sorry. I messed everything up. I wrecked it.'

Thomas says nothing.

'And that thing . . . that . . . business with Nicolas. That was just . . . that was nothing. That was stupid. I mean, he wasn't even a good kisser. He had this really long tongue and — '

'Don't bother with the details, Kat.'

I look at him in case he might be smiling but he is not.

'And I'm not trying to wreck what you have with Sarah now. I'm glad you're happy. You deserve to be happy. You're a good man. I was . . .'

'You were what?' He leans forward as if he really wants to know.

'I suppose I wasn't able for you.'

Thomas pulls back. 'I see.'

'You made me so happy.'

He says, 'Did I?' like he doesn't really believe it.

I nod. 'You did. And I could never make you that happy. It's not in me.'

Thomas studies me. As if he's lost and I'm some class of a map. 'So?' he says. 'What are you saying?'

'I'm apologising. For everything.'

Thomas shakes his head. 'I wish you weren't such hard work.'

'So do I.'

'What about Faith?'

'I don't know. I . . . I've wrecked that too.'

'Did Faith tell you that? Or did you decide?'

'Her brother rang me. Her little brother, Milo.'

'What did you say?'

'I was pretty short with him.'

'Yeah, but when he gets to know you, he'll know you don't mean it.'

'I don't think so, Thomas. I don't think that's going to happen.'

'Why not?'

'It can't work out.'

'You don't know that.'

'I don't know how to make it work. I've left it too late.'

'Isn't that a matter for Faith to decide? Not you.' His tone is as barbed as wire. He could be talking about something else. He could be talking about lots of things.

He stands up, pats himself down, which makes not the slightest bit of difference to any of the wrinkles in his clothes. He adopts a jocular tone. 'So what about the pair of us, then? Are we actually going to end up as friends?'

'Jesus, no. I couldn't be friends with you.'

'Nice.'

'No, I mean . . . ' Christ, being honest is hard work. And exhausting. I don't know how Ed does it.

'What?'

'I can't be friends because I'd be . . . hoping it could be something more. And thinking about *Grey's Anatomy*.' There. I said it. It wasn't that bad. Thomas doesn't even look surprised. The cheek of him.

He smiles. 'That was pretty good, mind.'

I nod.

He moves towards the door. Then he turns and opens his mouth and looks as if he's about to say something and, for a moment, I have an enormous feeling of well-being. As if he's going to say something that will change everything. Then he says, 'You'll let me know about Ed, won't you?'

Disappointment tastes sour. Like gooseberries.

I swallow it down. 'Of course.' I'll get Dad to ring him. I don't think I'll ever be able to talk to him again. Not after everything. Not when everything is wrecked and you're the one who wrecked it.

He nods.

He bends his head and ducks through the door. Then he turns and says, 'Take care of yourself, Kat.' This is goodbye but I don't say it. The word is stuck in my throat like a fishbone. Instead, I try to smile and he nods again and walks away, and I watch until he disappears along the curve of the corridor.

Finally, I can use a word that I've never had any cause to use before. Magnanimous.

I am being magnanimous.

It doesn't feel as good as I thought it might.

And I can't even have a drink. Not for a whole bloody year.

I was right about the Christmas tree. Dad shouldn't have bought it so early. It's starting to smell. It smells a bit like Mrs Barber's perfume. The bottle is so old that the picture and the words aren't there anymore. It just looks like an ordinary bottle that used to be white, I reckon, with yellow crusty stuff round the lid. I don't know why she doesn't throw it away. She says being wasteful is nearly as bad as being a robber, so maybe that's why.

We're on our Christmas holiday now. The bad thing about the holiday is that there's no lifesaving class. Damo has gone into town with his mam to see the lights and have their dinner in McDonald's. Damo's not into the lights but he likes McDonald's. He asks for a chicken burger meal and a chicken burger and his mam says that's dead greedy, but she gets it for him anyway. She says it's because it's Christmas but she gets it for him other times too. Even when it's not Christmas.

This will be the first year when people know I don't believe in Santa so I'm not sure if there'll be anything under the tree on Christmas morning. I probably shouldn't have let on that I didn't believe until Boxing Day. At least I'll probably get a present for my birthday.

I don't know if Ant and Adrian are coming home for Christmas. Faith didn't know when I asked her last week. I don't want to ask her again and I don't know their mobile numbers.

The only presents under the tree are the ones I put there. I'm not good at wrapping so I just bought those gift bags you can get in the pound shop. They're great except that if you look inside, you can see what the present is. I don't think Faith has looked inside hers yet so she probably doesn't know that I got her a keyring with an Irish leprechaun on it. I got it in the airport in Dublin when she went to the loo. His eyes light up green when you shake it. She has keys for the house as well as the Funky Banana so it will be handy to have a keyring to keep them all safe. I got her chocolates too because Mam always said that if you want to cheer up a woman, you could do a lot worse than give her chocolates and make her a cup of tea.

I go downstairs. Faith is sitting at the kitchen table doing the books. I say, 'Would you like a cup of tea?'

She picks up a piece of paper and looks at me. 'Whose number is this?'

'I don't know.'

'Milo?' Which means you have to answer the question again but differently this time.

'I don't know.'

Faith hands me the piece of paper. 'It's an Irish telephone number. A Dublin telephone number. I didn't call it so it must have been you.'

I'm trying to come up with something to say but I can't so I say nothing.

Faith points at the piece of paper she's handed me. 'The call was made at twenty past one in the morning.' She looks at me. Rubs her eyes and pushes her hair away from her face. Her hair could do with a brush. And a wash, to be honest. Mam would call it a wren's nest.

I'm about to answer. I get ready to answer. I've my mouth open and everything, when Faith says, 'And don't bother lying to me because I'll know.'

I close my mouth.

'Milo?'

'I rang her.'

'Who?'

'You know who.'

'No. I don't.'

'I asked her to come over.'

'Milo, for Christ's sake, what were you thinking?'

'She said she — '

'DON'T. Don't tell me what that woman said. I don't want to know. You should never have rung her.'

I look at Faith then. At her dirty, tangled hair. She never used to have dirty, tangled hair. There are crumbs on the kitchen floor and plates and cups and knives and forks in the sink and on the counter and they're all dirty too. There's scrambled egg stuck to a plate. It's been there since yesterday, I think. It'll never come off in the dishwasher. It'll have to be scrubbed and it'll take ages. And the Christmas tree. The drooping Christmas tree that smells worse than Mrs Barber's ancient perfume. And it's nearly dark. It's only about three o'clock in the afternoon but it's nearly dark anyway.

'Milo? What's the matter?' Faith's voice sounds far away, as if she's in a different place to me. It's probably because I have my hands over my eyes and ears.

'Milo?'

I shake my head but I don't think I can be quiet for much longer. It feels like there's something inside me. Like a volcano or something. We learned about Etna in school the other day. Miss Williams said that Etna is one of the most active volcanoes in the world.

'Milo? Milo, don't. I'm sorry. I shouldn't have shouted at you.'

I'm crying now. Like a girl. Not like Carla, though. She never cries. Not even when the girls call her a tomboy and don't invite her to their birthday parties. They say she wouldn't like it on account of the fact that they put make-up on their faces and make their hair go curly with a special machine. I don't think Carla would like it either, but you never know, do you? You never know with girls.

I don't think I can stop. I have my fingers across my eyes now but it's no use. I'm roaring crying and I can't stop. If Damo saw me, he'd give me a dead arm and call me a gay, which is just about the worst thing you can be, Damo says.

'Milo, stop. Please. It's not your job to fix things. I'm supposed to do that. I know I'm doing a terrible job.'

I can't say anything because of all the crying I'm doing, but if I could, I'd say, 'You're not doing a terrible job.'

Faith pulls me by the arms to the other side of the kitchen and sort of pushes me onto the couch. She holds one of my hands for a second but then she lets it go.

'Mam would lambast me if she were here.'

I try not to but I cry a bit harder, all the same. I suppose I've always known that Mam's not coming back. Not ever. I know that. I'm nearly ten. I'll be ten in three days. Christmas Day. I'll be ten on Christmas Day, which is the one day of the year when I can eat Christmas cake and birthday cake. At the same time, if I want to. Mam said she got me for Christmas. When I was a kid, I used to think that I came all wrapped up. Like a present. Of course I don't think that anymore. People know a lot more things when they're nearly ten. I know that Mam will never lambast Faith and not just because she never lambasted Faith or any of us, but because she's never coming home. Not ever. I'll never see her again and I know that Mrs Appleby says I can close my eyes and see her face in my head and remember her like that, but it's not as easy as that. Closing your eyes and seeing her there, in your head. I can see her most of the time but sometimes I can't and I'm worried about that. Like maybe she's leaving my head as well, and I don't want her to, but I don't know how to keep her there.

Anyway, if Mam were here, everything would be different. It would. I wouldn't be crying for a start. No way. And Faith wouldn't know that Mam isn't her real mam and that her real mam is somebody in Ireland called Kat, which is short for Katherine, who doesn't want to be anybody's mother even though she is. Even though she is somebody's mother.

And there wouldn't be crumbs on the floor all the time, or scrambled eggs stuck like glue to a plate, or a drooping, smelly Christmas tree in the sitting room three days before Christmas Day. And Faith wouldn't have dirty, tangled hair. She would have shiny, clean hair and she wouldn't be here all the time, making a mess in the kitchen or getting me to answer her phone and telling Rob she's in the shower again.

I say, 'She wouldn't lambast you.'

Faith sits on the couch beside me. She says, 'I know.' And then she starts crying. We're like a tag team in a relay race because now I'm not crying. Now I'm trying to think of something to say that will make her stop. She's crying like somebody who might never stop and I'm glad I can't see her face because of all the dirty, tangled hair round it. I think, if I saw it, it might set me off again and I hate crying because it gives you a headache and makes you dehydrated because of all the water that comes out of you. I stand up and pull some kitchen paper off the roll so Faith can blow her nose when she stops crying.

She stops and I hand her a piece of kitchen roll. She says, 'I should be doing this for you, not the other way round.'

I say, ''Sall right.'

Faith says, 'No. It's not all right. You're the one who's upset. Christ knows, you've every right to be.'

'I'm fine now. I'm not sad anymore.'

She looks at me funny. Like I'm one of those cryptic crossword puzzles that Mam used to do. Faith said she couldn't do them because she wasn't clever enough but Mam said that wasn't true. It was patience. That's all Faith was missing.

She says, 'What's your secret, Milo?'

I say, 'Which one?' as if I've got loads, which isn't true. I've only got the one that Carla told me. About her dad not having a job anymore on account of the shop closing down. No one else knows except me and I haven't told anyone. Carla made me promise that I wouldn't tell anyone. Not even Damo. As if I'd ever tell Damo something like that. I know he's my best friend but he'd blab it to his granny, if he still had one.

Faith says, 'Mam was right, you know.'

I say, 'About what?'

'About you.'

'What about me?'

'She said you were a tonic.'

'Is that good?'

'It means there's something about you that makes people feel better.'

'That's not true.'

'It is.'

'I haven't made you feel better.'

Faith goes ahead and hugs me then, and because she does it so quickly there's no time to dodge it. Faith's not a hugger, as a rule, so it doesn't last too long. Not like Mam. When Mam decided she was going to hug you, it went on and on for ages.

In fact, Faith's hug goes on a bit longer than I thought it would. And even though her hair is a bit dirty and she smells like a cigarette, it's actually not that bad because Faith happens to be one of the softest people I know so it sort of feels like you're being hugged by a marshmallow.

When she stops, she says, 'It's not your job, Milo. To make me feel better. I should be making you feel better.'

I say, 'I don't feel too bad.'

Faith says, 'But you do feel a little bit bad, don't you? It's normal, you know. To feel a little bit bad. There's no harm in it.'

I don't explain. About the crumbs and the scrambled egg and the Christmas tree and the dark of the house, even though it's only three o'clock in the afternoon. I don't say any of that. I just nod and Faith nods too, like I've said something that she agrees one hundred per cent with. The door into the sitting room

386

is open and you can see the Christmas tree from here. Faith looks at it. Like she's just noticed it. The drooping branches and the pine needles on the floor. She looks at it for ages.

I decide to say this: 'Mrs Appleby thinks that things can seem a bit worse. At Christmas time, I mean.'

Faith doesn't say anything for a while. She looks at me but I know she's not really looking at me. She's thinking about something entirely different. Turns out she's thinking about Christmas because she says — all of a sudden — 'Christmas.'

I say, 'Yes. It's in three days. Did you forget about it?'

She says, 'Sort of.' I don't know how you can sort of forget about something. Especially Christmas. I hope she hasn't sort of forgotten about my birthday too.

She says, 'I'm going to sort it out,' as if Christmas has sprung a leak or something and she happens to have just the thing to fix it.

Something is different. In the days following Ed's procedure — Ed's successful procedure — something feels different. Or perhaps it is me who is different.

I'm having funny thoughts.

Not funny ha ha.

Funny weird.

First of all, there's Brona. She rings to find out about Ed. I tell her and she says how pleased she is that the operation went well, and then she comments on how happy I sound and how she's never heard me sound so happy. Not ever. And I say it's because I've never been this happy. Not ever. This is difficult for someone like me to explain but I try. I feel like I've been given a reprieve. Like I was on death row and some lawyer in a John Grisham novel found some obscure piece of precedent law that meant I could waltz out of death row and skip on out of prison and take one of those Greyhound buses they're always taking in America and just . . . just be on my way. And, peculiar as that may sound, that's how I feel. And the really weird thing is that I don't just leave it there, the thought that is banging against the walls of my mind. No. I go right ahead and share the thought with Brona.

She tries to take it on the chin but she's pretty shocked. I can tell. And then, instead of giving her a moment to digest all this talk of happiness and the John Grisham novels and the obscure pieces of precedent law and the Greyhound buses, I go right ahead and tell her all the other stuff too. The stuff about me not writing. Not having written in months. Not a paragraph. Not a sentence. Not one single word. All the lies I've told her. I can't even call them white lies or half-lies. They were nothing but fully formed, gigantic lies.

She doesn't say anything for a while and then, finally, she says, 'I see.' Which is pretty damned good of her when you take everything into consideration.

'I'm not myself,' I tell Minnie.

'Thank Christ for that.'

'I need your help.'

'OK.' I love Minnie because she is the type of person who says, 'OK,' when you ask for help instead of asking what kind of help it is you need.

'Do you know how to organise a press conference?'

'No, but I know a woman who can.'

Minnie always knows women who can.

Minnie says, 'You sure about this?'

'Yes. I'm sure.'

Neither of us say anything for a moment and then she says, 'Why now? Why are you going public now?'

'I'd prefer people heard it from me, before that

man sells it to some British rag. Besides . . . ' I pause.

'Besides what?'

'It's just . . . it's time.'

Minnie nods. 'Yes, it is. It's time.'

Later, she rings. 'It's on for Friday. Ten a.m.'

'But that's the day before Christmas Eve.'

'You got plans?'

'No, but . . . '

'Be there at ten past. Tamara, the PR, will have the place stacked with journos. She's drip-fed them just enough to whet their appetites.'

My stomach contracts, like I'm on a rollercoaster that's inching its way to the top of the track. 'Thank you, Minnie.'

There's no going back now but, in spite of this, the happiness persists.

I'm happier than Ed, and that has never happened before. Not ever.

He says the same thing every day. 'When can I go home?'

'I'm not sure yet. We'll ask the doctor.'

'Will I be home for Christmas? I don't want to be here on Christmas Day.'

'You'll go home when the doctors say you can go home and not a minute before that, get it?' But even though my tone is as snappy and taut as ever, Ed senses the happiness and he's not delighted with it, to be honest. I suppose I can't blame him. It's not always easy when the shoe is on the other foot.

He says, 'You look different.'

'I know.' It's because I'm smiling. It happens every time I see him. I get the feeling again. The reprieve. John Grisham. The Greyhound bus. The happiness.

Ed says, 'Why?'

'I'm happy because you're OK.'

'I don't feel OK.'

'Well, you are, so stop feeling sorry for yourself.'

'I'm not feeling sorry for myself.'

'You are.'

'It's boring in here.'

'I'll read you a story. It's one I wrote.'

'You can't write stories.'

'I can, Ed. That's what I do. I write stories.'

'That story was written by Killian Kobain. It says it on the cover.'

'I'm Killian Kobain.'

'No you're not, Kat.'

'I am.'

'You're not.'

'I am.'

Ordinarily, Ed can beat me hands down in this type of conversation. Today, he just shrugs and says, 'What's it about?'

'It's about a policeman called Declan Darker who solves mysteries.'

'Are there lovey-dovey bits in it?'

'No.'

'OK then. You can read me a chapter and see if I like it.'

Later, when Mum and Dad come to visit, Ed says, 'Kat writes stories.'

Mum looks at me. 'Really?'

Ed grabs my sleeve. Pulls it. 'You do, don't you, Kat? You do write stories.'

There's nothing else to say except, 'Yes.'

Dad looks at me. 'I didn't know you did that, Kat.'

I shake my head. 'Nobody did.'

Mum says, 'What kind of stories?'

'Crime novels. I use a pseudonym.'

She says, 'Crime? That's a . . . a fairly popular genre, isn't it?'

'Yes.'

She says, 'So you do it in your spare time? When you're not . . . doing your technical writing? Is that it?'

'No, I, ah, I do it full-time. I'm not a technical writer. I never have been.'

She smiles then and I'm not sure but I think there is a suggestion of pride in that smile. If she were a different type of person altogether, she might punch me on the arm and call me 'a chip off the old block'.

Dad says, 'That's lovely, Kat. What's your pseudonym?'

I say, 'Killian Kobain.'

Mum says, 'Good Lord,' and Dad says, 'Oh my goodness,' because, while I'm pretty sure that neither of them has read a popular-fiction book in their lives, both of them have heard of Killian Kobain. The body of a hermit was found in a cave in Malawi recently and there was nothing in the cave apart from his body, a bow and arrow, the hide of a rhinoceros and a copy of The Lost Girl, which was the first Darker book to be made into a film.

I don't say anything but I smile. I can't help it.

It's around this time that I realise that the happiness I feel is not all about Ed. Not just about Ed. It's like a curtain is being pulled open, and when it opens all the way you can see someone standing there and it turns out to be me. I'm standing there. I'm there for anyone to see. I'm as plain as the nose on your face.

I've never been in Scotland for Christmas before. I've never been anywhere for Christmas before. Except home, I mean. It looks like Christmas in Scotland, on account of the snow. Me and Ant and Adrian and Dad build an igloo. Faith told Adrian that if he was coming to Scotland, he'd have to make an effort. She made him swear. He said, 'Cross my heart and hope that fat bastard keels over of a heart attack and dies.'

Faith said, 'ADRIAN!'

Adrian said, 'I'm joking, sis, take it easy.' He winks at me and smiles so I'm pretty sure he really is joking.

Faith makes Ant promise not to call Celia fat, or an adulteress or a home-wrecker or a gold-digger.

It's warm inside the igloo. Ant said it's because air gets trapped inside the snow and acts like an insulator. I say, 'What about our body heat?' and he says, 'I was just getting to that.' Afterwards, we build a snowman. Except Adrian puts two snowballs on the snowman's chest and says it's a snowwoman and Dad says, 'Grow up,' and Adrian throws a snowball at Dad's head and then there's a big snowball fight, and Faith says I'm the only one with any sense because I was the best at dodging the snowballs so my clothes aren't as wet as everyone else's.

Celia hasn't had the baby yet. She's gone to the hospital three times so far to have the baby but then she came home. Dad calls them false alarms, but not in front of Celia anymore.

Christmas is the day after tomorrow. It's turning out to be not so bad. There's tonnes of food in the fridge, for a start. The house is dead neat, even though it's huge. Dad is good at being neat and tidy now. When Celia's not in the hospital having a false alarm, she gets really mad if there's a buttery knife on the worktop or if someone has forgotten to flush the toilet. When she notices something like that, she puts her hands on the bottom of her belly as if it's about to fall off and she shouts, 'HAMISH,' which happens to be Dad's name, and then Dad has to come and tidy up the mess or flush the toilet and make her a cup of raspberry tea and massage her back until she tells him to stop. Celia's belly is way bigger than Dad's now.

Celia has a birthing pool. It's in a big room upstairs that has nothing in it except a really long mirror attached to the wall. The birthing pool looks a bit like a paddling pool. Celia says the room will be her office after the baby comes out but, as far as I know, Celia doesn't have a job anymore. Not since she started being Dad's girlfriend.

Me and Faith took the train to Scotland yesterday. Ant and Adrian got a lift from London with one of their friends who was driving home to Edinburgh for Christmas. Rob said he'd drive us but Faith said she needed to think about things. I don't know why she couldn't think about things in Rob's van. Maybe it's because the heater is broken. It's hard to think when you're freezing cold. I know because the radiator was broken in our classroom last month and Miss Williams said we all had brain-freeze because no one could do the mathematical patterns.

The train was much longer than the one we take to

395

London. Nearly as long as the Hogwarts Express, I reckon. I sat beside the window and Faith said, 'Order whatever you like,' when the man came with the trolley. I got crisps and a Mars Duo and a can of Coke and a packet of Starburst. The seats were dead comfy. Faith fell asleep. I didn't because there was too much to see out of the window.

I like the way the world whizzes by when you're on a train and there are no traffic jams so you can just keep on going. And I don't have to ask if we're there yet because I can tell myself, from looking at the names of the stations when we stop and then looking in the timetable we got at King's Cross.

When I was a little kid, I wanted to be a train driver. Now, I'm going to be a lifeguard when I grow up but I still like going on trains.

Dad met us at the train station. He gave me a high-five then took Faith's suitcase and put it on the ground and he hugged her real tight and they stood like that, in the middle of the platform, for ages, and everyone had to walk round them and they didn't even notice. Afterwards, Dad picked up Faith's suitcase and put his arm across her shoulders. He said, 'We're going to sort things out, OK, kiddo?' Faith didn't say that she could sort things out for herself. And she didn't tell him not to call her kiddo either. She just nodded and walked along beside him, like she was really tired.

Christmas decorations are pretty much the same in Scotland. Every single room in Dad and Celia's house has Christmas decorations in it. Not just the sitting room. Even the birthing pool has got tinsel all over it. Celia says she's having the baby at home because she heard about a woman who went into hospital to have a baby boy and she came home in a box. I don't know what happened to the baby. Celia didn't say. I hope he didn't go home in a box too, I really do.

The first time Celia thinks the baby is coming, she gets Dad to phone for an ambulance.

Dad says, 'Will I not phone Carol?' Carol is the name of the nurse who is in charge of filling the birthing pool with water and helping ladies who are about to have babies in their own houses.

Carol's name and number are in Celia's birth plan. She showed me the plan. It's four pages long. Celia typed it out herself. She can type ninety words a minute, which is one and a half words every second. I did the sum. It's long division.

Celia is in the hall, on her hands and knees. She's making a noise like a bear I saw once on a wildlife programme.

When she's finished making the noise, she turns to Dad and shouts, 'RING 999.'

Dad says, 'Don't worry, pet, I'll drive you to the hospital.'

Celia shouts, 'There's no time to drive. The baby is coming RIGHT NOW.'

When they come home from the hospital and Dad has put Celia to bed, he tells Ant and Adrian to stop laughing, and then he makes us promise that we'll say nothing about the birthing pool or Carol or the false alarm when Celia is in the room.

We promise.

I think Dad is glad we're here. He cooks haggis, even though Celia doesn't let him eat haggis anymore. Dad says it's traditional to eat haggis in Scotland and that he's only cooking it for us and he's not going to eat it, but I catch him picking some off Ant's plate when he's dishing up. I don't say anything and Dad winks at me and says, 'Good lad.'

Haggis doesn't taste as bad as you'd think. He serves it with mashed potatoes and turnips and brown sauce. Celia has to stay in her bedroom on account of the smell.

Faith says, 'We won't stay long.'

Dad says, 'Stay as long as you like.'

Faith says, 'OK. We'll stay for a week. If that's OK.'

Dad says, 'Of course, of course, that's fine. Stay as long as you like.' He always says the same thing a couple of times. Like he doesn't think anyone's listening.

I'm watching a programme about pandas. I don't know what they're going to do when the bamboo runs out.

Dad says, 'I took my eye off the ball for a while.'

Faith says, 'You've been busy.'

'Once the baby comes and things settle down, I'll pitch in more. I'll come down more often. Things will be better. I'll be better. I promise.' He puts his hand on top of Faith's and they sit there on the couch like that for a while.

Faith says, 'I still can't believe it.'

Dad says, 'Your mother and I should have told you. A long time ago.'

'No, not about that. About Mam, I mean. I still can't believe she's gone.'

Dad says nothing to that.

Faith says, 'Sometimes I forget, you know. Something happens. In a lecture or at band practice or something. And I think: Mam will get such a kick out of this.'

It's a good job Ant and Adrian weren't pandas

because only one of them would have survived. The mother chooses which one. I don't think Mam would have been able to choose. She said one was as bad as the other.

Dad says something about 'the boy'. He hardly ever calls me Milo.

Faith says, 'No, there's been too much upset already. He needs to stay in Brighton. That's where his home is.'

Dad says, 'OK then. Once the baby comes — if he ever does — and Celia gets used to him, I'll come to Brighton more often. Once a month, if I can. And the boy will come and visit. Won't you, son?'

Nobody knows what sex the baby is going to be, but Dad keeps talking about him as if he's a boy already.

I say, 'Could Damo come too? Sometime?'

Dad blesses himself and says, 'Saints preserve us,' but he's smiling so that means there's a chance that Damo could come too. Sometime. I'll just have to tell him what to do about babies. Damo doesn't have any little brothers or sisters so he won't know.

The man on the programme says that baby pandas are born pink and blind and toothless, which is a bit like humans. Humans can see only shapes and colours when they're born. And their eyes are blue. Mam said my eyes were blue when I was born and then they changed to brown. And I reckon Faith's eyes were blue when she was born and then they changed to green.

Faith is talking about the Funky Banana now and how Jack wants to buy it. I don't mind selling it if Jack wants to buy it. I bet he'll still give me free stuff when I call into the café. Damo too. Jack says we're like beans and farts. You never get one without the other.

Dad nods and agrees with everything Faith says but I'm not sure if he's listening anymore. He looks pretty tired, and later, when I say, 'Dad?' he jumps and says, 'Yes, of course, son,' as if we're in the middle of a conversation instead of just at the beginning of one. And he's wearing the same shirt he was wearing yesterday, when he picked us up at the station. It's got brown sauce down the front.

Faith's phone rings again but this time she takes the call. She stands up and says, 'Hi, Rob,' and then she leaves the room.

Baby pandas stay with their mams until they're one and a half or maybe two. I'm glad I wasn't born a panda.

Dad is snoring now. Upstairs, I hear Celia getting out of bed. She's making the bear noise again. I put my hand on Dad's shoulder and shake him a bit. His eyes fly open and he says, 'Yes, of course, son.'

I say, 'I think the baby's coming again.'

# 1

Minnie books the Grand Hotel for the press conference, which is a short walk from the apartment. She hires two security guards. Huge ones. I laugh when she tells me but Minnie's face betrays not even a hint of a smile.

She says, 'You asked me to take care of it. I'm taking care of it.'

Turns out she's right. She's always right. We do need them. When the room is full, the two of them stand at the door and present their joint bulk to any other journalists trying to get in.

They also come in very handy when the journos swarm like bees at the end, blocking the door, poking their microphones in my face and pointing their cameras at me. I'd say the photographer from *Heat* won't be waking up and smelling the coffee anytime soon, with that stump he's got now, where his nose used to be.

I tell them everything I know about Killian Kobain and Declan Darker. Afterwards, Minnie says, 'That's all, everybody. Thanks for coming.'

She has to shout into the microphone to be heard over the barrage of questions being hurled towards me. I answer a couple of them before one of the journalists at the front stands up and says, 'Are there any other skeletons in Kat Kavanagh's closet?' Because he has one of those booming voices, it punctures a hole through the

401

babble and gets people's attention, and there is a lull and everyone looks at me and waits.

Minnie nudges me.

I look at her.

She cups her hand over the microphone and whispers, 'You don't have to answer that.'

I shake my head, then look at the man and I say, 'Yes. There is something.'

★ ★ ★

Dad is already at the apartment when we get back from the press conference. In the car park. The engine of his car is running. Mum is in the front seat. I say, 'I thought we were going to meet at the hospital?' Ed is being discharged today. We all want to be there.

Dad says, 'I'll drive in. There's no need for everyone to take their cars.' He has a thing about paying for parking at hospitals. He calls it a 'scandal', which is a pretty strong word for him. Minnie, who rarely lets her car out of her sight — it's a silver Jaguar XKR-S — agrees to leave it at the apartment and let Dad drive all of us in. 'Just for the day that's in it,' she says.

Ed insists on saying goodbye to every patient, nurse and doctor in the hospital before we are allowed to leave. 'I'm glad to be going home but I'll miss the hospital too.'

I say, 'What'll you miss about it?'

'The nurses, mostly.'

Minnie says, 'Don't let Sophie hear you saying that.'

Sophie is the jealous type. I don't think she'd

boil a bunny but I'd say she'd have no qualms about, say, a gerbil or a hamster.

I'm glancing through the leaflet the nurse gave me about the pacemaker. 'The doctor says you have to go back for a check-up in a few weeks. See how the pacemaker is settling in.'

Ed looks worried. He unbuttons his shirt again and shows it to us. We can see the outline of the pacemaker beneath his skin. It is about the size of a matchbox. He says, 'I don't like it. It makes me feel scared.'

Minnie says, 'You're like the bionic man, so you are. They've rebuilt you.'

Ed looks at Minnie. 'I might have died, mightn't I?' He's fond of a bit of drama.

'It'll take more than a dodgy ticker to get rid of you, I'd say.' She's looking at Ed like he's her brother too. She never treated him any other way. I touch her arm and squeeze it. Just a small one. But a squeeze all the same.

A small smile gathers round her mouth.

I say, 'How's Baby Driver coming along?' Maurice took Minnie's name when they got married. He had to, really. He has a surname that happens to be on one of Minnie's blacklists.

She says, 'Week fifteen. Nine centimetres. About the length of a Curly Wurly. My stools are black but that's just the iron supplements.'

I say, 'That's great,' before she can fill me in on any more details.

Dad's car is just outside the hospital, with the engine running. Mum is in the passenger seat, even though she's supposed to be a keynote speaker at a writing conference in Prague. She shrugged when I mentioned it earlier. I help Ed into the car. Mum looks at him. 'There's a blanket there, if you're cold.'

Me and Minnie sit by the windows and Ed is in the middle. Like when we were kids. I tuck the blanket round Ed's knees and the smile he gives me is so huge and so true, I have to turn away. Minnie finishes tucking the blanket and she nods at me, and that's when I realise just how big today is. How huge.

The surgeon called Ed 'lucky'. I wouldn't have used that word. But that's the word I think of now. On this leg of the journey. The home stretch.

Ed is lucky.

We all are.

Dad drives to my apartment first. Minnie needs to get her car and I need to get a toothbrush and some knickers. Ed wants me to stay for a sleepover. I know he's milking it but I don't care.

There's a traffic jam from the railway bridge, through the Diamond and on past the Garda station. I don't take much notice. Malahide is one of those towns that people like to visit at all times of the day and night. It's Minnie who realises. She looks out of the window and says, 'That's weird.'

I say, 'What?'

Minnie lowers her window and sticks her head out. 'There are five television trucks ahead.'

I lean forward, into the space between the two front seats. I say, 'Oh yeah,' and sit back.

Minnie looks at me. She doesn't say anything.

We inch along. It's only when we get through the village and along the curve where the coast road begins that things become clearer. The car park in front of my apartment block is black with trucks. Television trucks. They've spilled onto the road, on double yellows, across driveways, along the edge of footpaths. One is on the slip that leads to the beach. Another has secured an elevated position up on the grass verge, where no vehicle has a right to be.

Mum says, 'What's going on?'

Ed nudges me. 'Maybe there's a celebrity staying in your building, Kat.'

Minnie looks at him. 'You're right, Ed. There's a celebrity in Kat's building.'

Dad says, 'Really? Who?' He is a closet celebrity-gossip-gatherer. I have seen copies of *Now* and *Closer* in his study.

Minnie points at me. 'It's Kat, you great eejits.'

Ed says, 'I'm not an eejit. And Kat's not a celebrity, silly. Her picture's not in any of the magazines Dad has in his study.'

Dad flushes. 'Someone left those magazines there.'

Mum says, 'What about the ones in the bottom drawer of your filing cabinet? Did someone leave them there, as well?'

This strikes us as funny, probably because Mum rarely says anything that you could brand 'humorous'. She is as serious as Tolstoy's *War and Peace*. It's just the way she is, I suppose.

Minnie looks at me. 'Kat, listen, you can't go in there. You'll be mobbed. We'll have to go to

405

your parents' house.'

Dad says, 'What if they follow us?' His hands grip the steering wheel so tightly that his knuckles are white. He would be hopeless as a getaway driver.

Minnie says, 'Kat, duck down. So they don't spot you.'

But I don't duck down because this doesn't seem real. None of it. Even though I can see them. The hundred-strong army of the type of media that you would be well within your rights to call paparazzi. On my doorstep. Waiting for me. I can see them. But I don't quite believe it. Not yet.

The line of traffic is static. Dad's car is stuck, right outside the apartment block. It feels like we're in the eye of a storm. Outside, the activity is frantic; inside, it's the type of quiet that seems too quiet. Just as I'm about to take Minnie's advice and duck down, someone shouts, 'Oi!' When I turn to look, there's a man in a truck and he's pointing at Dad's car. He's pointing at me. And suddenly my heart is hurling itself against my chest, like a battering ram. I yell, 'DRIVE!' and Dad — who is notable as a driver only because most people can jog alongside the car when he's at full tilt — rams the gearstick into first and swings out into oncoming traffic, narrowly missing the bumper of a mustard-coloured Ford Focus being driven by a man with a poodle on his knee. The man and the dog are in matching yellow jackets. It's funny the things you notice when you're being chased by a television truck. Dad guns the car and it roars up

Bath Lane, which is a narrow little one-way with a nasty bend. There's a dodgy-as-hell bit when Dad's car mounts the kerb, but apart from breaking some lower branches off a tree, there's no real harm done.

I keep my eyes on the rear window. The television truck is behind us and gaining. The driver shouts into a mobile phone.

Minnie yells, 'Take a right at the end of this road.'

Dad says, 'There's a STOP sign!'

'Well, stop first. Then take the right.'

Dad stops. Mum roars, 'CLEAR LEFT,' and Dad smiles at her before he shoots out onto the road, his tyres making a satisfying screeching noise against the tarmac.

Minnie shouts, 'Take that little left at Vinny Vannuchi's.'

I have to pitch in there. 'It's not called Vinny Vannuchi's anymore. It's the Scotch Bonnet. It's been the Scotch Bonnet for ages.'

Ed says, 'Is that the restaurant that has the spicy chicken wings I like, Kat?'

Dad yells, 'Am I turning left here or not?'

Minnie and I yell, 'YES!' at the same time and then Minnie looks over the top of Ed's head towards me and says, 'This is like *Cagney and Lacey*, isn't it? Except we're in the back seat.'

*Cagney and Lacey* was our favourite programme when we were kids. When we weren't watching it, we were playing it. We both wanted to be Cagney. We had to take it in turns to be Lacey. Neither of us wanted to be married to Harv.

407

Minnie shouts, 'Turn left here. Up into St Margaret's Park.'

Dad turns left so quickly I get thrown against the window and, for a moment, it really is like an episode of *Cagney and Lacey*.

Behind us, we can hear the roar of the truck.

Minnie says, 'Pull into someone's driveway. Look, down that road there. It's a cul-de-sac. They won't find us down there.'

Dad does as he's told. He pulls into an empty driveway and performs a pretty dramatic emergency stop. We wait. Nobody says a word. Minnie hisses, 'Get down, everyone,' and this time I do as I'm told and so does everyone else. It doesn't take long to become 'media savvy', it seems.

After a while, Mum says, 'This is ridiculous.'

I say, 'I couldn't agree more.'

Ed says, 'How come the television trucks don't chase you, Mum?'

Once we start laughing, we can't stop. If someone passes by, they would see an ancient green Lexus shaking, with what looks like nobody inside.

Dad waits a full twenty minutes before he drives away. He takes the back roads to Raheny, through Donaghmede and Kilbarrack. The rest of the journey passes without incident. It's only when we turn onto the Howth Road that I realise I have more to learn about media savvy-ness.

There are more trucks. Television trucks. Outside my parents' house. Only two of them but enough to give me a jolt, nonetheless.

Ed yells, 'Holy smoke!' when he sees them. He's enjoying all the cloak and dagger.

Dad says, 'I can't drive around for much longer. We're nearly out of juice.' He never says 'juice'. He says 'petrol'.

Minnie says, 'If we go in there, we're trapped. We'll be like fish in a barrel.'

That's when Mum says, in a quiet voice so we have to strain to hear her, 'I want to go home.'

Dad says, 'OK.'

And that's how we end up barricaded inside the house where I grew up, with the media, swelling in numbers by the hour, camped outside the door and up and down the street.

We pull down the blinds. Put on the kettle. Ed says he's starving but when I check the fridge there are a few stalks of celery, a tub of natural yoghurt, a hard triangle of Edam and a withered bunch of thyme. Looking in this fridge it's hard to believe it will be Christmas Eve tomorrow.

Dad says, 'I'm sorry. I haven't had the chance to go shopping.'

Ed says, 'But I'm hungry.'

I say, 'I'll ring Domino's.'

Minnie says, 'How's that going to look on the news? World famous author stuffs face with Domino's Mighty Meaty?'

In the end, I find potato waffles and fish fingers in the freezer, possibly left over from the days when I used to live in the house. I steam the celery to make it a bit more healthy-heart-ish for Ed but he refuses to eat it because I forgot to chop the stalks into chunks and I tell him I'll do it now but he says, 'It's too late, Kat.'

Sky News have the story running on a loop.

*The revelation today, of the author of the hugely successful Declan Darker series of novels, has sent shock waves through the publishing world, the reading world and the world at large. Katherine Kavanagh — known affectionately to her friends and family as Kat — revealed today, at a press conference, that she has been writing under the pseudonym Killian Kobain for almost twenty years. Following a short statement from Kavanagh, the writer left the press conference, refusing to answer any questions. The media-shy Kat is hiding out at her parents' house in Dublin, where her brother, Edward, who is autistic, is said to be recovering from the recent removal of a brain tumour.*

There's no point screaming at the television screen but I do it anyway. With each report comes a fresh inaccuracy.

*Kat Kavanagh received a six-figure advance in the spring of 1992 when she submitted a mere three chapters of Dirty Little Secret, which she had written longhand into several shorthand notebooks, to publishers Hodder & Stoughton.*

That's rubbish. Minnie sent the entire manuscript. And I used legal pads. And it was July. That's bloody well summer, the last time I checked.

*Brona Best — Kat Kavanagh's editor for the past twenty years — spoke today of the lengths that she had to go to, to protect her top writer's identity. Describing Kavanagh as deeply paranoid and unpredictable, Best said that, with*

*Kavanagh's murky past, the writer's behaviour is understandable.*

Brona rings almost immediately. She is weeping. 'I . . . I . . . I ne . . . nev . . . never . . . told them that . . . Kat . . . I swear . . . I di . . . I di . . . I didn't t-t-tell them anything.'

It takes me ages to get her to stop crying. Eventually I have to yell, 'Stop crying,' which works a treat.

Brona says, 'They're camped outside on the street. The phones won't stop ringing. One of the camera crews has rented a scissor lift.'

'Why?'

'I don't know. We're on the sixteenth floor, for Christ's sake.'

Brona never blasphemes. Things are serious.

'Look, Brona. Don't worry. It'll blow over. Just keep your head down and your mouth shut.'

Brona starts crying again. Quietly this time.

She says, 'You were right.'

'About what?'

'The leak. It came from our office.'

'WHAT? HOW?'

'Bloody Harold.'

'Harold? Jeremy's boyfriend?'

'Ex-boyfriend, remember? Apparently, he was up to his neck in debt. He was an addict.'

'A drug addict?'

'Cosmetic surgery. He's had everything done. He looked like Joan Rivers in the end, Jeremy said. Anyway, he must have been poking around Jeremy's home office and he found something about you. Jeremy is distraught. He's in the disabled toilet, crying his eyes out.'

'Why is he in the disabled toilet?'

'Privacy.' It seems like a strange word now, in the circumstances.

For a while, neither of us says anything. It's nice, actually. A fleeting moment of peace.

Then Brona says, 'Is it true? What you said? About having a baby?'

I say, 'Yes,' and Brona begins to cry again. A soft little cry. It makes a terrible sound.

Eventually she says, 'That's s-s-s-so saaaaaaaaad.'

It was only a matter of time before they uncovered Thomas, I suppose. They find him in one of his five stony fields, putting up a fence. He's wearing a long sheepskin over a suit, the trousers of which are tucked inside the wellingtons. The bright pink ones. With the yellow buttercups. The camera has to pan up for a good while before it reaches his face.

Seeing him on the television is a terribly strange sensation. His face is so familiar. I know it so well, like the way to somewhere you've been going to for years. You just go. You don't have to think about it.

And yet, there is something strange about it too and I think it's because Thomas is on the television and I've never seen him on the television. I've seen him in my home. In my bed. All over my life. And I miss it. I miss seeing him. This much I am certain of. To be honest, it feels good. To know something for certain.

The newsreader — Dawn Handel — is in the middle of a story about me getting a D for my English paper in the Leaving Certificate, which is the first thing they've said that is one hundred per cent true (Mum took it as a personal affront and didn't speak to me for weeks after the results came out). Dawn stops in the middle of a sentence about Sister Rafferty, who was my English teacher back then, and who surely must be festering in the grave by now. She cocks her head and touches her ear with her fingers. She says, 'Breaking news now. We are going straight over to a farm in County Monaghan' — she pronounces it 'Monag-Han', which I don't think the locals are going to like — 'where our reporter has caught up with Thomas Cunningham [Cunning-Ham], Kat's partner.'

I cover my face with my hands. Then I splay my fingers so I can see through the gaps and I watch his face on the screen. That familiar face. The face that I know off by heart.

Ed shouts, 'It's Thomas. There's Thomas. Thomas is on the television!' This brings Mum, Dad and Minnie running in from the kitchen, where they have been talking in low, urgent voices. On the screen now is a reporter with a microphone. He's a small, skinny little fellow with huge, black glasses. The microphone covers most of his face. He looks like he's getting smaller until I realise he's sinking. Every so often, he pulls one foot out of the black mud and it comes away with a guttural sucking sound that is picked up, clear as a bell, by the microphone. The persistent rain over the past few days has turned Thomas's five stony fields into a mud bath.

He says, 'I'm here in County Monag-Han at a

413

farm that is owned by Thomas Cunning-Ham who, we understand, is engaged to be married to Katherine Kavanagh AKA Killian Kobain.' He pauses to let the import of the sentence sink in. His feet sink a little deeper into the mud.

Behind him, the camera picks up Thomas, who has put down the hammer — thank Christ — and is walking towards the reporter.

Thomas says, 'Can I help you?' His tone is about as helpful as a hearing aid for a blind man.

The journalist says, 'Is it true that you are engaged to be married to Katherine Kavanagh?'

Thomas says, 'No.'

The journalist says, 'But you were romantically involved with Kat Kavanagh, were you not?'

Thomas steps forward and the journalist steps back. Thomas says, 'Get off my land.'

The journalist says, 'Did you know? That she wrote the Declan Darker books?'

Thomas says, 'I know a lot of things. And one of those things is that you're trespassing on my property.'

The journalist says, 'Do you know who fathered the child that Kat Kavanagh gave away when she was just fifteen years old?'

Thomas says no more. Instead, he picks up the journalist with both hands. It takes him longer than it should because he has to pull him out of the mud, which is now up to the journalist's shins. He walks to the bit of the fence he's built so far, and deposits the journalist on a haystack on the other side. Then he wipes his hands on the trousers of one of his two good suits and looks right at the camera, and that's

414

when the screen shudders as if whoever is holding the camera is running backwards — and why wouldn't they? — before it goes dark and then switches back to the studio, where Dawn Handel is there to pick up the pieces.

She says, 'More from Mark Simms in Monag-Han a little later on. And now, over to the sports desk.'

Minnie finds the remote and switches off the telly. She goes to the kitchen and switches off the radio. I hear her put on the kettle. She returns with her iPad. She says, 'You're trending on Twitter.'

I say, 'So?' because I don't see what difference that makes, in the general scheme of things.

Minnie says, 'And you're on the front page of all the evening newspapers and I don't just mean the Irish ones. Look.'

She hands me her iPad and I scroll through the headlines.

**THE NINE LIVES OF KAT KAVANAGH**

**KILLIAN KOBAIN GETS IN TOUCH WITH HIS FEMININE SIDE**

**I GAVE MY BABY AWAY, SAYS BEST-SELLING NOVELIST KAT KAVANAGH AKA KILLIAN KOBAIN.**

**KAT KAVANAGH REVEALS HER DARKER SIDE**

**LIKE MOTHER LIKE DAUGHTER**

**—JANET NOBLE IS KILLIAN KOBAIN'S MOTHER!!!**

**KAT'S 'DIRTY LITTLE SECRET'**

**DARKER SECRETS AT HODDER & STOUGHTON**

**KAT'S GOT THE CREAM AS SALES OF KILLIAN KOBAIN'S LATEST BOOK SOAR**

I stop scrolling.

I look at Minnie. She's looking at me as if she expects me to say something. I say, 'What?'

'What about Faith?'

Now they're all looking at me. Mum and Dad and Minnie and Ed. As if they're waiting for an answer to a question.

Minnie says, 'It's only a matter of time before they get to her.'

'I know, and I . . . I am going to talk to her, it's just . . . '

Mum says, 'You have to talk to her now.'

Minnie nods, 'Unless she's living in a hole in the ground, she'll have heard it. She'll have heard you. Telling the world about her.'

Ed says, 'She doesn't live in a hole, Minnie. She lives in Brighton. With Milo.'

Mum shakes her head. 'I don't know why you had to bring it up at the press conference, Katherine, I really don't.'

'I had to say it. They would have found out sooner or later. I had to be the one to say it.'

Dad calls a halt. 'I think we should all sit down. Take a breath.'

Mum glares at him. 'I suppose you'll be wanting to make us tea next.'

Dad stands up. 'That's a good idea,' and he goes and makes tea and manages to find a packet of chocolate digestives, so we sit round the dining-room table and drink tea and eat chocolate digestives and we try to make sense of things. Dad has Faith's number. He says I should ring her. Mum says, 'No.' She says I have to go to Brighton. I have to see Faith. Talk to her. I have to explain.

I don't know how to explain. I have no explanation.

'I can't go to Brighton. I can't even get out of the bloody house.'

And that's when Minnie leans forward and smiles her malevolent smile and says, 'You can.'

I say, 'How?'

'I have a plan.'

It's me who notices first, which is weird when you consider that I never watch the news. Well, hardly ever, on account of it being either dead boring or dead sad, like when a lady gets cut up into little bits and put in a suitcase by a man who lives in a basement with a dog and a hamster. That happened once. It was on the news so it's definitely true.

Celia is taking a nap. I reckon she's tired from all the trips to the hospital and back.

*Harry Potter and the Goblet of Fire* is on after the news. To make the time go a bit faster, I blow a Malteser from one end of the mantelpiece to the other with a straw, and that's when I see her. On the telly, I mean. I'm pretty sure it's her. I recognise her from the photographs in Ed's room. Even if I hadn't seen the photos, I'd probably know who she is because she looks exactly the same as Faith, except she's old. I pick the Malteser off the mantelpiece, put it in my mouth and turn up the volume on the telly.

She's sitting on a chair behind a desk like the desks we have at school. There's a microphone on the desk in front of her and she's talking into that. I don't know who she's talking to. There's a glass of water beside the microphone and she keeps picking it up and taking huge gulps out of it.

She might look a bit like Ed too, if she smiled.

That's when Faith and Dad and Ant and Adrian come into the room.

Dad says, 'We're going to play Scrabble.' Dad is really bad at Scrabble. He always makes up words. He uses the internet too, which is against the rules.

Faith looks at the telly and says, 'Jesus.'

Dad says, 'What's wrong?'

Faith says, 'SSSSSHHHHHH.'

Ant and Adrian say, 'What about Scrabble?' at the same time. Sometimes they do that. It's probably because they're twins. And they love Scrabble. They mostly always win.

Then Faith tells everyone to BE QUIET and Ant says, 'Time of the month?' and Adrian says, 'Shut it, scumbag,' and Dad says, 'Do you want Celia to come down here again?' and after that everyone shuts up.

The woman on the telly points at something and nods her head and suddenly there is a man on the screen. In fact, there're loads of them. And women too. They're sitting in chairs. Rows and rows of chairs. They have notebooks and pens and they're writing things into the notebooks with the pens.

The man says, 'So, er, Kat, is it all right if I call you Kat?'

Kat says, 'I can't stop you.'

'So, er, Kat, could you tell us why?'

Kat says nothing.

'Er, what I mean is, why have you kept your writing success a secret for so long?'

Kat throws her eyes to heaven, exactly the same way that Faith does when Ant and Adrian say they can't do the books because they've got a date or a pain in their toe or something. 'To avoid this.' She waves her hand around the room, so everyone knows she's talking about them.

A woman with really tight curls and a really tight suit says, 'If that's the case, then why are you telling us now? After all these years?'

The camera switches back to Kat. 'Because someone found out and has been harassing me, trying to extort money out of me.' Then she looks directly into the camera and says, 'The police have been notified and it's only a matter of time before that person is uncovered.' She looks exactly like Faith, when Faith says things like, 'I'm going to find out sooner or later so you may as well make things easier for yourself and tell me now.'

For a moment, nobody says anything. Then it seems like everyone in the audience starts asking questions, all at the same time.

Ant says, 'This is boring. When is *Harry Potter* coming on?'

Adrian picks up the TV guide. 'I hope it's the first one. The first one's my favourite. When Hermione's hair is all fluffy and huge.'

Ant says, 'Hermione is a nerd.'

Adrian shakes his head. 'I like women with big hair.'

Ant says, 'Freak.'

Faith watches the telly.

Dad puts on his glasses and looks at the woman on the screen. Then he looks at Faith. Then back at the woman on the telly. But I don't think he works it out. Not yet.

It's probably because he's really tired. Yesterday, he called Celia 'Beth'. Then he tried to put kitchen roll in the toilet roll holder in the bathroom and he forgot to put chicken in the chicken and broccoli bake. There's something sticky in his hair and I don't think Celia is talking to him.

On the telly, a small man with a big belly looks at Kat and asks, 'Are there any other skeletons in Kat Kavanagh's closet?'

Kat looks at the man for ages before she says anything. A woman who looks like a headmistress and is sitting beside Kat covers the microphone with her hand. She says something but I don't know what it is. Kat shakes her head and turns back to the small man with the big belly. She says, 'Yes. There is something.'

She picks up a pen, rolls it between her fingers. In the room, you can hear papers shuffling and people doing those coughs that people do when they don't actually have a cough.

Kat says, 'I had a daughter when I was fifteen and I put her up for adoption.'

Silence now. Not even shuffling or coughing.

Ant and Adrian look at Faith and say, 'Jesus H!' at the same time. I reckon they've copped on to it. You wouldn't think it, but they pretty much got all As in their A levels.

Dad sits on the couch so heavily that I think it might break, but it doesn't. It holds.

The people on the telly start asking questions, all at the same time. Cameras flash like lightning strikes.

A woman in the audience leans so far forward in her chair that she nearly topples out of it. She straightens herself and then says, 'Have you ever met your daughter?'

Someone else — I can't see who — says, 'Why did you give her up for adoption?'

'Has there been any contact with your daughter?'

421

'Does your daughter know that you're Killian Kobain?'

'Who is your daughter?'

'What's your daughter's name?'

'Where does your daughter live?'

And then someone — a man with a very shiny head, like it's been polished — says, 'Why are you telling us this now?'

Kat puts her two hands on the desk in front of her and studies them as if she's trying to learn them off by heart.

Then she looks up at the man and says, 'I'd prefer you to hear it from me.' She stands up then and says, 'I have no further comment.' And she walks away without turning back and the people in the room are on their feet now, shouting questions after her and taking pictures but they're just pictures of the back of her, because Kat never turns round.

Then it's back to the newsreader woman, who says, 'Janet Noble, Katherine Kavanagh's mother and winner of the Man Booker Prize, was unavailable for comment.'

Ant says, 'Holy F — ' and Dad says, 'Mind your language, young man,' before Ant even has time to say the F word. He often calls him and Adrian, 'young man'. It's because he doesn't always know which one is which.

The weather report is on now. The weather lady starts with: 'My goodness. Think I'll have to take my poster of Killian Kobain off the wall, eh?' before she starts on about the weather.

There's a weather warning, she says.

A chance of a storm, she says.

It'll blow over, she says.

Soon-ish.

Faith snaps off the television. She sits on the couch really suddenly, like her legs stopped working.

Ant says, 'That's her. Isn't it?' He sits beside Faith and picks up one of her hands, and instead of telling him to sod off, she lets him. She just sits there and lets him.

Dad — who sometimes forgets he doesn't have hair on his head anymore — brushes his fingers across his forehead like he's taking a fringe out of his eyes. He says, 'Do you mean . . . ? Is that . . . ?'

Faith nods. 'Yes. That's her. That's my . . . mother.' Faith doesn't sound mad. She sounds like Damo's mam when Sully is getting ready to go to the war.

Dad says, 'But I . . . what do you . . . how can . . . ?' I think he could do with a lie-down. He really could.

Adrian says, 'Well put, Father.'

Faith says, 'I don't believe this.' She's gone as white as a sheet. I hope she's not going to have a heart attack. George Pullman said his grandfather went as white as a sheet before he had his heart attack and dropped dead on the spot.

Dad says, 'I don't understand this. She wouldn't even see you. When you went to Dublin. And now she's on the telly and . . . '

Ant says, 'Sky News.'

Faith says, 'Oh Christ.' She looks like something terrible has happened.

Dad says, 'Now she's on Sky . . . saying that she's this big-shot writer who also happens to be your mother. It doesn't make any sense.'

Adrian says, 'I wouldn't imagine the two events are entirely unrelated.' He rubs his chin with the tips of his fingers when he says this, like he's a right old know-it-all.

Faith looks at Adrian and says, 'What do you mean?'

Adrian says, 'Some journo was snooping around, trying to out her. Threatening to reveal her identity. And, at the same time, this woman she's never met rocks up, claiming to be her daughter.'

Faith says, 'Claiming?'

I say, 'Faith's not lying, you stupid idiot. That woman really is her mother. We saw her name on the computer in the office in London. You tosser.' I'm really mad now.

Dad says, 'Milo, that's not very — '

Adrian says, 'I'm only trying to offer an explanation for the seemingly impromptu press conference that we have just witnessed, as I was, in fact, requested to do by your good self, Faith.'

Faith starts to cry. I turn to Adrian and say, 'Now look what you've done.' It's only then I realise I'm shaking. I think it's because I'm mad and I'm not even sure why I'm mad. I think it's to do with Christmas. And Mam. Mam loved Christmas. She should be here at Christmas time. I don't mean here, like in Scotland. Just, here. With us. And she should be Faith's mam. Her real mam. That's the way everything was before. Everything was fine before.

Adrian says, 'Put a sock in it, Milo.' He doesn't even look at me when he says that and that's when I go for him. Because I'm not the type of fellow who usually goes for people, Adrian is not expecting me, so he sort of topples right over, which isn't as bad as it sounds because he was standing near the couch and he mostly lands on that. Now that I have him down, I'm not exactly sure what to do so I just curl my hand into a fist and punch him a few times. In the shoulders, mainly. A couple on the chest and one on the arm. He yells when I do that so there's a chance I've given him a dead arm. I did that to Damo once. By accident. He couldn't write for the rest of the day. Well, that's what he told Miss Williams anyway. He didn't say it was me, though.

Adrian says, 'Get off me, you little runt.'

Faith says, 'Fuck off, Adrian. Don't talk to him like that.'

Dad says, 'Faith, your language . . .'

It's Ant who clamps my arms to my sides and drags me off Adrian. I'm yelling and roaring like I don't want him to pull me away, but I'm glad about it really. I reckon Adrian would have flattened me once he got his bearings. He usually makes mincemeat out of Ant when they scrap.

I'm in the middle of saying something like, 'Lemme go, I'm going to knock his block off!' or something like that, when Dad says, 'Can you PLEASE stop shouting? Celia is trying to get some rest. PLEASE!' Even though he's pretty much shouting himself. Adrian struggles up out of the couch and his hair is sticking up in a clump at the front, like an arrow. He looks at me with a sort of half-smile on his face, rubbing his arm like it's sore or something. He says, 'Not bad, kiddo, not bad.'

I say, 'I beat you,' because it's true, and he says, 'I let you win,' and Dad says, 'Can you all please SHUT UP!' There's a cabinet in the corner where Celia keeps stuff that her grandparents owned. Things like china shepherdesses with long thin staffs in their hands, and silver thimbles and glasses that are called sherry glasses. Everything in the cabinet rattles across the glass shelf in a way that Celia won't like one little bit. And I'm just about to point this out to Dad when Celia rushes in and says, 'I think the baby's coming.'

Everybody groans apart from Dad, who says, 'Are you sure this time, pet?'

Celia doesn't look very sure but she nods anyway.

Dad says, 'You're positive it's not indigestion. Like the last time?' and that's when Celia bursts into tears and says something like, 'Why is nobody on my side?' At least, I think that's what she says. It's hard to make it out on account of the crying. Dad looks at Faith and says, 'We'll talk about this when I get back.' Then he adds, in a lower voice, 'I shouldn't be long.'

I say, 'What do you mean, a decoy?'

Minnie says, 'You're a crime writer. You know what a decoy is.' She's talking to me and typing on her iPad at the same time. And I'd say there's not one spelling mistake in whatever it is she's typing. She's one of the best multi-taskers I know.

I say, 'Well, yes. But you can't be the decoy. You don't look anything like me.'

Minnie says, 'We're the same height and build. I'll just put a hat on my head and wear sunglasses. They'll be expecting that. Recluses always wear hats and sunglasses.'

I say, 'I am not a recluse.'

Minnie peers at the iPad, types something, presses Enter. 'Minnie!'

'Yes?'

'I'm not a bloody recluse.'

'They don't know that.' Minnie nods towards the window and I look out. They're everywhere. Sky's got the biggest van. It's more truck than van. I'd say RTE are embarrassed, with their little Hiace. It's bedlam out there. They're interviewing anyone who happens along. We saw Mrs Byrne — the next-door neighbour and chairman of the Residents' Association — on the lunchtime news. 'We always thought Kat was a nice, quiet kind of a girl. We had no idea.' Mrs Byrne scurries away, looking around her as if I'm about to jump out of a bush and write her into a story.

I shake my head and say, 'I can't just take a plane to England.'

Minnie presses Enter again and says, 'Give me one good reason why not, and you're not allowed to say 'Ed'. There's not a bother on that fella.' We both look towards the couch where Ed is lying, eating what's left of his hospital grapes and watching the *Coronation Street* omnibus.

I say, 'I can't just . . . arrive. On her doorstep. I don't even know her address.'

'We have the name of the café.'

'But . . . I can't just appear . . . with no notice.'

'No notice is better than notice, in a case like this.'

'But . . . '

Minnie switches off her iPad and says, 'There.'

'What?'

'I've booked you on the morning flight to Gatwick. Tomorrow.'

'But tomorrow is Christmas Eve. I can't just show up on Christmas Eve. The café might be closed.'

Minnie continues as if I have said nothing. 'From Gatwick, you get a Southern service straight to Brighton. You'll be there by lunchtime.'

'No, Minnie, I can't. I can't go tomorrow. It's too soon. I'll wait till after Christmas. St Stephen's Day, maybe.'

'Too late, I've already booked your flight and your train.'

'You've done all that already?' Minnie nods. 'Just now?'

Minnie nods again, this time adding one of her smug smiles. I can't blame her, I suppose. She really is a tour de force.

I say, 'But . . . after everything that's happened in the last few days, I'm in no fit state to do this. I need to gather my wits about me. I'm exhausted.'

Minnie says, 'You're not exhausted,' like it's a fact rather than merely an opinion that she happens to hold.

'I won't know what to say.'

Minnie pats my shoulder and says, 'You'll think of something.' I know I'll go in the end. I have no choice. Arguing with Minnie is one of the most useless and exhausting pursuits any human being could engage in. She's as relentless as a tank.

We end up eating chilli con carne on Christmas Eve, which happens to be one of my favourite dinners, on account of the kidney beans and the chilli peppers. Dad said he was going to cook his speciality for us on Christmas Eve, which is steak and chips, but he's still at the hospital with Celia. The baby hasn't arrived yet but the doctor said that Celia was exhausted with all the coming and going so she should stay another night. She's asleep now, Dad said, when he phoned. I told him to get some sleep too and he said, 'I think it might be on BBC Four.' He sounded like an actual zombie when he said that.

Ant makes so much chilli that there'll be enough for Christmas Day too, even though there's a turkey hanging on a hook in the pantry. Dad got it from a friend of his who's a farmer. It still has feathers. Dad was going to show me how to pluck it. It's starting to stink a bit. I hope we don't have to eat it. It would seem too much like Christmas if we had turkey.

Adrian mashes up avocados and garlic for the guacamole. I put the garlic bread in the oven and Faith sets the table. Adrian flexes his shoulder every now and again and says, 'You've got a good right hook, all the same.' He winks at me when he says it so I'm pretty sure there're no hard feelings.

Every time the news comes on the telly, they show the woman again. Saying the same thing about her books and about Faith being her daughter, except she doesn't say Faith's name and she always says, 'No comment,' when the people ask questions about Faith.

The newsreader says, 'Sales of the Declan Darker series of books have surged, since the revelations about their author, Katherine Kavanagh, who has been writing under the pseudonym Killian Kobain for nearly twenty years.' There's a shot of people in a bookshop but you can't see what books they're buying. Not really.

Faith says, 'That worked out well for her.'

Ant says, 'What?'

'That little publicity stunt.'

Ant shakes his head and says, 'Hardly. The woman must be up to her crow's feet in loot.'

Faith and Adrian turn their heads towards Ant and say, at exactly the same time, 'Shut up.' In fairness to Ant, he's pretty easy-going. He just shrugs his shoulders and spoons some more chilli and rice and sour cream and salsa onto his plate, and eats his way through it. Then he says, 'I bet she never washes her tea towels. She probably just throws them away when they're dirty. And her socks too.'

Adrian says, 'So that's what you'd do, is it? If you were rich and famous? You'd stop washing your tea towels? Let's hope your lotto numbers come up really soon.'

Ant says, 'It's weird, isn't it? Dad got Milo the Declan Darker game for Christmas — what's it called? Mind Games, or something.'

Adrian says, 'But that's rated eighteen. And it's on Xbox. Milo is . . . ' He looks at me. 'How old are you, Milo?'

431

I say, 'I'm ten tomorrow.'

Adrian says, 'Oh shit,' which probably means he's forgotten to buy me a birthday present, which is the really bad thing about having your birthday on the same day as Christmas Day.

I look at Adrian. 'But I don't have an Xbox.' Mind Games sounds legend.

'He got you an Xbox too.'

Ant says, 'It's not fair. Dad never tries to buy our love with good pressies anymore.'

Adrian says, 'Yeah. Remember the quad bikes?'

'That was some summer.'

'You're not supposed to tell me what present Dad got me.' An Xbox! And an Xbox game! For me! And even though I know I shouldn't, I can't help wondering if he got me the goggles too.

Later, Ant comes up from the cellar with cobwebs in his hair and says, 'I've found the good stuff.' He's got a bottle in each hand and one tucked under each armpit. They're covered in dust. He puts them on the table.

Faith picks one up. 'We can't drink this. It's nearly eighty years old.'

Ant looks at the label. 'Probably past its 'best before'. We'll be doing the old man a favour.'

Adrian pops the cork and I get the glasses. Four of them. Faith says I'm too young to have wine but she pours cranberry juice in my glass, which looks pretty much like wine and tastes way nicer.

Ant says, 'A toast.'

Faith says, 'Let's just get it drunk before Dad gets back.'

Adrian says, 'Let's drink a toast to Mam.'

And they look at me and I pick up my glass and we

all clink and say, 'To Mam!' like it's her birthday or something.

My eyes don't sting. I feel a bit happy, I think. Maybe it's because Ant made the chilli and Celia's baby might come soon and I'm getting an Xbox and we don't have to eat the turkey tomorrow. Mam made the best chestnut stuffing in the world at Christmas time.

Minnie's decoy plan turns out to be pretty formulaic. She could have lifted it from any number of mainstream films; *Ocean's Eleven* or *Mission Impossible*.

She arrives at my parents' house the following morning in a taxi since her car is still barricaded into the car park of my apartment block. We saw it on the telly. She's dressed for business in a military-style black leather coat with enormous golden buttons, black tights, high black leather boots, and a black peaked cap.

She leaves in my trench coat and trilby, a pair of my ankle boots and an enormous pair of dark glasses. The hat is vital because of its 'dual functionality', according to Minnie. It looks like a hat a reclusive writer-type would wear and you can tuck your hair under it. She completes the 'disguise' with one of Dad's golf umbrellas. I say, 'What do you need the umbrella for?'

Minnie says, 'To beat them with if any of the fuckers get too close.'

I don't have to look out of the window to see what happens. I watch it on the telly. When Minnie steps onto the driveway, they descend like a pack of wolves on a lamb. Except that Minnie Driver is no lamb. She holds the umbrella like a sword and pokes anyone within poking distance. One man carrying one of those fluffy things that look like a feather duster gets it in the stomach. He drops the duster and doubles over. You can't hear him but I'd say he's roaring with the pain. That umbrella has a particularly long, pointy bit at the end and she went in deep with it. Another journalist — a woman — gets a straightforward whack on the head with the rolled-up middle bit. She staggers against the belly of an incredibly fat man and sort of bounces back on her feet. She turns to smile a grateful smile at the fat man and he emits a stoic nod, as if this is not the first time his belly has been involved in such chivalry.

After that, the crowd parts obediently, and Minnie strolls to Dad's car, gets in and scorches out of the driveway. No one's ever scorched away in Dad's car before and I can tell he's a little worried. I say, 'Minnie's a good driver,' and he nods and I look at the screen again and I can't help smiling. There is something a little magnificent about Minnie Driver.

One of the reporters is saying that it's like a scene from a Declan Darker novel, which is nonsense. None of my characters have ever used an umbrella, other than to stave off the rain. There is a scramble for cars and vans and trucks as they prepare to give chase.

Mum lends me her walking stick, and I tuck my hair inside one of Ed's woolly hats. It itches terribly. I pick up the overnight bag Mum has packed for me, and the keys to her car.

'You're sure you don't mind me taking the car?'

Mum shakes her head. She pulls my hat down so it covers both ears. It's the type of itch you can't scratch. 'How long do you think you'll be gone?'

I shrug. 'I don't know. It depends.'

Mum steps away from me, her arms held tightly by each side, her back ramrod straight. She says, 'You're doing the right thing.'

I nod, although it's impossible to know if this is true. But she seems pretty convinced so I allow myself to be buoyed by her certainty.

I point to the window and say, 'I'm sorry. About all this.'

She tucks a stray strand of my hair inside the itchy hat. 'Adds a bit of colour to my quiet life.'

'You like your quiet life.'

'Maybe I like it a bit too much.' I don't say anything. Instead, I touch her arm and she pats my hand, and then she wraps her arms round me and suddenly she's hugging me and I feel the warmth of her face against mine, the skin there soft and delicate, smelling of the same talcum powder I remember from when I was a child. She stops as suddenly as she started. Pats me down. Like she's checking I'm still in one piece.

Dad says, 'Do you have enough money, Kat?'

Mum turns on him. 'For goodness' sake, Kenneth. She got paid one and a half million pounds for the film rights to *The Right to Remain Silent*. Of course she has enough money.' I didn't tell her that. She heard that on *Morning Ireland*.

I say, 'I'm fine, Dad,' and I kiss his cheek.

I take a breath and go into the den, where Ed

436

is playing the Wii. He says, 'Do you want a turn, Kat?'

I say, 'I have to go now.'

'To see Faith?'

'Yes.'

'And Milo?'

'Yes.'

'Are they going to come and see us again?'

'I don't know.'

'Tell them to come soon. It's really hard work keeping my bedroom tidy every day.'

'Why are you keeping your room tidy?

'In case they come for a sleepover. I already told Faith that she could sleep in my room the next time she comes, and Milo would probably come too so he'd have to sleep on the top bunk because he's never had bunk beds, and kids love sleeping on top bunks, don't they?'

When I hug Ed, he feels solid in my arms and I say it again, in my head: Thankyouthankyouthankyouthankyou. I don't know who I'm thanking but I am thankful, nonetheless. That he is here. That he is OK.

I put on my mother's tweed coat and pick up the walking stick. Stoop my back a little. Practise hobbling a bit. For authenticity. I find another golf umbrella in the cloakroom and arm myself with it. Just in case.

But, oddly, Minnie's plan works. It wouldn't have the nerve not to. The remaining journos watch me like hawks and take a few pictures and shout a few questions at me from a distance, as if they're worried about the umbrella or not really expecting an answer. I make it to Mum's car, open the boot and get the suitcase inside, then open the driver's door and get myself inside. It takes ages to get the key in the ignition with the shaking of my fingers. But I needn't worry because the journos have lost whatever minimal interest they may have had in me. They are here for one thing and there is an air of dejection about the place, which I can only assume is because the one thing that they are here for is not here anymore. Or so they think. My hands on the wheel are slick with sweat. I turn the key. I have a terrible feeling that this is the exact opposite of the right thing to do. But in spite of all these things, in spite of everything, I start the engine. I even remember to drive out of the driveway and down the road like an old lady: slow and steady.

Slow and steady wins the race. That's what Mrs Higginbotham used to tell me and Ed.

There are several moments when I want to stop. Turn back. Go home and hide in my apartment, like I have been doing for the past while. Years, really.

Like at the airport when the gate is about to close and I haven't boarded yet.

Like on the plane when I hear several passengers talking about Killian Kobain and Declan Darker and Kat Kavanagh.

Like when the plane lands and the captain's voice says, 'Welcome to London Gatwick. Weather is cold and bright with snow forecast for later, so it looks like it might be a white Christmas after all.'

But I don't stop, or turn back. I don't go home and hide in my apartment.

I keep going.

It's the strangest thing.

I disembark at Gatwick. I look at Minnie's instructions and follow them to the letter. Now I'm on a train to Brighton. When I get there, it's lunchtime, just like Minnie said it would be. I get into a taxi and say, 'Take me to the Funky Banana, please.' It sounds even weirder when you say it out loud.

The taxi driver puts the car in drive and moves into the lunchtime traffic. He is taciturn and therefore unlike any other taximan I have come across and I have come across a fair few in my time, being a great believer in drinking and not driving. At least I was until the bloody Ed situation. Day eight. Three hundred and fifty-seven days to go.

I clear my throat. 'The traffic's pretty bad, isn't it?'

'Could be worse.'

Silence again. I'm twitchy as a pulse.

I wish Minnie were here. It would be . . . nice, I suppose. To have someone here. With me. Someone in my corner, so to speak. I haven't thought about what I'm going to say. I just got on a plane and a train and now here I am, in a taxi with a non-verbal taxi driver, and suddenly the back seat of the cab feels enormous, with just me here. And I've nothing prepared. No lines to say.

It's only when I see the café from the top of the street that I realise I was hoping it would be closed. The awning in front of the café is one of the brightest yellows I've ever seen, and I'm delighted that I don't have a hangover because this yellow is so bright it would surely take the sight out of your eyes if you weren't in the full of your health.

The sign that pokes out at a right angle from the café is in the shape of a banana. A fairly ordinary-looking banana, to be honest.

The taxi driver pulls up in front of the café. It's packed with people in good form, eating and talking and smiling and even laughing. There's a lot of joviality, which is weird when you remember it's Christmas Eve.

The taxi driver puts the car in neutral and sits back, without saying anything. The meter reads twelve pounds forty-five pence and I give him twenty pounds. I don't even say, 'Keep the change.' I just get out of the car. It seems like the least I can do.

The café is quirky by accident rather than design. There's quite a bit of yellow. There's a sizeable amount of banana-inspired food. Banana and chocolate-chip milkshakes I can understand, but most people would have to draw the line at banana-infused tea, wouldn't they? Minnie would tell me to think outside my box of Lyons teabags, but I don't think even she or Maurice would have the stomach for it. There is not one matching chair in the place but because they've been painted such bright colours, it works somehow. I sit at the only vacant table. It's the one nearest the door, which means there'll be a draught and

440

I'll catch my death of cold, on top of everything else.

I sit down. There's a hint of Ireland about the place. The clock, for instance. Green and shaped like a shamrock. And the dish of the day is Irish stew. The weird thing is that, even though I'm not crazy about stew, when the waiter comes to take my order, I say, 'Stew, please,' and he says, 'Good choice,' as if he has sensed my hesitation and wants to assure me that I'm doing the right thing.

The Christmas tree in the corner is real, hanging with all manner of wooden fruit, among which bananas feature prominently. Oddly, I've ordered a glass of milk with my stew, as if I'm six and not so close to forty I can see the whites of its eyes. Well, I can't drink a proper drink like wine because of the deal I made with God, which is crazy when you consider that I don't even believe in God. But something won't let me disregard the promise. Just in case.

I don't think Faith is here. In the café. There's just the waiter, who is a Maurice Minor, which is Minnie's name for not-quite-a-man-not-quite-a-boy, and a fully grown man I can see in the kitchen every time the Maurice Minor opens the door. He's got long dark hair, which is in a high ponytail and tucked neatly inside a hairnet. He's chopping shallots with one of those gigantic, shiny blades that could separate a head from a body with a single swipe, if you were in that humour.

It's only when I realise she's not here that my shoulders descend from around my ears. In fact,

441

it's only when I realise she's not here that I notice my shoulders are up around my ears in the first place. I take them down. They ache, which means they've probably been up there for quite some time. And that's when I realise that I'm glad. Well, relieved anyway. That she's not here. And that's when I ask myself what it is I'm actually doing here. What it is I'm hoping to achieve. And exactly what I am planning to say if I ever do meet her.

The truth is, I don't know. I don't know the answer to any of those questions, but instead of leaving and getting in a taxi, then a train and a plane and going home to Dublin, where I happen to know the answers to lots of questions, I stay. It's like being in the dentist's waiting room. It's crowded and heavy with that dense smell of too many bodies in one small space. And you're afraid. You're terrified. There's a chance of root canal. But you stay. For some reason, you stay.

The stew comes in a pasta bowl with a plate of soda bread on the side and a dish of thick, yellow butter that is guaranteed to coat your arteries with the best kind of cholesterol. When I ask, I'm told that the milk is full-fat. 'It's the only kind we have.'

I butter the bread, dip it into the dark brown gravy, spear a piece of beef with my fork, add a baby carrot, a stick of celery, a chunk of turnip. It's good. It's very good. Even if you're someone like me, who doesn't eat this type of mush, you'd have to concede that it's good. Mrs Higginbotham would have said that a stew like this one would warm the cockles of your heart. I never really knew what she meant by that until now. I hadn't realised how cold I was until now. Or how hungry. It feels like an odd time to be hungry, but there you have it. Turns out I'm hungry. I haven't felt hungry in ages. I end up eating everything and use the rest of the bread to mop up the remains of the gravy.

When the waiter comes to clear away the plates, I am amazed to discover that I've drunk every drop of the milk. That'll look good on the scales tomorrow. 'You'll have dessert.' He states it like it's a fact, so I nod and ask what's good and he says, 'The Funky Banana, of course,' and I say, 'Yes, please,' as if I know exactly what a Funky Banana is.

When the waiter returns with the Funky Banana — which turns out to be a sort of ice — cream sundae in a tall glass with caramel and chocolate and sprinkles and, of course, bananas jammed in — I manage to say something.

I say, 'I'm looking for Faith.' That sounds a little born-again so I say, 'Faith McIntyre.'

The waiter looks at me. Like he knows me from somewhere. But whatever it is he's about to say, he decides not to say it. Instead he says, 'I'll get Jack.'

My heart is hammering inside my chest and I haven't even had one spoonful of the Funky Banana yet. It's like I'm on a path now. And I can't turn back, even if I wanted to, and, let's face it, I want to. I really want to.

Jack turns out to be the man in the kitchen.

He has removed his hairnet, which I find oddly gratifying.

He has two mugs of coffee in his hands. He stops when he gets to my table and stares at me. Then he says, 'You're that woman. On the telly. Aren't you? You're Killian Kobain.'

I glance about to see if anyone has heard, but no one is listening. I say, 'Yes.'

Jack puts one of the coffees in front of me and sits down in the chair opposite me. 'You're a dab hand with an umbrella, I'll give you that.'

'That wasn't me. That was my friend. Minnie. It's a long story.'

Jack leans forward. 'So, you're looking for our Faith?'

I nod. He wipes his floury hand on the front of his apron and extends it towards me. We shake hands. He's got baker's hands. Soft and fleshy and warm. Great hands for kneading dough, I'd say. You can't lie to a man with hands like that. Or maybe there just comes a time when you have to face up to things. Stepping up to the plate, Minnie would call it. Telling the truth, Ed would say. And Thomas? I don't know what he'd say. He probably wouldn't believe it. What I'm doing. He'd be too shocked to say anything.

I say, 'I'm Faith's . . . biological mother.'

Jack takes it in his stride. He says, 'Oh,' and he looks at me more closely. 'You look very like her.'

I say, 'She came to Dublin looking for me but I . . . I wasn't able to meet her. She's not expecting me. Is she around?'

Jack shakes his head. 'She's gone to Scotland. With Milo. They're spending Christmas with

444

their dad. It was a last-minute thing. I don't think she could face it, in the end.'

I say, 'What do you mean?'

Jack sweeps a hand around the café. 'Christmas. This is the first Christmas since Beth's death. You know she died, don't you?'

'Yes . . . I was involved in that accident too. My car was a write-off but I walked away with hardly a scratch.'

Jack says, 'Jesus. That's incredible.'

I nod.

He drags a hand down his face. 'Poor Beth.'

I put my hand on top of his and sort of squeeze it, briefly. I don't intend doing it. It just happens. I put my hand back round my mug of coffee and say, 'Were you close? You and Beth?'

He smiles. 'I knew Beth for years. We worked together in various restaurants and hotels over the years and then she set up this place and asked me to come and work for her. We had some great times here.'

I say, 'I'm sorry.' I can't think of anything else.

Jack nods.

I say, 'How is Faith? With . . . everything that's happened?'

'Not great, I suppose. She's been angry. With Beth. For not telling her about being adopted. And busy too, looking after Milo. I think she sort of forgot how sad she was, you know?'

I say, 'Yes,' even though I don't. I don't know.

Jack says, 'Faith asked me if I knew. Since me and Beth were friends, she assumed . . . But I didn't know a thing. All I know is that Beth loved Faith to bits. They were so close, those two.

More like sisters than mother and daughter.'

For the first time, I get a sense of this girl. I get a sense of Faith. And her mother. I don't mean me. I mean her real mother. Beth. The woman who reared her. Who never told her because she loved Faith too much. She didn't want her to feel that she was missing out on anything. Didn't want her to know that someone had given her away.

Didn't want her to know that I had given her away.

That's what I did.

I gave her away.

My hands tighten round the mug of coffee on the table. So tightly my fingers are white. So tightly, the mug might shatter. Jack says, 'Are you OK?'

'I'm fine, thanks.'

'What are you going to do now?'

'Do you happen to have Faith's address? In Scotland, I mean?'

'Yes, but it's Christmas Eve. You'll never get a flight now.'

'I will. I'll go stand-by or something. I'm here now. I have to keep going. I don't know what else to do.'

Jack looks at me for a moment, then gets up and says, 'I'll be back in a minute.' When he returns, he hands me a piece of paper. There's an address on it. I put it in my bag.

'Thank you.'

We shake hands again and he says, 'I suppose it's not a great time to ask for your autograph?' and I say, 'No, it's not.'

446

'Next time?'

'Yes.' And then I smile and I have no idea why. Perhaps it's because Jack thinks there will be a next time, and he knows Faith so I take it as a sign. A positive sign. That maybe, just maybe, things might work out OK in the end.

When I step outside the café, it has already begun to snow.

For the first time ever on Christmas Day, I don't wake up at five o'clock in the morning. I wake up at my normal time, which happens to be eight o'clock. I suppose it's because I don't believe anymore.

I am reading the instruction manual for the Xbox. Dad says he'll bring me to a shop when he gets a chance and get me a game that's suitable for my age. He says I can keep the Declan Darker game and play it when I'm older.

I got goggles too. They're the Speedsocket Mirror ones, which means that they cost twenty-three pounds but, so long as I don't lose them, which I nearly definitely won't, they'll last me until I'm around twenty or maybe even older than that. They're blue and I'm wearing them at the moment, just to get used to them.

Faith got me a book about sharks, and a new swim bag that's got a waterproof bit for your togs. Ant and Adrian got me a London bus moneybox with two tenners already in it, to go towards my London saving fund.

I say, 'What London saving fund?'

Ant says, 'You're coming to London. At half-term. You're going to stay with us for a couple of days.'

I look at Faith to see if this is true. She's smiling so it must be.

I say, 'Can we go on the London Eye?'

Adrian says, 'It's compulsory, mate.'

I say, 'Legend,' and everyone smiles, all at the same time, even Celia, who is in better form now because she's had a good rest in the hospital and when Dad brought her back this morning he made her poached eggs on toast, which happens to be her favourite breakfast.

Dad is wearing the apron I got him and making a lamb vindaloo, because a nurse in the hospital told Celia that a hot curry and a glass of full-bodied red wine might do the trick. Dad says, 'I've got a lovely bottle of red in the cellar. It's nearly eighty years old. Worth a fair bit now, I'd say.'

That's when Ant and Adrian put on their jackets and the scarves I got them and say they are going out.

I don't have the lamb vindaloo for dinner. It's not because it's too spicy for me. It's just that there's loads of chilli leftover from yesterday and I have that instead cos it's my favourite. Nobody mentions the turkey with all the feathers hanging on the hook in the pantry.

I'm watching *Pirates of the Caribbean* when the doorbell rings. Faith is texting Rob. They've been texting all day. I don't know why they don't just phone each other. I really don't.

Celia is sitting in the rocking chair with her feet in one of those foot massager things.

The doorbell rings again.

Faith says, 'Milo, will you get the door?'

I say, 'I'm watching the movie.'

'You've seen it a million times.'

'It's the really good bit.'

'Milo.'

I get up and step into the hall. The front door is

made of coloured glass and through the glass I see her. The woman. She has long dark hair, like Faith's. She's wearing a purple coat. I've seen the coat before. In a photograph in Ed's house. I'm pretty sure about that. I'm nearly positive.

I stop walking. I say, 'Faith?'

She says, 'What?'

'I think it's for you.'

'What's for me?'

'The door. I think it's for you.'

'How could it be for me?'

'Just come out here, will you?'

I hear her sighing, putting her phone on the table beside the couch, getting up. She walks into the hall, looks at the woman on the other side of the door, then looks at me.

She says, 'Why don't you answer the door?'

I don't say anything and she shakes her head and tousles my hair as she walks past me. She says, 'You can be so weird sometimes, you know that?' and she goes right ahead and opens the door.

I make myself scarce.

I end up saying, 'I should have called first.' After all the time I've had to think of something to say, that's what I come up with. Hours I have spent, waiting on stand-by at Gatwick airport for planes to Edinburgh that never arrived, or got delayed or cancelled, while the snow fell and fell until you couldn't see the runways anymore and the airport could do nothing but declare itself closed and people wept and roared at airport staff as if they had personally cancelled Christmas. I spent the night on a red plastic chair and finally managed to squeeze myself onto a flight to Glasgow. The airport at Edinburgh was closed because of the snow that kept falling and falling as if it would never stop. From Glasgow, I got a train to Edinburgh and a taxi to the address that Jack scribbled on the back of an envelope. I could not give an accurate or even approximate account of what thoughts rose and fell in my head in all that time. Which is disgraceful when you think that I could have spent at least some of those long, dreary hours coming up with something better to say at this door than, 'I should have called first.'

Even as I press the bell at the imposing door of the large, modern house in Edinburgh's leafy suburbs, I haven't yet come up with that killer line. I'm still rummaging around for something brilliant to say.

'I should have called first.' I think I say it because it's Faith herself who answers the door and this throws me. When I see her face, I get a sensation of being picked up and hurled against something solid. A brick wall. I don't know how I can be this unprepared. I've had nothing but time to think about everything. Surely, I should be more prepared. But I'm not. She looks like me. She looks like my daughter. If we walked down the street together, people would know. People would say, 'She's cut out of that woman.' I wouldn't have to say a thing.

'I should have called first.' My mouth is dry. For the first time since it began to snow, I feel the cold. It's digging into me like a spade.

Faith says, 'Yes, you should have.' She is wearing jeans, a T-shirt with some band on the front I've never heard of, a cardigan that goes down to her knees. In spite of the cold, her feet are bare. She looks so young. I bet she gets asked for ID all the time. I did too, when I was that age. I bet it really pisses her off.

I say, 'I'm sorry. I just . . . It was a spur-of-the-moment thing. I just left Dublin and . . . I kept going.'

Faith says, 'It's Christmas Day.'

'I know. I'm sorry. I got delayed. All the flights . . . with the snow . . . '

'It's not a good time.'

There's almost a feeling of relief. When I realise she's not going to let me in. I won't have to come up with something else to say. Some

452

explanation. Something that might make everything seem all right.

I say, 'I'm sorry,' again.

Faith says nothing. Her hand is on the latch. She wants to close the door. I want her to close the door. But, instead, I hear Minnie's voice in my head. She says, 'Strap on a fucking pair, would you?'

'I was fifteen when I had you.'

Faith says, 'I know.'

'I was . . . very young and . . . '

Faith says, 'We were all fifteen at one time or another. Not everyone does what you did.'

My teeth are chattering with the cold. There is snow on my eyelashes. I blink it away. 'I know. I'm sorry.'

'Sorry's not much use to me.'

'I know.' I don't say sorry again because she's right about that. I see Faith looking at me, waiting for me to say something that she can relate to. Something that she can understand. There's nothing. I've got nothing.

She pulls at the neck of the T-shirt and that's when I see it. The pendant that Ed bought for her, flashing silver in the pale light of this day. It's been a long day. The longest day, maybe. But I feel the unfamiliar tug of hope when I see the pendant. That has to mean something. Doesn't it?

All of a sudden, Faith says, 'What do you want?'

It's not rude, the way she says it. It's curious. Like she really wants to know. I sense an opening here. An opportunity. I have to be careful with it.

Make it matter. I don't think there'll be many of these. I don't deserve many.

'I want . . . I'd like us to be friends.' Friends? Why did I say that? It sounds so bloody twee. Is it even true?

Faith says, 'Friends?' Like she thinks it's twee as well.

I decide to stick to my guns in spite of a feeling that's spreading through me. It's not a good feeling. It's a combination of hopelessness and foolishness. Despite this, I say, 'Yes. Friends.'

Then she says, 'Are you friends with your mother?'

And I have to say, 'Not really.'

The feeling — the hopeless, foolish feeling — has reached my perimeters. It's all over the place. I ignore it. I say, 'But . . . maybe . . . since we're a bit different . . . maybe that means we could be friends.'

Her fingers tighten round the latch. 'I have enough friends, thank you very much.'

That's when I say, 'I don't. I've hardly any, actually.' I say it like I'm just realising it. I am just realising it. I'm realising a lot of things.

'Do you expect me to feel sorry for you?'

'No, of course not. It's not something that's bothered me before. I never thought about it. I don't think about much, to be honest. Nothing important anyway.'

A man appears on the doorstep. Maybe fifteen years older than me. Balding, swollen around the middle, exhausted-looking. I don't think I've ever seen a human being look so spent. He smells of curry.

He looks at me and says, 'Oh,' and even though we've never met, he knows who I am. Immediately. I don't have to explain.

He turns to Faith and says, 'Faith, love, would you let the poor woman inside the door, at least?' I'd say he's her father. Her adopted father. Adoptive? I'm not sure of the correct terminology, which seems wrong.

I say, 'No, not at all. I don't want to intrude. I just . . . '

Faith says, 'You just what?'

I have never felt more like walking away in my life, and there's no better woman for walking away. Let's face it, I've walked away from all sorts. I have never felt less like talking but, somehow, I manage to say something. 'I just wanted to talk to you, that's all. I think.'

'You think?'

The man says, 'She'll catch her death, love. She's not dressed for these temperatures. Look at her hat, for the love of God.'

Automatically, my hand reaches up to touch my hat. It's a Fedora. I'm wearing my Fedora. Nonchalant chic, Minnie calls it. I don't know what I was thinking.

Faith stands at the door. I see her deliberating. It's in the way she shifts her weight from one bare foot to the other. Her toenails are a metallic blue but the toes, the toes themselves, they are all mine. Long, skinny things with a slight bend along the second one. The one beside the big toe. At the top, just before the nail. That's where the bend is. I used to think it was something to do with all the unsuitable shoes I ever wore. Now

I know it's not. It's hereditary. Genetic. The thought gives me a jolt that seems physical. I feel like I am being felled. Like a tree. In my head, a lumberjack is shouting. 'TIMBERRRRRRRR!' as I topple. I put my hand on the glass pane of the porch, to steady myself.

The man says, 'I wouldn't put your hand there, if I were you, love. You'll leave prints and Celia is just bursting at the seams to find someone to go through for a shortcut, if you get my drift.' He smiles at me as if I know exactly who Celia is and why she should be bursting at the seams for someone to go through for a shortcut. He leans towards me and whispers, 'Hormones,' with one of those winks that some men favour when trying to induce empathy.

Faith opens the door a little wider. She says, 'I suppose you'd better come in.'

Suddenly I am glad about the man. The exhausted-looking man with the winky eye who smells of curry. I am glad that he is here. I step inside.

The house is a study in modernity. Everything is huge and shiny. You can see your face reflected in most of the surfaces. Where there should be walls, there are either empty spaces or glass. It's open plan gone feral. There is nowhere to hide in a house like this. I follow the man, who follows Faith. We're in a room now that spans the width of the house. I don't know what to call it, this room. It's got a kitchen, a dining-room table, several sofas, a couple of flat-screens, a sideboard and a dresser. In the corner, a woman with an enormous belly rocks back and forth in a chair.

Her legs are stretched in front of her, covered with a tartan blanket, which is the only piece of fabric in the entire, gargantuan room. Her feet are bubbling in a foot massager, like two enormous joints of meat.

She says, 'You're the lady on the telly. You're Faith's mother.' Her voice echoes round the room, bouncing against the chrome and the marble and the glass.

You're Faith's mother . . . Faith's mother . . . mother . . . mother . . . ther . . .

I look at her belly. It seems impossible that I was once like that. That the angry young woman in this gigantic room that doesn't know if it's a kitchen or a dining room or a sitting room, was once inside me. Was once part of my body. Part of me.

I hear Minnie's voice in my head and she's saying something like, 'Would you ever cop onto yourself?'

I cough. Stand up straight. Extend my hand. 'Hello, I'm Kat Kavanagh. It's lovely to meet you.'

The woman with the enormous belly has the two must-have qualities of 'the other woman'. She is both pretty and young. Not much older than Faith, I'd say. Late twenties. Thirty, tops. Her prettiness is of the generic variety. Blonde hair, blue eyes, high cheekbones, creamy skin.

She sits up a bit straighter and holds out her hand and I stretch my hand across her belly, careful not to touch her bump. She shakes my hand and shakes her head, all at the same time.

She says, 'Celia,' like it's an order rather than her name.

I'm about to say something, I don't know, like, 'When is your baby due?' but she cuts me off with: 'You wrote all those books. And nobody knew who you were.' She drops my hand but she is still shaking her head from side to side. 'What a strange thing to do.' She has a curious look on her face. As if I'm something the cat has dragged in and she's trying to work out what it is. I find myself thinking about what the man said. About the handprints on the porch window.

When it is quiet in a room like this, it is exceptionally quiet. Deathly quiet.

I say, 'When are you due?' Are you due . . . you due . . . due . . . due . . .

'I'm overdue, can't you tell?' Overdue . . . can't you tell . . . you tell . . . tell . . . tell . . .

She sighs. 'I thought the stress of having this lot up for Christmas would do the trick. But it hasn't worked.'

Faith says, 'Give it time. We've been here only a couple of days.'

In a way that is not meant to be kind, Celia says, 'It feels like you've been here for weeks.'

One of the doors into this cavern of a room bursts open and a boy runs in. He is wearing goggles. There are swimming trunks over his jeans.

When he sees me he stops and takes off the goggles. 'Hello. You're Kat. I saw you on the telly.'

I find myself smiling. 'You must be Milo.'

458

'I am.' He walks towards me and reaches his hand out.

I take it. 'You have a good handshake.'

He smiles. 'How's Ed?'

'He's much better. He got home from hospital yesterday. Or the day before yesterday, I think.'

Faith says, 'Milo told me he had an operation.'

I look at her. Force my voice to sound ordinary. 'Yes. On his heart. He had a pacemaker put in.'

Celia says, 'He's the autistic boy, isn't he?'

'Ed is my brother. He's got Down's Syndrome.'

Milo says, 'He's brilliant at Super Mario Galaxy.' And now I know what Dad meant when he said that Milo was one of those kids you'd want on your team. I smile at him again and he says, 'Would you like a cup of tea and some chocolate?'

I look at Faith and she looks at me and nobody says anything, and then Faith says, 'Could you make a pot, Milo?'

Faith's father chimes in, 'And some Christmas cake. There's some in the cupboard.'

Celia says, 'You're not supposed to eat Christmas cake, remember?'

'It's not for me, darling. It's for everyone else. It's Christmas Day, after all.' He smiles a tight, tired smile that slides off his face as soon as it reaches it.

'Well, Kat doesn't look like the type of woman who eats cake.' Celia looks at me. 'You don't mind if I call you Kat, do you?'

'That's my name. And I happen to love cake.'

This is not strictly speaking true. I love cigarettes and I love red wine, but in the absence of both, then Christmas cake and tea made by a ten-year-old boy will do. Besides, Celia is the type of woman who makes me want to disagree with everything she says.

'I'm Hamish, by the way. Faith's dad.' I shake his hand. I like that he doesn't say 'adopted Dad'. Or 'adoptive' or whatever the right word is. He just says 'Faith's dad'. And he says it in a way that brooks no argument. Not even from Faith, who, I am guessing, might be the argumentative type. 'Sit down, for goodness' sake.' He puts his hand right into the hollow at the small of my back, the way men of a certain age and disposition do, and leads me to the table, where he settles me into a chair. It's one of those chairs that're all style and no comfort. White and hard. Faith is standing at the door, as if she is about to leave. I have to think of something that will make her stay. And I have to try to get rid of Hamish and Celia. Even though I don't know what to say to Faith, I do know that there are things I need to say. I am hoping these things will come to me when the moment arises.

There's a period of about thirty seconds when no one says anything. It's excruciating. It's like writer's block, only worse. Page one of one. The blank page.

Say something.

I can't think of a thing.

That's when Hamish pipes up with a timely, 'So, tell us a little something about yourself, Kat.'

'Well . . . ' And that's when Minnie says, 'They don't want to know your favourite colour, Kat.'

'I had Faith when I was fifteen.'

I see Faith's fingers tighten round the handle of the door, but before she can open it and leave the room Celia smiles and says, 'We had a name for girls like you in school.' And I nearly kiss her because Faith releases the handle from her grip and approaches the table. She doesn't quite sit down but she hovers beside a chair, as if she might.

In my head I'm saying: ThankyouCeliathankyouCeliathankyouCelia. In real life, I say, 'I thought I was in love.'

Celia makes a sort of snorting noise. Faith pulls the chair out and asks, 'What was his name?'

'Elliot. Elliot Porter.' It feels strange. Saying his name out loud like that. After all these years. I feel nothing. I thought I would feel something. But I don't. He was only sixteen back then. Just a kid. Maybe he's changed. People change, don't they?

If Thomas could hear what I was thinking, he'd say, 'You've changed.' I'd deny it but he'd say, 'You have. You're giving people the benefit of the doubt.'

That's true. I never thought I'd turn out to be someone like that.

'I didn't realise I was pregnant until I was about seven months.'

Celia does a proper snort this time. She says, 'I knew after three days. Hamish came in reeking of that terrible aftershave he used to wear and I

461

just threw up everywhere, didn't I, Hamish?'

Hamish nods briefly and says, 'Go on.' Celia gives me a look that could curdle milk.

Faith perches on the edge of the chair. She looks at me for the first time. Really looks at me, I mean. She says, 'Did you ever think about keeping me?'

I say, 'No.' I say it as quickly as I can. To get it over with. 'Things were different then. It was 1987. I went into labour on my friend's couch. It was the first my mother knew of it. I was in shock. We all were. We did what we thought was the best thing at the time. For everyone. I've never really thought about it until now. I haven't allowed myself to.'

Faith says, 'What's different now?'

'I don't know. I think . . . maybe . . . I am.' And it's only when I say it out loud that I realise it's true.

That's when Celia doubles over and emits a screech. It is animalistic in its intensity.

Faith rolls her eyes. 'Here we go again.'

Celia throws herself off the chair, onto all fours, and screams, 'The baby, Hamish. The baby's coming.'

Hamish kneels on the floor beside her and gathers as much of her as he can into his arms. 'Hush now, hush now, ma wee darlin'.'

Milo approaches the table carrying a tray with a teapot and mugs and spoons and a plate piled high with Christmas cake. He says, 'Is Celia having the baby again?'

Faith says, 'Yes.' Then she turns to me and whispers, 'This isn't the first time she's gone into labour.' She puts the word 'labour' in inverted commas. Faith is nearly smiling and, again, I feel an enormous rush of gratitude towards Celia.

I take the tray from Milo. 'Should we phone for an ambulance?'

Hamish looks up. 'No, they said we're not to call for an ambulance again.'

Celia lifts her head. 'But I really AM in labour this time.'

Faith says, 'That's what you said the last time.'

Milo says, 'Yeah, but remember *The Boy Who Cried Wolf?* There really was a wolf that last time.'

Hamish says, 'Shut up the lot of you. Just . . . help me get her into the car.'

I'm closest and, even though I'm pretty sure he didn't mean me, I bend down and arrange Celia's arm round my neck. Hamish hooks her other arm round his neck and, together, we half drag, half carry the howling Celia to Hamish's jeep, already blanketed with snow. Just as we are hoisting her across the back seat, water gushes from between her legs. At first, she is delighted. She says, 'LOOK! My waters have broken. I TOLD you I was in labour!' to no one in particular, before she realises the import of the leakage and begins to wail and thrash. She locks her arms round Hamish's neck and refuses to let go.

'You have to let go now, pet. I need to drive to the hospital.' His voice is muffled because his mouth is crushed against Celia's cardigan, which is a mohair one. Incredibly itchy against his face, I'd say.

463

In response, Celia emits a long wail, like a foghorn.

Hamish manages to push his mouth away from the cardigan long enough to shout, 'Kat!' There's a long hair hanging from his lip.

'Yes?'

'Can you drive one of these things?'

'Well, I . . . '

'Could you drive us to the hospital?'

For a moment, I'm too surprised by the request to reply.

'She has a death grip on me and there's so much snow. Faith is nervous about driving the jeep at the best of times.' His look suggests that this is not the best of times and I can't say I blame him.

'Well, I . . . '

'It's not far.'

'I don't know the way.'

'I'll direct you. Please, Kat. I need to stay in the back with Celia. She's petrified, the poor wee mite.'

'OK.' There's nothing else I can do.

In the end, the baby comes at a minute past midnight so, technically, his birthday is Boxing Day, but because I hadn't gone to bed yet when he was born, it was still Christmas Day so me and the baby are sort of half-brother twins.

The baby is called Christian but Celia says we're not allowed to call him Chris or Christy.

In the hospital on Boxing Day, Dad lets me have a go of feeding the baby. He says I have to make sure the teat is full of milk, which is trickier than it looks. I'm not allowed to hold the baby yet in case I squash him, on account of him being so small. The bottle is nearly as big as the baby. He sucks pretty well, though. Dad says he's going to be a great grubber.

'You're a big brother now, Milo. You'll show this young fella a thing or two, won't you?' It's actually nice being somebody's big brother, even if you're just a half one.

Kat and Faith are outside, in the corridor, when I come out. Kat stayed in a hotel last night. Faith went to the hotel this morning. She didn't even have any breakfast before she left the house. She just got up and went to the hotel. She looked like she'd gone to bed in her clothes and didn't bother going to sleep.

Kat says, 'I just wanted to say goodbye, Milo, before I went back to Ireland. It was lovely meeting you.' For a moment, I think she's thinking about hugging me or something, but in the end, she doesn't.

Faith says, 'I'll be back in a minute,' and disappears down the corridor.

I look at Kat. 'Will you come and visit again?'

She smiles. 'I'd like to.' She looks better than yesterday.

When Faith comes back, she is holding three cans of Coke and three chocolate muffins. 'Are you hungry?'

I say, 'I'm starving.'

Faith says, 'I was talking to Kat.'

Kat says, 'Yes. I am,' even though she doesn't look like the type of person who eats chocolate muffins. I reckon she's more of a salad and fruit type of a person, like Miss Williams.

I eat with my hand under my mouth so I can catch any crumbs.

I say, 'I'm glad the baby is a boy.'

Kat and Faith say, 'Why?' at the same time, which makes them sort of smile at each other. They seem a bit shy, like new kids in class.

'Dad says I can teach him everything I know.'

Faith says, 'Ha! That won't take long.'

'I know loads of stuff. Lifesaving, for example.'

Kat says, 'Ed's been talking about doing a lifesaving class ever since he met you, Milo. He wants me to do it with him.'

'Have you ever done lifesaving before?'

'No.'

'I bet they have lifesaving-for-beginners classes in Ireland. They do in Brighton.'

Kat smiles. 'I'll Google it when I get home. Although I'd feel a bit old, doing a beginners' class. I'm nearly forty, you know.'

'You don't look that old.'

'Well, I am.'

'Coach always says it's never too late.'

'That's what Thomas says too.'

Faith says, 'Is Thomas your boyfriend?' Girls always want to know about boyfriends and kissing and stuff.

Kat shakes her head. 'He was. For a long time. We were pretty close, actually. He even asked me to marry him. After the accident.'

She looks at Faith then. 'I'm so sorry, Faith. About your mother.'

Faith nods. 'So am I.'

I say, 'Ed said you were in the same accident. The same one as my mam.'

'Yes. I was.'

'How come you didn't die?'

'I don't know. Thomas said it was a miracle.'

Faith says, 'Thomas sounds lovely.'

'He is.'

I say, 'Then why didn't you marry him? After the accident. When he asked you.'

Faith says, 'Milo!'

'What?' I ask, even though you're supposed to say 'pardon'.

Kat says, 'I don't really know, Milo. I was worried.'

I don't ask her what she was worried about. But I know that it's a horrible feeling. Being worried. Nobody says anything for a while. Kat's only eaten half of her chocolate muffin. The rest of it is on a napkin on her lap. I don't ask if she's going to finish it. I think Faith would kill me if I asked her that.

When Kat stands up, the rest of her muffin falls on the floor, which means that Faith definitely won't let me eat it now. I pick it up and put it in the bin. It nearly kills me. Kat says, 'Thanks, Milo.'

'You're welcome.' I try not to think about the chocolate muffin in the bin but it's hard.

Kat says, 'I should be going.'

Faith doesn't say anything.

Kat says, 'Do you want me to drop you home first? I could ask the taxi driver to drop you and Milo off at the house on the way to the airport.'

Faith shakes her head. 'We'll wait for Dad.'

Kat picks up her handbag. Unzips it. Then zips it again. She looks like she's looking for something but she can't remember what it is. Then she says, 'I'd love you to come to Dublin sometime.' She says it really quickly, like she's in a hurry.

Faith says, 'We already came to Dublin.'

Kat goes red, like Miss Williams when Damo told her about a bit of her skirt being stuck up inside her knickers that day.

'I know. I'm sorry. I wasn't . . . I should have come to see you. I did the wrong thing.'

Faith nods, like she's agreeing.

I say, 'I wouldn't mind going again. To Dublin. We didn't get to do much sightseeing the last time.' Faith glares at me. I reckon I'm in for it when Kat leaves.

Kat looks at Faith. 'Will you think about it? Milo could come too. I'll pay for the flights.'

Faith crosses her arms. 'We can pay for our own flights.'

'I know, but I just . . . I really want you to come. Both of you.'

Faith says nothing for ages and then she says, 'OK.' I don't know if that's OK, you can pay for the flights. Or OK, I'll come to Dublin. Or OK, me and Milo will come to Dublin. Or what?

468

Kat looks at her watch. She says, 'I'd better get going.'

It's only when Kat puts her hand on Faith's hand that I notice they have exactly the same fingers and thumbs. Really long, pointy ones. Mam said that Faith should have been a pianist. But having long fingers is handy when you're playing the violin too.

Kat says, 'I'll see you.'

She picks up her case and walks down the corridor.

When I look at Faith, there's a tear hanging off the edge of her jaw. I say, 'Are you crying because you're happy or because you're sad?' Sometimes adults cry when they're happy. Damo's mam does that all the time. Like when she watched Kate and William's wedding on the telly, she roared crying. She used up a whole box of tissues.

She wipes her face with the back of her hand. 'I think I'm just tired.'

'I think you're happy.'

'Why would you think that?'

I shrug my shoulders. 'I don't know. It's just a feeling I have.'

It's the thirteenth of March.

It's Tuesday.

Things are not bad.

In fact, they're all right.

I haven't had a drink for twelve weeks. In return, Ed's pacemaker has settled in fine. He's had a check-up and the doctor says he's in great shape. I think I probably could have a drink and Ed's pacemaker would still be fine, but if it wasn't, I'd have only myself to blame. That's what happens when you make a deal with someone that you don't quite believe in. You can't take the chance.

I look at the calendar. Six weeks since Faith and Milo were here for a weekend. Four weeks until they're coming back for another weekend. Easter. Rob is coming too. They're staying with me. Milo is staying with Ed. In the top bunk. Ed is delighted that Faith is not staying. He likes her and everything but, this way, he doesn't have to tidy his room. Milo told him that there was no need. I haven't met Rob before. I'm predisposed to disliking him. That's just the way I am. Minnie says that I'm to count to ten before I open my mouth. Every time I go to open my mouth. Count to ten. I'm practising. It's difficult. But I'm trying.

Fourteen weeks till the baby's due. Minnie's baby. It's a boy. They got a 3D scan. A handsome boy, Minnie says. 'He's got a brilliant side profile,' she says and she shows me a photograph, and it's true, the baby has a side profile that is nothing short of brilliant. It's remarkable, really.

I'm forty now. I turned forty nine weeks ago. It was pretty low key in the end. Me and Minnie and Ed and Mum and Dad went out for dinner. The only thing I insisted on was no champagne. I said, 'You can drink anything else you like, I don't care. But no champagne. This is not that type of celebration.'

Ed says, 'What type of celebration is it, Kat?'

'It's an 'I'm not dead, I'm forty' celebration. So, you know . . . low key.'

'That sounds good. Not being dead.' When Ed smiles, I smile. I can't help it. Milo is right: I do look like Ed when I smile.

That's when I say, 'You're bloody well right, Ed,' and I clap my hands together and roar, 'CHAMPAGNE!' and because it's a pretty posh type of a place, the staff don't comment on my rudeness. Instead, the waitress rushes out with a bottle of chilled champagne and five flutes. I fill three of the glasses with champagne and order fizzy water with a splash of blackcurrant for me and Minnie. Then we raise our glasses and Ed says, 'Here's to being forty and not dead.'

Everyone says, 'Being forty and not dead.' We clink and drink and that is the end of that.

Eight weeks since Minnie rang with the news.

She didn't tell me straight off. We talked about all sorts at first.

We talked about baby names: Maurice if it's a boy and Minnie if it's a girl.

We talked about my efforts to track down Elliot Porter. So far, I've managed to speak to two of his ex-wives and a couple of ex-girlfriends, and have reason to believe he may be prospecting for gold in South Africa. I just want to tell him about Faith. I should have told him a long time ago. I should have done a lot of things a long time ago. But all I can do is start from here.

We talked about Minnie's recent craving for yams. Turns out they're pretty hard to get your hands on at this time of year.

It's only when I say I have to go because I'm meeting Ed for our next lifesaving class, that Minnie brings it up. She says, 'I suppose you've heard?'

I say, 'Heard what?'

Minnie says, 'About Thomas.'

My stomach does its usual backwards somersault.

'What about him?'

'The engagement's off.'

'With the *Farmers Journal*?'

'Yeah.'

'Why?'

'I don't know. One of his colleagues told me. He didn't go into the gories.'

I want the gories.

Minnie says, 'Are you glad?'

'I don't know.'

'Tell me!'

'I think so.'

'You made a right hatchet job of that.'

'I know.'

Her voice softens. 'Maybe it's not too late.'

'I'm pretty sure it is.'

We leave it at that.

And Killian Kobain? Well, it's been just over eleven weeks since I dropped that particular bombshell. Eleven weeks of the media jumping out of various bushes and popping up behind me in the queue at the supermarket. I have to be careful what I put in my basket now. No more family-size pepperoni pizzas. How would that look in the 'Guilty Pleasures' section of the *Metro*? Yes, they still hang around the car park of the apartment block, on slow news days. My neighbours know most of them by name now. Mrs O'Dea insists on 'outing' them. 'I see you there, Paddy Miles, you dirty little scut. You should be ashamed of yourself, writing for that rag of a paper.' Paddy — who is a dirty little scut — gives her the one finger and she, quick as a flash, gives him the two. She means well, Mrs O'Dea. She really does.

And twelve weeks since I saw Thomas. At the hospital. He was my lesson, I suppose, and I learned him off by heart. That's just a fact. Twelve weeks since I started moving on. I'm still moving on. It'll take a while. That's what Minnie says and she knows everything. I'll just keep on moving on until I don't have to move on anymore. Maybe I might even meet someone. Milo says that his teacher, Miss Williams, has a boyfriend and he reckons she's even older than me.

Ten weeks since Nicolas from number thirteen sold his story to the the *Irish Daily Mail*. They called it 'My night with the Wild Kat'. Someone gets paid good money to come up with headlines like that. I swear to God.

Today, I've done four things.

I have spoken to my mother on the phone.

I have arranged to pick up Ed at the café after work and bring him to our next lifesaving lesson.

I have gone with Minnie to one of her ante-natal appointments because Maurice couldn't — some Genius convention in Geneva — and because, it turns out, the most independent woman in the world doesn't like going on her own. So I went. And we both looked at the monitor and admired the baby's brilliant side profile. It really is something else.

And I helped Dad in his garden. He says there's not much to be done there at this time of the year but we did things anyway. There is something calming about pushing your hands into the earth. It's getting the muck out from behind your nails afterwards that's the problem. We saw the tips of green shoots pushing their way up through the muck. Dad said, 'They're the first of the daffodils. Your mother loves daffodils.' This is something I did not know. I am moving on and learning things at the same time. You'd hardly know me.

Actually, five things. I emailed Faith. We email a lot. Nearly every day. I'm better on the email than the phone. I've always been better on the page than in real life. But I do my best to be as honest as I can. I want her to know me. The proper, horrendous me and not some fictional account of me, because, let's face it, we all know how good I can be at that.

'Verrucas, corns, bunions and all.' That's what Minnie says. It's not easy showing someone your bunions. They're not pretty. But that is what I am trying to do, nonetheless. It's pretty exhausting but then, when I get an email from Faith that says, in the subject box, 'SOMETHING AMAZING JUST HAPPENED!!!' in capitals and exclamation marks, it's worth it. It really is. She tells me about Rob. About the band. The tour. The conflict with Rob about the band and the tour. She hasn't got it worked out yet but I have. I haven't told her. I'll wait till nearer the summer, when things are a bit safer between us. But I have a tour of my own planned. For Milo. Some time in Scotland with his little brother and his dad. And then some time here with his uncle Ed. In the top bunk. They have taken to writing to each other. Proper letters with stamps and what have you.

So tonight, I'm tired. It might not seem like much but that's a lot of activity for a writer with writer's block who is moving on and learning one new thing every day.

I lie on my couch and work my way through a bowl of Funky Banana — Milo gave me the exact recipe — and that's when it happens. That's when the idea comes.

It's not like my usual ideas, which are more like fragments of ideas. This one is more than that. It is fully formed. I can see the beginning of it. The end. Even the middle.

I move to my desk. Quietly. As though the idea is like a wisp of cloud that will blow away at the merest sound.

I sit down. Open a notebook. The one Ed gave me for my fortieth, even though I don't use notebooks. But this idea seems somehow too fragile for the laptop. Oddly, I find myself thinking — believing — that this story needs the gentle scratch of a pencil against the page.

'Jesus wept.' That's what Minnie would say to that.

I pick up the pencil.

I begin.

# 13 March 2012; Brighton

Mr Edward Kavanagh
24 Howth Road
Raheny
Dublin 5
Ireland
Europe
The World!
The universe!!
The Galaxy!!!!!!!!!!!!!!!!

Dear Ed,
Thanks for the football for Christian. I gave it to him when he visited us last weekend. Celia took the batteries out of the puppy that I bought him. I don't think she liked the barking or the song. She likes peace and quiet. I don't know why she got a baby because babies are pretty noisy, most of the time.
I'm sort of supporting Chelsea now too. You're right. That penalty shouldn't have been allowed.

477

Damo says the ref should have gone to Specsavers, ha ha!

No, I'm pretty sure the valentine's card wasn't from Carla. She didn't go red or anything when I showed it to her. And she said it was slushy. Maybe it was Lorraine. She's always talking about love and stuff and the other day, during break, she kept chasing me even when she wasn't it. Faith said I should keep it because it's my first card, but I put it in the bin in the library when me and Carla were there, helping Miss Rintoole.

I think the jump you're talking about is the straddle jump. It's when you jump into the pool and try not to let your head go under the water. I can't believe you and Kat are learning that already. We didn't do that one for ages. Coach has arranged for the intermediate class to visit the Brighton lifeguard station next Saturday. I can't wait. They're going to bring us out in the lifeboat if the conditions are calm.

Faith told me about the plans for the Easter holidays. That's legend. I'll bring my goggles and my togs and maybe we could go to the pool and practise lifesaving. And you can come to Brighton to visit me and Faith sometime. You could meet Damo and Carla and we could go to the Funky Banana. Jack owns it now but he says I can bring my friends anytime. Even Damo, so long as he promises not to touch anything again, or talk to any of the customers.

Have to go now. Faith and me are cooking fajitas tonight, which happen to be one of my all-time favourite dinners.

Ant and Adrian are coming home at the weekend. Ant is bringing a girl and I think she's his girlfriend. Her name is Julia but Ant calls her 'Mouse'. I don't know why. Maybe she's really small. Or quiet. Rob said he will come to our house and cook something special for all of us when Ant and Adrian and Julia/Mouse get here. He says he'll bring dessert too, which will probably be Mars bars even though Faith says Mars bars are not dessert. Rob is mad about Mars bars. So am I, especially Mars Duos.

Yours sincerely,
Milo McIntyre

PS. I'm putting in a Petr Cech card because (1) he's the best goalie in the entire universe and, (2) I have two of them now.

PPS. Hunger Games is coming out in ten days!!!!!!! It's 12A but Sully is coming home from the war next week and he said he'd come to the cinema with us, to make sure that I get in this time.

PPPS. Tell Kat not to worry about being the worst in the class. Coach says everyone can be good at lifesaving so long as they practise a lot.

# Epilogue

## 1 July 2012; Dublin

### I

This is the first book launch I've ever attended.

Faith says, 'Are you nervous?'

I still get a jolt when I see her. The very fact of her, standing here, beside me. She is taller than me. Thinner. But there are similarities. The long, dark hair. The pale skin. The green eyes. She doesn't look like me but she looks like a version of me.

I shake my head. 'Actually, no. I thought I would be nervous. But I'm not.' This is not bravado. It happens to be true. I should be as nervous as a hedgehog chancing a beach road on an August bank holiday. But I'm not.

She nods then. Smiles. The dimple dents her right cheek. Ed's dimple. She says, 'Anyway, there's no need to be nervous about the book.' Her copy of *Lifesaving for Beginners* is tucked under her arm, like a clutch bag. Now my mouth is dry and my heart is banging against the wall of my chest, like a drum solo. I had already decided — before I sent her the book, before I'd finished it — that I wasn't going to ask her if she'd read it. I definitely wasn't going to ask her what she thought of it. I wasn't going to say a word.

481

'Did you read it?' I feel like someone's just plugged me into the mains.

Faith nods.

'And . . . ah . . . what did you think of it?' Goosebumps rise on my arms, like I'm standing in a draught.

'I thought it was brave. And honest. And I really like the way it ends.'

I'm glad I'm sitting down. The relief would have floored me.

Faith puts her hand on my arm. A brief touch. 'Good luck.' Then she walks towards the door of the office, which is a small, cluttered room at the back of the bookshop. 'See you out there.' When she leaves, I twist the rod at the edge of the window and the venetian blinds tilt. The bookshop is teeming with people. Journalists and photographers mostly. You'd think, after six months, interest would have waned. Heads turn as Faith disappears into the throng in the green linen dress that her mother called her 'Ireland' dress.

I scan the crowd again but it's only when I don't see him that I realise I'm looking for Thomas. He's a journalist after all. It's not beyond the bounds of possibility that he might be here. No matter how many lambs his ewe bears, he's still a journalist. He could easily be here.

But he's not.

# II

Minnie bursts into the room, gripping a clipboard in her hands. A pen is clamped between her teeth like a bit. She looks at me. Plucks the pen from her mouth. 'Good,' she says. 'You're here.' She scores a tick on a page that's attached to the clipboard, like I'm an item on her 'to-do' list. I probably am.

The clipboard is Natasha's, the PR Brona hired to handle the launch. Except that at exactly 9.13 this morning, Natasha got text-dumped by her boyfriend of seven and a half months who was on the cusp of moving into her one-bed in Notting Hill. Now she's in the Turk's Head drinking tequila and leaving increasingly incoherent messages on her ex-boyfriend's mobile which he has — thus far — failed to return. The cad. That's what Brona called him.

Minnie has stepped into the breach. She's in her element. 'PR's a doddle,' she said, in front of Natasha's assistant, who curled his hands into fists so Minnie couldn't smell his fear. She's put him on name-badge duty.

'You ready?' She inspects me from the feet up, nods and scores another tick on her page. She doesn't comment on the effort I've gone to. The red dress with the matching shoes and the fitted black leather jacket. But she ticks me off her list and that's something.

I say, 'Yes.'

'Good.' She takes a walkie-talkie out of the pocket of her jacket and presses a button. Static hisses through the speaker and she winces. She presses another button and says, 'We are leaving position D and will be at position A in T minus twenty seconds; do you copy, Alistair?'

A man's voice with an English accent, high and halting, quivers down the line. 'Er, yes, Minnie. We — I mean I — I'm reading you, ah, loud and clear, as it were.'

Minnie looks at me. 'Fall in,' she says and I do because Minnie is on a roll and so, I suppose, am I. The crowd parts like curtains and we make it to the podium at the other end of the bookshop in exactly T minus twenty seconds.

Brona introduces me. She says lovely things, all of which are untrue to a greater or lesser degree. She calls me 'charming' and 'cooperative'. She says it's always been a 'pleasure' working with me. She tells them about my work ethic, which she describes as 'exemplary'. HA!

Minnie can't wait to get her hands on the microphone. For a moment, standing on the podium with her huge blue eyes and her blonde hair in a plait down her back and her belly swelling against the silk of her pale pink maxi-dress, she looks adorable. She looks like the type of woman who might make cupcakes and help little old ladies across the road. Then she snaps on the microphone and says, 'Kat won't be doing a reading so if you want to know what the book's about, you'll have to buy it. If you have a question, put your hand up. If I point to you, ask your question. If I don't point to you and you ask a question anyway, you will be removed from the premises.' She nods towards two enormous men swaddled in sombre black suits and wearing matching black wraparound sunglasses. The same pair from the press conference, which seems like a long time ago now. They stand on either side of the entrance, silent and unmoving and a little bit magnificent. Minnie ends with a curt, 'Kat will sign copies of the book afterwards. Form an orderly queue in single file at the right-hand side of the shop.'

For a moment, nothing happens. It's hard to know where to look. Then, one by one, the arms go up until the bookshop is a sea of disembodied hands, all waving at me. Minnie points to a journalist near the back and barks, 'YOU.' The journalist — a woman with a meaty red face — looks at Minnie and points to herself with a questioning expression and Minnie nods impatiently, hands me the microphone and so it begins.

'Kat, first of all, may I offer you my congratulations on the book. I finished it last night. I couldn't put it down.'

Killian Kobain would know what to say to that but I can't think of anything.

She goes on, 'The book is not a Declan Darker book.'

I would have thought that was pretty obvious.

'Why did you decide not to write another Darker book?'

Finally. A question. I look at the front row where Mum, Dad, Faith, Milo and Ed are sitting. Milo looks like he's been attacked with Dad's Brylcreem because his fringe is pasted against his head. He smiles at me and gives me the thumbs up sign. He uses both thumbs. I wink at him and then return my attention to the journalist. 'It was time to write something new.'

Hands go up. Minnie points at a middle-aged man wearing a beanie hat in the second row and shouts, 'YOU.' I'm surprised because beanie hats on middle-aged men are one of the items on Minnie's pet-hate list. She says they're a foil for either baldness or sticky-out ears or a combination of both and that they fool no one.

The man in the beanie hat says, '*Lifesaving for Beginners* is about a teenager who gets pregnant and gives the baby up for adoption. Is it autobiographical?'

I've been dreading this question but it's not unexpected. The details of my life have been wrapped around a fair amount of fish and chips in the last few months. I say, 'No, it's a work of fiction,' and I'm about to leave it at that and then I don't. This keeps happening recently, since I finished the book. It's like I'm springing leaks. I'm coming out. I keep coming out. I take a breath. 'But it's true to say there's a lot of me in this book. I didn't realise that until I read it myself for the first time. I had buried that part of myself. That fifteen-year-old girl. I hadn't thought about her. I abandoned her, in a way. And then I read the book and there she was, on the page. It was like meeting someone I used to know but hadn't bothered to keep in touch with. It was a shock. But it was something I needed to do.'

There is silence in the room. I've been taciturn these past few months. The media has interpreted this silence as aloofness. They've

486

called me cold. Remote. They were not expecting this. This deluge. Neither was I. And neither was Minnie by the look of her. Shocking Minnie is no mean feat but it seems like I've managed it. Then the man in the beanie hat opens his mouth to ask another question and this brings the unshockable Minnie back because she hits him with a tart, 'You've asked your question,' before pointing to a woman on the other side of the room and roaring, 'YOU.'

She says, 'What genre is the book?'

I say, 'I don't know.'

Minnie points and roars again, 'YOU.'

'How long did it take to write the book?' A high-pitched voice near the back of the room that turns out to be a burly man with a ferocious-looking beard.

'Six weeks.'

There is a pause then. A collective intake of breath. But it's true, that's how long it took me. Six weeks. Beginning to end. With no need for editing other than a few apostrophes that were in the wrong place at the wrong time. I've never been great with apostrophes.

Six weeks. Writing and sleeping. That's what I did for six weeks; that's all I did for six weeks. Brona said, 'See what you can do when you put your mind to it?'

Minnie points and roars, 'YOU,' at a skinny youth with enormous glasses perched on a long, narrow ridge of nose.

'Some commentators are saying that your second novel, *In the Dark*, is loosely based on some of your real-life experiences. What's your response to that?'

'*In the Dark* is about a serial killer who buries his victims alive in shallow graves in Leitrim.'

'Yes, that's the one.' He seems pleased with me.

'I've never been to Leitrim.'

'But the killer was adopted. And the book is the only one that's set in Ireland, isn't it? That's the point I'm making.' You have to wonder if some of them have been to any sort of educational facility.

I look at Minnie and she points to another one and roars, 'YOU.'

'Is it true that you had a nervous breakdown when you were sixteen?'

'No.'

'Seventeen?'

'No.'

'Eighteen?'

I shake my head. 'I'll save you the bother of counting up to forty, shall I? I've never had a nervous breakdown, although I'm not ruling one out.' This generates some titters around the room. Nervous ones.

More hands. Minnie takes her time. She points and roars, 'YOU.'

'Is it true that you got the name Killian Kobain from the back of a Cornflakes box?'

'No, it was Sugar Puffs.' Some of them are writing that down. I swear to God.

And on it goes.

Someone asks about the dedication. I was wondering when that might come up. Killian never dedicated his books to anyone. 'You've dedicated the book to Beth. Is that your daughter?'

I say, 'No,' and Minnie's about to bark 'YOU' at someone else when I say, 'Beth is my daughter's mother. I dedicated the book to her by way of thanks.'

'YOU.'

A small, narrow woman with a pinched face says, 'Your mother once likened the writing of crime novels to painting by numbers. How do you respond to that?'

'She's changed her mind. She says it's more like join-the-dots now.' I look at Mum who squirms in her seat but manages a small smile. I feel a rush of affection. This hasn't been easy for her. But she's doing her best.

Minnie says, 'One more question,' and the room is a collection of hands and somehow Minnie manages to pick one. 'YOU!' she roars, even louder than before, as if she knows that her PR career is nearing its end and she wants to go out with a bang.

'Are you going to write any more Declan Darker novels?'

I say, 'Yes. One more.'

'Why just one?'

I don't answer immediately and into this pause, someone shouts, 'She's going to kill him!' As if Darker is a real live person and I, a killer who may very well bury people alive in shallow graves in Leitrim. There are gasps around the room and, for the first time, I think I get it. How much people like Declan

Darker. Love him, even.

I say, 'No, not necessarily. But he's getting on, you know. Maybe I could retire him. Buy him a cabin in Montana. He'd love that. I could even marry him off. Maybe he finally meets someone? Falls in love? Gets happy? Why not? That sometimes happens. Doesn't it?'

Someone shouts, 'That's outrageous.'

Minnie says, 'That's it. No more questions,' and the hands come down and an orderly queue forms in single file down the right-hand side of the bookshop, just as Minnie instructed.

## III

The queue starts from the little table at the top of the bookshop, where I'm sitting, snakes to the door and spills onto the street. After an hour my hand is as rigid as a claw and my face aches from smiling into people's cameras. I motion Milo over. 'See how long the queue is now,' I whisper. The news isn't good. 'Another fifty or so,' he says.

'Or so?'

'Seventy-three to be exact.' He smiles at me and somehow I manage to sign more books, smile into more cameras and even hold a woman's baby while she rummages in her bag for her copy of the book.

Beside me I feel Minnie tense. I look up. Her eyes are trained on the door. She picks up her walkie-talkie and presses a button. 'We've got a situation at six o'clock. Over,' she whispers into the radio. She looks at me. 'Stay there.' Then she walks with a huge degree of purpose towards the door. I stand up and that's when I see him. In the queue, at the door, the top of his head reaching for the architrave. He nods when he sees me and the grey curls bounce, like an Irish dancer's wig. He's wearing the skinny black jeans that I bought him on a mini-break in Donegal. The white T-shirt with the hole in the back where his goat got at it when his rigged-up clothesline collapsed. No jacket. In one hand, a copy of the book. My stomach contracts.

The hired goons and Minnie bear down on him. Thomas stays where he is, oblivious to the imminent danger. I say, 'Excuse me,' to the man at the top of the queue who looks at his watch and shakes his head, tutting, like I'm a train that's been delayed.

I move towards the crowd. The goons are on either side of Thomas, waiting for the signal from Minnie. She nods at them and they move closer to Thomas, sandwiching him between them. I push through a particularly thick knot of people and burst through the other side. 'Stop!' I say, stumbling over someone's handbag on the floor and falling against one of the goons, who feels as solid as a brick wall. He puts his gigantic hands on my shoulders and places me back on my feet. Minnie looks at me. 'He claims he's only here to get the book signed. But I can have him removed from the building. Just say the word.' Then she looks at Thomas and smiles. 'No offence, Thomas. I'm just doing my job.'

Thomas smiles back. 'I didn't know you'd

gone into the security business.'

'Sideline,' Minnie says.

Thomas looks at me as if he's about to say something, and I'm dying to know what it is he's about to say when Minnie declares, 'Decision time, Kat. In? Or out?'

'I . . . ah . . . in.'

'You sure?'

I look at Thomas. 'If you want to. Stay, I mean.' He nods, amused.

Minnie looks at the goons and says, 'Stand down,' in a disappointed, resigned sort of a way and they take a step back at the same time, like a pair of gigantic dancers, oddly graceful.

Minnie takes my arm and frogmarches me towards the table. On the way, I pass Milo. 'Can you count them again?' I hiss at him. He nods.

Back at the table, the man is still looking at his watch and shaking his head and tutting. I'm signing his book when Milo comes back with a hefty 'Fifty-seven.' Thomas is at the end of the queue. I square my shoulders and keep on signing. Inside my head, there are questions. Doubts. Second guesses. Worry. But there are other things too. There are possibilities.

I notice that my inscriptions are becoming more flamboyant. Caution is in my hands and I am throwing it to the wind.

Before, my inscription was always the same: their name. My name. The end. Now I was going all out.

*Kat xxx*

*Love, Kat xxxx*

*Lots of love, Kat xxxxxx*

*All my love, Kat xxxxxxxxx*

I can't stop smiling. Thomas is here and I'm like Brona now. I'm calling it A Sign.

*To Ger, best of luck with the driving test, will keep fingers crossed! Loads of love, Kat xxxx*

*To Barney, so lovely to meet you. Hope she says YES!! Best of luck, Kat xxxxx*

*To Siobhan, you'll never know if you don't ask. Ring him!! Love Kat xxx*

*To dear Michael, your kind words mean the world to me. Lots of love, Kat xxx*

And the weird thing is, I mean it. Every word. I'm on a high. I'm on a roll.

Faith arrives at the table. 'You OK? Can I get you anything?' I look at her and I get the jolt. I say, 'Can you get me the book I signed for you?' She hands it to me and I re-open it at the page where I signed it earlier. The page where I wrote her name, then my name. Now I write, in big, looping lettering, *Thank you for coming to find me. Lots and lots of love, Kat xxxxx* I make her promise that she won't read it in front of me. She promises and I hand her the book and she opens it and reads the inscription right there in front of me. She nods and says, 'You're welcome.'

The book I signed for Minnie is still on the table. I open that and write, below the place where I wrote her name and my name, *Even if I had lots of friends, you'd still be my best one. Kat xxxxx*

Later, Minnie will read it and say, 'Soppy cow.'

I look at Milo, who is keeping count. He flashes ten fingers at me, closes his hands, then a further seven. Seventeen people left. I keep going.

Now there's just one woman in front of Thomas. One woman with an enormous rucksack on her back. She struggles out of the bag, sets it on the floor and opens it. Inside are books. Stacks of them. She removes them one by one. Places them in two piles on the table. Eighteen in total. Nine in each pile. The Declan Darker books. Two sets. She explains about her neighbour, who is in hospital having her varicose veins done. Would I mind signing all of them? One set for her and the other for her neighbour? The veins are bad. They're the bulgy variety. The operation hasn't been as successful as she'd hoped.

You can't argue with bulgy veins. I say, 'My pleasure,' and I start signing. Even the cramping of my hand is not enough to quell my outpourings of affection.

'What's your neighbour's name?'

'Dolores.'

*To darling Dolores, so sorry to hear about your troubles. Hope you are back on your feet very soon. All my love, Kat* xxxxxxxxxx

I write eight more variations of that, then I start on the other pile. The woman's name is Kerry. I start to write. 'No,' she says. 'It's with a C. And an ie.'

'Cerrie?'

'That's me. And could you sign this one for my boyfriend?'

*To Des . . .*

'With a Z.'

*To Dez*
'This one's for Florence.'
'With an F.' My little joke.
'No, with a Ph.'
'Phlorence?'
'That's it.'

I sign and sign. I'm nearly there. Behind Kerry — Cerrie — Thomas is on the phone. I hear his voice, soft and low. Wispa bars. My mouth waters.

'Here's the last one. Can you make it out to Lola?'

'Sure.' Lola. You can't go wrong with Lola.

'Eh, there's an H at the end,' says Cerrie. I add the H — Lolah — and Cerrie smiles. 'You're much nicer than I thought you'd be.'

'Er, thank you.' It takes her ages to put the books back inside the rucksack. I try to help but she says no. They have to go back in chronological order. I don't say, 'Have a safe trip back to the asylum, won't you?' I say, 'No problem. And thank you for coming. And give my best to Dolores, won't you? And to Dez, Phlorence and Lolah, of course.'

Eventually, she hoists the rucksack on her back, turns and leaves.

'There you are.' That's what Thomas says when I look up. He smiles his old familiar smile and says, 'There you are.' I feel like he's right. Here I am. It's taken me so long to get here but I made it in the end.

I say, 'I've missed you.' It slips out. I'm still springing leaks, it seems.

He looks shocked. I can't blame him.

He doesn't say, 'I've missed you too.' I decide not to take it as A Sign.

Instead, he says, 'You never got in touch.' He sounds hurt, like he wanted me to get in touch. A feeling surges, like a tide coming in. I recognise the feeling. It's hope.

'I thought about you every day. I missed you every day.' I say it real matter-of-fact. It's the only way I can manage. 'I just . . . I didn't want to call you. I didn't want to presume. And I knew you had your own stuff going on . . .'

'You mean Sarah?'

I nod.

'That was a mistake.' I stand up. He doesn't call it a disaster, which I would have preferred. But a mistake. That's something. Someplace to start.

I say, 'I know all about mistakes. But it's like Samuel Beckett says, about failing. You have to try again. Try harder. Fail better.'

'Fail better?'

'Yes. That's my plan. I'm going to fail better. No point in setting expectations too high, with my track record.' That earns a smile. A small one.

I move around to his side of the table. Stand beside him. Close enough to touch.

'I'm not expecting you to forget about everything that's happened. For us to pick up where we left off. But I want you to know things about me. I want you to know everything. Like all those times I said no, I really meant yes. Yes to everything.'

He looks at me then. Right at me. 'Yes to everything?'

'Yes.'

'Like bog snorkelling? Yes to bog snorkelling?'

I think about bog water between my toes, damp and dirty. I say, 'Yes.'

'Yes to a weekend in Leitrim?'

I think about Leitrim. All those cold lakes. The endless grey skies. I say, 'Yes.'

'Yes to fishing? Fishing in Leitrim?'

An image of a bucketful of bloody fish guts swims to the surface of my mind. I dunk it with both hands. I say, 'Yes.'

'Kite-surfing?'

I see myself in a full-body plaster cast. I say, 'Yes.'

'Kayaking?'

'Yes.' That one's a doddle, as Minnie would say.

'Down the river Liffey.'

Oh Christ, the Liffey. The stinking, sludgy, smelly Liffey. I look at him and I say, 'Yes.'

He smiles but he doesn't ask me anything else. It's like he's run out of things to ask. I'm at the end of the road. The possibilities are dwindling. This is it. This is how it ends. It's like someone is about to shout, 'Lights out.'

But then I remember that I've nothing to lose. So I go right ahead and say, 'I was wondering . . . will you be hungry on Friday night around eight?'

'There's a fair to middlin' chance.'

'Because I was thinking — if you're not busy or anything — you could come over on Friday night for dinner.' I put my hands behind my back. Cross my fingers, like Milo does when he's hoping for something good.

'Are you cooking?'

'Ah, well, I . . . '

'I'm just messing with you.'

'I'll get really nice takeaway. And cheesecake from the deli.' The bait is on the line. There's nothing more I can do.

Thomas shifts from one enormous besandalled foot to the other. 'Well . . . I suppose it would do no harm to talk. And I could collect those cords.'

'The yellow ones?'

'They're beige.'

'Sure. You could pick them up.' Now is not the time to mention that I threw them off the balcony one night in a fit of wine-induced pique. They snagged on a gutter. They're still there, as far as I know.

And that's when Thomas says, 'All right. Friday night, so. I'll see you then. We can . . . talk.'

I nod towards his copy of the book. 'Do you want me to sign that?'

'Sure.' He hands me the book. I pick up my pen. Open the book. Bend my face to the page. I've thought about it so many times. What I would write if he asked me to sign the book. I went through dozens of inscriptions. Clever ones. Pithy ones. They've deserted me now, like rats off a sinking ship. I suppose I never really believed that I'd have to come up with something. I never thought he'd ask me to sign it. Why would he? After everything?

But here he is. Asking me. I close my eyes and write the first thing that comes into my head. I hope Minnie never reads it.

To Thomas,
You were right.
When you said I loved you.
Whatever happens, I know this much is true.
Yours
Kat

# Acknowledgements

The terrible thing about acknowledgements is that there's always someone you forget. Like Avril Rankin. Avril taught me everything I know about dog pounds and rescue centres during the writing of *Finding Mr Flood*. I can't believe I forgot to thank her, but I did. So here I am remembering. Thank you Avril. For everything.

My sincere thanks to the McGowan family, especially John, Sinead, Mary, Bernard, Dave and Lyndsey-Anne. For sharing their stories with me and for their hospitality and generosity.

A huge thank you to Aine Maguire-Keane, who told me her story with her usual sincerity and charm and good humour.

Thank you to my local G.P., Cathal Martin, who provides me with medical conditions for people who don't exist and — more importantly — tells me how to make them better.

Thanks to the Adoption Association of Ireland who helped me with the research for this book.

Thanks to the Arch club in Portmarnock, for facilitating me.

Thank you to Neil MacLochlainn for telling me the way things are in schools in the U.K.

A big debt of gratitude is owed to Eileen Kavanagh who read a draft of this book and was so generous with her time and her expertise in providing invaluable feedback and insight. I will return the favour any time.

Thanks to my sister, Niamh Geraghty, who reads the many, many drafts of my books and laughs at the bits that you're supposed to laugh at. Even if I had other sisters, you'd still be my favourite one. And to Niamh MacLochlainn, who read the manuscript in one sitting and who is always so generous and supportive with her feedback.

Huge thanks to the staff at Hachette Books Ireland and Hodder & Stoughton in the U.K., especially my editors, Ciara Doorley and Francesca Best. I have learned so much from your patient and careful work on my books. Thank you for helping me tell my stories.

An enormous thank you to my agent, Ger Nichol, who is always in my corner. Thank you for believing in me, even when I don't. Especially when I don't.

Writers need readers. Otherwise, you're just alone, in a room, talking to yourself. It still surprises and delights me when someone contacts me to let me know that they've read a book that I've written. It's even better when they say that they enjoyed it. And some of them aren't even related to me. So a huge thank you to all the people who read my books. I really, really hope you enjoy this one.

I am, as always, indebted to my family: my parents Breda and Don, to whom this book is dedicated. This is one small thing I can do for you in return for the many huge things you have done for me over the years. And to my children

Sadhbh, Neil and Grace. They are the people who live with the person who writes the stories. They have their own stories to tell about that experience and those stories aren't always good . . . So thank you all, for your patience and your love.

And to my friend, Frank MacLochlainn. Thank you for your friendship, your support, your understanding and your love. I couldn't do it without you.

Finally, to Maeve Binchy, who died this week. I will never hear your stories, on the page or the radio or the television, again. I will miss that. I will miss you. You inspired me. You told me that I could do it too. You told all of us. Thank you so much.

Ciara Geraghty, 8th August 2012

We do hope that you have enjoyed reading this large print book.

Did you know that all of our titles are available for purchase?

We publish a wide range of high quality large print books including:
**Romances, Mysteries, Classics**
**General Fiction**
**Non Fiction and Westerns**

Special interest titles available in large print are:
**The Little Oxford Dictionary**
**Music Book**
**Song Book**
**Hymn Book**
**Service Book**

Also available from us courtesy of Oxford University Press:
**Young Readers' Dictionary**
**(large print edition)**
**Young Readers' Thesaurus**
**(large print edition)**

For further information or a free brochure, please contact us at:
**Ulverscroft Large Print Books Ltd.,**
**The Green, Bradgate Road, Anstey,**
**Leicester, LE7 7FU, England.**
**Tel: (00 44) 0116 236 4325**
**Fax: (00 44) 0116 234 0205**

*Other titles published by*
*The House of Ulverscroft:*

## BECOMING SCARLETT

### Ciara Geraghty

In Scarlett O'Hara's life, everything goes according to plan. Until now . . . Scarlett has returned to her childhood home, her plan in tatters and a baby on the way, while John Smith — Scarlett's boyfriend — has left her to join an archaeological dig in Brazil. Worse still, she's unsure who the baby's father is . . . even though she's slept with exactly four-and-a-half men in her entire thirty-five years. Scarlett throws herself into her job as a wedding planner, but even that's not going smoothly, because she has growing feelings for her most important client's husband-to-be . . . In the end it's the person she thought she knew best — herself — who surprises her the most, as she tries, for the first time ever, to navigate life without a plan.